The creator of this sinister parable, the most prolific and popular American writer of his time, was born in 1806 in Charleston, South Carolina. He died in 1870, ruined by the Civil War.

With a text established by James B. Meriwether, this edition has a significant Introduction by Donald Davidson and Mary C. Simms Oliphant. James B. Meriwether is a professor in the Department of English at the University of South Carolina and a member of the Executive Committee of the Center for Editions of American Authors of the Modern Language Association. The late Donald Davidson, a noted poet and critic who was a member of the group known as "The Fugitives," taught at Vanderbilt University. Mary C. Simms Oliphant, co-editor of *The Letters of William Gilmore Simms*, is a granddaughter of the novelist and still maintains a residence at his plantation, "Woodlands."

Volume II of the Centennial edition will consist of uncollected *Stories and Tales*, edited and introduced by John Caldwell Guilds.

THE WRITINGS OF

William Gilmore Simms

CENTENNIAL EDITION

VOLUME I

THE WRITINGS OF

William Gilmore Simms

CENTENNIAL EDITION

VOLUME I

Voltmeier

or THE MOUNTAIN MEN

Introduction and Explanatory Notes by
Donald Davidson & Mary C. Simms Oliphant
Text established by James B. Meriwether

UNIVERSITY OF SOUTH CAROLINA PRESS
COLUMBIA

CENTER FOR EDITIONS OF
AMERICAN AUTHORS

AN APPROVED TEXT

MODERN LANGUAGE
ASSOCIATION OF AMERICA

®

*The publisher gratefully acknowledges the assist-
ance of the Friends of the University of South
Carolina Press in meeting the manufacturing costs
of this book.*

GENERAL PREFACE TO THE CENTENNIAL EDITION

Work on *The Centennial Edition of the Writings of William Gilmore Simms* officially began in 1964, when the University of South Carolina and its Press undertook to support the first stage of the project. At that time I became general editor, and the following year James B. Meriwether became textual editor. But the planning of the edition had been in progress since 1960, when a committee called together by Donald Davidson and chaired by Edd Winfield Parks, with Professor Meriwether as textual advisor, established the general scope and the editorial policy of the edition. The project received the formal endorsement of the South Atlantic Modern Language Association and the Southeastern branch of the American Studies Association in the fall of 1960. Although the Louisiana State University Press expressed interest in publishing the edition as early as 1961, it was found that the editorial work could most efficiently be done at South Carolina, where nearly all of the relevant manuscript and printed materials are located. The decision of the University of South Carolina Press to publish the edition made it possible to begin work on the first four volumes in 1964.

The Centennial Edition of the Writings of William Gilmore Simms will present a critical, unmodernized text of Simms's selected prose and poetry, in accordance with the textual principles and standards established by Fredson Bowers in the Centenary edition of Hawthorne, and those prescribed by the Modern Language Association Center for Editions of American Authors in its *Statement of Editorial Principles: A Working Manual for Editing Nineteenth Century American Texts*. The Editorial Board has decided first to undertake certain of Simms's less well-known and hitherto almost inaccessible works, concentrating upon previously unpublished manuscripts and material never before brought together in book form. The first fifteen volumes of the Centennial edition include *Voltmeier*, *Stories and Tales*, *Paddy McGann* and *As Good as a Comedy*, *Social and Political Essays* (the first four volumes), a volume of selected poetry and drama, two volumes of short novels, a selection of literary essays, *The Wigwam and the Cabin*, *Guy Rivers*, *Richard Hurdis*, *Border Beagles*, *The Cassique of Kiawah*, *The Yemassee*, and a bibliography—but not the Revolutionary Romances or the Kentucky tragedy volumes, for instance, which will be added if additional funds become available.

When so many have played significant roles in making the Centennial edition of Simms possible, only general debts of great magnitude can properly be acknowledged in this Preface to the edition as a whole: to the late Alexander S. Salley, whose collection of Simms, now in the South Caroliniana Library of the University of South Carolina, is invaluable; and to Edd Winfield Parks and other members of his 1960 committee—Donald Davidson, C. Hugh Holman, Louis D. Rubin, Jr., the late Randall Stewart, Arlin Turner, and Mary C. Simms Oliphant—whose early leadership was indispensable. The Editorial Board wishes particularly to acknowledge its indebtedness to the Advisory Committee, created in 1964, who have given unselfishly of their time and knowledge, always to the benefit of the edition: Clarence Gohdes, Duke University, chairman; Matthew J. Bruccoli, Ohio State University; Jay B. Hubbell, Duke University emeritus; and Willard Thorp, Princeton University.

John Caldwell Guilds

March, 1968
Columbia, South Carolina

ACKNOWLEDGMENTS

The editors of this volume are very grateful to the following scholars who assisted in the preparation of the introduction and notes: Rupert E. Palmer and Heinrich Meyer of Vanderbilt University; Arlin Turner of Duke University; and Dean Emeritus Francis W. Bradley of the University of South Carolina. Our especial thanks are directed to the staffs of the South Caroliniana Library of the University of South Carolina and the Joint University Library, Nashville, for their unfailing courtesy and assistance. Financial support for the preparation of the text was granted by the Committee on the Humanities of Vanderbilt University and the Committee on Research and Productive Scholarship of the University of South Carolina. For their aid in connection with our research in the United States Court records of the Allen Twitty case, we wish particularly to thank Beverley S. Simms, David H. Dantzler, and Warren R. Wilson. The assistance of Ralph Maultsby and Mrs. E. E. Barr was invaluable in tracing geographical details and property deeds in North Carolina. We are also grateful to Senator Strom Thurmond and O. B. Hartzog for their assistance in making available to us material for our background research.

D.D.
J.B.M.
M.C.S.O.

NOTE: *The death of Donald Davidson occurred on April 25, 1968, when* Voltmeier *was in page proof. His early leadership was indispensable to the initiation of a collected edition of Simms, and he never failed to give generously of his time and knowledge once the project was under way. The Centennial edition of Simms has lost one of its most loyal and devoted supporters, and the Editorial Board a close friend and irreplaceable co-worker.*

CONTENTS

INTRODUCTION

I

On December 11, 1868, William Gilmore Simms wrote to his New York friend of many years, Evert Augustus Duyckinck:

I am approaching the close of my Mountain Romance of "Voltmeier" which is to be published serially, and which is, as I think, in some respects, one of the most remarkable books I have ever written. Consult with Widdleton touching his new edition of my writings. Now that the election is over, and Revolution has every thing its own way, we should have the millenium that was promised us in that event—Peace and Plenty. Widdleton may now begin the new edition with my Revolutionary Romance of *"Joscelyn"*, of which the greater portion is written. . . . The tale of "Voltmeier" may be made to follow next winter. Both books I hold to be among the most excellent of my prose writings.[1]

The promised millenium was not delivered by the Grant administration—not even to the liberated Negroes who had heard so much of "Kingdom Comin' and the Year of Jubilo"; certainly not to Simms or the South in general, or to the nation. The hoped-for new edition of Simms's writings was never published. But *Voltmeier, or The Mountain Men* duly appeared in an ambitious new weekly magazine, edited by Orville James Victor and published in New York by French and Wheat. The novel ran for twenty-six weeks, beginning with the issue of March 6, 1869. Two years previously (January-December, 1867) Simms had published *Joscelyn: A Tale of the Revolution* as a serial in *The Old Guard*. At the time of his

---

[1] *The Letters of William Gilmore Simms,* ed. Mary C. Simms Oliphant, Alfred Taylor Odell, and T. C. Duncan Eaves, 5 vols. (Columbia, S.C., 1952-56), V, 181.

letter to Duyckinck, Simms was probably revising *Joscelyn* for the expected new edition. Simultaneously, he was writing a third novel, *The Cub of the Panther*, which also was published serially in *The Old Guard* in 1869; and he was taking notes for a fourth novel, never written, in which young George Washington, at the time of Braddock's fatal campaign, was to be a central figure.[2]

Of the three completed novels *Voltmeier, or The Mountain Men* now becomes the first to appear in book form and thus to fulfill in some symbolic measure the urgent hope of William Gilmore Simms's last years.

It is a characteristic Simms novel, though—as might be expected— not so teeming with masculine vigor and bold action as *The Forayers* and *Eutaw*, not so warm in human comedy and good humor as *Woodcraft*. Yet it still mines with much real success from the deep and rugged veins of American frontier life that gave these and other novels of Simms their hardiness and validity. *Voltmeier* has, too, the vices of construction and style found in Simms's preceding novels —the vices largely of his period, which neither Simms nor his contemporaries, even the greatest of them, ever fully overcame, if we judge them by mid-twentieth-century standards. Read a century after its inception and serial publication, *Voltmeier* certainly fulfills in various ways Simms's own good opinion of his work as he expressed it to Duyckinck. It has moments of real excellence, some of them startling in their graphic power. Whether excellent or not in all respects, it is without doubt "in some respects" one of the most remarkable books that Simms wrote.

In *Voltmeier* the aging (though not broken) Simms returns with obvious fondness to his best field—the Southern frontier. The scene is, to use Simms's own terms, "the border range between South & North Carolina." More specifically, it is the wild upper reaches of the French Broad River, in the deep valleys and lofty mountains of southwestern North Carolina, where, in the early years of the nineteenth century, great herds of cattle, horses, and hogs still roamed what was then called "the Cherokee range." The herdsmen were Southern frontiersmen, predecessors of the cowboys of the trans-Mississippi plains. On occasion they rounded up their herds, large

---

[2] *Letters*, V, 171.

or small, and drove them over mountains and valleys to distant markets. Among these, naturally, as in the trans-Mississippi West of later days, were desperadoes and outlaws as well as honest and gallant men. In *Voltmeier* Simms once more makes good use, in his familiar manner, both realistic and semi-humorous, of these generally low-grade characters. These southern frontiersmen, good and bad, are the "mountain men" of his alternative title.

But Leonard Voltmeier of the main title—Voltmeier *alias* Bierstadt, *alias* Old Grizzly and other names—is a different sort altogether. A German adventurer in America, the friend (as Simms represents him) of Goethe, an intellectual, and also apparently something of a practical scientist, Voltmeier leads a double life. As Bierstadt, or Old Grizzly, he rides a black horse, and is a veritable king of outlaws—a "big operator" in modern terms. From his remote mountain cave where he keeps a skilled German engraver at work and the "Wolf Den" that is his headquarters, he carries out large-scale counterfeiting in North Carolina and the South, and with it robbery on no small scale. Though robber and counterfeiter he is nevertheless a Robin Hood who does good to the poor. As Voltmeier, he rides a handsome white horse, is an eminent and respected planter and "rancher," owner of a magnificent estate called Keovala, father of the beautiful Mignon, and a connoisseur of music and poetry.

It is the introduction of this singular personage into the upland frontier of the Old South that makes *Voltmeier* different from Simms's preceding novels. Apparently no moral scruples have checked Voltmeier's career until young Fergus Wallace, son of the woman whom he once loved and his "half-nephew in fact," is shot and seriously wounded by two of his henchmen, Brown Peters and Swipes, who are joined in the later stages of their operations by a more polished ruffian named Gorham. Their mission is to waylay and rob a courier who is en route to the Cherokees with their annual stipend from the Federal government.

When Voltmeier—in his role as Old Grizzly—bends over the wounded and unconscious Fergus and identifies him, from his watch and from the papers that he carries, as his "half-nephew," his two lives begin to converge dangerously. As Voltmeier he must arrange to have the young man nursed back to health at Jake Harness' house, and then, eventually, brought to Keovala, but in carrying out this plan he must risk exposure as Old Grizzly. He experiences a surge of deep emotion. A sense of guilt awakens and with it a sense of impending doom. It is at this point that Simms begins to emphasize Voltmeier's Faustian character and to develop the theme of atonement.

Can Voltmeier solve his personal problem and somehow atone for old wrongs and more recent crimes without deeply injuring his daughter Mignon and his ward, Fergus? Once Fergus is brought to Keovala, the two young people fall in love. If all goes well, they will marry, with Voltmeier's blessing. But they know only the rich and brilliant Voltmeier of Keovala plantation who loves literature and music, and can quote Goethe. Of "Old Grizzly" the counterfeiter, mastermind of illegal operations that have their seat high in the rocky gorges of the French Broad River, they know nothing. Voltmeier has already made partial atonement in rescuing Fergus, healing his bullet wound, and taking him into his Keovala mansion. He plans to avoid exposure of his double life by abruptly ending his criminal operations and returning, with the young couple, to his native Germany.

But the secret enemy, Gorham, the "Black Dog" of Old Grizzly's own band, guesses that Bierstadt wears another face than the one he wears in the counterfeiters' Wolf Den. With malice and great shrewdness Gorham plays the spy upon his employer. He plots to ruin Fergus and Voltmeier and to take Mignon for himself. The plot against Fergus almost succeeds after Gorham plants counterfeit bills on the young man, gets him arrested, and even stirs up a lynch mob against him. Gorham's scheme fails when Voltmeier—though in this instance technically innocent—writes a letter of confession to the Court and takes upon himself the guilt of the crime with which Fergus is falsely charged. Then comes a series of rapid, dramatic scenes in which Gorham and Voltmeier—as pursuer and pursued—thread dark, wooded ravines and gallop along dizzy precipices. The novel ends when Voltmeier, bleeding from Gorham's bullet and dagger, grapples with his adversary on the brink of a gorge near the counterfeiters' den and drags Gorham with him to death in the rocky torrent far below. It is a somber ending, not unlike the last scene of *Moby-Dick:* "Two arms for a moment appeared above the waters, one hand still grasping a knife, and striking wildly; the other thrown up in air, and grasping vaguely, as if seeking for some support, and then all disappeared" (p. 424).

II

In what respects, exactly, did Simms consider this work of his last days "remarkable" and "most excellent"? He does not say. Undoubtedly he took pride in his portrayal of Voltmeier since in this central character he at last builds up to something like heroic and tragic dimensions his early conception of the man who has an advanced intellectual education without a correspondingly thorough moral education. In some sense Voltmeier is Guy Rivers or Richard Hurdis or Ellis Saxon of *Border Beagles* more firmly realized and more clearly motivated. But the psychological novel, though it always attracted Simms, was not his true métier. The twentieth-century reader soon perceives that Voltmeier is by no means a Captain Ahab or a Reverend Mr. Dimmesdale, although he does have some generic resemblance to that celebrated type of romantic sinner. Simms's genius is for straight narrative action, not for delicate or profound exploration of motive. He is never at his best when digging into a conscience or a consciousness. The nineteenth-century fictional tool provided for such digging—the "dramatic monologue" borrowed from stage soliloquy and "aside"—served him no better than it served his British and American contemporaries. If the attitudinizing monologues of Voltmeier could have been translated into the "stream-of-consciousness" medium of more modern fiction, particularly if they could have been disciplined by the limited point of view so cunningly developed as a modern technique, *Voltmeier* might present a more shipshape effect and therefore give more satisfaction to twentieth-century scholar-critics and to readers habituated to current techniques. We should also bear in mind that serial publication enforced upon Simms's novel—as upon the serialized versions of Hardy's and other nineteenth-century novels—a rather sensational content along with an often incoherent, scrappy structure. Simms himself says, writing to John Esten Cooke during Christmas week of 1868: "I am not good at serial writing, but it compensates better than any other now." [3] And he was in great need.

Still, the novel *Voltmeier*—which Simms would have insisted exemplifies the art of the romance rather than of the novel—is likely to leave a strong impression even upon a modern reader. The critic must seek to discover why this happens. It therefore seems proper to examine some circumstances that may have influenced Simms's personal estimate of *Voltmeier*.

The probability is that *Voltmeier* was for Simms a revival of the more vigorous and joyous days when he had written the early group of his Border Romances and, as a hardy southern supporter of the "Young America" group, had taken a stand in his *Views and Reviews* for a truly American literature no longer dominated by the "tyranny" of British literary authority. "The airy structures of our imagination," he wrote, "born of a like sky and atmosphere with that of Greece, should not shrink from comparison with those of Dodona and Hymettus. Our Olympus rises at our will, and the divine spirits which we summon to make sacred its high abodes, clothed in a political freedom superior to that of Athens, with less danger of having their supremacy disputed and their rites disturbed, should surely bring to their altars a priesthood no less great and glorious." [4] So said the Simms of 1845. The Simms of 1868–69, wrecked by war and poverty, his political freedom lost, ailing in body, troubled in mind, his State under the rule of carpetbaggers backed by Federal bayonets—that Simms still *must* write or perish utterly. Whatever may be said of *Joscelyn* or *The Cub of the Panther*, written at furious pace during these last years, *Voltmeier* is much more than a "potboiler." Simms wrote it also, truly enough, *calamo currente;* but for certain reasons *con amore.*

The distant origin of the novel—and probably its first conception—appears to be the hunting trip that Simms took with some friends to the general vicinity of Mt. Tryon in North Carolina during the autumn of 1847. In that year, after returning to Charleston from his usual summer trip to New York, Simms arranged to go with his family to Spartanburg, which he had never visited. The South

[3] *Letters,* V, 191.
[4] *Views and Reviews in American Literature . . . First Series* (New York, 1845), p. 19.

Carolina up-country would afford relief from the heat and summer fevers of the Woodlands area, but he also planned to inspect nearby Revolutionary battlefields. On July 15, 1847, Simms wrote his friend James Henry Hammond that he would leave his family at Spartanburg and "push for King's Mountain & other places, gleaning scraps & glimpses for revolutionary & other illustration." [5] To his New York friend James Lawson he wrote from Spartanburg on September 23: "Tomorrow, I expect to set off on a visit to the mountains of North Carolina. I shall be gone a week or ten days when I begin my slow descent to the low country. My purpose is to visit as much fine scenery, and to see & hear as much as I can. I shall make a book of it. 'A chiel's among 'em taking notes, & i' faith, he'll prent 'em!'" [6]

Three weeks later, Simms was back in Charleston and on October 19 wrote Robert Taylor Conrad, Philadelphia journalist and editor:

I am here again, on the seaboard, after a two months ramble among our mountains. I have been for some weeks the occupant of a camp among the hunters, beyond our remotest bounds of civilization. I have slept with the howling of the wolf & the sudden shriek of the panther in my ears, and have eaten my steaks of venison, fresh from the haunches of the buck, eight hundred feet above the Atlantic levels. I could make you a series of descriptive sketches that might tell much better than most of our foreign travel,—and may do so. [7]

These sketches appear never to have been published, though perhaps the episodic and descriptive poem "Tselica," which still exists in manuscript, [8] was what he had in mind. But the journal entries he made (excerpts from which are published in the explanatory notes) reveal how carefully he gathered in 1847 the material for a novel not written until twenty years later.

Nor is *Voltmeier* the only work in which Simms drew upon this 1847 excursion. The short novel *The Cub of the Panther* and two

[5] *Letters,* II, 330. See also Simms's letters to Perry (II, 333), to Duyckinck (II, 286), and to Lawson (II, 345).

[6] *Letters,* II, 350.

[7] *Letters,* II, 351.

[8] In the Charles Carroll Simms Collection, South Caroliniana Library, University of South Carolina.

lectures on the Appalachian region which Simms gave in the North in 1856, which still exist in manuscript, also show the extent to which Simms put his eyes and ears to work on that trip. And though he was already thoroughly familiar with the mountain country of *Voltmeier* from a five weeks' tour on horseback in the summer of 1842 and from a third visit in 1849 (on a journey ending at Warm Springs, Georgia), these writings are most of all indebted to what Simms saw and heard on the free and foot-loose camping trip with the hunters in 1847.

From the notes he took on this trip it is clear that in general the route followed by Simms and his friends in 1847 is that followed by young Fergus Wallace of *Voltmeier* in his mountain journey from Spartanburg to the vicinity of "Mills Gap at Mount Tryon." Two of the characters in the novel—Major Henry and Dr. Columbus Mills—bear the names of persons well known to Simms. Indeed, Mills was a kinsman, at whose house Simms was visiting when the 1847 hunting trip took place, and was, in fact, the chief guide for the trip, at least in leading Simms to points of special interest to him. "Mills Gap" appears both in the 1847 notes and the novel, and Simms drew pencil sketches of the "Range" and "Highest Peak of Mt. Tryon," with the notation that they were made "From the West porch of Dr. Mills's House" and from the "North Window" (See illustrations facing pages 432 and 433). Simms climbed Mt. Tryon on September 26, 1847, and had a sweeping view of the peaks and ranges visible from that point. On Tuesday, September 28, he noted that "we left the foot of Mt. Tryon, on a visit to the range called the Balsam Mountains in N.C." From this point on, the notes are rich and detailed in their description of the wide terrain and the ways of hunters, campers, and above all, the mountain people of the area.

When the party, after ascending Balsam Mountain, traverse the upper reaches of the French Broad River, Simms gives much attention to wild life—to the ways of bear, deer, wolf, panther, bees, hornets, ants. On the higher parts of the Balsam, they have their first hunt, during which a bear leads the dogs an exciting chase among precipitous rocks and turns to fight the dogs on the brow of a cliff, above a torrent, much as Voltmeier and Gorham grapple in their fatal struggle in Chapters 73 through 76 of the novel. Other touches in the novel, particularly in the scenic descriptions, greatly generalized though these are, may derive from other parts of the long mountain trip, which included a ride to Caesar's Head and a journey—passing the Green and Broad rivers—to Hickory Nut Gap.

Most important of all is the likelihood that Simms derived the suggestion for the central figure of the novel from the last-mentioned part of his journey, since at this time he visited the house and farm of "Allen Twitty, the famous counterfieter." From Dr. Columbus Mills and others, during the hunting trip, Simms must have gleaned some details of the sensational trial, involving Allen Twitty and various other North Carolinians, that dragged on for many years in the Federal District Court at Raleigh. Allen Twitty, himself a man of a prominent North Carolina family, was indicted on general charges of counterfeiting, along with a number of unsavory ruffians accused of operating a widespread business as his confederates. Twitty is evidently the model or prototype that Simms used for the fictional Leonard Voltmeier in his character of Bierstadt or "Old Grizzly."

The Twitty case came up for trial almost yearly between 1805 and 1815. Trial proceedings were delayed—no doubt intentionally "obstructed"—by the failure of material witnesses to appear, by forfeiture of bonds, by grants of *nolle prosequi* on certain counts, by numerous continuances, and even by requests for postponements by the prosecuting attorney. All of the persons arrested were eventually acquitted.

In its public aspects, the case may be followed in the columns of the Raleigh (N.C.) *Register*. The prominence of some of the accused persons soon made it a *cause célèbre*. Brigadier General John Moore (to take one notable example) had reached "the heights of eminence" in the social and political life of the State. He had been a member of the Commons for fifteen of the years between 1788 and 1806, and in the latter year had been Speaker. But he had been so "obnoxious" and active in bringing the counterfeiters to trial that he was charged by the gang with being himself concerned in their counterfeiting operations. General Moore was actually arrested and temporarily imprisoned. It took the combined efforts of the local bar and shocked citizens of the surrounding country to extricate him from danger.

The prisoners at the bar were said to be "fiends in human shape," but so "influential and hardy" were they (it was alleged), and so able and prominent was the counsel for the defense, that the Judge had balked at authorizing their arrest. The people (it was claimed) were "all under influence of fear or favor." Allen Twitty, the master counterfeiter, boasted that he would have no difficulty, at any time, in procuring bail for at least $20,000.[9]

So deeply had the case impressed itself upon the popular memory that, when Simms visited the mountain country forty years after its beginnings, actual details of the trial and its circumstances were topics of common discussion among his hunting companions. His host's kinsman, Ambrose Mills, had served as one of the Justices of Peace involved in the proceedings. One of the most interesting facets of the impression made upon Simms himself by what he heard is the memorandum he made to himself (in the 1847 notes) to remember Twitty's many "virtues."

From the *Letters* we may suppose that Simms began the actual composition of *Voltmeier* early in 1868. Certainly he wrote most of what we now have between January, 1868, and January, 1869. Yet the opening sentence of the novel, with its reference to Spartanburg as it was "at the period of our narrative, some forty years ago," strongly suggests the possibility that Simms may have begun a draft of *Voltmeier* soon after his return from the mountain expedition of 1847. "Forty years" previous to 1847 would place the narrative in the period when the operations of Twitty and his associates came to light; but forty years previous to 1868, the time when Simms was desperately looking for material that would make a novel and bring in cash, would not be particularly appropriate.

That Simms, rummaging among his papers, found and hastily incorporated in *Voltmeier* the opening passages of a novel begun in 1847, can only be conjecture. But it is clear that his three mountain trips of the 1840's, and particularly that of 1847, were a major source for several of his later writings. The chief of these, of course, is

---

[9] The editors have been fortunate in having access to the entire body of the court proceedings in the Twitty case, now filed with the records of the General Services Administration, East Point, Georgia. (See also Explanatory Notes, p. 433.)

Voltmeier, and mention has already been made of *The Cub of the Panther* and the two "Apalachia" lectures of 1856. In addition, the tall tales "How Sharp Snaffles Got His Capital and Wife," first published in 1870,[10] and "Bald-Head Bill Bauldy," still in manuscript[11] but to be published in a later volume of this edition, probably owe something to these trips. The opening scene of "Sharp Snaffles," where the hunters lounge and compete in the big "Lie" of tale-telling, may well picture the camp of the Simms party in the autumn of 1847; and the tone of "Sharp Snaffles" echoes, as do parts of *Voltmeier,* the happier days of Simms's life.

Hardly less important in Simms's mind than the revived frontier setting, obviously, is the German element, which Simms develops with a zest that reflects one of his paramount intellectual interests from boyhood to old age. We do not have here what is often dismissed as the "Gothic" tendency of Simms's earlier romanticism. Leonard Voltmeier is shaped as a power-seeking Faustian character whose moral dilemma is intended to resemble that of Goethe's hero. That Voltmeier's daughter is named Mignon suggests, perhaps, that we are to look for something of Wilhelm Meister in him, too. The idealized nineteenth-century Germany to which Voltmeier hopes to escape is as Arcadian as the land of Mignon's famous song in *Wilhelm Meisters Lehrjahre:* "Kennst du das Land wo die Zitronen blühn." When Voltmeier brings the rescued Fergus to Keovala, Mignon proceeds to teach him German. Soon the two young lovers are reading together Schiller's *Maria Stuart.*

The name "Voltmeier" seems to be a hybrid of Simms's own coinage, with "meier" as the German part and "Volt" conjectured to derive from the name of the Italian physicist Alessandro Volta, if only on the somewhat implausible grounds that Voltmeier (as Bierstadt) guards his mountain hideout by electric wires—from which the prying Gorham receives a shock—and provides for the complete destruction of his operations center by the electric detonation of hidden explosives. The electric detonation is of course anachronistic. It is hard to guess what Simms had in mind. But it is not hard to realize that in representing Voltmeier as a German intellectual

[10] *Harper's,* XLI (Oct., 1870), 667-687.
[11] In the Charles Carroll Simms Collection.

Simms recalled the buoyant days of the eighteen-forties and fifties when he was reading widely in German literature, both in the original and in translation. In those years Simms was the dominant figure of a little Charleston circle that met regularly with their native German friend and teacher, Augustus Sachtleben, to read and discuss German literature. One of this circle was James Warley Miles, Episcopal minister and classics professor, who sat at Simms's bedside when he died. To Miles he wrote, in a letter of uncertain date: "Meanwhile, Sachtleben has got back & proposes that we shall resume our German readings—the old Class. We are to meet at my wigwam [Simms's Charleston House on Smith Street] on Thursday night at 8 P.M. and look to see you there. We now propose to take up the Egmont of Goethe. Don't fail us." [12] In 1829, Simms had written admiringly of *Wilhelm Meister's Apprenticeship* as second only to *Faust*. In prose fiction he rated it as "the master-work of the great author of Germany." [13] In the eighteen-sixties Simms was not alone in that estimate and must have taken satisfaction in imparting something of a Goethean aura to the major character of a large novel. It is the Goethean aura, whether authentically Goethean or a Simmsian-Carlylean notion about Goethe, that raises Leonard Voltmeier above the picaresque figures of the Border novels.

III

The agony that went into the composition and serialization of *Voltmeier* is a story in itself—a story not paralleled in the annals of American literature and almost too distressing to be related here in all its painful details. Simms apparently began work on the novel early in 1868, perhaps by late January of that year. The *Southern Home Journal* of Baltimore announced in its issue of January 4, 1868, that "Wm. Gilmore Simms is . . . writing a serial for the Southern Home Journal." [14] Simms had indeed committed himself to that enterprise and to much more. By this time he had re-estab-

[12] *Letters,* V, 326.
[13] *Southern Literary Gazette,* I (March, 1829), 384.
[14] *Letters,* V, 84n.

lished connections with the staunchest of his Northern friends. To Duyckinck he wrote, from Charleston, January 20, 1868:

I am about to commence a story for which I am to get $600—if I am ever paid; I have been a loser some $300 since I left New York, writing for periodicals; and now doubt all of them. I have commenced rebuilding at Woodlands; but a single wing of one story giving me 4 rooms on a floor. These must suffice for the present. . . . The money goes out very fast, and the work goes on very slowly, and I am every now & then troubled with the vexatious question—of what use! However, even as a temporary shelter for my family, it is absolutely needful, and if we escape being driven out or massacred within the next two years, it will have pretty much paid for itself.[15]

Simms's expressed fear of "being driven out or massacred" is one of the relatively few references in his letters of this period to the turmoil of Reconstruction, which by 1868 was developing its ugliest phenomena in South Carolina. For governor the State had a carpet-bagger from Ohio, one Richard K. Scott, an official of the Freedmen's Bureau, notorious for his corrupt and oppressive administration. But Simms doubtless had more particularly in mind the threats of the newly organized Union League, a militant, secret, and actively violent Negro organization. Even so, foremost in Simms's thought were food, clothing, and shelter for his family. For funds to rebuild one wing of the twice-burned house at Woodlands, he had sold at a sacrifice his valuable collection of Laurens manuscripts to the Long Island Historical Society of New York. "Aside from the special fund for this building," he wrote Charles Gayarré, on March 13, 1868, "I have not a dollar of resource, save what I work for from day to day." [16]

By the time of the Gayarré letter Simms had written "500 pages MS. note paper, of this work [Voltmeier]." By May 3 he reported to M. C. M. Hammond that he had completed 640 pages of the novel, "having about 360 more to write between this & July." Also he was doing other writing—journalistic hackwork. "I write column after column for the Courier—& contrib[ute] occasionally to the

---

[15] Letters, V, 106.
[16] Letters, V, 116.

Magazines, and all for [a] sorry compensation."[17] A little over a month later, on June 12, Simms wrote from Charleston, in much discouragement, to his son William Gilmore Simms, Jr.: "I am not well. My digestion is bad, & I need better food than I get here. . . . I am uneasy at not hearing from the Baltimore publisher, who has failed to acknowledge . . . the last 155 pages of MS. sent him, and does not as yet respond to my call for a money instalment. It is very vexatious."[18] Meanwhile, two periodicals that owed him for contributions—*Southern Society* and *Southern Opinion*—failed to remit a cent. Against one of them Simms filed a suit for $250. He did not have money enough to pay "an ugly little balance" owed to the workmen who were rebuilding Woodlands.[19]

Simms was overworked, disgusted, ill, but not defeated. He retired from Charleston to Woodlands. There he resumed work on *Voltmeier*—writing, presumably, in the little one-room brick outbuilding today preserved as his study—but broke off relations with the *Southern Home Journal,* and wrote Duyckinck that he would go to New York in August.

On arrival in late August, Simms wrote his son that he was ill with "the severest attack of chill & fever that I have ever had to endure."[20] Nevertheless he was soon making plans to go to Great Barrington, Massachusetts, also to Boston, and back to Yonkers, and most especially was intent, through his old publisher, J. S. Redfield, "to procure a prompt answer from Mr. Victor," editor of the new *Illuminated Western World,* to whom he wished to offer "a collection of *short* stories, suitable for periodical publication."[21] In mid-September, Simms was in New York again—taking quinine daily and writing his son about paint and shingles for Woodlands. Also he had been in touch with Mr. Victor. On October 3, still lingering in New York, he wrote Victor and offered him, not a book of stories, but his novel:

I propose "Voltmeier" to you, for the first use, for Seven Hundred Dollars, three hundred & fifty to be paid on the sheets already in your

[17] *Letters,* V, 126.
[18] *Letters,* V, 138-139.
[19] *Letters,* V, 153.
[20] *Letters,* V, 154.
[21] *Letters,* V, 156.

hands, & in advance of the residue; the remaining three Hundred & fifty to be paid on the delivery of the completed MS. of the work, which I undertake to complete with all possible expedition.—I could wish to take home with me the last chapter of the MS., now in your hands, in order to weld the two sections together in the most art-like manner.[22]

In a postscript Simms made it clear that he wished to retain the right to publish *Voltmeier* in any new edition of his works.

By October 29 of this busy and tormented year Simms, back again at Woodlands, found himself simultaneously at work on three books—*Voltmeier, The Cub of the Panther,* and the romance planned but never written dealing with Washington during Braddock's campaign. He may also have been revising *Joscelyn* for the projected but never realized new edition of his works. On December 1 he wrote M. C. M. Hammond: "I am now working on a dead horse, that is to supply material for money already advanced . . . . Here for six weeks have I been toiling religiously day by day, and in that time have written nearly a thousand pages MS. such as this, not including a vast deal of correspondence, &c."[23] Throughout the the autumn and early winter of 1868, Simms's letters abound with references to the progress of *Voltmeier*—which he twice calls "Voltmeier, or the Mountain Robber"—and with indications of the pressure that he felt in keeping ahead of the printers, who by Christmas were evidently setting the first installment of *The Cub of the Panther* for its January debut in *The Old Guard.* Not until January of 1869 was he able to finish *Voltmeier.* On January 18 he wrote Victor:

The residue of the MS. of Voltmeier has gone forward by express, sent from here two days ago. I trust it will reach your hands in safety. It is sent to my agent who will deliver it to Mess'rs French & Wheat, and I have drawn in his favour for the balance of Three Hundred Dollars, which I beg you will see to the payment of, as I labor under some pressing needs, with no other resource but that money. You will find that Voltmeier considerably exceeds in the number of pages my own estimate; and instead of 1000 of my small pages, it reaches 1255, or thereabouts. This, if not a gain to you, is so much loss to me. It will show you that I have been conscientious, in labouring duly to develope the story, as one eminently of art. Let me entreat you to enter upon the task of abridging it,

[22] *Letters,* V, 166.
[23] *Letters,* V, 177.

with great tenderness and caution. Try, on the contrary, the experiment on your readers, of an art-romance—a something which passes above the sensational, into the psychological & largely imaginative; subordinating and using the passions without suffering their domination. I think you will find enough in 'Voltmeier' of the sensational; enough for pictorial illustration on a bold scale, for the most gluttonous of your readers; but much besides for that higher class to which in your work as already published, you seem to appeal.[24]

Editor Victor evidently did not use the "great tenderness and caution" in "abridging" that Simms implored him to exercise upon a manuscript admittedly over-long. For example, we may doubtless blame on Victor's incautious cutting the failure of the serialized novel to clear up the mystery of the peculiar amulet given to Fergus by Major Henry and greatly emphasized at the beginning of the narrative. Simms would hardly have been guilty of *that* omission. He must have intended for the amulet to carry dramatic weight in the meeting of Fergus and Voltmeier. Victor also did not exploit Simms's suggestion that he might use scenes of the novel for "pictorial illustration on a bold scale."

IV

With *Voltmeier*, Simms's work as a writer virtually ended, except for what little he might still have to do on *The Cub of the Panther* and the stories he left in manuscript, "Bald-Head Bill Bauldy" and "The Humours of the Manager." His last formal composition was his address, "The Sense of the Beautiful," delivered on May 3, 1870, before the Charleston County Agricultural and Horticultural Association. After the event he wrote Lawson that he was "feeble, & exhausted from delivery, but contrived, by sheer will, to hold out & hold forth to the last." [25] The same words would apply with equal force to the entire incredible struggle of Simms as writer, during these years, to support his family, rebuild the Woodlands house, somehow maintain the plantation, keep in touch with friends of North and South, and give aid and sympathy to the needy of

[24] *Letters*, V, 197.
[25] *Letters*, V, 313.

all degrees, despite the extreme social disorder and danger around him, despite heartbreaking losses and disappointments, and above all despite the racking abdominal illness that finally proved fatal. From February, 1869, to the end, his letters refer frequently to his illness and exhaustion, but soon carry assurances that he is feeling better. Simms attributed his condition to overwork. His letter to Paul Hamilton Hayne, of December 22, 1869, sums up vividly the circumstances referred to in various other letters:

For my part, and for the last six months, I have been literally *hors de combat*, from overwork of the brain—brain sweat—as Ben Jonson called it,—and no body sweat—no physical exercise. In the extremity of my need, I took contracts in N. Y. in the autumn of 1868 for no less than three romances, all to be worked, at the same time. I got advances of money on each of these books, and the sense of obligation pressing upon me, I went rigidly to work, concentrating myself at the desk from 20th. Oct. 1868 to the 1st. July 1869.—nearly 9 months, without walking a mile in a week, riding but twice and absent from work but half a day on each of these occasions. The consequence was that I finished two of the books & broke down on the third, having written during that period some 3000 pages of the measure of these which I now write to you. [Then, after describing his symptoms] From July, when I went North, to the present moment, I have been suffering more or less acutely, and at no time without constant abdominal uneasiness. . . . You are aware that I was burned out by Sherman, and had to rebuild, restore, replenish & provide. You may ascribe all my physical sufferings to this necessity, for this could not be done without money, and my only capital was in my poor brain. And my brain has played the devil with my bowels, and that these have not yet played the devil with my brains, is due to a resolute will & to a good physique.[26]

His own distress, great though it was, did not prevent Simms from aiding others. In 1866 Simms befriended Henry Timrod, already mortally ill, by peddling the twenty remaining copies of Timrod's *Poems* at rare book prices to Charleston friends, for the impoverished poet's benefit.[27] This is but one of many instances of the wide play of Simms's generosity and immense energy, even when Death was already beckoning him.

[26] *Letters*, V, 282, 284.
[27] Edd Winfield Parks, *Henry Timrod* (New York, 1964), p. 45.

What sustained him, besides that "resolute will" and "good physique" mentioned in his letter to Hayne? Surely it was the impulse that made Simms above all else a writer, with a passion for storytelling not equalled among his American contemporaries. To the last, Woodlands plantation demanded ceaseless attention. The affairs of his State, the South, the Nation excited and at times absorbed him. Editing diverted him. Politics tempted him. In the final years War and Reconstruction all but crushed him. Still he was a writer, faithful to his art as he conceived it. Out of his early devotion grew Simms's conception of a national American literature, boldly outlined in his "Americanism in Literature" article of 1845 [28] and related essays. Specifically, in his lengthy article, "The Epochs and Events of American History, As Suited to the Purposes of Art in Fiction," Simms took his stand with Philip Sidney, the great Humanist of Elizabethan England, in asserting the superiority of literary art over history.[29] While claiming a certain distinctness and newness for American literature, he nevertheless placed it within the broad stream of British tradition—and therefore of the West European tradition that all possessed. To his own historical imagination he gave a range that covered much of the immense territory of "Epochs and Events" set forth in this article. With varying success—it must be acknowledged—and often in unseemly haste, Simms explored, in his romances, biographies, stories, poems, and miscellaneous writings, our American history from its remotest colonial origins on down, with special attention to neglected phases of Spanish and French exploration and settlement in the South and Southwest, the Caribbean area, Central America, and even the South American continent. In Spanish and Spanish-American history alone, Simms ranges over more than a thousand years, from the eighth-century conflict between Arinn Goth and Catholic Spaniard depicted in *Pelayo* to the clash of Mexican Santa Anna and the Texans which is the subject of his drama, *Michael Bonham*. It is true that many of these works, ambitious though they are and moved by a genuine and scrupulous

[28] *Southern and Western Monthly Magazine and Review*, I (Jan., 1845), 1-14; Simms's review of an oration of the same title by A. B. Meek.
[29] *Southern and Western Monthly Magazine and Review*, I (Feb., March, 1845), 109-127, 182-191.

historical consciousness, are written in the diffuse and sententious prose that afflicted romantic fiction of the time, whether from American, British, French, or other hands. Simms is better, perhaps is near to his best, when forced to concentrate, as in some of his stories—for example in his less well-known stories like "Marie de Berniere" or "The Maroon."

Ill though he might be, fatally ill, distraught by grief, Simms wrote, wrote, wrote, beside the blackened ruins of his house, and so kept to the end the devotion of his youth. So did Walter Scott write, in his time of trouble, and Honoré de Balzac, pressing to round out, even if in extreme haste, his *Comédie Humaine*. Simms died on June 11, 1870. What wonder that when his body was prepared for burial, the fingers of his writing hand could not be straightened. His friend Paul Hamilton Hayne, writing in 1885, reported that at Simms's death one of his admirers said, "I made garlands of laurel and bay, and wove too a cross of white immortelles, which I placed in the poor emaciated hands of the corpse, the *fingers of which refused to take any other position than their natural one, drawn up as if to write!*" [30]

D.D.
M.C.S.O.

---

[30] Hayne, "Ante-Bellum Charleston," *Southern Bivouac*, I (Oct., 1885), 268.

Part I

VOLTMEIER
or The Mountain Men

Chapter i

FERGUS

Spartanburg, the chief town of the District of that name, in the State of South Carolina, with a present population of some four thousand inhabitants, was, at the period of our narrative, some forty years ago, simply a village, with a population which did not exceed one fourth that number. A showy and imposing town now, with fine churches and colleges, it was then a pretty mountain hamlet, occupying an undulating surface, dotted with neat cottages, a score or two of shops confined to one street, and occasional small farmsteads, which agreeably diversified its general aspects to the eye of taste. Contiguous to the mountains, they hung upon its northern border in long, irregular elevations, rising from several hundred to as many thousand feet, and sending their blue peaks aloft, as if to sustain the great arch of heaven that spanned them with an azure which admirably harmonized with their own. These mountain outlines made the boundaries between the two sister Carolinas, and constituted the first steppes to that grand range known by the red men of this region as the "Apalachian;" by those of Virginia as the "Alleghany," and commonly, by their white successors, as the Blue Ridge—the great back-bone of the country—separating, or rather connecting, the States of the Atlantic with those which spread themselves along the waters of the Gulf of Mexico.

The store, or more properly shop, of Brigham & Co., was one of the largest and most pretentious in the way of trade, of the place. The building was of brick, tolerably capacious, and its stock in trade was comparatively large. The shelves were well filled with dry goods; and the counters below and above, together with large portions of the floors and gangways, were crowded with the usual varieties which country stores are usually required to keep. Boxes and barrels, packed and marked, were ranged outside along the pavement. The concern of Brigham & Co. evidently was a flourishing one.

I

Within the store, his coat off and sleeves rolled up, a young man, who might have been twenty-one or thereabouts, was busily engaged in weighing, packing and marking. Great bundles of goods, neatly put up, tied and labeled, were accumulated upon the counter. Boxes stood ready to receive them as they should be prepared. Crockery ware, iron ware, glass ware, medicines, calicoes, cloths, groceries— everything, in short, which farmers and planters might need or desire, had been thus gathered together by the vigorous industry of the young shopkeeper. There was no delay in his operations. His eye cast for a moment upon the order book, and in the next his hands had gone to their work, of meeting its requisitions; and as each order was completed, the articles were boxed or barreled, the package marked, and borne or rolled out upon the sidewalk, to take its place with such as had already accumulated there. But, though the young man's movements were all full of animation, his countenance exhibited none. It was marked by an expression of anxiety which almost amounted to pain. The eye was dull, though large, and of a fine gray. The forehead was broad and full. All the features were finely moulded, exhibiting character, as well as sym- metry and beauty. His figure was tall and slender, but manly, and the carriage was easy, and marked with a natural grace. The tem- perament was the sanguine, rich and warm of complexion, indicating zeal, energy, and eagerness of impulse; though it was evident that these had been somewhat subdued by a training of circumstances which had finally taken the aspect of an habitual care. The sadness of his countenance, while restlessly at work, was still predominant in all his features.

At length he paused from his more active labors, gave a glance over his order book, checked off the several articles enumerated, made several memorandums, closed the book, proceeded to wash face and hands in water kept in the rear of the shop; and, this done, he put on his coat, and after a moment's hesitation, as if in doubt, he suddenly moved forward, and emerged from the store into the street, making his way to a post, some twenty steps from the shop, where two men were engaged in conversation. To one of these persons he simply bowed respectfully, and then addressed the other—a compact, hard-featured person of dogged aspect, small, fox-like eyes, and a sinister expression of countenance.

"I have finished all the orders, sir, and beg that you will now suffer me to go home—perhaps for the rest of the day."

"Go home—and for the rest of the day? Why, man, what are you thinking about? It is hardly eleven o'clock! You can not have finished half the orders."

"They are all finished, sir."

"What! the hardware for Colonel Birdsall, and that long order from Jones & Whipple?"

"All, sir—"

"Impossible! You did not *come* till eight."

"True, sir; but the orders are all supplied, nevertheless."

"Bring me the order book."

It was brought him; and, with the book in hand, he proceeded to examine the marks on the several packages on the pavement.

Meanwhile the third gentleman, a person apparently of thirty years of age, of short figure, but amiable expression of face, had taken the youth by the hand, with an earnest pressure, and said tenderly:

"And how is your mother to-day, Fergus?"

The moisture grew in the youth's eyes, as he replied:

"Very feeble, Major; she is sinking fast. I know not how soon—"

Here Mr. Brigham returned; and thrusting the order book into the young man's hands, said impatiently:

"I don't see, sir, how I can spare you to-day. Who's here to attend in your absence, now that Archy Mason is away?"

"He came back last night, sir."

"And why has he not shown himself to-day? It is now nearly twelve o'clock."

"He will be here by twelve, sir. I have seen him. He was very tired when he got into town late last night, and slept late this morning."

"And whose fault was it that he came late? He should have been back by sunset. Always some excuse for dilly-dally! But, whether he comes or not, I do not see how you can be spared. He is but a boy, who can't be trusted to put up orders and answer questions."

"But the orders are all closed already, sir, and—"

"Look you, Mr. Fergus Wallace! I don't relish these incessant calls upon your time and mine, which every now and then take you off for a day at a time, on every idle pretext—"

The young man's cheeks flushed; and in accents inclining to be vehement, he replied quickly:

"Pretense, sir! my mother is probably dying, while I am parleying here!"

"Parleying! Ah, parleying! and with *me!*"

"Yes, sir. I know not how long she will live—and I must go to her, whether you consent or no."

"Ha! well, sir, depart as soon as you please. But you will remember to remain away until *I* shall *please* to solicit your return!"

The young man gave a single, but expressive look, to the gentleman whom he had addressed as "Major," then bowing slightly to both parties, he turned away, and was at once speeding up the street in a walk that might almost be called a trot. When he had gone the Major said:

"Brigham, you are quite too harsh with that young man."

"Major, you know not how these young fellows bother me. Here's that boy, Archy Mason, who should have been back before sunset last evening; he idles away his time on the road, and I reckon, does not get back till midnight, and oversleeps himself in the morning; and here's this Fergus Wallace, who is just as full of pride as if he were the lineal descendant of the great Sir William himself, that you read of in the Scottish Chiefs—he comes to me every third day in the week, with the pretense of his mother's great illness and danger. He has had the same story in his mouth for the last three months—and I'm sick of hearing it. I wish the old woman would get well at once, or die and be done with it!"

"For shame, Brigham, for shame! the young man has told you nothing but the truth. Mrs. Wallace has been sinking for months, and now the end approaches. Mrs. Henry was with her last evening, and she assures me that she can hardly survive the next forty-eight hours."

"Indeed! You have it from your wife, then. If you had told me that, I'd have let the young man go at once without any words."

"And why should you not put full faith in *his* words? Did you ever catch him in a lie? Do you suspect him of any dishonesty? Have you not, now, Mr. Brigham,—I put it to your conscience,—have you not always found him truthful and honorable in all his dealings? were I to put you on the stand, to-morrow, as a witness in respect to his character, would you not be forced to say that he was as upright a youth as you have ever known?"

"Well, Major, since you put it in that light, I confess I should have to say so—"

"And still, for all this conviction, you wantonly wound his sensibilities by showing that you doubt his veracity."

"You're too hard on me, Major! I did not mean *that*—all I meant was that I thought him unreasonably apprehensive of his mother's danger."

"And even the *unreasonable* apprehensions of a *son* for his *mother's* life, are to be respected, Mr. Brigham. That they are *unreasonable*, does not make him *untruthful*, if his fears are honestly entertained. Now let me tell you that you have lost one of the best securities for your own successful business, in losing that young man."

"Oh! he'll come back!"

"Don't you believe it. He has too much pride for that, after what you have said, and the treatment you have shown him."

"Well, I'm willing to believe that he has the pride of the old Devil himself, but he'll come back. He can't help it! He can't live upon nothing; and places at three hundred a year are not to be had for the asking, let me tell you. Times are too hard, clerks too plentiful, and good situations too few, to be parted with because of a few hard words from master to man."

"You do not know Fergus Wallace, Mr. Brigham. Hard words, I grant you, might be forgiven; but hard feelings, never, by a man of his character. I said you do not know Fergus Wallace. I do. You tell me of three hundred dollars as his salary. You do not know that, for this year, I myself have paid him, for his services to me, a salary of half that amount."

"Services to you, Major?—"

"Yes; he has been drawing up papers for me, for nine months; drawing them at night, after his day's work in your shop has been done—drawing them by the bedside of his widowed and diseased mother. At first I gave him employment for *her* sake, knowing how little they had to live on; but very soon I employed him for my own sake, as I found him not merely very useful as a copyist, but remarkably intelligent as a lawyer."

"As a lawyer, Major?"

"Yes, as a lawyer! He has been reading law for two years under my instructions. I supplied him with the books, and his progress has been wonderful. I hold him to be one of the most promising young students I ever met, and this very season he will apply for admission to practice in all our courts."

"What good will that do him, and how will he support himself, I wonder, till practice shall come in?"

"How? Hark ye, Brigham, and judge for yourself of your chance of getting him back to drudge for you all his time, at a salary of three hundred dollars."

"Well, Major, I'm curious."

"Well, he comes to *me*, hereafter, and not to *you*. I had resolved, months ago, to take him into my office, the moment he is admitted, giving him five hundred a year as my copartner in the law."

"Well, Major, I don't think this so friendly on your part—taking my clerk out of my hands in this way, when I've been giving you all my business for the last five years, and paying you, perhaps, as handsomely as any client you ever had."

"Beautiful consistency, Brigham! You drive a clerk from your house, and complain that another takes him in! You deserve to lose him; and he is quite another person from what I think him, if he ever darkens your door again, though you should bait your clerkship with three thousand, instead of three hundred dollars. Yes, Brigham, he *has* pride, and great should be your shame for so wantonly insulting it. Good morning, Brigham. And when you have a good clerk, good officer, agent or servant, see that you do them honor, if you would prove yourself either a good trader or a good Christian."

The Major left him, and Brigham, silent of speech, but savage of mood, shook his doubled fist at the back of his lawyer, and returned within the shop, which was his temple.

Chapter II

MOTHER AND SON

The cottage was a very poor one, some three miles from the village, nestling humbly in a little hollow of the hills, and half buried from sight by overcrowding foliage, which had been left for many a day unpruned. It was a little farmstead, of some five acres only, that of the widow Wallace; not absolutely sterile, but almost totally lacking of cultivation. A small garden of half an acre lay back of the dwelling, where a few meager sprouts and common vegetables might be seen, not to *grow* exactly, but to exist. Poverty was the most conspicuous of all the present objects; poverty without and poverty within,—poverty and sorrow,—and silence,— soon to be that of death!

A shiver passed through the whole frame of Fergus Wallace, as, lifting the latch of the decaying door, he passed into the humble habitation. He entered with cautious footsteps, as if he dreaded to disturb some sacred slumber. It might be that last sleep of all, which is always felt to be sacred. He paused, breathing slowly, and half stifling his breathing, when he had entered the narrow passage from which the rooms, all on one floor, opened on either hand. He looked to one of the chambers, and having, as it were, gathered up courage for the movement, he approached the door.

His footstep was now heard. A faint voice from within called him by name. The keen ear of a mother knew that footfall of her son by infallible instincts. The door was opened for him by a little girl, the daughter of a poor neighbor. She had been for the last hour the only companion of the widow.

"Is it you, Flit?" said Fergus, gently tapping the child upon her head.

"Yes, Mr. Fergus, I've been staying with your mamma, while *my* mamma went home to see to Wattie."

"Thank you, Flit."

7

"No, don't, Mr. Fergus. I'm so glad to stay."

"Well, mother." And he seated himself beside her, kissing her on the brow as he did so.

"It is well, my son! It will soon be better;" and she smiled faintly, but sweetly, to her son's eyes, as he gazed earnestly into her own filmy orbs. A placid resignation—its beautiful calm—overspread features which had once been beautiful, but which were now wan and lusterless, save where a single spot of crimson—very small, but very bright—kindled, like an eye itself, upon either cheek.

The heart of the young man seemed to quake within him as he gazed. He was silent, and gave expression to his fears and feelings only by that long straining gaze, and that fond pressure of his hand on hers. He sat there in silence for a while, when the widow said to the child—

"Go now, Flit, my dear—go home to your mother and help her to nurse little Walter."

"Please, Ma'am Wallace, I'll come soon again if mamma will let me."

"Oh! she'll let you, Flit. Go now, that's a good child."

"Good bye, ma'am. Good bye, Mr. Fergus."

"Good bye, Flit." And the little thing, not more than eight years old, went, seemingly with reluctance. Silence—deep, expressive silence—followed her departure for a while. Fergus Wallace had no questions to ask, no consolations to offer. He had no hopes; and when he looked round the little apartment, and saw the meagerness of its possessions; when he beheld the vial of medicine upon the toilet, and bethought him of a thousand delicacies which might sweeten somewhat the bitter of that cup of life, from which life was now permitted to take its only draught; and that this life of the beloved one was going out in comparative privation of everything that wealth might bring, and affection would desire to bestow; very sad, if not bitter, were the thoughts that gathered in his mind.

Day by day, during the whole term of his mother's decline, had he been haunted by this visible presence of Poverty—powerless to drive it away. He sometimes diverted a small sum from the daily expenditure—not often to be spared—in procuring her some foreign delicacies—but, with his poor salary, this was to be done rarely. Occasionally some good neighbor brought her a jelly, or an orange, some sweetmeat or fruit or beverage; but the poor lady had few friends who were able very frequently to contribute in this manner. Mrs. Henry had only recently sought her out, under instructions from her husband, who, though long knowing young Wallace, had not, till a few weeks, been aware of the extreme condition of his mother. The son's pride had kept that secret. Her visits were now frequent, and her gifts constituted the greater part of those little delicacies which found their way to the widow's chamber.

"Mother," said Fergus, abruptly breaking the silence. "I have brought you some oranges just from the city. Will you suck one, or shall I peel it for you?"

"Oh! thank you, Fergus—thank you. I was craving some grateful acid. My dear boy, how well you know what I wish. Peel me one quick, Fergus, and give me piece by piece."

She sucked the grateful juices with avidity, and her eyes absolutely brightened as she did so.

"It is so cool, so grateful!"

Fergus smiled sadly, as he thought over the struggle with himself, that morning, when about to buy the three oranges which he had brought. They would take the last money from his pocket, and he had drawn his month's salary in anticipation, and Major Henry was also in advance to him some twenty-five dollars. He thrice approached the basket of oranges on the stand of the village grocer, and as often receded from the temptation; but the recollection of his mother and her preference for the delicious fruit, prevailed, and his compensation fully came when he beheld the dying woman so happy in enjoyment of the gift.

"Now, dear Fergus, I feel better. The orange has taken the bitter taste of that physic out of my mouth. Put up these pieces—I will suck them after the next dose. There, now, sit by me! I wish to talk with you."

"Will you not fatigue yourself too much, my dear mother?"

"I must not mind fatigue *now*, my son; what I *have* to do, or say, must be said and done quickly—*now*, if possible. It will be good two hours before the Doctor comes, and dear Mrs. Henry told me she would come in the evening. What I have to say can be all said in two hours. Push up the bolster, my son, my head is too low."

He obeyed her tenderly, doing the offices of the nurse as gently and easily as a young woman might have done. He had for a long time performed such duties; and, working all the day, had not unfrequently been the sole watcher at her bed-side all the night.

"Now, bring me yon desk, my son—your father's desk, my son. Do not part with it if you can help it. It is a fine one—English make, you see, and all complete, with his dressing-case in it. He was very fond of this desk, and wrote his letters every night upon it. He was a man of business, Fergus, though unfortunate. He was too honest to be very lucky. But"—

She paused, and was breathing with difficulty.

"Mother, you fatigue yourself. I know all these things—"

"Wait! wait!"

Gradually she recovered and continued:

"*You* must wait on me, Fergus. I will say as little as possible—only what is necessary. Open the desk, my son, and hand me the sealed packet you will find upon the top."

He did so.

"This letter," said she, "is to your half uncle, Leonard—Leonard Voltmeier. The name is German, as perhaps you know. When your grandfather died, his widow married Voltmeier, a very smart and handsome German, who came to this country as a wine-dealer, the partner of an European House. Leonard Voltmeier, his son, was the half brother of your father. There were four years difference in their ages. Voltmeier, *his* father, failed in business; but your grandfather's large property had been all settled by will upon your grandmother, and that became the sole support of the family. From the first, Voltmeier seemed to take a dislike to your father, and even when he was a young man almost of your age, undertook to beat him, which he had often done when your father was a boy. Your father ran away, got to be a clerk in Wilmington, and afterwards set up business for himself. It was then he married me. He let your grandmother know all about it; but she was very angry, and refused to let him bring me to see her. Your poor father always said that Voltmeier was at the bottom of that business, and that he no doubt dictated the letter. Voltmeier I had known before my marriage. Your father was a proud man, and never tried any more, until after old Voltmeier died, which he did suddenly one day, of apoplexy. His mother consented to our coming, and wrote a civil letter enough to me. It was civil, but not cordial. We went to see her, and soon found that Leonard Voltmeier, your father's half brother, was quite the master of the house. He was a very smart and handsome man, like his father—perhaps a handsomer man, though I could never see it. But he was handsome, and he was certainly smart. He seemed to me to know everything. His father had sent him to Germany for his schooling when he was a mere boy, and there he learned to know everything, and, I'm sorry to think, to believe in nothing good. He always spoke contemptuously, and even bitterly, of all things that we poor home-bred people are accustomed to consider sacred. To your father he showed dislike, if not disrespect, and they finally quarreled. Neither your father nor myself ever got a cent of your grandmother's property, and there was a considerable property left, I hear, in two counties of North Carolina. When I last heard of Leonard Voltmeier, he was flourishing and reputed to be rich. He was smart enough to make himself so; he could do almost anything, was a great reader and student, and despised your father as a merchant. This letter is to him."

"But, mother, how is it to be sent?"

"It is not to be sent. It is to be carried,—and you, my son, will be the bearer."

"What! Seek *such* a man? Why should I so humble myself, mother?"

"Beware, my son, of what was called the family pride. Humility is the foundation of all the virtues, as well as of success—that humility which is content to do, and to suffer in the line of duty."

"But, *is* this my duty, mother?"

"It is! It is a duty to yourself, and—to—me! That letter, which has been the labor of weeks, daily, when you were absent at the store, may have a saving effect on your uncle. It tells the melancholy story of our trials, of your father's sorrows, and of our privations; and, though it does not say so, in words, it shows conclusively that all was due to the cruel treatment of us, by his father and himself. It will show, from your father's own lips and letters, that I was a dutiful wife to him, and on his death-bed, he avowed that he never once regretted having married me. If your uncle has heart or conscience, *you* must afford him, as I do, the opportunity—the most precious of all things to men guilty of wrongdoing—of making atonement. This is a duty which, as a Christian man, you owe to your uncle,—not considering the blood of your father which flows in his veins. And, Fergus—Leonard Voltmeier owes something especially to—me!"

"Mother, this will probably interfere very greatly with my own future fortunes. I have not told you that I have been studying law, for nearly two years, with Major Henry. The Major tells me that I will make a good lawyer. You know what he has paid me from time to time for writing for him. But he hints at something better, and I have reason to believe, that, as soon as I shall be admitted to practice, he will give me a share in his business."

"Well, this visit to your uncle can only delay you for a season. Should your uncle do nothing for you,—and that you can soon find out,—it will be easy to return to Spartanburg."

"But my place may be occupied by another."

"Have faith in God, my son! Major Henry is a good man, who will not treat your claims lightly, and you can plead my commands! —ah! my dear Fergus, forgive the words—no! no! not commands, my dear son, but entreaties—your dying mother's last prayers to you, —to do as she implores."

"Mother, dear mother, I will obey you. I will do what you desire. But, how am I to find my uncle?"

"That will not be difficult, I think. Leonard Voltmeier is not the person to suffer from obscurity. He will be a marked man wherever he lives—if he still lives, of which I can say nothing. You will find him in one or other of the counties the names of which are endorsed upon the packet; and in these counties there are other parties whom your father knew, whose names are also given in this memorandum, which you can consult. They must some of them still be living, and they will probably be able to inform you of all you need to know."

There was a long pause after this. The narration of the dying lady was broken frequently by temporary exhaustion; and she now lay silent, breathing heavily, panting, as it were, rather than breathing. Having rested a while, she resumed, though with evident effort.

"Fergus, my son, do you know what day this is? It is your birthday."

"I had forgotten it, mother!"

"Poor boy! The heart must be very sad, and the head suffering, when a youth forgets his birthday."

Fergus murmured unconsciously, from Shakspeare—

"They tell me 'tis my birthday, and I'll keep it,
In sober pomp of sadness."

"What is it you are saying, my son?"
"Nothing,—only some lines of poetry."
She resumed:
"But *I* did not forget your birthday, and I have a gift for you."
"A gift, mother?" smiling very sadly.
"Yes, a gift! Your father's watch. I have kept it sacred to myself
—sacred even from poverty! That which he gave me, when we were
married, was sold to help pay for this poor homestead; but though
often pressed for the means of life, parting week by week with some
one of my little collection of precious things, I could never bring
myself to part with this of his. It is now yours: and oh! Fergus, if
you can, keep it as sacredly as I have done. Nay, put it on now," she
said, seeing he was about to lay it aside—"wear it from this, your
birthday—your *birth*day, my son, and my—"

The sentence was unfinished. A deep groan from the breast of
Fergus told her too surely that the word—"death-day"—need not
be spoken by her to be comprehended by her son.

Chapter III

PASSING THE VALLEY
AND SHADOW

It was *not* her death-day. There was still a further respite. She
rallied that afternoon and was able still further to commune with
her son, however feebly, and to enter into such family details as
were only too painfully interesting to both. They were such as
she felt it her duty to deliver; many, indeed, respecting his father
and other parties, which had hitherto never been revealed. These
details placed him in possession of a long and touching history which
before he had only in part conjectured. They made him familiar
with all that family history which a good son, properly sensible of
what is due at once to self and to society, ought to wish to know.

The poor woman had addressed her mind, in her last remaining
hours, to every matter which could seem to bear upon the fortunes
and the future of the youth. His journey in pursuit of his uncle
Voltmeier being resolved upon, she proceeded to counsel him as
to his progress; to suggest the routes which he should take with
the better prospect of discovery; and how to provide the means of
travel. The little farmstead was to be sold, with all its small ap-
pendages of furniture and stock. With the funds from the sale he
was to procure himself a strong, serviceable hackney; while what
should remain of his money was estimated to be quite sufficient to
meet the expense of travel, and to support him, for a certain period,
in his search; after that—but here all counsel must fail, or deal in
generalities only.

"This done, my dear son, I commit you to God! Have faith in
God! Strive earnestly and honestly, according to your best powers,
and the promise of God will not fail you. I can do no more. I shall
pray, my Fergus, as I have prayed daily and nightly, in your behalf;
and if it be permitted me, though unseen by your eyes, mine shall
keep that watch over you which has been kept, without weariness, for

twenty-one years. In all this time you have proved a dutiful and dear son to me. It will be a sweet consolation to you, oh, my best beloved, in future hours, to remember these as the last words of your dying mother. They come from her very heart of hearts, and she breathes them with prayer and in blessing on your head!"

He had fallen on his knees beside the bed, and his face was buried in its folds beneath her hand. With feeble effort she raised herself forward, and her lips were bent down upon his forehead. Her prayer and blesssing, a feeble murmur from the lips, but with wondrous emphasis from her soul, were inaudible to his ears. But, if the good God should hear—and who can doubt that the earnest soul-utterance of such a mother will appeal instantly to Him?— what need that the object of the prayer should hear also. He, indeed, could well conceive what words were spoken, what invocation made, with what keen interest and tender love! and—could he question the efficacy of such a prayer in the progress of his future life? He felt, gliding through his whole frame, a new consciousness of security and strength, and his courage and his will grew accordingly.

The mother resumed her position upon the pillows, though with effort, and lay back with eyes shut, and hands folded together, as if in continued though silent prayer. Still kneeling beside the bed, the face of the youth remained hidden from sight among the bed-clothes. A sob at moments was heard, half stifled in utterance; and then the hands of the mother sought his head, and her long wan fingers stole fondly into the thick volume of his dark brown hair.

And thus the two; when the door quietly opened, and the good Mrs. Henry came in, accompanied by the good Mrs. Bobo, both of whom had been in frequent attendance, both seeking to supply, at intervals, to the invalid, those little comforts, those delicate consolations, which one loving woman knows so well how to administer to another. These two were soon followed by other ladies; and a little while after came the worthy but humble woman, Mrs. Harkis, another poor widow with two children, little Wattie and little Flit. The two latter were left at home—Flit to watch over the little sick brother.

The small room in the cottage was now quite full. It is not surprising that a death-bed should prove an attraction to so many living witnesses. The awful solemnity of that transition from life to death, compels a fearful and trembling, though intense curiosity, which is legitimate as natural. What doubts, what fears, what conjectures, agitate the thoughts and kindle the imagination of the spectator! There is a soul about to take its flight to an unknown and mysterious realm of equal doubt and wonder. That soul has been with us for years, clothed in a form of beauty, and speaking to us hourly through thoughts, feelings and associations, by which we knew how beautiful in itself it was, and now it departs even as a bird leaving forever its nest; but we see it not as it flies, and we know not whither it goes! we ask when it shall awaken to its new condition;—in what condition—what superior wings of beauty shall it put on;—to what more elevated skies shall it soar;—and what are the joys and blessings, what the being of loveliness and happiness which it shall attain! In a few hours, and that frame which now breathes before us, and whispers sweetly in our ears, and smiles upon us with such a loving sadness, will be cold, senseless, inanimate, making no answer when we call, and looking no longer back with eyes of affection, to the affection that looks only through its tears!

The dying woman has a smile for all of her friends. She whispers to the bended ear of each in turn. They sit beside her in silence for a while, and then one of the ladies reads from the only book which has been found proper to such an occasion. The reading over, all sink down for a while in inaudible prayer; and the invalid faintly speaks—

"Thanks! thanks! dear sisters: it is a great kindness. Oh! the beautiful words of God. Oh! the sweet promise of the Blessed Saviour! Have mercy, O Father, on us all! Have mercy, O God, upon HIM!"

Her hands are close pressed upon the brow of her still kneeling son.

Mrs. Henry and Mrs. Bobo are to sit up this night. The night is closing in, the sun is sinking lower and lower among the western mountains. But a few crimson streaks are left flushing their great brows, and warming faintly the dusky horizon. The chamber of the dying woman becomes silent, all of the guests have gone, but the two ladies, and these prepare themselves for the vigils of the night. Each knows her task. The training of woman for the death-bed is proverbial. They have a special endowment as nurses and watchers. They minister together or in turn. The bed-clothes are re-arranged—the bolster and pillows re-adjusted. The attenuated frame of the sufferer is gently raised, and, wearied on the one side, she now reclines upon the other. The supporting cordial is given— the medicine, how vainly, but with the fond hope that it will delay that hour of final and fearful struggle which is yet certain to come; and all is done which art counsels, or nature can desire. Silence and quiet prevail; only the hard breathing of the invalid, and an occasional whisper among the attendants occur to assert the continued presence of life.

A harsh voice is heard without. It is the physician, Dr. Simpson; a rough, half savage person in voice and manner, but kindly and gentle in fact, generous and sympathetic—good kernel, rough outside—who hides a world of charity in an ungracious manner. The patient starts at the voice as if from slumber. The ladies soothe her to quiet, while Fergus steals out from the chamber and joins the doctor at the door. At the same moment Major Henry comes up.

"Well, Fergus?" from both the new comers. He comprehends the questions.

"She seems inclined to sleep. We thought her sleeping, but at the sound of your voice she started."

"Ay," said the doctor—"my voice is anything but a flute, and I fear it sometimes scares her! But, sleeping or waking, I must look at her."

And, with the words, he proceeded to pull off his boots where he stood, and entered the chamber only in his stocking feet.

"We will remain out here for a while together, Major, if you please."

"Why not? the night is pleasant, Fergus, and I come to spend one half of it with you."

"Thank you, sir, you shall have my bed."

"Oh! I shall hardly sleep. It is your company that I desire. We will talk together. I had some conversation with Brigham after you left, and I think I've made him heartily ashamed of himself. One word, however, and but one, on that subject—do *not* return to that man, no matter what offer he makes you. There are better things in store for you, and it will be my pride to see that you make, what I feel that you can make, a first-rate lawyer. You must not throw yourself away any longer in the inferior business of weighing groceries and packing boxes. Enough on this head for the present. Let us stroll for half an hour."

The two strolled away along the hollows of the hills. The moon rose, wan and beautiful, above their tops, and looked down with that sad smiling which so wakens the sympathies in loving hearts. By inexplicable associations, Fergus thought of the soul upon its flight—of the wan, pallid face of his mother, and her faint whispering accents—of all that had been between them, of love, and care, and anxiety, of doubt and hope, for the long period in which he had been conscious of her love and of his own.

The tears gathered in his eyes, and he walked on unconsciously, while, to divert his mind, his good friend, Henry, discoursed to him of "Bacon's Abridgment," "Chitty's Pleadings," and the "rule in Shelley's Case," and was perfectly satisfied that Fergus Wallace, being so excellent a listener, would prove a most admirable pleader! The excellent Major—with a wonderful proclivity to fun and the humorous, could only keep himself from falling into these veins by sternly concentrating himself upon the serious topics and regimen of the law.

The doctor, meanwhile, stood at the bedside of the patient, silently listening to her breathing,—she again slumbered,—and, seeming to count her pulsations from these faint utterances of her lips. He turned away finally in silence, whispering to Mrs. Henry, as he left the room:

"Let her sleep! Do not disturb her on any account."

"Anything favorable, doctor!"

"Favorable, madam! She is dying;—sinking rapidly; may go out in her sleep, and be happy in doing so; possibly in a grateful dream of life! She will pass like an infant, from play to slumber; or if she should waken, it will be for only a brief term of breathing life! no more! She will probably last through the night. Let her sleep. No more medicine. Nothing, unless she wakes, and shall call for it."

Such was the verdict, which the unmusical voice of the doctor hardly suffered him, and only with some effort, to deliver in a whisper. He encountered Major Henry and Fergus on his way out of the lane, and simply announcing that he would come in the morning, he put spurs to his horse, and went off in a canter, as if seeking to avoid all questioning.

Major Henry went off also, about midnight, and Fergus then silently returned to the chamber of his mother, and seated himself beside her, in patient watch. Mrs. Henry then retired to her chamber, while Mrs. Bobo continued her watch. And so through the night— the patient still sleeping, and somewhat more soundly than had been the case with her for several nights before.

Day dawned, and still she slept. Fergus continued wakeful and watchful; and Mrs. Bobo, after whispering him to call her, if needed, retired to the neighboring chamber.

It might have been an hour after this, when, with a faint moan, the patient appeared to wake, and, with the feeble utterance of the words "my son," brought back the young man from the most wretched of reveries, to the consciousness of the immediate occasion of his wretchedness before him.

He bent his ear to her lips. Her hands were feebly lifted to his face, but simply passing over it, sunk down again beside her. But he heard the whispered words—

"Light! window—air!"

He rose and threw open the window. The broad light of day had come, and faint gleams of sunshine stole through the aperture. He could then see the lessened brightness in her eyes. The film was glassing them gradually. But she spoke—

"Great sea! what billows! But the sun is upon it! mighty voices, rolling like the organ! But the song! the song! more light—let me hear!" Silence for a while.

He stooped beside her. His cheeks were pressed to her own, and she half turned to him her face. Sliding his arm beneath her head, he brought her face up fully to his lips—he looked into her eyes. They were rolled up.

"Mother, mother!" he cried, involuntarily, "look upon me once more, my mother!"

She seemed to comprehend him. The balls of the eyes rolled back to their accustomed places. The light for a moment kindled them with expression; they smiled; the mouth smiled; and then the wan, pale vacancy passed over all, and there was no more answer!

"Oh! mother! mother! mother! One more look, dear mother, but one, but one!"

He received no answer; and, for the moment, had no further voice! all was still,—until the door quietly opened, and little Flit stole in, stole up beside him unnoticed, and gazed upon the scene with a stare of terror and wonder.

"Oh! Mr. Fergus," at length said the child, whom he had not yet noticed—"Oh! Mr. Fergus, what is it?—can it be—"

"Death, Flit! this is death!"

Then the child burst out into sobs as if its little heart would break, and ran out of the room, shrieking—

"She can't speak to me any more!"

Her cries brought the ladies into the chamber, and with a heavy heart, Fergus resigned the corse of his mother to their gentle and melancholy cares.

Chapter IV

THE AMULET

To dwell upon the scene of Fergus Wallace's sorrow, is to give painful interest to a story which involves much of that young person's heart-life; but there is, henceforth, in his career, so much that calls into action all the more stirring elements of his character, that we hasten the narrative, and pass the sad period of his bereavement with a word. Mrs. Wallace was buried with the simple rites of a simple people—the gentlest of hands and the kindest of hearts doing for the dead those last rites, which it is the precious privilege of humanity to offer to those we have loved, when at last they are called from us forever. Fergus' bereavement was, indeed, great, but with the heart and hopes of youth, it was not the crushing, blasting sorrow, which the older feel when the one worshiped is torn away. The young man for a brief time dwelt in the deserted rooms, where everything was so precious in its associations; then, arousing, he prepared to obey the injunctions of his mother, to sell off the little property and effects, by which to obtain money for prosecuting his journey of search for his uncle.

The good Major Henry came forward, not alone with his advice, but his assistance.

"Go, Fergus, if you must, but remember that, return when you will, my offer is open to you. I shall only be too happy to receive you into my office."

Thus encouraged and assisted, Fergus was not long in his preparations. The little property was sold at a fair price, a superb horse was provided; the pressing offers of Brigham, for his future services, were rejected, much to that person's astonishment and anger; the day preceding that fixed for his departure on his mission came.

"Well, Fergus," said the Major, "everything is pretty much set-

tled, I believe. I have attended to what little law matters were necessary; and, with a light pocket, a thin pair of trowsers, a porcupine
saddle, and a hard-trotting horse, you may be on the very high road
to fortune, for aught we know. I could wish, my boy, that your heart
were only as light as your pocket!"

"It is strong, my dear Major, and as firm as it is heavy!"

"Keep it so, Fergus, and beware of the bright eyes of the tender
gender, till you have been at least five years at the bar."

"No fear, sir. With my horse Hamlet I may almost say:

'Man delights not me, nor woman either.' "

"Oh! put off your dolefuls. Remember, you are about to go into
battle, and there must be no clouds upon your spirit, making you
hang back in the action. And, holding life to be a long warfare, and
knowing that you are about to penetrate one of the wildest of our
mountain regions, where you will meet all sorts of customers, I have
prepared for you a paper, to be used or shown at any period when
you may find yourself in difficulty. I wish you to read it. You will
find it difficult to understand, as it involves a mystery which I can
not explain to you. But read."

Fergus read as follows:

"To the First of the Seven!—B—Stadt, Greeting:
"Should you meet with the bearer of this remembrance, value him—
take care of him—serve him; for you shall know him as my friend, and
one of the apples of mine eyes. I love and honor him, and hope to make
a great man of him! Do thou also do him honor and give him welcome.
He carries with him *two* tokens to prove that he comes from *me*—one in
his *bosom*, another in his *memory*. When he has given you these, you will
know that he is the proper bearer of this letter.

(Signed.)   JAMES ED. HENRY.
Spartanburg C. H." (no date.)

"There is certainly something mysterious in this missive. Is this
all?"

"No. Here is a bit of ivory upon which you trace, beautifully cut
in German characters, the three figures:

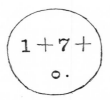

"This you will suspend about your neck by a string. You note the small hole in the figure O. Now, you might be robbed of these, and they might be found useful in other hands. To make them so, exclusively to yourself, you must memorize two doggerel lines—

> 'One to seven, and seven to one,
> Count as you will, there yet is none.'

You can memorize these two lines; but never repeat them *until you have shown the letter, under exigency, and never repeat them in the hearing of more than one person.*"

"I confess, Major, you greatly rouse my curiosity."

"And can only in very slight degree satisfy it. The person who will understand these tokens and words, is one whose life I saved almost at the peril of my own. He was in a great civil danger and I saved him as a lawyer. To do so, I had to take a journey, now several years ago, among these very mountains which you are about to penetrate. It is a very wild region still; it was a thousand times more so then; and I narrowly escaped with my life. In brief, a woman saved me from murder! In this region of country, the person to whom this missive is addressed was a sort of feudal baron among the professional hunters, many of whom were so many outlaws. Well, I secured the required evidence. I traced him through *seven aliases,* but, to this day, have never found out his true name! This is the mystery in these lines. I saved him by an *alibi* at last. If a criminal, he was a great one, and on a bold scale. He was grateful for what I had done, and gave me the largest fee that I ever got as a lawyer. In doing so, he forced upon me this little amulet, as he called it, and gave me these lines, jesting with me at the time, that with seven of his names, I had not yet found the true one. But he instructed me in the use of these tokens, just as I have instructed you. A few words more, and

I have told you all I need or should repeat. Bierstadt was the first of the seven *aliases*. How many more he enjoyed can not be said. We will call him by this *one*. Bierstadt, great criminal as I believe him to have been, was, even under the rudest of disguises, one of the most perfect gentlemen I have ever met. Capable of descending to, and putting on the rudest, wildest, most uncouth looks, habits, and manners, and of imitating wonderfully every *patois* in this country, he is yet admirably well read, a subtle casuist; can speak the French, and perhaps other foreign languages, and is so ingenious in argument that he needed little to have made a profound lawyer. He is, I think, a good deal of an artist, since he cut the figures on that ivory tablet, with his penknife, while sitting in this very office, and he plays exquisitely on the flute."

"An admirable Crichton."

"Yes, indeed,—well, he continues grateful for what I did, and the peril I incurred in his behalf, and, every year, I receive some present from him. How it comes, I know not. I find it here, left in my absence, either at home or office, with my name upon it, and the words *'From one of the seven.'* That is all! He lives still, I take for granted; since it is within the last nine months that I received one of these proofs of his equal remembrance and existence. Now, Fergus, I have told you all that I can tell you. You will readily see, from what I have said, that this person, should you encounter him, is one capable of doing you good service in an emergency. My letter, I think, will make him eager to do so."

In two days more, Fergus Wallace was on his way to the mountains.

Chapter v

"I'M CUR'OUS."

At the foot of one of those gorges, or "gaps," as they are called in backwoods parlance, which constitute the few common passes through, or over, or into the grand chain of the Apalachian, stood one of those small dwellings which, almost exclusively, form the habitations of the people in this region. It was a frame house of moderate dimensions, yet, when the travel was comparatively small, it served the purpose of an hotel. The human habitations are few, and only dot the occasional hill-side, or roost in little valleys, which seem scooped out of the mountains, for better protection against the winds of winter. Generally speaking, the people are very poor, and cultivate the smallest possible tracts, in which they rear a little corn, peas, some few vegetables, and an occasional tobacco patch.

From this class, it is but a step to the wild, lawless men of the mountains. Far away, along the line of the great hills, from Virginia to Georgia, stretch fastnesses as wild, savage and unknown as when, two hundred years ago, the feet of the Cherokee trod them; and, to-day, amid those retreats, dwell men as wild and rude as if the signs and sounds of civilization were forever banished. In some sequestered spot one bold spirit would settle, and, in time, become a kind of baron among the rough people, who dispensed his bounty freely, and in return received such homage as at once assured his safety and his prosperity; or, if he were disposed to act the part of leader or chief of the bad characters whose haunts were among the hills, he could maintain his two-fold character of planter and outlaw, unmolested and unwatched.

In one of the basement-rooms of that little hostel above referred to, sat two persons, men, seemingly deeply interested in the examination of certain bits of paper, upon which might be seen, not read, certain memoranda written in ciphers, dots, numbers, and very curious characters. They did not appear to find the work easy, of deciphering these characters; nor shall we undertake to do so.

25

The men were both, evidently, of low character; but they were also singularly unlike. One of them was a huge barbarian, in a costume that was more like that of the red, than of the white man. He wore his hunting-shirt of buckskin, his leggins of the same material, but, partly over these, was a pair of boots, of ordinary make, but manufactured of untanned leather. His hunting-shirt was opened at the breast, displaying a vast thicket of hair, which might have entitled him to a close cousinship with Esau. His face, as well as form, was massive, and deeply tinged with a rich, dark crimson, which might be ascribed to the free use of the pale white beverage, corn whisky, which stood in a huge half-gallon bottle, conveniently beside him. Enormous whiskers and moustache, and a shock of hair, thick as Samson's, and as black as Cocytus', impressed you with the idea of leonine strength, if not of leonine character. The eyes were great also, and protruding. The head was large, but the posterior regions preponderated too greatly for a proper moral or mental balance. His voice was loud and insolent; his action spasmodic and angular.

His companion was a ruffian also; but was of a very different order. He was small of person, below the medium size, but compact of build, muscular, with short arms as legs; clad in common homespun, which, like the costume of his companion, showed signs of travel and hard usage; and he wore common shoes, undressed, such as are made for negroes. The study of this man lay wholly in his face; and it was a study. The eyes were small, and of a dull pea-green color; the cheeks were sunken and sallow; the mouth was large, but sinister, curling upwards at the corners; the ears were singularly small; the hair and beard were of the most carroty complexion. He spoke little, with caution, and in tones so low, that his companion had occasionally to require that he should repeat what he had said. Both men carried their rifles; the long weapon of that class, which, by the way, was manufactured in the mountain region, by Deckard, as far back as the days of the Revolution. [The art continued in this precinct; and it was thought by many that the *native* mountain rifles of North Carolina were better than any of foreign importation; and this was their reputation some thirty years ago, if not now.] Both also wore bowie-knives, which they carried in a belt behind them, on the right hip, as sailors carry theirs, convenient to the grip of the right hand.

The larger man filled his cup and drank.

"I don't see, old Swipes," said he, as he swallowed a stoup that might have satisfied a giant, "I don't see this thing so cl'ar. Here's the sign of Moggs' cabin—that's cl'ar; but what's this figger-work? what does that mean?"

"Well, that's Clough's, I reckon."

"Well, supposing that's correct, what is the onderstanding then?"

"Why, I suppose that he means that we'll find him at *Moggs' first* or at Clough's *next*. But, I don't see that that's a matter of any consekence. You know, if we gits the money, we can easily fix it to meet him somewhar."

"Somewhar! Oh! no doubt about that. We kin meet him anywhar, I'm thinking. By the limping Jeremiah, Swipes, he's everywhar! Did you ever know such a pusson? You can't find him out, do what you please. Hyar he tells *you*, set out, in this quarter, and you'll happen upon a pile; and then he says to me, you go in this track, and *you'll* git the pile."

"Well, we gits it, pretty much as he tells us."

"But that's *not* enough. Dern my buttons, but we tried every way to find out whar he twigs it! I sees him just when *he* pleases, and no other time. I've tried my best to *find* him out, and, onless he said the word, I might jist as well have tried to find a needle in a haystack! He's an onpossible man to find."

"But, why do you want to find him? He's good enough as he is, for us. He *finds* for us. He puts us on the trail, and we have a fair share of what runs into the net."

"But, dern it, Swipes, I'm not satisfied. I wants to see how the machinery works. I'm cur'ous, you see."

"I sees that, cl'ar enough, but I don't see the sense of it. I only knows that we gits the profits jist as much as he."

"I don't know *that*, Swipes. I rather reckon that he makes a hundred to our one; and ef so, I don't see why we shouldn't have our fa'r share. He's a gentleman, and a rich man, I'm sartain, ef we could only find him out."

"You'd better rest easy, Brown Peters, when you know you're well off. Ef you're a-doing well, what's the use of poking into another man's secrets? Ef he wants to have secrets, let him have 'em! I'll keep my own, I know!"

"But, dod dern it, I'm cur'ous."

"Oh! be done with the cur'ous! *I'm* doing well."

"But we does all the hard work, Swipes!"

"We does what we're *good for* to do, and he does what we *kain't* do; and that's the reason and sense in all kippartnerships. Don't you see? Ef you *kain't*, let me just give you a piece of warning. Don't let your being cur'ous make you kill the goose! it lays golden eggs for us! Do you wants to go to the plow ag'in?"

"Divil take me first!"

"Well, then, you jist stick to your business, and toe the mark as the master marks it out."

"But I hates—"

"Oh! blast the hates! let's look to business. Here's the writing."

"Stop, till we takes a pull togither."

"Hyar's to you."

"And to you."

And so they drank together.

"Now," said the fellow who had been called Brown Peters—though this may be only an *alias*—"now, what do you make of *that?*"

"That's the mark of the fellow that's to bring the Cherokee money from Government."

"Twelve thousand dollars—"

"Sixteen thousand dollars."

"Good! I like the bigger figger! well—"

"Well, you see the other mark?"

"What does that mean?"

"It means *to-day.*"

"No! *to-morrow.*"

"And this? what of this?"

"Why that's the chestnut tree turning, along the gap;—and you see the next;—that's the painted *red boulder* what the Injins painted."

"And thar we sets the trap. You at the one, I at the other, and he kain't pass us both."

"And how does he find out when this man's to come?"

"Ef *he* finds out, we don't, you see; and if twan't for *him*, we'd never find out. You knows that!"

"But how does he git to find out these things?"

"Well, now, Swipes,—" mysteriously— "you're cur'ous. I'll tell you what I thinks. He's mixed up with them members of congress, and one-half of them are jist about the condemdest rogues in all creation. They don't think it any offense against the people to lie, and I'm pretty sure of one thing, that any man what will lie will steal. I knows it by experience."

"But they gits a share, without running any of the risk."

"To be sure they does!"

"And we've got to do the work."

"That's so."

"I'm a-thinking, Swipes, we don't git altogether our shar', considering the risks."

"Nonsense, Brown, how would we know of this man and this money, at all, ef twan't for *him*, and those members of congress? Thar's a man to put the dogs on, and thar's another man what takes the stand, and does the shooting, and so you know where you *air*. Now what's the word?"

"Wall, I must say, I begins to see the sinse of the figgers, and so, if we fix the fellow, we takes the *findans* to Mother Moggs', and thar we meets with *him*."

"Jest so! But thar's some other things I must show you about the bills."

"Ah, yes! Well, show away." And the two outlaws put their heads together.

We need not pursue these details any further, especially as the conversation was interrupted by the entrance of the landlord, who produced a fresh bottle, joined the two, and they all drank and chatted together.

But, after the arrival of the landlord, there was no more talk of business, and no further details. It is to be supposed that the landlord knew his guests very well, or suspected their quality. But no landlord questions the guests who pay! Swipes threw down the reckoning. It was in a bank bill of the State of *North* Carolina. He examined it rigidly, and said, with a smile:

"Right stripe this time, Swipes."

"All right!" was the reply of Swipes. "Hev to look, though, you know."

"No questions axed, I reckon," said Peters, "and the road free."

"Go ahead, fellows, and take it smooth."

Horses were saddled, and the pair rode off. Towards sunset a fresh traveler appeared at the "*station*," in the person of Fergus Wallace.

Chapter VI

THE ANGEL IN THE HOUSE

Tom Thrasher, the landlord, sate in the same apartment, a back room of the house, in which the two confederates, "Swipes" and "Brown Peters," were engaged in the discussion of the undefined work which they had in hand. He was busied in the examination of a pile of paper money which he had before him. His attention was divided between this examination and the discussion of an ample tumbler of strong waters, such as he had served out to his visitors. At the close of each *count,* the money being assorted according to its several denominations of one, two, five, ten, and twenty, he swallowed a potent mouthful of the beverage, and rubbed his head and ears with satisfaction, while he smacked his lips and rolled his eyes, expressing, more markedly, at the close of the count, his pleasure, by a sound something like a grunt grafted upon a guffaw! It was a hoarse guttural growl of a laugh, which, however uncouth and unnatural, was yet evidently significant of delight, according to the nature of the beast.

"All right," said he, at length, folding up the pile of bills compactly. "They don't put off any of their *chaff* and *blink* upon Tom Thrasher! They knows better! Let them once try it, and I'll blow the game. They knows it! Well, it settles a long score of Sundays! We're square off now, 'till the new turn begins. Good fellows, both! Swipes is sly, and keeps a still tongue in a long head; as for Bully Brown, he'd rowel me sometimes if he dar'st. But he won't try, for he knows the weight of my knuckles, and the sharp eends of my tusk and grinders! An he's only sassy when the liquor rises too high in his swallow! But what's thar to do now? Them fellows are on a big drive! They're fighting shy of their talk to-day! I reckon Swipes don't let Brown know all about what's to be done till he finds himself a-doing it. Sly fox, that Swipes! But, I reckon I'll hear of something afore long, and then I'll know how they've been speckilating. Well, what's the fizzle now?"

This, to a pale, thin woman, of whitey-brown complexion, who, at that moment, made her appearance at the door. She was his wife, and there was something like terror in her face, as she heard his sharp question, made in tones more like those of a prairie wolf than a human being. Her own trembling tones were almost indistinct, as she replied:

"Thar's a young man at the door."

"Well, what does he want?"

"He wants to come in and stay."

"Well, let him! What do I keep tavern for, do you think? Ain't it 'Entertainment for man and beast'? What sort of a critter is he?"

"He's a young gentleman."

"A gentleman, eh? Ha! Them fellows know'd it, you see! That's what they've been calkilating! Let Tom Thrasher alone for putting two things together. I sees the connection. Well, what do you stand thar for? Ax the young *gentleman* in; do it sweetly. He's a pretty young gentleman, I reckon; and is for gwine through the 'gap' in the morning—that is, if he doesn't take the track to-night. Is thar a room? Don't think! Ha! ha! It's a rough road for young gentlemen to travel, day or night. The rocks tumble, now and then, upon young *gentlemen*, and hurts their heads and constitutions. But that's none of my business. I'll take a look at this young *gentleman*, and see if his head's a hard one."

And, finishing the contents of his goblet at a single gulp, he followed his wife to the front.

Fergus Wallace had already entered, and received the welcome of the woman, which appeared to be a reluctant, if not a cold one. The landlord was more cordial, boisterously so, and when he cried out: "How are you, young gentleman?" it seemed to Fergus like the salutation of a great bear about to be followed by a squeeze. It *was* followed by a hearty squeeze of the *hand*, the region being one of a rough democratic character, recognizing few of the artificial distinctions of society, sometimes resenting them as impertinences, and deferring greatly only to those which represented *money!* At the first glance, it did not seem to Tom Thrasher that the new comer was a man of *money!* The old experience of the landlord made him a shrewd judge of character and resource, at a few keen glances at his party, and he thought to himself:

"This kin hairdly be the person they're a'ter! He don't look as ef he had the flash. I reckon he's only some clark on a collecting bout. He's got a mighty good horse for sarvice, however."

Putting up the horse in the stable, he examined him more closely; lifted his feet and exclaimed—

"Them shoes is new; put on only a day or two ago; and I knows the fit! They're by that nigger blacksmith in Spartanburg. The fellow's only a clerk or shopkeeper, and he hasn't done much collecting as yet. Yet, there's no telling. He seems a shut-mouth;—he's close. And them old chaps knows what stakes they're got on the kairds. Phew! It's nothing to *me*, and ef they play or ef they don't play, I can do the whistling. I reckon, sometime in the eend, they'll be bringing, one or t'other, some of the grist to my mill!"

Fergus Wallace was somewhat taciturn, it is true; but not an absolute "shut-mouth," as the landlord had styled him. The latter was full of his questions, and was answered very civilly; quite sufficiently, but in few words.

At the supper-table, which had very good cheer upon it, venison steaks, and hot breadstuffs, he was helped freely by both landlord and wife, the former saucing his meats with his speech, and the latter waiting upon the table—a frequent habit in this rustic region—as modestly as if a servant only.

At length, in the course of the repast, Fergus caught her eye fixed upon him with a degree of earnestness which compelled his attention. He noted, also, that the woman seemed as carefully to watch, at the same time, that the eyes of her lord and master should not detect this gaze upon the stranger. There was a sadness in the woman's glance, blended with earnestness, which conferred upon her features a certain degree of intelligence, such as it did not possess when under the eyes of her husband. Then it was vacant quite, and the expression was little more than an idiotic stare. But the landlord left him little opportunity for continuing his study of a countenance which had yet impressed him curiously.

"I reckon you're for the '*gap*,' *stranger?*"

"To-morrow, sir; at sunrise."

"And which way do you strike?"

"That I've to find out when I cross the ridge."

"Close!" was the aside of the host. Then, aloud—

"You know your route for a part of the way, I reckon."

"No, indeed; but you, perhaps, can help me. Where can I put up to-morrow night?"

"Well, riding some thirty miles or so, you kin strike old Bonner's, always, ef you keep the main trace. He keeps a 'stand.'"

"And he, I suppose, can give me further directions?"

"Yes, I reckon; but it's a strange way to travel without 'zackly knowing whar you wants to strike."

"That is truly a misfortune; but it's one not to be helped."

"You're not going among the Chirrikeys?"

"It may be; but I don't know yet."

Landlord—*sotto voce*—as he went out—"A rigilar shut-mouth! draws in his head like a tarrypin, whenever you pokes a question at him. Them fellows knows their man. I shouldn't wonder now ef he ain't the very fish that they ixpects to git in their net to-morrow."

The host had gone to the stables. Scarcely was it evident that he had left the house, when the wife passed rapidly round the table to the side where Fergus still continued to sit, and, in low tones, her countenance really brightening into intelligence, and her voice still tremulous, being warmed with evident interest, said—

"Young man, the mountains are wild places, and dangerous. There are bad men among them, and if you have much money, or anything to tempt the robber, keep a sharp look-out. Keep your pistols ready—"

"I have no pistols!"

"No pistols? No weapon of any kind?"

"None."

"Good Heavens! and what are you to do?"

"Trust in God, my good woman."

"That's very well said; it's a good trust; but, in the mountains, it's well to have the arm of flesh ready. God's word is not much read among the wild people of the ridge. Is it so that you *have* to go through the 'gap' to-morrow?"

"It is so! It must be!" said the young man, gravely.

"Then, may God speed you safely. But keep sharp eyes on every hand. Don't stop at any call; but whenever you hear, suddenly, either sound of man or beast, put spurs to your horse, and keep him at a gallop, till you get out of hearing. You'll be safe for to-morrow, at least, if you get to Bonner's by night. Ha! Hush!"

With the sound of the host returning, the woman glided away from all proximity to the young man; her face, so recently excited with vivid expression, relaxed as suddenly into the dull vacancy of ignorance and apathy, if not of idiocy; and she was quietly employed in removing plates and dishes from the table, when her husband reappeared in the apartment. He gave a searching glance from one to the other; then, as if satisfied, proceeded to draw from a cupboard the large bottle of spirits which we have already seen.

"You've got a mighty good horse of your own, young man, that'll carry such a pusson as you for a thousand miles, without any feel of the strain; and ef you'll be content to do but a hundred miles every three days, he'll take you to the eend of the world, and be the better for it at the eend of the journey. But see that you don't push him in the beginning. At a walk, only, he'll take you five miles an hour, and that's quite as much as you should do crossing the mountains. Ride slow and you ride sure."

Fergus recurred instantly to the wife's recent counsel that he should ride *fast;* but he said nothing. He ventured upon a few questions, after a while, touching the mountains and the people; asked after the chief persons, best known; and listened earnestly to the names given him; but neither of the parties derived much information from the dialogue, which could enlighten them in any degree, or satisfy what might be called their curiosity. The questions of Fergus gave no clue to his objects, nor did the answers of the landlord tend to remove a single pebble of difficulty from the way of the traveler.

At length, with a great yawn, the host rose and said:

"Now, young man, what do you say to an eye-closer? What'll you take? Shall it be a warm toddy, or a good sup of peach and honey."

"Thank you, sir, neither! I never drink."

"The deuce you say! You *never* drink. Why, what's to become of you in a world of sperrits? Ha! ha! ha! You hain't had much of an edication in the wide world, I reckon; and I reckon, moreover, you've never been much in this mountain country of ours! Does I jedge rightly when I thinks you don't smoke neither?"

"I do not."

"Nor chaw?"

"I have never used tobacco!"

"Then the sooner you learn the better! Tobacco is a great sweetener of the senses, stranger. It takes a man's brain like a charm. It operates like some fine music; like a soft horn blowing among the mountains, when the night's a-coming down, or when the moon's rising. It quiets all the narves, jest like a good medicine that opens a quiet way to sleep. Rich men can do without tobacco, perhaps, having other things; but tobacco's the poor man's blessing, next brother to good strong drink. Hyar's to you, young man, and a pleasant journey in your dreams."

Fergus rose. The "eye-closer," like the "stirrup-cup" of old, was the signal for departure for the bed.

"Will you have me wakened soon in the morning? I wish to make an early start."

"I'll do it, myself;" was the reply. He had already shown Fergus the way to his room, before supper, carrying up his light little valise; and now, the young man, with his *dip* candle in hand, made his way up stairs, and to his chamber, alone; leaving the landlord in the act of replenishing his tumbler. He had hardly entered the room, and closed his door, and was winding his watch, when he heard a shuffling in the passage leading to his door, and a fumbling at the handle of the latch; but, in the moment after, the harsh voice of the landlord was heard—

"What the blazes are you doing here, woman?"

"I just came to bring a coverlet for the young man's bed," was the subdued, but still audible answer.

"Give it to me," was the stern response, "and git down sta'rs, and mind your business down sta'rs."

A moment after, he opened the door without knocking, and strode in, bringing the coverlet, of white cotton, homemade, with fringe; an article to be commonly seen in these precincts.

"My wife sends you a coverlid, young man, though it's sich a warm and pleasant night, that you'll hardly want it."

Fergus noted that he had come up stairs, and made his appearance, without shoes, and *in his stocking feet.*

After lingering a few seconds his visitor bade him good night, and took his departure.

Then Fergus heard murmured voices from below, and an occasional growling, or roar, from the master. It occurred to him, as a suspicious thing, that this man had stolen up without his shoes; and it also occurred to him that the wife's bringing the coverlet was simply a pretext, possibly to give him some additional counsel and warning. He inferred from this that the husband was no better than he should be, and that the wife, poor, pale, wan, and spiritless, was yet the "*Angel in the House.*"

In how many guises do the angels appear! Happy if we could only know when we entertain them.

Chapter VII

IN THE "GAP"

The circumstances were suspicious. The hints of the woman; the entrance of the man to his chamber, in his stocking feet; his close following of his wife; and a general knowledge of the wild country which he was about to penetrate—all were well calculated to occasion, in the mind of Fergus, a lively sense of insecurity.

But, he had heart of firmness; a calm head, and an easy conscience; and, meditating his situation, he quietly secured his door, wound up his watch, tightened the belt about his body, which contained his little money, and prepared himself, after prayer, for sleep.

His prayer was made in silence, upon his knees, even as he had been taught to make it, while his head rested on the knees of his mother.

Prayer is a great sedative for thought. It wonderfully calms the pulse which is excited; and, when fervently made, it banishes fear, and allays all anxiety.

Fergus Wallace well knew that the only secret for mental repose lay, first, in the proper performance of duty. For all the rest, faith taught him, then, to throw himself wholly upon God. He was in God's hands now! without weapons, the arm of flesh could avail him little! His faith was strong, as it was, from long training, habitual; and, with a wonderful calm, he laid himself down to slumber, and soon slept as placidly as an infant with the arms of a mother thrown around him.

He slept, unconscious of a dream, and awoke at daylight, invigorated for his journey. His landlord evidently had been up before him; and, ere he was dressed, was thundering at his door. The breakfast was in readiness; but ere they sat down, Tom Thrasher had prepared for his guest, as for himself, the inevitable dram of peach and honey. This was the "eye-*opener*," "the peep of day," "the phlegm-cutter;"—for by these, and sundry other flash names, was the draught distinguished.

38

It was with great difficulty that Fergus could escape the entreaties of his host to partake with him; and it was, evidently, to his great disgust, that he found the young man firm. Still, the potent beverage was not to be lost, and Tom Thrasher was not the man to shirk double duty at the bottle. He drank both stoups himself, and professed himself in better health than before.

At breakfast, Fergus could perceive, at times, the eyes of the woman turned upon him, with glances full of significance; but at moments only, when in the business of the breakfast, the looks of the host were diverted from her; at all other moments her countenance wore that expression of vacancy which seemed most natural to it. Had she desired to communicate anything to him, as Fergus thought from her looks that she had, no opportunity was afforded her. Tom Thrasher never left the room till the meal was fully discussed. The youth had no longer any excuse for lingering at the breakfast-table.

"And now, stranger," said the host, "ef so be you *will* start, and must be off, your horse is ready at the door; but, if you'll stay a day over, we can give you a famous deer-hunt to-day. There's a party of *five* of as keen hunters after venison as you ever see'd, to brush the sides of yonder mountain with me to-day; and ef we don't give you a chaince at a big buck, thar's no snakes in all Flurriday! what say you?"

Fergus thanked him for the invitation, but declined it; alleging the necessity of his going forward.

"What have I to pay, sir?"

"Oh, a mere sarcumstance—nothing to speak of—one dollar and a quarter, lawful currency."

He paid it; the host then caught up his little valise, walked with him to where the horse stood saddled in waiting, and hitched to a swinging limb, fastened the valise to the saddle, and held the bridle while the youth mounted.

He bade him farewell, and the landlord, with a growling civility, and rough shake of the hand, wished him a pleasant journey.

As Fergus, wheeling his horse, looked round to the dwelling, he caught a glimpse of the woman at one of the upper windows. He could not well distinguish the expression in her face; but, for a moment, he perceived her uplifted finger, as it were in the act of warning him to caution. She could do no more. He bowed his head involuntarily, and rode away.

"Well," said the landlord, aloud, as Fergus rode along the hill-side out of hearing, "I wished him a pleasant journey, but I said nothing about its being a safe one. That 'gap' is a great place for sarcumstances, transactions, and other accedents. Ef he kin make his ride a pleasant one, I'm sure I don't begrudge it to him; and, for that matter, I've no 'jection to his making it safe too,—*ef he kin!* That all depends upon what sort of luck he was born to. I only knows that thar's a set of varmints now on the scout, that'll hardly let him pass free of toll, ef they thinks him able to pay scores ac-cordin' to quality."

The woman had been soliloquizing also.

"Lord send the poor young man a safe deliverance! I tremble for the poor traveler always when I see those two ravenous wolves and tigers on his track! And such a handsome young man! I wonder if he has a mother living? If he has, she should be praying for him now, with all her might,—with all her heart, and soul, and strength, and may the good Lord help her, so that she may not pray to no purpose."

Up, and up the mountain-side; and the "gap" opens; and Fergus, looking back, has lost sight of the slope to the valley, which he had so lately left. He is in a gorge which sunlight rarely penetrates—a cold, damp channel, as it were, with boulders on each hand, and, occasionally, a mass of rock incumbent over his head, and the heavy trees cast their great shadows along the narrow pathway, helping to make more sombrous still the gloomy route. Not even a bird-chirp is heard; all is a death-like stillness, and the very air seems to sleep!

Fergus has never been *among* the mountains. He has only beheld them from a distance. They naturally inspire him with awe, which blends, however, with those grave, sad feelings of his heart, which have also given their complexion to his mind. Deep in meditation to forgetfulness, he rides forward, hardly heeding the progress of his horse; at one moment he is suddenly awakened to his situation by finding himself on the very edge of a precipice, from which his horse recoils. He looks down into the monstrous gorge below, the great tops of trees, an hundred feet beneath him, hiding its dark recesses from the sun's eye and his own. He hears a fall of waters, the rolling of a stream over crags and boulders; and, at one moment, he beholds a flash of white, more like a spiritual form, leaping from the mountain. It is a tiny waterfall. The murmurous sounds continue in his ears as he winds along the mountain ledges, ascending,—still ascending,—till he reaches the crest of the heights, and beholds the grand sea that seems to spread everywhere before him; the blue billows, flashing with their white caps, a perfect illusion of the sea,— and rolling themselves upward, as if to embrace the heavens!

Wonder upon wonder, and all how gloriously grand and beautiful; and his reveries carry him back to that vague period of creation, when, under the sovereign will, the earth was rolled into mountains; the waters into the boundless valleys of the immeasurable sea; and suns, and stars, and systems, took their places in this most beautiful world, beneath the azure cope and curtains of the heavens! And so riding, so musing, forever in silence, and forever making discoveries new to his eye, and shaping and coloring every thought and fancy, the day sped on; the sun rose to his utmost altitude; the mountain seas, beneath his gaze, flashed with more frequent white crests upon their somber brows, and the fascination grew into a spell that bound him with thought and silence, as in some grand deep cavern of the genii. His was a poetic mind, of quick imagination, and a lively fancy; and images of beauty, strange, wild, weird and fantastic, came to him unbidden; like so many nimble pages, who, born of human susceptibilities, are ever ready to anticipate the needs of thought, whether for study or relief.

But, from the great heights, the pathway began to descend. The slope downward became rapid. The prospect grew momently more and more bounded. The mountain-tops were no longer visible; the sun threw no smiles upon his pathway. He seemed to be descending into the very bowels of the earth. The gorge deepened. The huge boulders ran beside him on either hand, and sometimes hung threateningly over him, held seemingly rather by a will of their own, than by any natural purchase of earth or tree; a breath would fling them down, crashing as they came, and covering, with their unbroken masses, everything below!

Silent in his awe, he rode on as if fearing by his breath to precipitate his doom. Again he hears the murmur of mysterious and unseen waters. Again he sees the flash of a white form as it leaps the crag, and is lost among the great glowing tops of the forest trees that shoot upwards from unknown depths. The road winds frequently; now, with broad sweeps of space; and now, short, with sudden turns, following the irregularities of the mountain, or avoiding the edges of an obtrusive precipice or gulf.

And still the silence prevails; not even the cry of beast or bird appeals to human sympathies, and kindles them to activity. Fergus felt himself suddenly shut out from humanity; and chilled, he shudders, as if with some presentiment of ill. He asks himself if there be spiritual instincts. The old tales of childhood recur to his mind; the dreams of classical and oriental faith and fable; the vague faiths of humanity, in spite of science and philosophy, in the supernatural. He almost fancies that he hears the voice of his mother, in a faint, feeble wail, borne on the sudden breeze, and imploring his return. Certainly, he has heard a sound.

He listens, his ears now keenly alive.

"It is surely a whistle."

It might be of a bird!

Farther on, he hears it again; more faint, as if a sigh out of the very silence!

He remembers the counsel of the wan, sad woman at the inn, and urges his horse forward more freely. But here the "gap" narrows, and so circuitously, that he fears to put the beast to his speed, or even to canter, lest he should find himself upon the edge of the sudden precipice.

The horse trots forward. He wheels him around a bold projection of bald rock, sees a longer stretch than usual before him, of straighter track, and spurs the animal into a canter. At that moment a harsh voice, from under cover, cries out—in his very ears:

"Stop you thar'!"

It is the usual salutation of the hunter to the buck, when he would arrest him in his progress, and, compelling the beast to pause and wheel, afford him an opportunity for the use of the unerring rifle.

The cry now, however, only serves to impel Fergus to the more free use of his spur, and with quick instinct he plies it earnestly. The steed plunges forward into a full and fast gallop.

There is a rushing in the thicket; pebbles roll down from the heights. Another and another whistle, and now a shout, and Fergus again plies the spur. The warning of the woman is in his ears, as if from a trumpet.

"Don't stop to answer any call! Ride fast! *Don't* ride slow!"

He obeys her! His blood rises with the increased speed of his horse. He begins to think of weapons—if he had them. He feels, now, that it would be better to confront his enemy with some, any instrument of death or murder, than to fall a miserable unresisting victim. His blood and brain equally warm with this conviction, and a bitter feeling of mortification mocks him with his inability to fight. He can only fly! He has again driven the spur into the steed, sending him headlong forward, though the pathway closes in front, and he knows that the curve which he must now make, will be an abrupt one.

It is!—short, sharp, and perilous.

Suddenly he falls from his saddle—falls clear, and the horse passes headlong from under him! A sharp rifle-shot rings through the woods at the same moment, and calls up the dull echoes from the opposite rocks. Fergus Wallace lies insensible at their feet, with the hot blood issuing from his breast!

Chapter VIII

"WOLF-DEN"

In a deep hollow of the hills, hidden from the sun, in a lonely mountain gorge, verging upon those rich bottoms where the laurel so crowds its shoots with leaves of sombrous green as to make a perpetual night, in which the bear loves to harbor during the dog-days, stood the stone hovel, built of rude boulders, which, to all those who knew the spot, was styled the "Wolf-Den."

It was an ancient place of human harborage, if its occasional tenants, in any degree, had kindred with humanity. It might have been a structure originally of the Cherokees. It was apparently old enough to have been so, but its interior indicated something more of art than was common to the red man; and within, it proved a comparatively comfortable refuge in a tolerably severe winter climate.

On the outside, with its irregular walls coated with green lichen, it seemed only fit for the habitation of that ugly beast from which it took its name. Surrounded by a dense undergrowth of green, yet stunted shrubs and trees, you might happen upon it by accident, but would scarce be like to see it, unless shown, by any wandering glance. It was entered by a hole, rather than a door, in one of its sides, and the only daylight that ever penetrated its interior came through certain crevices, where an occasional boulder had been dropped, or thrown out from the walls. These were stopped with a plaster of clay within, keeping out the cold winds, while the recognized and legitimate chinks, serving for windows, were stuffed with dried rushes, which were removable at pleasure. A huge chimney recess, of mixed boulders and clay, afforded a fireplace, and the huge pile of wood beside it showed the party in keeping always ready for its instant use. The floor was strewed with rushes. The roof was covered with a dense coating of clay, well held together by a judicious mixture of that straw, of the lack of which the Israelites complained so bitterly when required to make brick for the Egyptians.

From this apartment, a hole in the wall, which you had to stoop to your knees to enter, conducted you into another, of smaller, but somewhat superior pretensions. Here was bed and bedstead; and there was more light, and something of a fireplace also; a table of pine, a rude chair of oak with seat of cowhide, and a shelf on which stood a tin basin and a pail of water, and over it a looking-glass, four by six. But the structure was of the same materials as the other—rude boulders, coated with clay, all the chinks being well closed, but without any attempt at smoothing the surface. The chimneys did not rise apparently above the roof, and if they gave out smoke at any time, this was scarcely perceptible from without, winding its way as it did through a densely massed shrubbery which completely lapped them.

Within, you could see that the roofing was sustained by a heavy flooring of unsquared logs, which spanned the entire area, and, until they rotted down, were quite capable of sustaining the incumbent clay with which they were covered. Such was "Wolf-Den," and it is to be hoped that the description is not only enough, but that it is adequate to the claims of the fabric.

In the main section of this uncouth hovel, might be seen, at the moment when we penetrate its secrets, an old woman, its regular inhabitant, who might have made a becoming figure as the Witch of Endor, in a tableau of the Asiatics. She was as tall as the ordinary race of man, and as gaunt as Don Quixote. Her skin was as perfectly tanned, and of very much the complexion of a side of harness leather. She had possibly once been white. She might now be well mistaken for a daughter, or mother, rather, of the whole race of red men. Her eyes were sunken in great greenish hollows, from which, under provocation, they darted a red, serpent-like sort of ire, expressive of violent passions and a vindictive spirit. Her cheeks were as sunken as sallow, but the cheek-bones were of singular prominence. The mouth was great, but sunken in also, the teeth being all out; and the chin, sharp and coming to an absolute point at the extremity, protruded fully half an inch below the mouth, and formed a singular correspondence towards approximation even, with the enormous and sharp nose peering above it. She might have been a first cousin to Methuselah in age, from her general appearance, but for the erectness of her person. She had no stoop in her narrow shoulders, and betrayed, in all her movements, a degree of vigor quite in contrast with her seemingly great age. Her garments were of the simplest kind of the country; a frock of tarnished yellow homespun, which hung upon her person rather as a sack than a garment, secured by a belt of common black leather about the waist,—in which she carried a good sized knife,—and by shoulder-straps of cloth. Partly covering these was a sort of tippet of homespun also, which served to hide in some degree a long skinny neck, and a withered brown bosom.

She was employed—indeed, she was rarely unemployed—about some culinary office at the moment when we first beheld her, a pot was on the fire, simmering with water; and a sort of shambles or dresser, for preparing the meats, extending along one whole side of the hovel. On this dresser lay several sections of meat, apparently venison, while overhead hung a large mass, a haunch, in fact, well-smoked, of what had once been one of the fattest of the brown bears of the mountain ranges. A few boxes and barrels, with pots, kettles, and a single stool, made up the contents of the hovel.

An hour may have elapsed since the moment when Fergus Wallace was shot down by the unseen assassin, when the ears of the woman were suddenly elevated, like those of a steed about to *shy*, from nervousness or fright. She left the fireplace, proceeded to the door, and stood to listen. Soon, the echo of horses' feet could be heard striking the occasional boulders in their path, and a few moments brought two horsemen, leading a third horse between them, to the entrance of the hovel. They led the steeds to the rear, fastened them in a close thicket below, and worked their way round to the entrance. The two men were those whom we so recently encountered at the tavern of Tom Thrasher; the steed which they led was that so lately ridden by Fergus Wallace.

Where was he?

Had they left him to perish, a prey to vultures and wolves, in that gloomy pass of the mountains where he fell?

Alas! for the poor mother, and her unavailing prayers!

"Is it you, old Swipes?" demanded the woman from within, before opening the door.

"It's both of us," was the answer.

"What? is Brown Peters here again!" demanded the woman, as she undid the fastening, and admitted them.

"And didn't you expect *me*, too, Mother Moggs?" asked Brown Peters.

"Well, I did reckon, arter I gin you that scalding of hot water, that you wouldn't be much in a hurry to show your face to me again."

"Better not say nothing about that business, you tarnal old sarcumstance, or I'll give you such sass for your supper, that you'll forget your breakfast, forever arter;" responded the fellow sullenly, and with a very savage look.

"Do you say so, my honey?" returned the woman, with an equally savage leer, as she grasped, and drew from its sheath, the sharp knife at her girdle. "And I'm a thinking, if you was to try it, Brown Peters, the divil would soon git his own!"

"Hush! shut up!" said Swipes. "Get us something to eat, Mother Moggs."

"Git you something to eat! you ain't got time for that. Here's Old Satan himself been a waiting for you this hour, and—hush—he'll be a hearing you, I reckon!"

"*He's* here, is he?"

"Yes, I tell you;" pointing to the inner door, with an air of mystery somewhat coupled with an expression of fear, or awe rather.

"Hush! He's at some of his devil's work now, for the benefit of your precious souls."

"Well, I'm glad he's come! 'a short horse is soon curried,' and we kin know all about this business in the twink of a mosquito's wing. Ahem! ahem!"

The two last ejaculations were uttered with emphasis, as if designed to be heard. But it was perceptible, from the subdued tones of the speakers, that they also shared somewhat in the awe, in respect to the unseen party, which was so clearly expressed in the woman's look and language.

The moment after, the inner door was opened, and the unknown, stooping low to do so, made his appearance, emerging from the little opening in the inner chamber.

The new comer was apparently a very old man, whose white beard and hair almost completely enveloped head, face, and chin, and dropped down, broadly and thickly, a full foot over his breast. He was tall and broad-shouldered, and stepped firmly, but stooped considerably, apparently from his great age. Large and expressive gray eyes, an eagle nose with wide nostrils, were significant of moral power, at some earlier period; but the sunken mouth indicated the loss of teeth, and, when he spoke, this deficiency was evident enough, the lips sinking in at every utterance.

"You are come?" he said, in hoarse, deep accents. "Well?"

"We've done it; but with what luck, kain't be said so sartain," was the prompt reply of Peters.

"Enter," said the old man, as he pointed to the inner apartment. They obeyed him; a fire was already blazing within, and the table set out before it. The blaze diffused a vague red light over the gloomy chamber. When they had entered, the superior said to the woman—"Go forth to the peak, Moggs, and watch till the horn is blown."

She disappeared. He bolted the outer door closely behind her, then passed back into the inner chamber.

"What report?" he demanded.

"He came, jist as you said, and we treed him, and got the money, but not what you said it was—only a poor two hundred and thirteen dollars, South Carolina bills."

The money was placed on the table. The brow of the old man was clouded.

"That is strange! What more did you get? He must have had papers. These will explain all. There should have been twelve thousand, at least."

"Yes, there was papers, but neither on us kin read writing, you know. Here they are! and there's the chap's watch, but what's the good of it now, 'cept for the gould, is not easy to be said. It's pretty well battered by the bullet."

"You didn't shoot him, surely?"

"Had to do it! couldn't ha' stopped him if we hadn't! You see, when I holler'd to him to stop, he jist druv in his spurs, and went off at a gallop; going at full speed down one of the crookedest twists of the road, jist where it turns down by the 'monkey rock.' Then it was that Swipes had to drop him."

"Haven't I told you a thousand times, never to kill when you can help it? never to take life?"

"But we couldn't help it! Swipes will tell you that nothing but a bullet could ha' stopped that horse."

"You shot the horse, then! Where's the man?"

"No! we didn't shoot the horse. That was Swipes' mistake. He shot the man."

"And killed him?"

"I reckon so! He was onsensible when we s'arched the body, and that's all we got for it;—them things, watch, money, papers, and the horse."

"And to get the horse, you shot the rider?"

"He's a mighty clever critter for a leap," said Swipes, justifying himself, as it were. "Good, too, for a quarter race!"

"Great God. What fools you are, to commit murder, and incur all the danger of it—for it is apt to find its avengers—for a miserable horse, when thousands are running wild among these mountains."

"But they have all of them got their owners."

"So had this horse his owner. The others you might pick up by the score, as you *do*, without taking life for it! It is the curse of the business, when you have to use such tools for it!"

The old man strode the room in a mood which silenced the two. He turned, suddenly, and took up the watch. It was shattered, but the bullet, after penetrating it obliquely, had glanced, without passing through it, and the watch was covered with blood. The reflection suddenly occurred to the old man that the wound might not be mortal.

"Where did you hit him?"

"So close to the heart that I don't think he drawed the breath of life a moment a'ter."

"Get your horses ready. We must see."

They turned to go out. As they did so, revolving the watch in his hand, the old man visibly started. He suddenly caught up the papers; and his fingers, hands—nay, his whole frame—trembled as he read the several addresses on the two packets which were in his grasp. The two rogues looked at each other significantly. The unusual emotion of the stern master spirit which had governed them, astonished them by its strangeness, and it was with quick instincts that they both at once conceived the notion of a mystery, which was to be withheld from them. As they still lingered, curious and watchful, the master recovered himself, and with stern glance, and in sterner tones, pointing with his finger, said:

"How! Why do ye wait? Begone, quickly! and get the buffalo sling wrapper. I will join you soon."

"It's mighty cur'ous," said Brown Peters. "What kin he be a'ter doing now?"

"Something's to come of it; you'll see," was the reply of Swipes, as they hurried to the horses. "It's only more grist to our mill."

"Great God!" exclaimed the old man, when he found himself alone. "What can this mean? Can it be possible?"

He gazed upon the back of the watch, where somewhat dim by age, but still visible, were to be read the two letters, "F.W."—nothing more.

Chapter IX

"HE LIVES."

The brief interval that was allowed to the mysterious old man, while the two emissaries were bringing up their horses, was devoted to a hurried examination of the papers, stained with his blood, which were taken from the bosom of Fergus Wallace.

These were, as we remember, two—one, the packet of considerable size, which had been delivered to him by his dying mother, the other the mysterious letter of Major Henry.

Dark and gloomy was the expression of the old man's face as he read; but, smoothing his brow, as the tread of the horses sounded from the entrance, he hurried papers and watch into his bosom, threw on his shoulders a blanket-cloak of large dimensions, under which, ready to his grasp, but concealed from sight, he fastened a brace of pistols. A small shagreen morocco case he drew from a recess in the wall, and, thus prepared, he joined the others at the entrance. His own horse had also been brought up, saddled and bridled, at the same time. This beast was of a deep coal-black, of great size, strength, and fleetness.

"Have you got the buffalo-sling?"

"All ready, sir," was the reply.

"Go on—lead the way."

The tones were stern, but calm, with no show of that emotion which had been shown them in the "Den," and which had been even somewhat increased by his hurried examination of the papers.

"Fast! faster!"—and at the command they went on at a half-canter, in spite of dark towering woods and mountains, and a narrow and winding pathway, such as we have already described, verging frequently along the edge of the abyss. But these riders were all born mountaineers, and knew every foot of the pathway, by night as by day.

It was not long ere they reached the scene of the bloody catastrophe. It was unchanged in all respects, as when the assassins left it. The same awful stillness, the same gloomy impending fortresses of rock, the same great towering trees, shaking idiot brows with the solemnity of a priesthood.

Fergus Wallace lay still insensible on the terrace where he had fallen. The mysterious old man dismounted at once and knelt beside him, for examination of his heart. He had water brought from a mountain rivulet, and sprinkled him in the face. Then, producing a flask of mountain brandy from his bosom, he poured some of it into the lips of the victim, but he did not swallow. The water application was continued to face and forehead. The bosom was laid bare, and the blood-stains washed away. The stream had ceased to flow; the blood which had already issued from the wound was clotted around the wound.

From the little morocco case which he brought with him, the old man produced a probe, which he applied with all the boldness, if not all the dexterity, of an approved chirurgeon. His experience seemed considerable, even if he had made no studies in the schools. A faint groan issued now from the wounded man, and he continued to groan with each new application of the probe. The two subordinates looked on in silent curiosity, much wondering at the skill of a superior who had proved himself competent to so many performances.

Groan after groan sufficiently testified to the continued presence of life in the wounded man, and rising, as if satisfied, the old man, speaking rather to himself than to his companions, said:

"'Tis as I thought! The bullet has glanced from the watch, and passed off along the side, making a great score beneath the arm, which it has barely grazed. He will do! He will live!"

He now poured the brandy into the patient's mouth, and a portion of it was evidently swallowed. Then the old man gave his instructions in the following words:

"You must now make amends for your blundering. You must carry him between you, as soon as night sets in, in the buffalo-sling, and lay him down, in silence, in front of Jake Harness' gateway."

"And what good will that do?" was the surly question of Brown Peters.

"Much! Enough that I know! Let me tell you that, if I had found him dead, I should have been very much tempted to put a bullet through each of your heads. You have mistaken your man! The other man has gone towards the 'Mills Gap' at Mount Tryon. There are suspicions of you, and the government gave orders to change the route. I find all *that* in the papers which this young fellow carried. When you have laid him down quietly, after nightfall, before Jake Harness' house, leave him, and work your way among the mountains as fast as you can go. By good riding you can still head the *'courier'* with the Cherokee money, before he can get through the gap. Ride slowly, till you lay the young man down, and let there be as little motion as possible."

"Why, Jimini, it's good eleven miles to Jake Harness'."

"You can *walk* it in three hours."

"I don't like to go about Jake Harness', eenyhow. He's jub'ous of me,—mighty suspicious; and I rather reckon has no love for any one bone in my body. He'd just as soon shoot me as swallow a dram of peach and honey. It's a word and a blow with him most times, and the blow first, when the other man's not to his liking."

"He need not see you, unless you choose to get drunk by the way, or do some foolish thing. It will be night, and no moon, when you get to Harness'. Just do as *I* tell you, and all will be right! As soon as you have laid the young man down at the gate, put the spurs to your nags, and don't draw bridle until you make the head of the 'gap.' Then see that you do your work without drawing blood, unless it's the blood of the horse."

"That South Carolina money of the young fellow, do you reckon it's *good* money?"

"Ah! I see, Swipes, what you're thinking of. It *is* good money. There it is—the whole—divide it equally between you. The watch you will allow me to keep."

"Yes, and much good may it do you. It won't lose time, I reckon, tho' it kain't keep it under present sarcumstances."

And the savage chuckled over his jest.

"Take this flask of brandy with you, Swipes, and, at every mile, pour a little into the young man's mouth. I look to you, Swipes, particularly, to see that you do not suffer Peters to move too roughly, or to drink up the liquor. That flask, alone, may be the means of saving the youth's life. And you will do your best to save it, if only to atone for this wretched blundering."

Some few more instructions, and, assisting the two to sling the wounded man in the buffalo-hide between the horses, the master started them on their way. To carry a wounded man in a sort of a litter thus, suspended between two men on horseback, was a very common process in all this region, even in colonial times, when the wars with the red men compelled a frequent resort to this expedient.

The old man rode back to "Wolf's Den," where he busied himself, in his cell, until night had fairly set in. Then, saddle-bags in hand, he went forth, mounted his own steed, the black—sable as night itself,—and led that of Fergus Wallace, all harnessed as before, with saddle and bridle, just as he was when captured by the assassins of his owner.

When thus mounted, the old man sounded his horn, and waited until the witch-woman, Moggs, came down from the rocky height, where she had been posted as a sort of watch. She stood before him in silence.

"See that you have no more quarrels with these men, Moll, and give them no liquor. Do not let me have to say this to you again."

"They allays brings their own liquor," was the reply. "I never gin them any."

"But you have it here! see that you drink as little of it, yourself, as possible. I have my eye upon you, when I'm a hundred miles away! Nothing that you do, or they do, escapes me. You were all drunk together, here, when you quarreled. You drink with them and of their liquor. Do not deny it. Beware, for if *I* should forbear to punish you, *they* will not. That fellow Brown Peters, when drunk, would as soon knife you as look at you."

"I knows that, too, your honor; but I'm as good as he with a knife, and I'm a leatle quicker to use it, ef he fools with me."

"Still, no drinking together, and no over-drinking by yourself; and, should they bring their own liquor, take an opportunity to break the bottle—"

"It's a jimmy-john what they carries."

"Break it, if you can."

"As ef that wouldn't raise the old divil quicker than anything else, your honor."

"They need not know it, if you are as quick of hand and eye as you pretend; watch your chance for what you do. They will give you chance enough."

"When will your honor git back?"

"Sometime before you've said your prayers," was the scornful answer.

"Oh, I says them every night, your honor, whenever I thinks of my poor boy, Ephraim. Hes'nt your honor hearn tell of him yet?"

"Yes! He's in jail in Yadkin county."

"And will—will your honor—"

"Yes, yes! I will have him out for you before many days. It may be you shall see him in a week or two."

"Lord be thanked—and—"

"No more," said he sternly, "but remember!" and thus saying he rode away.

"Lord! Lord! what a man! I do believe he's something of the old divil himself. He knows everything; and, I'm a thinking, he can a-most *do* anything. He's a most fearsome pusson!"

Chapter x

HOW THE FATES TAKE
THE SLOT

W hat were the meditations of the mysterious "Gray-Beard," the "most fearsome pusson," as he rode along the lonely mountain side, just as night was falling? He rode slowly, and, from the listlessness of his manner, yielding the reins and the way itself, seemingly, altogether to his steed, he appeared buried in the deepest thought. The horse of Wallace followed, led by a long halter fastened to the saddle-bow of the other, and within the easy reaching of his hand.

That the old man thought, deeply and sadly, perhaps, with some humiliating reflections, showing conscience and memory to be equally and actively at work, might well be conjectured by the groan, at intervals, which escaped from his bosom, without his own consciousness. As yet, it is not permitted us to penetrate the secrets of that bosom, and trace out its mysteries. We only know that his present and recent emotions were the fruit of some discovery which he had made in the sight of Wallace's watch and the perusal of the papers he had carried. These he had conned rapidly, during the brief interval between the departure of his subordinates for their horses, and while he awaited their return, in his cell at "Wolf-Den." In this perusal he was evidently startled into the exhibition of an interest which was remarkable in the case of a person who was evidently so capable of self-restraint and so superior to the exhibition of all excitement. That he was not superior to the feeling, we have seen. We may add that there were passages in the larger packet, which, in the absence of all scrutinizing eyes, filled his own with tears.

"What a fool I am!" he exclaimed, as he thought over these passages while he rode, and brushed away the unwonted waters from his eyes. "That I should be moved by a woman's letter or a woman's weaknesses! or even by those of my own ignorant youth. Pshaw!

56

What's Hecuba to me! And yet,"—after a pause, "it will not down at my bidding. There are still some fountains in the heart capable of overflow, though the snows cover them. They flow deep, in secret passages, like some of the hidden streams in these mountains; we can not drain them off, or dam them up, and there comes a day when the snows suddenly melt, and the rocks fall away, and the stream gushes forth and sings its secret as it goes along a pathway which it never knew before! And this hidden stream of mine—who would have thought it!" Again brushing the great hot drops from his eyes—"these dying words—like the rod of the prophet smiting the rock—have compelled the unsuspected waters once more to flow! Yes! She might well make this appeal to me, on behalf of this boy, if she had, indeed, believed that I loved her! And did she *not* believe? The appeal would seem to prove it now. Had she no love for me in return? Why not! Himmel! as I think—look back—remember, and now read—I might myself have been the father of this boy! And, but for *him*—my evil genius—how I hated him! how I hate him still! and hating him, I did wrong to her! she takes her revenge now for both!"

Again he dashed the big drop from his eyes; rose almost erect in his stirrups, and whistled to his horse, which started at once out of a slow walk, into a trot. The rider, a moment after, checked the speed of the animal, and resumed his musing.

"The Fates!" he exclaimed, "how they do pursue us! The Furies ever on the heels of Orestes! We may not baffle *them!* We may not cast them off! They have the scent of the sleuth-hound, and, once they take the *slot* of the game, they are at his heels till time shall pass into eternity! Time! Eternity! What idle words, without distinction! And that I should need to use them! I know not what damnable instinct it is—what thirst or rage—that keeps me at this work. I tire of it; and yet, the Fates! Will they not hound me on it, to the end of the chase? What a madness—not a passion, but an insanity! It is a nature! but what a gift of horror does it involve! Can I escape the fates! Can I refuse the gift—forbear its exercise—deny my nature, through a wile hostile to my endowments? Oh! the damnable perversity which makes me a master, yet keeps me for evermore a slave! and to the basest of all masters—one who feeds blood and brain with equal fervor, to escape from which is to perish!

It is a game, with the greatest stake on the board. Yet, wherefore play it out to the end? wherefore, but for this damnable phrenzy of the blood, that makes a phrenzy in the brain, and keeps it ever hot with the fever that makes all gaming a law as well as an insanity. It had not been thus had *she* but smiled; had *I* known—and now, here—her letter from the very grave! The Fate begins to show its hand! Something which I can not foresee must grow from this! The wonderful coincidences here have a vast and deep significance!"

So, musing as he rode, now falling into reverie, now passionately rising into speech, he alternately arrested and coerced the rapid motion of his steed, until himself arrested and brought back, as it were, to the ordinary business of thought, by the sudden and full stoppage of the animal.

The progress was thus suddenly stayed beside an enormous boulder, which jutted out into the road. As the rider discovered this object, he wheeled the horse suddenly about, and, rounding the obstruction to the right, he turned abruptly into a narrow avenue, the entrance to which was hardly discoverable by the passing traveler. The track was only wide enough for a single horse, and was too rocky to be well beaten, yet the beast was evidently well acquainted with his course.

It was now that his rider, for the first time, as if under the influence of a resolute will, seemed to address himself to the single purpose of going forward, which he did, in a trot. The route was dark; but an occasional star peeped down through the tree-tops, upon the still descending valley over which he sped. Soon, emerging from this path, he entered upon a wider track, and began to ascend. An hour might have elapsed when the cliffs grew to great frowning forms above him; and, anon, he rode along a ledge of rock skirted by a great abyss; and then the roll of rushing waters came upon his ears, very like the rollers upon the sea-beach after a storm. But the river was invisible, though still heard; and the woods and cliffs seemed to blend themselves together in a gigantic mass of thicket, and, with a sudden wheel of his horse again, the rider disappeared from sight, as if suddenly swallowed up in the earth.

For an hour all was still, save the voice of a murmurous wind among the gigantic oaks, and the ceaseless shock of unseen waters from below!

At the end of this time, emerging from the same thicket, came one who rode a horse as white as that of the other had been black. He was distinguishable, in the darkness of the night, only by the white steed which he bestrode. You could see the dark outline of the rider, cloaked like the one who went before, but nothing besides. The party, who now appears so vaguely upon the scene, rode now as rapidly as the other had ridden slowly. He partly went over the same ground, but, turning, after a short quarter of an hour, to the right, he entered upon what seemed a wagon trace, leading through a valley. He, too, was soon lost from sight, as suddenly as our first horseman, and only after the lapse of an hour did he reappear upon the scene.

Meanwhile, the two robbers, with Fergus Wallace slung between their horses, had made their tedious way, with a painful slowness, along the route which had been assigned them. They had faithfully, though impatiently, obeyed their orders, and still, an occasional groan from the buffalo-sling had given them equal intimation of life and suffering. At intervals, Swipes administered the brandy to the lips of the wounded man, doing little more than wet them with the liquor.

The two talked together as they went, the tedious slowness of their travel making them glad to employ the only agency which they possessed, the better to beguile their progress. But their dialogue was not such as to make us desirous to report it. At length, however, reaching a certain point of the route, by which they knew that they were approaching the dwelling they were bade to seek, a dog was heard to bark. They paused to listen.

"The old slut gives tongue," said Peters. "Let's stop here a bit, and wait! We kain't be more than a quarter from Harness'."

When all sounds had ceased, they resumed their progress.

It was now near midnight. The darkness of the night had increased. The sky, with few exceptions, was wrapt in cloud. But a few stars shone out with a twinkle, rather than a gleam, and they rode on into the darkness.

They paused at length, and, observing all the precautions taught by a long experience in stealthy progresses, they proceeded to lower their now unconscious burden to the ground. They were tender enough in this performance; and, this done, Swipes applied the brandy to the mouth of the patient, who lay motionless beside a gateway, opening in a pale fencing. Twenty paces from this gateway stood a small cottage, dimly perceptible only after your eyes had become somewhat reconciled to the thick atmosphere.

Their mission was accomplished. This was the Harness settlement;

and they mutually congratulated one another in whispers, that the travail was over. They had no care about the result. Once more did Swipes apply the brandy to the lips of the wounded man, as they prepared to leave him to his fate.

"He'll hardly git over it, I'm thinking," said Peters, "spite of all the old gray-beard said."

"I don't know," whispered the other—"he knows *so* much!"

"But he don't know everything."

"I'm not so sure of that," said the other. "I sometimes thinks he does. I knows I never lied to him yit, that he didn't find it out."

"Wall, let's ride!"

"Softly—slowly! lead your horse a bit, till we gits out of hearing, and has a fair start."

"Give's a swig of that brandy now; I'm fairly parched up for a drink. That chap won't want any more, and who's thar to give it him a'ter we're gone?"

Will he live? Will he die? They are gone, and neither cares to ask these questions, or to care for the answer!

In the darkness—in the very depth and darkness of the midnight— he lies, face upward, unconscious, to the unpitying stars.

The wolf bends over the gray crags of the brooding mountain, and sends a long howl of hunger through the air! The dog within the close crouches shuddering beneath the dwelling, and howls back an apprehensive moan.

There are no other sounds of life! There is no light visible within. But, suddenly, one of the sleepers of the dwelling starts up, as the blast of a horn, thrice repeated, is sounded at the entrance. Another moment, and several strokes resound upon the door of the house. Then a light is struck, a head peers out from the upper windows, and a voice somewhat impatiently demands:

"Who's thar now? Who are you?"

The answer to this question acts like magic. A strange, strong voice, responds briefly:

"Voltmeier! Come down quickly, Jake Harness, there's murder been done at your very door!"

"Murder! You don't say? I'll be down, Colonel, in a twink!"

Chapter XI

VOLTMEIER

A few moments delay, and two men appeared, emerging from the entrance, bearing a lantern. Here they were met by the stranger calling himself "Voltmeier," and recognized by one of them as the "Colonel." He led them quickly to the front gate, where lay the body of Fergus Wallace. The two men held the lantern to his face, and stooped to examine him.

"He's dead, I'm afeared, Colonel! There's no life in him!"

"Yes, Jake! I think there is life," was the answer of Voltmeier. "He's warm yet. I've felt him. I think it's a swoon only, from great loss of blood. Get an old door, Jaques, or any large long shutter, and let's take him into the house. You'll give him shelter, I take for granted."

"To be sure we will, Colonel. Poor fellow! who kin he be, and how come he hurt?"

"No matter these questions now, boys; get the shutter, and let's lift him in. It's important that I should examine him at once, and see where his hurt is."

They obeyed, and, while they were procuring the shutter, Voltmeier led his horse within the enclosure, and took him to a contiguous stable, with which he seemed to be quite familiar. He returned to the entrance in time to assist the two in lifting the still insensible youth upon the shutter, and bearing him into the dwelling.

This operation sufficed to answer the doubts of all parties, as to the continued existence of the wounded man. The motion of lifting and carriage, however tenderly performed, extorted his groans, which continued even after he had been laid down upon a pallet upon one of the floors in an upper chamber.

"Make a fire, Jake," said Voltmeier; "and give us as much light as possible."

Meanwhile, Voltmeier threw off his coat, and busied himself about the patient, handling him with great tenderness, but with firm hand, and like a surgeon, and an evident confidence in his own capacity to do so. At moments he applied a little brandy, or some other stimulant, to the lips of the wounded man, simply wetting them, as it were, but with no purpose to make him swallow.

When the lights were sufficiently kindled, and the brands were in full blaze in the fireplace, he proceeded to a more close examination of the wound. From this there had been a fresh flow of blood, since that first examination, which, as we have seen, took place upon the highway. This blood had also become clotted about the wound, and had need to be washed away. When this was done, the stranger drew forth from his valise a little shagreen morocco case of instruments, which very much resembled that in the hands of the previous operator. It was evident that there were at least two persons in this wild country, who were thus prepared with the necessary knowledge and implements for *extempore* surgical operations.

But the Colonel, so called, might have been a surgeon also. In the more primitive regions of the South, Colonel is simply a form of courteous address, like Mister in other places; and is sometimes found to supersede even the professional titles. The Colonel, Voltmeier, might very well be a physician.

"It's an ugly hole, Colonel, they've made in the poor fellow's jacket, whoever done it. I'm afeard the bullet's in him yet," said one of the young men, whom we have heard called by the name of Jaques.

"No! I think not," was the slowly uttered reply, as Voltmeier continued his examination. Then, rising from his knee, and resting for a while, he said:

"The bullet has evidently glanced. It has struck against some hard object, and glanced off, running around the muscle, and scoring its way in a long gash along the side. See where it has traveled."

He showed the wound, the course of the bullet, and where it had passed out of the coat, just behind the armpit, tearing flesh and muscle as it went.

"The aim," he continued, "was good for the heart; and had the bullet not struck against some hard object—a watch, perhaps—it must have been instantly fatal."

"But there's no watch," answered the other, examining the fob of the vest, and showing the garment.

"Yes," said Voltmeier; "but you see how the fob has been scored. He has been robbed of the watch, evidently, and, perhaps of all his money, whatever that might be."

"That's cl'ar enough now. He mought hev had a smart chaince of the grit in them pockets. He looks like a gentleman born, and has good clothing for a traveler."

"Almost too good! Fine clothing sometimes costs a man much more than his tailor's bill. Eh, Jake?"

"That's sartain, Colonel. And now, what do you think, Colonel— will he do? Will he git over it?"

"Yes; if you'll take care of him."

"To be sure we will, ef you says so. I reckon he's an honest man, and, belike, he's got friends and kin that'll be mightily worried about him, when they kain't hear. He kin stay here 'tell he's able to go, but *you'll* hev to do the doctoring, for none of we people knows nothing about it."

"But you can dress the wound when I show you how."

"Well, Colonel, we kin try; but we hain't got your fingers, and hard work don't make light work easy."

"But a light heart, and a good heart, Jake, makes it easy to learn how good things should be done. It will not be difficult when I have shown you. But we must make him drink some of this. Raise his head a little—gently—gently."

The liquor was poured into the mouth of the wounded man, and he was finally found to swallow. His eyes opened, then closed again when his head was laid back upon the pillow; and Voltmeier proceeded to dress the wound, which he did—in the estimation of the two mountaineers—according to the best rules of the art. He drew their attention to all his processes, and, when necessary, taxed their assistance.

"Ef the old woman, now, was not so half-blind, Colonel, she could do it like a charm. She used to sew, and knit, and spin, when I was a boy in the sapling, and she was as quick and spry in all nice things, as ef she was born with a needle in her hand and a gould thimble on her finger. But she kain't see now how to darn a stocking or baste a jacket. I'm a thinking, some day, to carry her down to town and git her a pair of specks."

"She shall have the specks, Jake, without your carrying her to town, which is a wearisome journey to an old person. I will bring her a pair, when next I go to the town."

"Oh, Colonel, you are too good. She'll thank you mightily; and, ef they only gives her the eyes to read over the Blessed Book when the Sunday Sabbath comes, she'll be a blessing you forever."

"She shall have them, Jake."

"But, Colonel, will you be able to git sich specks as will suit her eyes? She's quite nigh on to seventy, you know, and they do say that it's hard to choose eyes for old people, onless they tries a good many."

"I think I shall be able to suit her, Jake. I know something about spectacles, and glasses, and—"

"I don't know what it is *you* don't know, Colonel," was the quick complimentary retort; but the other did not seem to heed it. He held the pulse of the patient, counted the beats, and applied the stimulant to his lips, making him again to swallow.

"He has lost a good deal of blood. But this is faintness only— weakness—we must bring him up with brandy. He will gradually come to, if you only see that he has the stimulus when he seems to need it."

He gave them the necessary directions.

"What have you got to do this week, Jake? will you be much at home?"

"I kain't say that, Colonel. I ought to be seeing after my stock. I must salt 'em, and give 'em a count. We has to be always watchful about hyar; for we've got some most rascally tramping thieves, I reckon, that's to be found in all the Cherokee range. The Cherokees themselves are great robbers, but they do it on the sneak, and are a leetle too cowardly to make a break on a large scale. But thar's some of these mean whites, who are sassy enough to come into my mountain range, and, dern their bad blood, they don't stop, if they kain't do better, than drop a man with a bullet at a hundred yards, sooner than go off empty-handed. I've lost a matter of no less than three mules and two young horses in less than nine months latterly; and I'm thinking that ef I don't sell off a drove, I shall be a losing more.

I was jest a calkilating, only yesterday, to drive down some twenty head of mules, and see what bargain I could make at Spartanburg, so as to put so much safe into my pocket; and it mout be I shall go next week. But what's the trouble, Colonel?"

"It's this: this young man has to be watched and tended. It may be that he will be unable to ride for two weeks or more. That we shall see in a day or two. Now, I can trust you and your brother, Benjie here, to take care of him for that time, so that he won't suffer. I'll come as often as I can, to see how he gets on, and when he can bear to sit a horse. You see, Jake, I feel very much interested in this poor fellow. He reminds me of one I knew many years ago, and one whom I loved like a brother. I wish to save him as if he were my own son. Now, you need not go to Spartanburg with your mules. I need an addition to my stock, and will take what you've got to sell, at Spartanburg prices. All that I shall ask of you is, when the young man is able to travel, to set him on horseback, and you and he and Benjie, together, can drive your drove to my ranges, and then come over to me for the money. What say you to that, Jake?"

"It's a fa'r offer, Colonel, and will suit me to a button."

"Very well. It's understood; and—"

Here they were interrupted. The faint voice of the patient was heard in a feebly-uttered word—

"Water."

Voltmeier rose quickly, stooped to the youth, motioned to the young man to bring water, and administered it himself. The patient swallowed freely, opened his eyes for a moment, closed them again, and, while Voltmeier was feeling his pulse, seemed to sink into slumber. And so he continued through the rest of the night, which, however, was closely verging upon the morning. Once again, before daylight, he called for water, which was supplied him, and again he seemed to sleep; while Voltmeier continued his instructions to the two mountaineers, blended with such asides of conversation, incidentally, as seemed to interest the parties. They naturally spoke of the events of the night, and Jake Harness recurred more than once to the frequent outlawries of the region.

"How *you* kin ride, Colonel, as you do—come hyar in the very middle of the night, and never happen to be hurt by some of these rascals—I don't see; but I reckon they all knows the good you does;

and how you doctors the sick, and feeds the hungry, and helps the country every way. Ah! what a blessing it is whar a man has a big purse, and a heart that's big enough to use it like a white man and a Christian gentleman."

"It's my good luck, Jake," said the other, with a light laugh. "They don't happen to meet me when I ride. I always ride in dark nights, and never let anybody know when I start, and make it a rule, never, if I can help it, to carry money about me. I somehow never meet anybody when I ride."

"Well, that's strange! I tell you, Colonel, thar's as many robbers in these long, dark ranges of the Cherokees as you kin shake a stick at! I never trusts myself out among the hills at night, onless it's a grand necessity. They do say that thar's a grand army of rogues, kivering all the country, having their signs and countersigns, their passwords, and curious sounds, horns and whistles, and that they spreads away, all through the mountains, from Virginny to the Massassip; and that what they robs from one State they sells away off in another. They jest meet and hands over the plunder, from hand to hand, till your horse or mule, that you've lost in Carolina hyar, finds its new owner down the Red River, prehaps. That's what many people say and think, and some do go so fur as to say, that ef we're to save hoof or hide of horned or any other cattle, we'll have to turn out and hunt these robbers jest as we hunt down the b'ar and the painther."

"I hardly think it, Jake. This must be an exaggeration, at all events."

"But the cattle goes, Colonel."

"True, but—the wolf and panther take a portion, and the beasts will wander off, from pasture to pasture, and down among the cane bottoms, into the very jaws of the wolves, however much you salt them. But, here comes the sun!"

And, even as he spoke, a level shaft of rosy light passed through the open window, to be followed soon by a very shower of like arrows from the same glorious archer of the heavens.

Chapter XII

THE MOUNTAINEERS

The increasing light in the chamber, from the rapid rising of the sun over the surrounding heights, enables us now to take in the whole scene within, and to note the appearance, in detail, of the several actors.

There lay on one side of the room, still as if dead, the form of Fergus Wallace. He occupied a neatly spread mattress, covered with a milk-white coverlet. Beside him sate one of the two brothers, who, thus far, of all the household, had alone made their appearance.

Jake and Benjie Harness are tall and stalwart yeomen, farmers, graziers, and occasionally hunters. In the pursuit of their several occupations, they had shown equal industry, energy, and intelligence. They had prospered accordingly. It was easy to raise cattle in the rich pasturages along the sides and in the hollows of the mountain ranges; and the mountain lands, in that sparsely settled country, were so cheap that they possessed large and ample ranges of their own, upon which a thousand head of cattle might be fed. The farm produced Indian corn abundantly, sixty bushels to the acre being frequently the product of the fertile bottoms and valley lands.

As hunters, they were bold and adventurous, and bear and deer meat were always to be found hanging in huge masses from their rafters. The hides, and occasionally the hams, of these animals, were sold in the distant towns and villages.

They were hardy lads, these boys—the taller, Jake, being about twenty-five, and Benjie, twenty-one or two years of age. Big-limbed, broad-chested, with the muscles on their arms and legs like so much whip-cord; they were always ready to take the field, whether in plowing or hunting; and a few hours' sleep, after a hard day's work, sufficed to enable them to rise like young eagles, fresh for new flight, with every morning. In the features of both there was a frank, hearty manhood of expression, blended with a singular and confiding sim-

67

plicity, which was, of itself, almost conclusive of their good faith and honesty. Nor was their appearance in conflict with the fact. They had both full faces, with smooth, rosy cheeks, made richly brown by the sun. Each wore a massive shock of hair and heavy beard, of a reddish brown color. Their costumes were those of the mountaineers, in ordinary homespun of domestic manufacture—coarse and strong, with the overall, fashioned after the hunting-shirt of a hundred years ago. This hunting-shirt might sometimes be found of well-dressed buckskin, with long, hanging capes of the same material, and fringes at cape and skirts, made simply by long *slits* or slashes, along the margin of the cape or skirt itself, as was the habit of the Cherokee chiefs, when these claimed to be the princes of the land.

With a heavy fur cap, crowned, and with rifle equipped, each of these young men would have been conspicuous as young braves among the red men. See them as they dash, handsomely mounted, up the hill-side in pursuit; or on foot, present themselves upon a cliff, confronting the bear or deer, and you have such a picture as would be the admiration and the model for the dramatic painter.

The personal appearance of him whom they called the Colonel—Voltmeier—very unlike that of the two young men,—was yet much more marked and distinguished. He was taller than either, quite as erect, and, though simply clad, in a fashion not very dissimilar to their own, yet of superior material, had yet the unmistakable air and carriage of a gentleman, born and bred in good society. His head and face were of massive, but admirable proportions—the head rather square, yet lofty, and the face, though broad, yet rather spare of flesh. His hair, originally black, was grizzly now; he wore no beard, and his skin, which was at first sight better calculated to arrest attention and occasion remark, was of that deadly pallor, that marbleized whiteness, which we somehow associate with the presence of a passion at white heat; latent, perhaps, but ready to burst forth without warning, like some volcano, whose mountain-tops are yet covered with snow. A deep-set, but large gray eye, keen and piercing, which yet declared for nothing beyond vigilance, served to heighten the general effect of his features, and the color of the skin, in impressing the observer with the idea of powers and passions which had been wonderfully disciplined to subjection, without any forfeiture of vitality. The more you surveyed the aspect of this man, the more uncertain became your judgment in respect to his age. At a first glance, you would suppose him forty-five—hardly fifty—but a continued study of his features, especially in their immobility, would persuade you that he was fully sixty, or even more. At the end of your scrutiny, you would possibly doubt that he had passed beyond the middle line of thirty-five or forty; and, briefly, you would come to the conclusion that there are few persons possessed of such or more vital energies; one more strong of will, more ready in action, or more able in performance.

While we are making this scrutiny, the chamber is entered by an old woman—the mother of the two young men—somewhat decrepit, but full of animation, who probably counted some sixty-five years of life. She wore a cotton cap, from which escaped a generous flow of hair, perfectly white—long, silken hair, soft and fine, which hung down upon a pair of healthy-looking and fair cheeks, the wrinkles of which were not very pronounced. She had been a comely woman in her prime, no doubt, and was pleasant to look upon.

At her entrance, Voltmeier, who had just then been examining the features and feeling the pulse of his patient, turned quickly, but with great quiet of manner, and taking her hand, expressed himself very glad to see her, and see her looking so well.

"And I'm mighty glad to see *you*, Colonel; you always makes me feel quite bright when you come. But you don't come quite as often as I could wish, and you stay too short a time when you does come. You know we're always glad to see you."

"Hard work, my dear Mrs. Harness. It's not often that I can spare time to visit my best friends. I have too much to do."

"Well, I don't see why *you* should be a-working all the time, or so hard either, Colonel. Everybody says you're the richest man in all the Cherokee country."

"Why should that make a difference, Mrs. Harness? No riches can make up to a man what he loses by doing nothing. Idleness is the worst crime against God. Our happiness does not depend upon what we have, but upon what we do. What says the poet?"

Here he recited:

> "In *doing* is blessing,
> And he is most blest
> Who learns the grand lesson
> Of doing his *best*;

And the best gifts of heaven,
    Most fruitful of spoil,
Are the fields it has given
    For the *freedom of toil*.

No lack of the region
    For culture and art,
If the proper religion
    Be warm in the heart.

And in *doing* is *living*,
    In *striving* the *soul;*
The *gain* is the *giving*,
    The *march* is the *goal.*"

Here he paused abruptly, and gently led the old lady to a chair; he had continued to hold her hand while he recited. This done, he walked away to the window, and looked out for a moment. When he turned to her again, it was with the slightest possible smile upon his marble features.

"Well, Colonel," said the old lady, "that seems to be a sensible scripter'. Ain't thar some more of it?"

"Yes, but this is all I remember."

"Well, but, Colonel, I'm a-thinking that there must come a time for putting down one's work, and folding one's hands in the lap, and saying: 'Now, lettest thou thy sarvant depart in peace!'"

"When we can do no more—yes!—But, better die in the harness, my dear madam, at the plow, than upon the common, waiting for death, and seeing the birds of prey gathering around you, waiting for the moment when you can no longer lift a hand to drive them off."

"Well, Colonel, I reckon you're right, as you always air. But what's the to-do with this poor young man that they murdered at our very door? Benjie come to me and told me in the night who 'twas had come, but he wouldn't let me git up, tellin' me that I could do no good."

"He was right, Mrs. Harness."

"But you don't know what a good nurse I em, Colonel. And, now, do tell me, will the young man live or die?"

"He will live, my dear madam. I think I may safely say so."

"I'm glad of it, Colonel. But you're always so sartain of what you say."

This was said doubtingly, however.

"I think there is no doubt," said Voltmeier, going to the bedside.

"The bullet has narrowly escaped all the vital parts, and what he now labors under is simply loss of blood, and some injury to the muscles, which will occasion pain, and may retard his recovery some weeks; but can hardly, by any possibility, affect his life. It only needs that we should watch and nurse him carefully. He may be for some weeks a burden upon your hospitality and care."

"Oh! don't say that, Colonel. It'll be no burden, anything that we can do, for you, or for the poor young man either. That he should be murdered at our very door, and we not to know it, and nobody to help him? The bloody villains! But the gallows will be their portion yit. That's jist as sartin as that there's a God in heaven."

Voltmeier walked away to the window. The widow rose and followed him, saying:

"Trust the poor young man with us, Colonel. We'll do for him as well as we kin. I was always a good nurse, and ef 'twant for my poor eye-sight, I'd be jist as good as I was twenty years ago."

"Oh, mother!" cried Benjie, "the Colonel's going to bring you a pair of specks. He says he kin fit you, so that you needn't travel to the town to git sighted."

"Oh! kin you, Colonel?"

"I'll try, Mrs. Harness."

"You're so good, Colonel."

"Good! Oh, no! Good, indeed!"

"And you *knows* everything! Now, how kin you jedge about my eyes, unless you tries the glasses by my own eyes?"

"I can bring you several pair, you know; but I know something about glasses myself, and with a little examination of your eyes—sit down here."

He placed a chair for her in the very blaze of the sunlight. The eyes were closed instantly.

"Open your eyes."

She did so. He waved his hand suddenly across them, and she winced. He bade Benjie light a candle and bring it to him; then removed the old lady and her chair to a dark corner of the room, and, when the light was brought, he held it close to her eyes, severally, and watched keenly the effect.

"Well," said the widow, inquiringly, when the light was removed, "kin you sight me, Colonel?"

"I hope so."

He did not think it necessary to tell her that her imperfect vision was the work of time—that it was age, and not disease of the orb that made her sight imperfect. He ordered frequent washings of cold mountain spring water throughout the day.

Meanwhile, Fergus Wallace opened *his* eyes, looked around him, and spoke.

"What has happened?"

Voltmeier passed to his bedside and took his hand, saying quietly:

"Be at ease, my son. You are with friends, who will take care of you."

The youth murmured, and his hands were lifted as if to feel within his bosom. But the arms dropped listlessly. The feebleness continued. His eyes were closed again.

"There is no fever yet," said Voltmeier, as if to himself. "Let me have the brandy."

He merely wet the lips of his patient with the liquor. Another spasmodic effort of the wounded man, who, this time, carried his hand to his bosom, then muttered, rather than spoke, but the words were intelligible:

"The papers!"

"They are safe," was the prompt reply of Voltmeier, and the youth again closed his eyes, as if satisfied.

"But there were no papers, Colonel, when I stripped him," said Jake.

"True," was the reply. "But we need not tell *him* that—just now, at all events."

"That's sensible," quoth the old lady, to whom Voltmeier now again addressed himself.

"I will remain with you to-day, Mrs. Harness, and I hope, before I leave this poor fellow, to see him better, and—safe! I shall leave him, then, with you."

"And you think he won't die, Colonel?"

"Not this time! I trust to see him improving every hour. There may be some little fever, from the irritation of the wounded muscles;

but, with proper care, and frequent application of the remedies which I shall leave with you, I hardly doubt that you will find him stronger, and able to speak in the morning. But you must discourage much talking. He will do, if you will keep him silent; answer no questions. Tell him nothing whatever, only that he is with friends, and that all his papers and effects are safe. He'll do."

"I'm so glad! And I'm so glad you'll stay the day with us, Colonel."

"Oh, mother, you know the Colonel always stays the day with us when he comes."

"That's true; and why kain't you stay the night, too, Colonel?"

"No, my dear madam, I must travel to-night."

"Ah! you'll pay for it some day. That night traveling in these mountains is hard riding, and a man sometimes comes upon something harder than the rocks. You see what this poor fellow has come to?"

"My dear Mrs. Harness, one must ride where fate and the devil drive."

"Ah! lack! but there's no devil a driving *you*, and if you'll only put God in the place of fate and the devil, I reckon you kin stay to-night."

"Impossible!"

"Wall, Colonel, 'scuse me! I must go and see about the breakfast. It's lucky I kin give you a fresh venison-ham steak this morning! Benjie, boy, go at once and make up the fire, and cut the meat."

And the two left the room.

Voltmeier and Jake Harness alone remained with the patient.

"Jake," said Voltmeier, "whenever you can bring over this young fellow to Weimar, make your arrangements, if it be possible, to take a drove of horses over to Henderson, Asheville, and Flat Rock. There is a demand for good horses among these rich men from the South Carolina salts; and I have some twenty head that I think to sell off myself. The thing will pay you."

"I know that, Colonel, and I'll try to fix it to suit. I can git Pike to go along with me. Benjie must stay at home to see to things, and take care of the old woman, you know."

The feeble voice of the patient again summoned Voltmeier to the bedside.

"Where am I?" was the question.

"You are with friends."

"Have I been struck?"

"You have been thrown from your horse and slightly injured. You will be better to-morrow. Be quiet now. Be not impatient."

"But my papers?"

"Are safe, in good hands."

"Watch—father!"—his voice died away in a murmur.

"All safe! all safe!"

The young man slept.

"But was thar any watch?" said Jake. "I never seed any."

"I think it likely. The robbers evidently stripped the poor fellow. But we needn't let him know any of his losses until he recovers his perfect senses. Say nothing to him—mention neither your name nor mine."

The day passed. In its progress, the condition of Fergus justified the predictions of Voltmeier, and he felt the better satisfied to leave him that night to the tender cares of the Harness family. An hour after dark and he was gone—riding forth on his white steed into the deep valley and black shadows of the mountain gorges.

Chapter XIII

HOW TO RELIEVE THE WAYFARER

A day and night elapsed since the old man of "Wolf-Den" parted with his emissaries, sending them off with the body of Fergus Wallace, and on their further mission of robbery, perhaps of blood. He had himself mysteriously disappeared, as we have seen, in one of those wild and seemingly inaccessible nooks of rock and jungle, so many of which are to be found scattered throughout the ranges of the Apalachian chain.

It may have been twenty miles or more, as the crow flies, west from the farm of the Harness family, that we again meet with the two ruffians whom we know as Brown Peters and Old Swipes. They occupy a mountain hollow gorge and valley, one of those beautiful recesses of the mountains which seem shut in by nature, hallowed, and made secure from the intrusion of the world. On no side was there any visible outlet. The mountains rose into great massive towers, pinnacled with gray rocks, that stood up as so many sentinels, watchful against any intrusion. Great fissures, dells and hollows, scored the sides of these cyclopean elevations, as if, trenched by the storms and thunderbolts of a thousand years, their wounds only partially covered by masses of foliage, in which the oak found its loving companion in the vine, whose bright flowers, of all tints and colors, warmed the otherwise sterile aspect of the scene with all the glow of beauty.

In one of these hollows, scooped out, as it would seem, for shelter and security, and half hidden from the passing sight by masses of the densest umbrage, lay at length the persons of the two outlaws. They played at cards, and a jug, conveniently beside them, with a pewter mug, indicated probably their chief processes of refreshment. Fragments of bread and venison in strips, showed that they had dined on the spot. A little mountain rivulet kept up

75

a perpetual leaping from the bald brow of an impending rock immediately behind them, at the bottom of which the streamlet found repose in a beautiful basin, the water being clear as crystal. From this they drank; not blending the water with their apple brandy—such was their beverage—but employing it in small proportions, *after* they had swallowed their potations,—which were taken in no such stinted measure. Drinking thus, at intervals, and playing at *"old sledge,"* they seemed to give no heed to the surrounding scenes or to certain accessories, which, as we look about us, may well engage our attention.

At about twenty paces from where the ruffians lay at their play, sat a person, with head drooping, but occasionally lifted up and looking about him with a most lugubrious aspect of consternation and bewilderment. He was evidently a citizen, who had been caught napping; well dressed, in city costume, with the exception of his coat, which lay beside him. He sat uneasily, writhing about at moments, as if with a sense of pain, but giving utterance to no expression of it beyond what was visible in his uneasiness and his face. That was pale with terror. He had evidently gone through a trial which had effectually rebuked his manhood. A closer examination shows him to be tethered, his hands behind his back, bound at the wrist with strong thongs of buckskin, the chafing, as well as restraints of which, probably occasioned much of his uneasiness.

Near him stood a strong hackney, with saddle and bridle, ready for his rider, but halted securely to a sapling. A little beyond him lay a small valise, open, and apparently rifled. Some loose papers lay scattered about, documents and newspapers, and a few articles of clothing.

A robbery had evidently taken place. A further scrutiny of the scene discovers the two horses of the outlaws, securely fastened, and in part hidden in a dell of the mountain.

The captive was silent. The two gamesters pursued their play in comparative silence also, broken only by an occasional ejaculation. Silence was abroad upon all the heights. The wilderness of mountains and valleys seemed all to sleep, and but for that perpetual murmur of the mountain's runnel, in its perpetual leaps, sheeted in white foam, down to a like slumber with the scene, in the little fairy-like lakelet at the foot of the rocks, one might deem that all animation had passed out from the heart of nature into that of death.

At length, throwing down his cards, and rising with a yawn, stretching his great arms wide as he did so, Brown Peters exclaimed:

"And how long air we to wait here, Swipes, for that darn'd eternal black-snake; that vinegar-souled fellow, Gorham? I'm mighty nigh wore out with this waiting on a fellow that don't seem never to come up to time."

"Well, I reckon he'll be hyar soon now. The sun's two hours high yit, and he's had his work to do, I reckon; and a handful of it."

"He work—not he! He's a snake—a fox—and he uses our fingers for work. What old Grizzly sees in him for sarvice, I kain't see, Swipes, nor kin you."

"Be easy! I reckon he knows best."

"And when will we let this fellow loose? Did you ever see sich a scare! He's jist as much frightened now as when we first tuk him. How the —— could they trust such a critter with so much money?"

"We kain't let him loose you know, till we're ready to ride ourselves."

"Well, we'll hev' to put out before sundown, if we ixpects to make the 'den' to-night. What's the use of waiting for Gorham. He kin find his way to the 'den' without us."

"But he was to meet us hyar, you know, to help us work in this business."

"But the business is done without him. He never was much account when work was to be did."

"But, ef he comes, and we're off, how will he know that the business *is* done. He'll hev' to wait looking for us. Don't be in a hurry, Brown, we've time enough, I reckon. He's slow, but he's always sure."

"Yes, and dern'd sly. I never sees his eye, looking out sharp on one side, so, but I thinks of a rattle-snake in disguise."

"Better not be talking so in his hearing. You says some mighty sassy things to him in your liquor; and some day he'll be putting a knife into you."

"Who's afraid? I'm not—of him or any man of his riches!"

"But, what's the use of treading on a fellow's toes all the time?"

"Well, it's jist to see ef he's got any feeling in 'em! Now, he don't seem to me to hev' any of the feeling of the right human in him. He never drinks. He never plays. He never has a good word for a fellow. He never has a joke; and as long as we've worked and played and quarreled and fit sometimes together, I've never seed him laugh. Now, all that's onnatural. It's downright onhuman. When you find a fellow that's never yet larned to laugh, he's all over snake. Then, agin, I'm a thinking he's got the idea in his head that he's born to be a gentleman. See how nice he fixes up his ha'r; and how he carries sweet soap, with a strong scent, to wash his hands. And he's got a little brush for his teeth, and sich a splashing and washing of his mouth, he makes, every morning, is a vexatious thing to hear, perticklarly when we knows it's all nonsense and conceit."

"Oh! don't you bother about his ways and notions. It don't take a copper out of your pocket to put in his. And he does his business and you does your'n, and we all gits our share!"

"But you sees, Swipes, I'm a cur'ous pusson, and it's my way to be finding out all the secret of the article. I'm cur'ous about everything, and likes to s'arch in all the close bushes, and hiding-places."

"Yes; and some day you'll get your fingers into a rat-hole, or a snake-hole, and git a bite for your cur'osity."

"Leave me alone, Swipes. I'm cur'ous, but I looks before I leaps. Now, if I could only find out what's so strange in that old gray-beard Satan of our'n! That's the cur'ous that I wants to have a good peep into. Ef I could only find him out."

"You'd better try to peep into the house of the raal old devil himself, than show your cur'osity about that grizzly b'ar of ourn. I tell you, Brown Peters, if you don't know it for yourself, that, next to the old Satan, I do believe that old man kin *see* through everything, and almost *do* everything. I warns you that, jest while you're thinking, he's reading you like a book. I do believe he knows where all the gold mines is buried in these mountains, and the lead mines too."

"Ef he does, why don't he dig for em?"

"I reckon it's easier the way he takes to git his money."

"Well, we've made a fine haul to-day, I reckon. It's the biggest pile we've ever had in the net at one time."

"Yes, I'm thairsty to be at the counting. Hark! there he comes."

A child-like cry, like that which the panther makes, was heard from a neighboring crag.

"How well he kin do it," said Swipes.

"Snake or no snake, Gorham can mock the panther so that the beast her ownself would be taken in. Hear ag'in! It's fair beautiful how he does it."

"So he does; but the panther's a tricky, sneaky beast, and that sort of carakter suits Gorham nateral. There he goes it ag'in. Now, do you answer him. One, two, three!"

Swipes did so; and in twenty minutes after, the party was joined by the person of whom they had been speaking.

Their portraiture of this man was not ill-drawn. He was a slender person, very dark and sallow of complexion, thin features, with high cheek-bones, almost of the type of the red man, very black hair and beard, both long; the latter falling down in a heavy mass, nearly a foot long, upon his bosom, and the former rolled in heavy folds over his back and shoulders; a deeply set and piercing black eye, cold and calm, however bright, shining icily; long nose, attenuated to sharpness, and a medium forehead, of some breadth, but of little elevation;—these were the prominent features. His costume was something finer than that of his comrades, but still that of the backwoodsman. He walked slowly and quietly into the circle, saying nothing, but with his eyes traversing the whole area, and seeming to take in everything at a glance.

"We've had a long wait for you, Gorham," said Brown Peters. "You're cursedly behind time, old fellow."

"Yes!" was the quiet reply, but no excuse was given.

"We've done the work, you see. No thanks to you."

"Thanks to *you*, then," said the other, coolly. "I'm lucky in having such efficient associates."

"But, by gum, Gorham, it won't do that we should hev the work to do, and you share the gittings. That's onfair play, I'm a-thinking."

"There's enough for all, I hope," replied the other. "How is it, Swipes?"

"A big pile; but we leave it to old Grizzly to do the counting."

"Well, harness up. The sooner we ride the better. It'll take us till full dark to work our way out of the hollows and up to the hills. The old man will look for us at the 'den' by midnight."

"Where's your horse?"

"Down yon bottom."

"Well, go ahead! we'll join you. I'll onhitch this scary fellow and let him go. Shill I let him hev his horse?"

"Yes, he seems nothing remarkable, and a horse will tell a story and be a witness, very frequently, where a bank-note goes current, and gives no evidence. See him sent off in the right direction."

"Well, you carry this bundle of bills; you, Brown, take this, and I'll pouch the other. Wait for me at Buzzard Roost."

Some other brief dialogue, contemplating their arrangements, and the two disappeared, leaving Swipes to a conference with the prisoner. Him he approached promptly.

The poor fellow seemed quite exhausted, and begged for something to eat and drink. He had not got recovered from his fright, and asked hurried questions about what was to be done with him, which Swipes did not care to answer.

"Hyar," said he, "young fellow, is a bite of bread, and hyar's a good swallow of apple-jack first, and hyar's a hunk of venison. Ef these don't keep life in you till to-morrow morning, you'll be sure to die to-night. Thar's a drop of consolation always in the sartainty of anything."

"I might as well be dead at once," said the captive, mournfully, as he took the bottle in his grasp, and swallowed deeply of the brandy.

"That's jest as you likes it. We've let you off mighty easy."

"You've ruined me forever."

"Oh, you're young yit, and you'll rekover after a short seasoning in the mountains."

"I shall never be able to show myself in Washington again."

"I hear it's a mighty bad place, and a place where everybody steals is not good for anybody. Thar's but leatle chaince for much profit whar thar's so many competitioners."

The captive groaned bitterly, and craved another stoup of the liquor. It was given him. He had now been released from his bonds.

"Now," said Swipes, "I'm going to quit you."

"Oh, my God, no! Let me go along with you."

"Kain't be did, my beauty. You must take the other route. Ef you starts to come with us, or to follow us, we'll send you by a short cut to kingdom come. You don't know that country yit. You'll find it some day. Don't be in a hurry now to turn your horse's head to them parts. But you jest shape your course by the sun, jest westward, and you'll git to the Cherokee country. And you'll see the city of Jericho, and you'll hear all about Methuselah and Jerusalem, 'specially as you don't bring 'em the money they've been ixpecting. If they lets you off without axing you to leave your scalp, you'll be lucky. Don't say I didn't give you the right warning."

"My God! my God! what is to become of me? Can't you let me go with you, and hide me somewhere? I shall never be able to go back and show myself."

"Then go for'ard, man, and fight it out. Set your teeth fast together, with a stiff upper lip, and jump headlong into the dark. You've got a good hour by sun before you kin do that, and a good hour by sun, putting your spurs to use, will bring you to a cabin—more than one—whar you kin sleep without any danger of finding yourself in the wolf's belly when you wakens up in the morning. And so, I whistles you on your journey."

He rode off without further parley, while the miserable captive, now freed from his bonds, yet prostrate from despair, threw himself upon his face, and clutched at the rocks with his fingers, in an agony which no language was able to express. Bitter groans escaped his bosom, but no word his lips.

Chapter xiv

MOGGS

We have seen the departure of Voltmeier, riding away from the farmstead of the Harness family, after night had fully set in, and under the cover of its deepest shadows. He rode fast under the circumstances, seeming quite satisfied to leave his horse to find his way at his own discretion. The beast seemed at no loss, having no doubt traveled it repeatedly before. The wayfarer, had there been any on the route, might have heard the trampling of his hoofs on the stony ground; but he could only have seen the sudden flash of his white form, emerging, for a single moment, from the dark shadows of the night, to be swallowed up, in another instant, by the same somber sea. There was no moon; and but few stars were to be seen, faintly glimmering through the heavy mists which were now rolling up, dense as the smoke of a burning city, but without the glare which illuminates them from the deep, damp gorges lying all along the road.

We have seen from what mysterious depths of thickets and rocks Voltmeier had emerged, and how suddenly, on the night when he found the insensible body of Fergus Wallace in front of the Harness Cottage. We behold him now, once more penetrating this wild realm of obscurity, over which seemed to brood the silence and the gloom of death. Verily, could we trace the gloomy avenue under the light of day, or under any light, it would realize for us as perfect a conception of the valley and shadow of death, as it is possible for human imagination to conceive.

He has penetrated it without fear or hesitation. His horse goes forward without pause. One moment his white side appears limned against a massive black boulder, and in another moment he has gone from sight, plunging into the densest body of pitchy darkness that ever massed itself impenetrably before the mortal eye.

An hour may have elapsed after he had thus disappeared, when the silence was broken, and again by the heavy trampling of a horse. A large dark body emerges soon from the same gloomy avenue which had swallowed up that of the preceding rider. There is a vague outline of man and horse, distinguishable only by motion, from the thick shadows of the scene. Again we hear the footfalls of the steed, as he winds about the gorges, gradually receding as he ascends the hills, and lost from hearing as you follow, by the sudden roar of waters. A river rolls below! A cascade tumbles from above! You see a sheeted form for a moment, all foam, plunging from the precipice, and burying itself in the sea of black beneath.

The tread of the hurrying horseman is no longer heard, and you would follow in vain upon the track he has pursued.

It is midnight, and the silence from the mountain tops hangs like a spell of death over all the scene.

An hour more and you hear the trampling of other steeds. They come from the opposite quarter—from the West. Then you hear voices, and anon, three horsemen hurry by you at a trot, in Indian file; and they too are swallowed up from sight in an instant; their voices sounding in your ears in occasional speech, till they work around the next curve of the road along the mountain.

The woman, Moggs, the weird, witch-like woman, the keeper of "Wolf-Den," is wakeful. The fire blazes on her stony hearth. Vessels lie upon it containing food. Huge collops of venison, for steaks, are divided, and in waiting, in a great pewter basin upon the "*dresser.*" A supper for several evidently is in preparation. She is busy at this work. Her hoe-cakes already are baking before the fire; you can hear the water par-boiling as it begins to simmer. The woman now whets her knives; now wipes her pewter plates; now gets ready certain flagons of the same material, and now seats herself, knife in hand, over the fire, as if to rest and brood.

And, brooding, she soliloquized:

" 'Tain't bekaise I'm lonesome! I don't mind *that!* I kin go out and talk with the rocks. Thar' they stand always, in the same place, and I'm not called upon to move 'em. And then the sun comes up and warms 'em; and the moon, she rises jist the same here as for them people down in Spartanburg and Greenville. And I don't kear to see them, and they don't kear to see me. What would they look at in me, I wants to know? I don't see any good to come to me, gwine about among people. I had the feelin' once; but it's all gone now! Now, it's as much, if I gits my feed rigular, and my sleep when I wants it, and them, and the clothing, is mighty nigh all the things that most people wants. And I kin talk to myself when I chooses, and we never quarrels. I don't think, ef I had to choose now, I'd ever quit this one place, tho' it be what folks calls lonesome. Ef I hed only a cat now, for company like, I reckon I'd feel easier. But the cussed critters won't stay here with me. I've had a dozen, but they gits wild and goes off into the mountains, and down among the hollows, and then I reckons that the varmints eats 'em up. Thar' was Jim,—as big a cat as I ever seed,—and so fat; and how he could sleep, and sing in his sleep! I liked to hear him. And Poll-Puss; how I did love her, with her great round black head and black tail, and her carrot-colored body—all over! But I couldn't keep 'em any! Yet I always fed 'em well. They had meat whenever they wanted it, and the fattest—sometimes b'ar, and sometimes wenzon, one or t'other all'ays. Yet they wouldn't stay. I reckon they fed so much upon wild meat it made 'em wild too, and they went off to hunt for themselves. Now, ef I could only give 'em milk, I reckon I could keep 'em. But how to git the milk onless I had the keow. Ef we had the keow now, we could keep her close in a high pen, somewhar down in the hollow, where they hides the horses. I reckon old Grizzly would git me another cat ef I ax'd him; and I'd tell him about the keow too. He ain't too hard a man, a'ter all; and he kin do jist anything he wants to. Ef he says the word, old Swipes would git the cat, and he'd make the pen too for the keow, ef I ax'd him. He ain't like that brute, Brown Peters. I do think that Brown Peters is about the meanest varmint that ever crawled on the face of the airth. I do think, now, that he has hed something to do with driving off all them cats. He seed how I tuk to the poor things, and he hated them for it—and he ain't a bit too good to kill 'em, bekaise he seed me like 'em! Ef I only know'd *that!*—"

And she brandished the knife which she had kept all the while in her grasp, waving it over the fire, at each several suggestion of the objects in her mind.

"Yes! ef I only *knowed* it."

And the malignant, almost fiendish glare, which shot from her eyes at these words, would have spoken most emphatically to the fears of Brown Peters, could he have beheld it, and hearkened to the soliloquy.

Here her speech was ended, and she rose and proceeded to carve the venison into strips proper for broiling.

Suddenly she stopped, and appeared to listen.

"He's come. That's him. The old Grizzly heself."

The beating of a horse's hoofs is heard winding about the building. The old man of "Wolf-Den" leads the beast, a noble black, hardly distinguishable from the night in its kindred density of raven darkness, down the hollows to some cavernous hiding-place in the rear.

A brief interval follows, when his signal sounds at the entrance. The door is opened by the woman, and the venerable gray-beard appears, bent of form, feeble, seemingly, of movement, shrouded in a rusty cloak, and appearing to have long since overpassed the alloted period of human life. The woman muttered, as, without noticing her, he passed into the interior apartment, as she had said many times before:

"I reckon he's a thousand years old, like the man in the Bible that lived on grass."

She had confounded two very different scripture characters, but it does not matter.

Old Grizzly suddenly reappeared.

"Moggs," said he, very quietly, "you should have a cat or two here to keep you company."

"Oh, Lord! oh, Lord! Ha' marcy upon my soul! He knows everything. He knows what a pusson is thinking about. Ha' marcy, Lord, O, marcy! He kin look into the very body of a pusson, and see what's in her very soul."

The astonishment which thus forced her into involuntary expression, was followed by a look of consternation, subsiding into awe, which was ludicrous to behold. She stood staring at him aghast, mouth and eyes equally on the stretch—the former showing a single long projecting tooth, almost a tusk, upon one side, and a few irregular stumps upon the other; the eyes aglare with an expression such as they probably would have shown had she suddenly felt herself in the presence of Satan himself. Then she trembled all over, and sunk down upon the rude oaken chair, covered with bearskin, which was her *peculium,* and which neither Brown Peters nor Swipes were ever permitted to profane by use.

"Why, what's the matter, woman?"

"Oh land, sir! it's so scary to know——"

"To know what?"

"That you knows everything what a pusson is a-doing or a-thinking —jist the same."

He did not attempt to undeceive her. It was, perhaps, good policy, to leave her under this impression. He might have enlightened her very easily by suggesting that her soliloquy had been sufficiently loud to be heard without, and that he had, with his usual precaution, approached the entrance on foot some minutes before he brought up his horse. She had no sort of consciousness, indeed, that she had spoken at all; and, possibly, would hardly have believed him had he asserted it. He added, as he returned again within:

"The cat shall be here within three days; and after a while you shall have a cow also."

"Oh, land! oh, land! did ever a body hear the like! Have marcy, oh, Lord, upon a sinner!"

Chapter xv

SPOILS, AND A HINT
FOR THE FUTURE

An hour later and the three ruffians arrived at "Wolf-Den," and upon duly signaling were at once admitted; with their appearance the woman Moggs set her venison steaks on the fire. Brown Peters rubbed his hands gayly, and sniffed the pleasant fumes which saluted his nostrils, with the air of one who was blessed with a wolfish appetite.

"Ef you were only a *human*, old woman, you would hav' a right to a Cherokee husband," he exclaimed, irreverently, "sartin. You knows how to dish up a brile like a sensible human pusson."

The woman gave him an oblique glance, looking up from the gridiron, over which she was stooping at the time, with a fiery glance in answer, venomous and vindictive, which she could never have embodied in words. Then, as the same fellow was beginning to speak again:

"Oh, don't you be biting at me with your eyes, Moggs."

She silenced him by rising erect, and pointing silently to the inner room.

"Oh!" in more subdued tones, "he's here, is he? But," still more softly, "whar's he hid his horse this time?"

"What's that to me or you, Brown?" said Swipes, in a whisper.

"Only I'm a leetle cur'ous."

"Your cur'ous will cut your throat, some day."

This also *sotto voce*, to which the ruffian promptly replied, though still in under-tones:

"Perhaps, onless my hand and knife ain't quick enough for the throat of the other pusson."

"Hush," said the man called Gorham, who had so recently joined them, as he pointed to the door, then opening, of the inner apartment. The old man quietly emerged from it, stooping low, and looking feebler and older than ever.

"He's a-breaking down at last," said Peters, in a whisper, to Gorham.

But the calm, clear, emphatic voice of old Grizzly, as they irreverently called him behind his back, gave the most emphatic denial to this opinion. The tones of that voice indicated *power*. The glance of his eye declared it; and the *will* which spoke out in his words, and which imposed upon all the party, impressing them usually with the sense of their inferiority, made them in another moment wholly forgetful of his physical decrepitude. They felt themselves instinctively in the hands of a master.

"Business first before supper! See, Moggs, that you keep everything hot. We will soon be ready for your meats. Come in, men, follow me."

They followed him into his sanctum. There, though the season was mild and genial, they found the blaze of a cheerful fire. A huge flagon stood upon a table, and there was quite a display of pewter mugs.

"Will you drink?" said the senior.

Brown Peters was ready, Swipes not disinclined, but Gorham hung back, and seated himself in silence.

"Gorham drinks buttermilk, fresh from the churn," said the irreverent Peters, while the cold, but keen eyes of the old man deliberately scanned the features of Gorham. They were met by a blank, expressionless gaze of the other, who yet looked fairly into the eyes of the superior.

"I never refuses *my* liquor," quoth Peters; "nor Swipes his'n neither. I've been wrastling with Baldface, day and night, for a matter of twenty years, but I always *got him down*."

And the ruffian chuckled heartily over his own jest.

"He'll have his revenges out of you at last, Peters, and the danger is, that, when he gets *you* down, he'll keep you there!"

"Don't think so, old gentleman! Ef he throws me sometimes, I rekivers soon, and never too late for the business I've got to do."

"You've been successful?" said the senior.

"I reckon thar's a good haul. We didn't miss our man this time, and we hed no trouble. He jest give in, like the old coon, and come down, all in a trimble, at the p'inting of the rifle. You never seed a chap so scared. I'm a hoping, whenever they sends money ag'in for the Cherokees, from Washington, they'll always git a fellow to bring it, who knows how to shell out, without saying a prayer. Though he did pray, after a sort, like old Moses Smoke, who always blessed the Lord for what he didn't ixpect, though he always had a mighty big expectation."

"You have not injured the fellow?"

"Only a leetle bruise over the eye, when he run it suddenly ag'in my hammer here! I reckon it's hurt my knuckle jest as much as his peeper."

"And where and how did you leave him?"

"Jest whar we treed him. He was sound in body, but mighty sore at heart; and jest cried, like a sucking baby, when we were gwine to leave him. He beg'd to come along with us, but that couldn't be did, you know. We loosed him from his tights, and gin him his horse, and our blessings; told him how to put out, and how he should reach the Jerdan, and get to Jerusalem or Jericho, before night set in! I told him to ride fast, and p'inted out the road; and, jest to make him use his spurs, I said how the wolf and painter were always mighty hungry at this time of the year, and had a mighty strong appetite for the meat of tender young pussons jest from the big city. I reckon he's gone with a rush, after what I tell'd him."

The old man made no reply to this long narrative; and, each of the party approaching him in turn, presented his package, which he at once opened.

There was a brightening of the eyes of all parties as they beheld him unfold the several packages, and proceed to count the bills, which were mostly fresh issues, crisp and smooth, and bright and new, of the United States Bank—a "big pile," as Peters phrased it— and probably one of the largest "hauls" which had been made by the party for a long season.

Twelve thousand dollars was the final count, and the senior immediately proceeded to divide it in four equal parcels. This done, he said:

"Now each of you will count for himself."

"Well, thar's no reason for that," quoth Peters; "we've seed you do it, all fair,"—and he caught up his *own* pile, and thrust it into his bosom. So did Swipes.

Not so Gorham. He proceeded, deliberately, not only to count, but to examine the several bills, the cold gray eyes of the old man watching him with a fixed gaze, as if he were studying some problem connected with this person's nature. But he made no comment.

Gorham at length seemed satisfied, and soon buried the bills in his pocket, and remained silent.

"And now," said the senior, very gravely, "after this stroke of fortune, my good fellows, it is well that you should tempt her no more in this neighborhood. The loss of so large an amount of money will cause great excitement, and a searching inquiry; and, however cautious we may have been in our operations, you will all be objects of suspicion. It is quite probable that the government will employ a special police for ferreting out the affair; and, indeed, I should not be surprised, if they should send out a troop of soldiers for a general hunt through the Cherokee country. The Cherokees themselves will turn out *en masse,* and join the hunt, and whether they should discover anything or not, they will prevent any further operations here for some time to come. It is our policy, therefore, to lie low, keep dark, and, in fact, remove to regions more remote. Now, I have intelligence of good things to be done on the Lower Mississippi, and on the Red River, and thereabouts. There's a great demand for horses in Mississippi State, and, with the large sum of money which each of you now possess, you can go into a good speculation as drovers. If you will take my advice, you will set out for the southwest, without letting the grass grow under your feet. How are you all off for pole-cat paper?"

There were various answers; and the gray-beard, having carefully secured his share of the plundered money, produced a huge package of bills of various banks along the seaboard and interior, all looking exteriorly good in uninitiated eyes, but which were so many cleverly executed counterfeits.

In a wild, remote, and sparsely settled region, it made little difference, in respect to the circulation, whether these notes were spurious or genuine. The demand for a currency was large, and it was only an occasional note that ever found its way to the bank counter, to undergo its cross of condemnation.

At the rate of *ten* for *one*—a thousand of the counterfeit for a hundred of the genuine paper—the venerable senior exchanged goodly sums of the spurious notes for the crisp bills of the United States Bank; thus greatly increasing that capital in their several hands, which they were expected to turn into mules and horses—to say nothing of other things—in a long progress through the Southwest, from the Carolinas to Arkansas. It was a pretty operation in what was considered, by all the party, as a legitimate branch of business.

Much desultory talk followed, and some discussion. It was evident that the party were a little disturbed—not disquieted—by the scheme proposed. Their previous experience, however, had been such as to leave them in no doubt as to what should, or might be done; but there were other questions. Should they work together or separate? Old Grizzly had been the cementing link between them—their *head*—the master-mind, that had controlled and counseled their operations; and they had worked so successfully under his guidance, that each felt himself at a loss at the idea of having to go alone for the future. Each had already begun to conceive his novel embarrassments, while in the formation of their separate plans for the future. It was felt by each that a consultation between them was necessary; but this required another time.

There was silence for a while, after this suggestion of their superior. Meanwhile, the senior rose and said:

"Perhaps you had better take your supper now. You can consult together afterwards. I shall not be with you, as I propose to ride to-night. I shall meet you before you depart, on two occasions at least. It will be well that you should be about here during the week, lying close by day, and coming to the 'den' only by night. I shall then see you, and will advise further with you."

Then the silent man, Gorham, spoke but two words, but so deliberately:

"And you, sir?"

The eyes of the two men met. The look of the old man was quiet, but searching. That of Gorham was somewhat more eager than usual, but the eye was visibly hooded, and drooped beneath the steady glance of the superior; but, with only a moment's delay, the other replied:

"I propose to go to Europe for two years. Two weeks more will hardly find me in this country."

"Then we're broken up," howled out old Swipes. "What'll we do?"

"You can do as I have told you—as I have taught you. You can do nothing, if you please, but live somewhere else on what you've got. Perhaps that's the best counsel I could give you. But the danger is that you will drink—you will game—you will waste your money in a thousand ways. Were you wise and strong men, it would be easy for you to settle yourselves on good farms in Mississippi; buy a few negroes, and be at peace with the world; or you could establish yourselves in the West as drovers, buying your cattle in these mountains, and making handsomely at every trip. At all events, my plan is to put myself out of the way, and I am bound for Europe, as soon as I can hear of a packet. You, too, will find it wise to get out of the way as soon as possible."

The eyes of the old man and Gorham again met in mutual inquiry—the large, cold, gray eyes of the one, like those of a toad in the rock; the sharp, small eyes of the latter, like those of a serpent in his coil. And so, for some seconds, they exchanged glances, which were, in fact, moral studies.

Then the old man rose and said:

"To your suppers now, and I will leave you. Discuss the matter among yourselves, and I will counsel with you at our next meeting."

"Do you not sup with us?" inquired Gorham, respectfully.

"Not to-night. Beware now of strong drink, the cards and dice. Beware you, Brown Peters, especially. You know your weakness."

"Yes, I knows, old gentleman," replied the ruffian, braggartly, "but I knows, besides, that I've got the strength and the sense, too; and, drunk or sober, I reckon, I knows how to hold my hand ag'in any man's, old sledge, brag or poker, with old Baldface working all the time between, from elbow to elbow. But, there's Gorham, now; he's all sarpent! He don't drink, and he don't play; but on the sly, he's jest as cunning a Yankee sarpent as ever skinned his own shadow to git something for the Sunday market. I'd like to know how you're a gwine to give *him* good advisings. I'll tell you one thing, before you begin. Ef he thinks you're gwine to make anything by it your own self, he'll never take your advising."

Neither the senior nor Gorham seemed to notice this speech, but again their eyes met unconsciously, and those of Gorham again fell beneath the glance of his superior.

"What does this mean?" was the unspoken inquiry of the old man, to himself, as he bade them all 'good night,' while ushering them into the front apartment, where the hot, smoking venison steaks were awaiting them.

The demijohn of whisky was carried out by Peters, who, with Swipes, had evidently resolved to make a night of it. The old man slips a few pieces of silver money into the hands of Moggs, as he passed through into the darkness.

He was gone.

There was a wrangle between Swipes and Brown Peters about something or nothing, which lasted some twenty minutes, and when, at length, they sate down to supper, after taking each a hearty stoup of whisky, it was discovered that Gorham had gone also. He was nowhere to be seen, nor had Moggs noticed how or when he went out. He must have followed the senior very closely.

"You old hag!" said Peters, "you see nothing that you don't want to see."

The old woman had her retort.

"You beast!" she cried; "I sees everything I don't want to see, when I sees your tiger-baboon face."

"I'll smash your muzzle, you old heifer!" roared the indignant Brown, raising his fist to strike. Swipes seized his arm.

"Don't be a fool, Brown!"

"The old witch!"

Moggs looked wicked enough, with the long, sharp *couteau de chasse*, secreted behind her back, but grasped resolutely in her hand, and ready for the assault.

"But whar's Gorham?"

"Who kin tell? He's a chap that always has a hole to hide in, and a hole to creep out of."

"I'm mighty cur'ous!" said Brown. "He's on the track of old grizzly. I wonder ef they goes together. Ef I thought so!—"

"Don't you believe it. Gorham has no love for old grizzly."

A full hour had elapsed when Gorham as suddenly reappeared as he had disappeared. He gave no explanation of his absence; but looked sulky, and remained as silently as possible; taking his place at the board, and eating long after his comrades had finished their repast. They were drinking—anon playing—again quarreling; and he slept—or pretended to sleep.

Chapter XVI

HONOR AMONG THIEVES

—Or seemed to sleep.

Perhaps Gorham did *not* sleep. His comrades could not tell; but, somehow, their experience of the man was such that, whatever he did, said, or appeared to think, was matter of suspicion. They seemed to give him credit for a subtlety which was ever busied in some device, either for his own profit, or the hurt of somebody else. And the two, Brown Peters and old Swipes, grew, from suspecting, to dislike him, and, disliking and suspecting, they tacitly grew to fear him.

Looking at the seemingly sleeping man, Peters, in subdued tones, muttered to his companion:

"You kin no more tell what he's a'ter at any time, sleeping or waking, then you kin tell what a hawk spies when he's looking with all his eyes hafe a mile in the air over the top of Old Tryon. He's sly as a sarpent, and cunning as a fox, and kin creep into a hole without scaring the spider from his net. He's been a'ter old Grizzly!"

"What makes you think so, Brown?"

"Well, I kain't tell you edzackly, but I've seed the signs for a long time in him. He's watching the old man, and I'm a-thinking the old man ain't got his eyes altogether shet, while he's s'arching about. He's cur'ous."

"Yes, and you're cur'ous too! Set a thief to catch a thief! You sees the sign of Gorham, bekaise you're on the same sarch, Brown. I knows it: and what the devil is there to make you cur'ous?"

"Well, by Hocus-Pocus, ef you was a man of only hafe sense, you'd be cur'ous too. Ain't it cur'ous that we knows hardly nothing at all about old Grizzly; that we kain't find him when we wants to; that we don't know whar he's a-living; that we only sees him when he pleases, and only for just so long as he pleases; that he goes and comes as ef he rode on the winds; that he knows a'most everything, and puts us on the scent, or the trail, as ef he was the old devil's own attorney-gineral. I tell you, Swipes, I sometimes fairly sweats under the feel-ing of cur'osity. I've tried to track him more than once. I've started fair after him. I've trailed him for miles; then I've gone and got ahead of him and been on the watch for hours, and by the etarnal hokies, jist when I thought I hed got him fa'rly treed, I've lost him, and I always lost him jist at one p'int of the compass."

"And whar was that?"

"You knows whar the big rock that we call the 'Tumbling Terra-pin' stands, mighty nigh, a long stretch of laurel, so thick and bleak, that a b'ar would not be always willing to try to strike in and scratch his way through; where the airth seems to sink down suddenly, and jist opposite thar's a tumbling water that's always keeping up a sort of guzzling-guzzle-guzzle, and as you walks on towards it, the airth is all the time a-falling from under you, till you thinks you're a gwine down, deep down into the very infarnel pit that the preachers tell on; well, it's jist about thar that I've always lost him. You'd hear the hoofs of the horse a-coming, and you'd see a sort of flash, and then you'd hear nothing, and see nothing furder, only the guzzle-guzzle of that falling water, and the great black wall of laurel. Wall, it's three times I've tracked the old Satan to that very p'int, and thar I always lost him."

"Did you push into the laurel thick?"

"Didn't I—and the next thing to tell of is the most cur'ous thing of all. As I was a-breaking my way in, sometimes crawling on hands and knees, on a suddent I was knocked down, clean over, by a blow that warn't a blow neither; nothing seemed to strike me anywhar in perticklar; but I was jist struck somewhar and tumbled over. It was jist as ef an Injin arrow was shot through and through all my bones. I fair wiltered up and went over all in a shiver, and I then know'd that old Grizzly had to do with evil sperrits—perhaps with the old divil himself. Three times I tried it, and every time—"

At this moment the eye of the speaker suddenly turned to where Gorham was seeming to sleep, and he caught the glittering, eager eyes of the latter, wide, bright, dilating with impatient consciousness, and seeming to drink in every sign and syllable that was shown or spoken.

"Oh, you beast! Oh, you black-snake!" cried Brown Peters, start-ing up furiously and darting towards the listener. "To be purtending to sleep, and listening all the time to a gentleman's private conversing.

I've hafe a mind to squeeze your whole snake soul out of your caterpillar body."

And he took Gorham by the throat, before the latter could rise from his recumbent position, and with such a steely grasp of the fingers, as promised, if continued, to effect very soon that squeezing out of the soul from the body which he had promised. But Gorham struggled and flourished his knife savagely, and old Swipes got in between them just in time to prevent further mischief.

"Don't you, Brown! What a d—d fool you air when you're in liquor!"

"But, dern his rattles, don't you see he's been a-watching us and listening, and purtending all the time to be asleep? Is that fa'r play I wants to know?"

"Oh! dern you for a fool. You're drunk, Brown. Kain't a fellow shut his eyes, and lie down ef he pleases, and ef sleep won't come, how kin he help it; perticklarly as you talk so bloody loud that no man kin sleep easy onder your tongue. Shet up and let's have a drink, and try your luck ag'in at the kairds."

Where such are the parties, whisky, dice and cards are potent pacificators. Not that either of the two men were pacified or reconciled; they were only parted and divided. They had never liked each other; and the proceeding of Gorham, pretending sleep while watching and listening, was regarded by the more reckless ruffian as an act of treachery to his comrades. And perhaps it was, even if we apply a moral standard to the case. It sufficed Swipes, however, that he had prevented the present mischief, and he made no further effort to bring the two to a better understanding. Something he did say, however, to the effect that where men had to work together, they should be at peace with each other. But even this soothing remark only roused Brown Peters' wrath anew.

"Work together! Who wants to work with *him*, I wants to know? How much of the working does he do? He's always a disapp'inting us when we most wants him. Ef I has much more work to do with him, I'll work the snake out of him first. So look to it, my chicken, for I'll wring your neck before I'm done with you."

"And git the knife for your pains," said the other, coolly.

"What's that?" and with the pewter mug at his lips, Peters was about to turn upon the speaker, his eyes full of the renewing glare of passion, when Swipes caught him by the arm.

"Come! come!" said he, "there's been fooling enough already, and old Grizzly will be sure to hear of it. It'll be a breezy day ef he should hear what you've been saying! Think of that! He ain't the man to let you off with a scratch, ef he once knows that you've been taking his track, either on you. Ef Gorham's been watching you, you've been watching old Grizzly, and you say that Gorham's been at the same business. Ef so, you're both on you great fools; and sp'iling your own chances through your 'tarnal cur'osity. But where's the old woman—where's Mother Moggs? Ef she has overhearn you now!"

"She?—Moggs? She's on the rock, I reckon."

"Hush!"—in a whisper—"Step light—follow me! we'll catch her a-listening, too, I reckon."

Swipes was still sober enough to move lightly, and he succeeded in reaching the door and throwing it open, and there, even as he suspected, Mother Moggs was in the very act of rising from beside the door, where, "squat like a toad," she had been crouching—for how long none knew. They had not seen the moment of her exit from the apartment.

"You old hag!" roared Peters, advancing upon her with outstretched hand.

"Keep off—hands off, you bloody villain!" she cried, brandishing the familiar knife; "my knife is a-longing to slash your liver."

Swipes again interfered; and more mildly inquired:

"What air you doing hyar, Moggs?"

"What hev you hearn?" demanded Peters.

"I've hearn only a quarrel between two drunken fools—that's all."

"Let her alone, Brown. I reckon she knows what a fool you air, when your skin's full of liquor. Git up a while on the rock, Moggs, and keep a sharp look-out tell we calls you. Ef you hears anything—"

"I'll not go to the rock ag'in to-night; I've just come down from the rock. Thar's a painther (panther) out on the mountain. I hearn him cry."

"It's a pity you hadn't waited for him! He's mighty fond of tinder and delicate young women. What a sweet bite he'd hev hed of you, you old witch of Satan!"

The old woman answered him only with a look, which had more of her knife in it than her love.

"Git in, Moggs," said Swipes, "and git to your roost. You hed better sleep ef you kin; for we're in for it all night. We'll blow out the night with a breeze that'll scare off the painters."

The old woman went in, muttering:

"Ef you only had the proper sperrit, you'd go out and take his hide to-night!"

Brown Peters followed her with a curse, and the *show* of a kick; but his boot failed to reach her, and perhaps was not meant to do so. She had a sleeping corner in which she suddenly disappeared.

To drink again, after this episode, was a matter of course. Swipes took occasion to whisper to Gorham:

"The only hope is to git him dead drunk as soon as we kin."

But Swipes' process involved a nice little selfish calculation, as to the amount of money which might be won while the process was going on.

"Shill it be kairds or dice, Brown?"

"Oh! dice. Kairds are tiresome!"

"And what shall it be?"

"What you please. I reckon you've cleaned up a full hundred of my honest yairnings"—with a chuckle—"and you're greedy after more. You've got a most bloody appetite, old Swipes."

"It'll be a ten, eh? It's *your* turn for luck now, old fellow!"

"A ten!—make it a hundred while you're about it. Ef it's my luck, dern my buttons, but I'll put it to the strain. I'll make the sixes spin around to the tune of a *thousand* before I let the luck git out of my harness."

What need to survey the scene farther? We leave the two ruffians at play. The drink is freely plied; and, with a deep hole made in his lately acquired money, Peters finally sinks, face downward, on the table, in a sleep that looked very like a swoon. Swipes, too, slept after a while, having soberly put away the money he had won. The woman Moggs slept also.

Then Gorham rose up quietly, and made his way into the inner room, the sanctum of old Grizzly, kindling a light here, having first carefully extinguished the lights which had been burning in the larger apartment. When the day was about to dawn his light also was extinguished, but not before; and, without waking any of the sleepers, but the old woman, to close the fastenings of the entrance, he went forth, rifle in hand, and was soon out of sight of the den.

Chapter xvii

THE CAVERN

Down, down into the thick darkness of the deep gorges; winding away at the foot of the mountains, and lost, seemingly, in impervious thickets and inaccessible recesses—away, and along the dismal tracts of bay and laurel, that rose up, silent, massed like a solid wall, as defiant to approach as the mountain barriers themselves— gliding through one narrow opening after another, that, here and there, betrayed itself, but only to the experienced eye and the practiced footstep—now sinking suddenly from sight, as if fallen into a chasm—and now suddenly wheeling about and around some mighty boulder, and emerging into a pathway between and beneath great masses of overhanging and beetling cliffs—rising, at length, to the perception of a sheeted form, all white in foam, the little cascade comes tumbling from its rock, and now lost wholly from pursuit in the interminable thickets—the black horse and darkly-shrouded rider sped their way, where there seemed no way, until swallowed up from sight, and lost to hearing, in the great gulf and abyss of darkness, which hung over the unequal levels that rose along the margin of the great French Broad River, that grandest of all mountain rivers, which tears open the vast mountains, and with the twin forces of fire and water, splits wide the unwedgable rock, and, in grand upheavals and terrible convulsions, forces its way, under perpetual struggle; now with great leaps and plunges; now with constant chafings in a course of rapids; roaring and moaning as it goes, an incessant torrent; with charges, as it were, of battle; masses of infantry forever pressing on, with grand clash and bound of cavalry, while a dread artillery thunders to the echoes of crag and cliff, and faint wails, as of a receding bugle, blend at intervals in the awful orchestra, as if to soothe that rage in nature, which represents the unmitigable warfare of conflicting elements and agents! Now, could you have tracked the footsteps of this horseman; of that powerful black steed;

strong as a buffalo, yet gentle under the well-known hand and voice of his mysterious rider, as the oriental genii under the spellword of the wizard, you would have lost him just at that point of the main road which is formed of a solid plate of rock, lying level, completely covering the highway; on one side imbedded in the mountain; at the other overhanging a little precipice.

At this precipice, gradually descending from the first rock, is a series of ledges of rock, similarly flat, which conduct, one to the other, in regular order, in little falls of three or four feet.

Upon these ledges the steel-shodden feet of the steed make no impression. Though following each other in regular steppes of descent, they are yet placed obliquely to each other; so that your progress downward is winding and circuitous. Between them and the road spreads a coppice, which conceals them from all eyes that look downward from the highest elevation. From all the points above you behold only a great gulf below, and the traveler sees only a narrow tract, which he must follow heedfully, winding, as it does, beneath a great mountain with overhanging crags on one hand, and the ledge which defines the precipice upon the other. He will never, unless shown, conceive the possibility of the descent below by any horseman, but at the peril of being dashed to pieces in the unknown gulfs beneath, which his eye fails utterly to pierce.

Yet, had he been nigh enough to see, our horseman would have shown that there was nothing impossible, and little that was really dangerous in making the descent. When he had reached this point, which, from the gray surface of the rock upon the road, was easily visible, even in the night, he descended from his horse, drew the bridle over his head, led him to the first of the steps, and, first letting himself down, then gently speaking to the steed, the animal leapt, almost with as light a foot as his rider, and stood with him upon the second of the broad, flat plates of stone. He was then wheeled about to the left, conducted to a third descent, and this leap made, in like manner with the former, he now stood actually beneath that projecting ledge of rock, protruding from the roadside and utterly concealed by it from all eyes down-looking from above. And so, ledge by ledge, the horseman conducted the docile beast, from step to step, till he gained an even track of probably a hundred yards. Here he remounted, and rode on, winding his way through a range of spruce and balsam pines, until he reached a fissure of rock, barely wide enough through which to pass. Hemmed in by hills, crags, great boulders at one moment, and dense thickets at another, there was no seeming pathway; and the sinuous progress could only be made by a series of perpetual surprises and unexpected turns; and then only by one who had long before made the exploration of this wild labyrinth of nature.

Enough, perhaps, has been said for a sufficient comprehension of our horseman's progress. It required, after the descent from the public road, to be made mostly on foot, with the led horse slowly following. At length, rounding a gigantic and isolated boulder of massive granite, he passes under an overhanging crag, a mighty mass which jutted out from a series of rocks of like description, thrown together in such relation—crags on each side, at equal distances, supporting the masses above—as to make a cavern—a rude cyclopean apartment; the result, no doubt, of volcanic eruption.

Here, rounding the enormous boulder, which was isolated, yet appeared to close the entrance to this cavern, and certainly concealed it totally in front, our horseman had no sooner conducted the beast, than he whinnied with delight, as with the consciousness of home! There was an answering whinny from within—from the dark and vaulted recess, in which, at the opening, nothing could be seen! But, as you enter, light gleams in from numerous openings above. The rocks are no conglomerate—are simply and loosely thrown together, and one or two little streams of water penetrate perpetually through the openings above, and find their way and overflow several little basins below.

The black horse eagerly presses his way in, and lo! a beautiful white horse—spotlessly white, as the other is spotlessly black—awaits him, and whinnies shrilly at his entrance; and answering whinnies, one to the other, make all the echoes joyful. This little cavern, rude, but capacious, is put to the use of a stable. It admirably answers its purpose. It required but little work of man or art to adapt it to its uses. A few loose boulders are brought together, and the thing is done.

Could you pierce the darkness with your inexperienced eyes, you would see that there are stalls for three steeds, separated from each other by barriers of stone; that there are hollows in projecting rocks, contiguous to each stall, which hold corn; a rack of poles overhanging, which contain fodder, and numerous little basins contiguous, below and about, which are always overflowing with the cool streams penetrating from above.

Each beast knows his own stall. Those of the white and black adjoin, and either of these has but to pass his head over an artificial barrier of rock, to rub his nose against that of his neighbor. This they do, while the mysterious old man, in the darkness which he seems to love, takes the harness and trappings from his beast, and suffers him to feed or drink at pleasure. And, speaking to both animals, in the German language, a few words only, in soft and gentle speech, as to favorites well beloved and trusted, he leaves the Black and the White equally to ruminate together upon his conversation and his corn. He himself has more to do to-night!

Emerging from this little cavern, our wayfarer passed around the huge boulder, which, at some fifteen feet, covered the entire front of the secret place; proceeded onward, still circuitously, picking his way over vast *debris* of rock that seemed to have been shivered by volcanic throes of the mountain. Then he entered a gorge made by greater fragments, and, anon, the noise of rolling, rushing, and dashing waters might be heard, like the noise of breakers upon some rock-bound shore. The illusion, when the white foam of the river might be seen in perpetual plunge, and in its chafing rapids, was perfect as that of the sea, especially at night, when the eye failed to take in the deep forests, and the rugged cliffs on the opposite side.

Ascending some bold cliffs, our gray-beard still approached the falling waters, to which he gradually descended, pursuing a lower ledge of rock which ran beside the stream, which dashed its foam momently above the crags. Over this lower ledge he plied his way, the light foam of the wave being frequently dashed into his very face by the sudden currents of wind issuing from the opposite gorges of the dismembered mountain.

With the flash of the waters in his eye, with their hoarse murmurs in his ear, and with their foam sprinkling his face and bosom, and sometimes blinding his sight, the old man went forward with a deliberate, calm constancy, without hesitation or emotion, as one quite confident of his route, and assured of his own capacity for any encounter. Yet, great billows, wallowing and rolling over at his very feet, seemed like so many Fates or Demons, wrapt in terrors, and raging to devour.

At length he paused, set his feet firmly on a rising boulder, and stood on a higher ledge. Then stooping, he passed under a cliff, wound his way for a few paces beneath it, and stopped at what appeared to be a black mass, huge, mammoth-like, overwhelming, looking directly down upon the stream. He approached the mass, moving along a narrow ledge just wide enough for a single person. Below him, the waters rolled and plunged, and writhed and roared, as in a mortal agony. Above him, the rocks towered away, till they swelled into a grand mountain fifteen hundred feet above the river. He crouched where he stood, moved forward, turning his back upon the river, and was lost at once in the blackness of the overwhelming rock.

There was the rock, but the vast jaws in the rock, which swallowed him from sight, were those of a grand cavern! He rose from a crouching position, rose erect, seemingly a man of greater elevation than before: no longer stooping as with age, but as if suddenly reasserting his manhood in the very vigor of its prime.

A light burned in the background of the cavern, a strong light, that of a lamp of curious structure and peculiar powers of illumination; but from the place of entrance, and at the distance where it burned, it seemed little more than the faint flicker of a taper in the bedroom of the dying man!

The new-comer advanced. As he did so, the form of another person became apparent in the vault; an old man who sat at the table on which the lamp was burning, and who seemed curiously engaged, with certain small implements, in the measurement of lines and figures. He looked up as the other came on. Then he cried out, with all the eagerness of a child suddenly made glad,—

"Ah! *mein Herr!* You are come at last! I almost gave you up for to-night. But you are come, that's enough."

This was said in German. The answer was made in the same language.

"Yes, Gellert, I am come; but I am wearied. I have had much to do, and want sleep. You, too, are wearied. You over-work yourself."

"Ah! *mein Herr!* I could not sleep—my brain was troubled! *Mein Gott*, I have had such thoughts. My dreams trouble me. Ah! those dreams!"

"As I say, you over-work yourself! I, too, begin to feel that I am over-worked. We both need rest."

"Ah! you feel that at last! Ah! Well!"

"It will soon be over, I hope. I begin to see the end very soon, Gellert."

"Ah! and what shall the end be? That is what I wants to know."

"Rest, if anything. Who knows?"

"*Mein Gott,* you come to dat! Then I have not dream for nothing."

"No matter about your dreams, Gellert. We shall soon awake to certainties. Go to bed, old man."

"And you! You are tired. Shall you not go to bed, too?"

"Not yet! I could not sleep now if I were to try. I must first work off some thoughts, while my body is at rest. Go to bed, you,—sleep and dream!"

The tones were those of command. The old man obeyed, put up his implements carefully, rolled up some sheets of paper upon which he had been making calculations; and, finally, with a great yawn, retired from the table. A few moments after he was busied throwing off his garments, and disposing himself, at length, upon a rude pallet, which lay, almost out of sight, at the extremity of the cavern.

The new-comer, "Old Grizzly," as we may still call him, threw himself upon a rude bench of common plank, folded his cloak into a pillow, and, stretching himself also at length, and crossing his hands upon his bosom, shut his eyes, and seemed about to realize the sleep which he also desired.

But he did not sleep. He rose within half an hour, and taking certain packets from his bosom, stored away some of them in a box which stood in a crevice of the rock, and proceeded, by the lamplight, to the perusal of others.

"This d—nable *unrest!*" he murmured. "The question is how to be freed of that? What substitute for it shall I find? That is the problem! Shall I solve it? It will always be time enough to die!"

So he mused, so muttered, while he read. Great clouds gathered about his brow. His eyes darkened, as if with looking inward and upon the darkness. Then, as if desiring rather to escape thought than satisfy doubt, he exclaimed:

"At all events, *this* life must end! There is no need that it shall continue. I have, at length, a motive, and the clue to escape! It is in my power, by Providence, shall I call it? to atone at last. This boy—yes! Well, whatever happens, it will be quite enough if I shall have made my Mignon happy—my beautiful Mignon—my precious! I could bear the rack, could I see her upon the throne!"

Chapter XVIII

PRAYER

The night waned rapidly, and still this mysterious wayfarer, upon whom our eyes have been so long fixed, mused and read at intervals, sometimes brooding in a long deep silence, and anon breaking out into speech of passionate and perhaps incoherent soliloquy. One document, in especial, seemed to demand his frequent reperusal. It was that paper, written by the hands of a dying mother, which had been plucked from the bosom of the wounded Fergus Wallace. Over portions of this paper, which, from its length, and its effects upon the reader, seemed to embody a long and touching history, he seemed to dwell with keenly aroused and agonized interest and feeling. His soliloquies, incoherent, perhaps, in some respects, to the hearer, are no doubt expressive of a passionate remorse in him.

"Yes!" he exclaimed, "she might have been mine! I see it here! She would conceal from me the truth; but it will not be suppressed. It needed but time, but that patience which I had not then; but a certain degree of tendance and solicitude; but a little more of demonstrative kindness; and but a proper policy with my more fortunate and more prudent brother.

"He triumphed. How! By what arts; by what subtleties; by what wrong done to my heart in cruel misrepresentations to her?

"Was it so? Do I not wrong him still? It may be so. Certainly, the brave defiance which he gave to a father's and a mother's will, in periling fortune and their affections, in behalf of the woman he loved, was a shame to *me*, and necessarily cast a cruel doubt over the love which *I* professed—which I felt! But mine was—alas!—not then, a self-sacrificing love! I had not the magnanimity to surrender for one, however precious, all the other objects of life. Ambition stood in the pathway of love, and I lost that jewel which no after-triumphs have supplied to me. I wronged her love, in doing wrong to my own, and might have been happy in a possession, with such a happiness now, as none of my possessions can give. And now, it is too late! too late! Those bitter words—that terrible conviction—too late! too late!"

Here he paused, rose and strode the rocky floor of the cavern, with his hands clasping his head: This, for a while, when he resumed his seat and his soliloquy:

"Too late for happiness, yes; but surely, not too late for atonement. This is the last grand privilege of life; and this sad sweet voice appeals to me, from the very grave, and entreats, not demands, that I *do* atone; and prays, oh! how pitifully and pathetically, that I may be spared for the exercise of this grand privilege! She prays for me, for the prolongation of *my* life, when she is surrendering her own! She prays to *her* God for that mercy to me, which I denied to her and hers. Her rights, her husband's—my brother's rights—all denied them; and I in my rage and disappointment at defeat, in my ambition and desire for power, grasping all that inheritance which left them destitute to the last! Can I make this atonement now? Can I restore the dead to life? Can I compensate them for so many long years of suffering, privation and sorrow,—all fruits of my cruel wrong! How, oh! my friend Goethe,—thou who hast so frequently rung in my ears, that one word *'atonement'* as the last sublime privilege accorded by the Fates to man—how can *I* atone for these things? How repair the cruel hurts of my infliction, when the two chief victims both lie silent and senseless in their graves? Solve me this problem, oh! my master, if, in all thy various wisdom, thy wide search, thy deep philosophy, thou hast found the essential secret of thy search."

Another pause after this apostrophe, and another passionate striding of the cavern. He staid himself abruptly in his walk; returned to the table, took up the manuscript, fastened his eyes upon it, but without reading, and continued his speaking.

"And yet, does not this voice from the grave—this voice of the beloved one, of that one most wronged, who dies with the speech of forgiveness upon her lips,—does not she herself point out the way? Does she not commend to me this son of her affections,—the son of him whom I have wronged with her;—and, has she not said—the words are remarkable, as suggestive of what Goethe has so often said to him—'If you still live, Voltmeier, as I trust in God you do, you will—you should—be glad that you still have an opportunity to atone to me and to his father, for your wrong to *us*, by your justice to *him*. Do not, I pray you, forego this opportunity to win that grace of mercy from Heaven, which I have earnest hope will accompany *my* forgiveness. It is not too late, if you still live,—and that you *do* live, for mine and my son's, as well as your own sake, is the last fond and earnest prayer of her whom you once professed to love!'

"Poor Catharine!

"Yes; there is a sacred significance in this language. Something may be done. Goethe was wont to say: 'The earnest, religious *will* to atone, seconded by the resolute effort, in all possible ways at atone-ment, is, by a law of Providence, sufficient for its object; but, upon this object, the whole soul must be set, with all its will and all its strength, never once turning aside from the one paramount duty, which thus resolves itself into the last obligation of the mortal life.'

"And he meditated, I feel sure, this very solution of the problem, as furnishing the material for the fit sequel to his 'Faust.'

"It must be so.

"And—look at the coincidence—

"The boy falls into my hands!

"Another crime of mine, and he is about to perish from it!

"It is *my* hand that rescues him from the death, which my imple-ments would have executed upon him!—and that he should so fall into *my* hands, at the very moment when my crime has bathed my hands in his blood—that, in his insensibility he should have borne this precious document to its true address, opens before me the dreadful whole of this miserable career! But it opens also the passage to atonement! The opportunity is accorded me by God—Fate, Providence—what you will; and the question is: shall I find the courage, the will, the wisdom, for that new life which 'atonement' properly begins? I must try! I must try!—and the beginning must be prayer! What else? There must be a strength superior to my own, to enable me to fight this new fight."

The strong man sank upon his knees. He laid his hands upon the manuscript. He bowed his head upon it, and thus, for a while, in utter silence he remained.

Did he pray? In what language, and how harmonize those discords in soul and mind, which prayer is solicited to subdue? How, and through what process of humility, attain the required strength for the beginning of that new life?

Did the Deity hearken to that appeal which he has not suffered us to hear? We can not answer. We know not. The sequel may show.

Chapter xix

SCATTERED

We need not prolong this scene.

The night was rapidly speeding to the dawn, when the old man retired to a cell in the rear of the cavern, which seemed to have been specially scooped out for the purpose of a chamber. A little pallet was sustained on a rude frame-work of scantling and boards, sufficing for a bed, upon which he threw himself down, seemingly exhausted, and silence now prevailed throughout the vaulted apartment, not only during the night, but long in the next day.

The sun was careering over the mountain-tops, and leaping upwards like a courser rising out of the sea, long before either of the inmates of the cavern came forth to behold his progress. Midday, however, found them once more busied in a long and interesting consideration of their mutual and mysterious affairs.

In the meanwhile, however, he whom we have heard called "Old Grizzly," adopting the speech of his subordinates, seemed to have regained that decisiveness of tone, will, and general bearing, which he has usually shown. Whether he still reflects so severely on himself now, as before retiring last night; whether his conscience still pricks him with remorse; whether he adheres to his express resolution of atonement; or whether, as is but too frequently the case with poor humanity, his words have undergone a change with his recovery from temporary exhaustion, is yet to be seen. At all events, we find him exhibiting the same stern directness of purpose in his manner and language as belonged to his former character.

The will of a powerful organization, and an experienced and well-trained manhood, is still the prominent exhibition in his conduct. If he still adheres to his purpose of repentance and atonement, as declared on the previous night, *his trial is begun*. It will be a terrible one, in degree, with the mighty change which his resolution is to effect, and the suffering will be proportionally greater, as it requires to be endured in silence.

The cavern at midday was very nearly as dim as at midnight. The lamp burned all the while upon the table, giving a bright light to all upon it, and to a small surrounding precinct, but not extending to the extremities. To explore there, at any time, the tenants employed a smaller lamp, enclosed with glass, which protected the light from the little currents of air, which issued from neighboring fissures in the rock.

By the light upon the table we discover that it is covered with a variety of articles and implements, of the uses of some of which our experience tells us nothing. We see that there is all the apparatus for engraving. For this purpose there is every variety of tools. There are bottles at hand, which may contain acids; little gallipots which probably hold various dyestuffs. Fragmentary and unfinished specimens of printed engravings lie about, which show the hand of a master-workman. Some chests may be found in corners and crevices, and we note, in a spot not far from the entrance, an electrical battery, from which radiate sundry wires, passing out of the entrance, and curiously inwoven with the natural vines growing out of the shelving *debris* of the rock. The discovery of these wires will remind us of Brown Peters' description of the mysterious blow which he received while endeavoring to gratify his passion for the *"cur'ous."*

The master of the place—for such he was—emerged from the cavern at rising, and walked out to the edge of the little cliff which looked down upon the raging waters; still bounding, still chafing, at their perpetual struggle with the rocks; now broken into little cataracts, and surging in foam over massive black boulders, and then rolling away in swollen billows, each of which, clad in hues of green and yellow, seemed to envelope some demonic form. He seated himself upon one of the crags, and gave himself up to musing.

Here he was soon joined by the little old German from the cavern, who brought with him several bank-notes, to which he challenged the attention of his superior.

"You shall not be able, *mein Herr*, to say which is which. You shall tell me."

This was spoken in German.

The other replied in the same language, as, taking the bills in hand, he examined them with seeming carelessness, but with the quick eye of the artist, and suddenly pointing to a *dot*, he said:

"This is your copy; this the original. Compare, here, and note the difference. But it is well done, Gellert."

"Ah! *mein Herr,* you have good eyes. What eyes! I see! I have make too much of dat eye. But it is beautiful done, is't not so, *mein Herr?*"

This was said in broken English—the conversation being carried on, at intervals, in this patois—the German being still the chief medium of conversation, in which both the parties were experts.

"It is well done, Gellert. But this must all stop now. The work is pretty well over."

"How so, my master?"

"We have done enough. *You* are rich now."

"Rich enough to live, my master! but not for my grand experiments; not for my great discovery. Dat will take a great deal of money."

"Yes, and still you will have enough. We must break up here. You will be soon in danger here."

"Ah, *mein Gott,* what have dey been doing, *mein Herr?*"

"It matters not to say. There's mischief afoot, and we shall soon have government troops hunting through the neighborhood. I must make *you* safe, my good Gellert, and so you must go to Germany as soon as we can get you off. You can perfect your discoveries more successfully in Germany than here. You can live cheaper, and you can there be *safe.* Here, my poor Gellert, they will hang you, if they catch you."

"Hang me! Oh, *mein Gott!* Do not say such tings to me, mein Herr. Dey frightens me to death. What, wid rope 'bout dis neck— ach! It is very terrible to tink. It shall break my heart. Den, my inventions."

"You must escape while there is yet time."

"And I must leave dis beautiful workshop of mine in dis temple where I meditates de grand discovery; de perfection of all art; de great invention of all de ages—ah! miserable! I have lov' to live in de darkness here, and to listen in de night to de grand voices speaking to me from de waters; and I must be gone from it forever, never more!"

"Even so, Gellert. But you will be going back to your own beautiful country, and you will go back refreshed by your long intercourse with nature, to the full fruition of all that is beautiful in art. You love art, I know, Gellert, even as the mother loves her child; for man is the parent of art, even as nature is the teacher of man. You must go! In Germany you will be rich, Gellert, and you can there procure those agencies and that machinery for your inventions which can not be found here. You must go; but that will not forbid you to return when you desire, and when it will be safe for you to do so."

"But, mein Herr, how shall the troops know what I am, and what I do?"

"They will soon know, if *they should find you here.*"

"Mein Gott, that is true; but what if I shall destroy, burn up, cut to pieces, bury in the holes, and fling into the river, my tools, my machinery, all de proofs of what I have done?"

"Well, and with these destroyed, what can you do here? What then would you stay for? These tools, and implements, and agencies, my poor Gellert, are your very life. Destroy them, and you destroy yourself. *We* shall destroy them for you, Gellert. *I* shall *need* to destroy them."

"*You*, my master;" very reproachfully.

"Even so, Gellert. It would be much more painful to me to see you hung!"

"Och! Mein Gott! Do not, Mein Herr, say dis ting to me once more again! It is very horrible. And so, I must go to Jarmany."

"You must go, Gellert."

"And what for you? What shall you do? Will dey not have some rope for you?"

"Hearken, Gellert; I think not! but I mean to follow you soon."

"Ah! you will come!—you will follow me? Dat is good! I shall not lose you. You have been my friend, mein Herr. You have taken poor Gellert from the earth, and have made him rich. If you shall come to Jarmany, it shall make him happy. Wherefore shall you not go wid me? We shall be ever so much happy together."

"That is impossible, Gellert. But I hope to follow you soon—as soon as I can put my house in order."

"Mein Herr, you have loved me, and been my very good, most best friend. Have Gellert been true and faithful to you always, so that you shall never have say to yourself, Gellert is not behave himself right. He is not right, and true, and proper, and full of gratitude?"

"Never, my good Gellert. I have always found you grateful, and humble, and doing all I wished. It is one of my regrets now, my good Gellert, that I have too frequently required of you such tasks as now make your present danger—and mine! We need only part, however, for a season. You may expect me to follow you soon; and now, to show you that I am in earnest, let us commence the work of destruction at once. Give me those bills, Gellert. Follow me!"

He led the way into the cavern.

"Now," said he, "bring out all the impressions you have made from this new plate."

He was obeyed. Large piles of counterfeit notes were soon accumulated upon the table. The old man swept them from the table to the floor, casting upon the pile the new notes which Gellert had just brought him as specimens of fine workmanship. Then the master applied a taper to the pile, which was soon reeking in flame, and sending up its smoke on every hand.

"Ah! mein Gott!" was the exclamation of the poor artist. "Dey was so very beautiful! I shall never make such beautiful notes, no more again!"

"Never!" said the stern voice of the master; "never, Gellert! You will do better things! You will now fix your thoughts wholly on the grand invention."

"Ah! mein Herr! but it is most grand invention! De whole world shall say—"

"And in Germany you will be able to carry it out! You could never do it here. Here, you would be at this miserable business all the rest of your life. Now, for your tools. We shall give you freedom, Gellert."

With mingled groans and ejaculations, poor Gellert gathered up his tools, with as tender care as if they were designed for preservation, and not for sacrifice; but, heedless of this tenderness, the master swept them remorselessly into a sack, and the two went forth together, and climbing to a ledge which overhung a deep abyss in the river, a great maelstrom of surging and rolling waters, whose blackness indicated the depths below, the sack was dropped into the gulf, and from its weight, after a few eddies, disappeared from sight.

In this manner, all proofs which the cavern might have contained, suggestive of the recent occupation of its inmates, were swept away;

and Gellert, wringing his hands above the water, bemoaned the loss of his occupation even more bitterly than Othello. It had been his very life, as he had said, for many years, and that use which breeds the habit in the man becomes one of the most powerful despotisms in his nature. But the superior was inexorable.

"Now," said he, "my good Gellert, we must make the arrangements for your departure within the next three days. I will arrange to get you to Asheville, from which place you will take the stage. Your money shall be merged in bills upon New York, where you can have it changed to gold, or procure bills to Hamburg. But I will put you in the way of doing all these things."

We need not pursue these details, the discussion and arrangement of which employed the parties, at intervals, throughout the day. Gellert submitted, but he was a melancholy man. After night-fall, the master disappeared from the cavern, and in three hours after, Colonel Voltmeier, riding his splendid white charger, made his appearance at the cottage of the Harness family.

Here he was always welcome. As he expected, he found Fergus Wallace better, quite sensible, and anxious about his papers. He had been told that he had been discovered and his wounds dressed by a passing gentleman; but the name had been withheld by the special instructions of Voltmeier. The latter renewed the assurance previously given to the young man, that the papers were all safe, and should be furnished him when he was able to travel.

His wound was examined. Voltmeier spent most of the night at the cottage, but left an hour before dawn, having studiously avoided much converse with his patient, on the pretext of sparing him all chances of excitement.

Chapter xx

UNDER TORTURE

Five days have elapsed, and we have seen nothing of any of the several parties introduced to us in our previous narrative. But before that time was fully over, the woman Moggs had found a fine tabby at the entrance of *"Wolf-Den,"* purring at the entrance; as great a surprise to that witch-woman as if the beast had dropped from the clouds.

At the end of the five days "Old Grizzly" reappeared at the "Den", as suddenly and mysteriously as ever, bringing with him a rather large packet, carefully done up in cloth, and covered beneath his cloak.

He said no word to the old woman as he passed into his private cell. Here he remained for some time, silently and secretly occupied in performances which Moggs was not permitted to see. But her sharp eyes were satisfied that the bundle so carefully brought in was one of weight, and evidently a box or keg, though rolled up in canvas. Was it gold, or silver, or what form of treasure? The old woman became very much excited. "Old Grizzly" had come unexpectedly. It was *not* his night, and he knew that the three ruffians were to be absent. "And he never appeared with such a burden before! and it was so closely covered up!"

There was a certain little aperture—a mere fissure in the wall which separated the inner from the outer room, known to Mother Moggs only, as she thought. She had made this discovery in her researches, and it is just probable that her knowledge was not shared with any other parties. It had been a pretty little exercise for her, occasionally, when the master was at work within *his* den, to endeavor, through this aperture, to borrow some of the lessons of his art! With now an eye, and now an ear at the opening, she could catch glimpses sometimes of an interesting action, and at other times various utterances of soliloquy, which might tell much or nothing!

Using her eyes and ears on the present occasion, she discovered the wizard at his necromantic operations, the significance of which is not very clear to her as yet. He has unwrapped his bundle, and reveals to us a good-sized keg, which seems weighty, and may be full of gold! This, after much labor, he buries beneath the cross wall which connects while it separates the two chambers. He unfolds, subsequently, a series of long coils, which look, as Mother Moggs deems it, to be only so much plow-line. With this the old man busies himself, in making twines leading along the foot of the wall, until an orifice is reached, which opens a narrow channel from the interior of the den into the open area of the hill-slope. A sudden puff of fresh air, through this orifice, extinguishes the lamp which he has placed too closely to the opening.

He relights his lamp, resumes his work, which employs him for some time; then sits down at his table, jots down certain memoranda, rises, and emerges into the outer apartment, so suddenly and unexpectedly, as almost to surprise the woman, in her watch. She, too, had her *cur'osity*, as well as Brown Peters.

But, passing her without any apparent notice, the master took his way to the entrance, opened the door and passed out. He was absent for some time, lost to sight in the shadows of the mountain. How he busied himself without, it was no longer possible for the woman to see, but we may shrewdly conjecture that the business which now exercised his cares had something to do with that which he had carried on within.

It is certain that he crouched low at the foot of the wall without, in which lurked that crevice, the wind through which had extinguished his lamp.

From this point he worked his way down along a hollow, leading to the blended rock and thicket, where the horses of the party were usually kept hidden.

Finally he returned, calm and grave as usual, a little more bent than his wont, probably not so much from age as from unusual fatigue.

This time he spoke, on entering, to the woman, having first carefully secured both the outer and the inner door.

"Follow me here, Moggs."

She did so! He bade her be seated; but she continued standing.

"Your son is free, Moggs. He should be here to-night. He promised me."

"Oh! Thanks to your honor! You are so good. My poor Ephraim —my poor boy! And he's safe, at last, your honor? And there'll be no more trouble, sir, and he'll be coming here to-night, your honor, and—and—"

"Yes; he should have been here before this. Now, hear me, woman. You have that son to answer for! He is now safe; and I have so provided for him, and for you, that he may continue safe, if he pleases! But he is weak and easily tempted, unless you keep him from the bottle and—"

Here he paused, breaking off suddenly in what he was going to say,—and pausing, as if to weigh his language.

"And from old Swipes and Brown Peters, you would say, your honor."

"*You* have said it, Moggs! Now, hear me. I have arranged with Ephraim as to what he is to do. You are willing to live with him, are you not?"

"I wants nothing better, your honor."

"Well, see that he carries you away from this place within five days. He knows where to go. There's a nice farm and cottage, and a cow—and with your cat—"

"Oh! sir, I thank you for the cat. I know'd 'twas you! It's hard to say what you don't know, and what you kain't do. But, Lord love you, your honor, I'm to leave 'Wolf-Den!'"

"Do you like it so much that you want to stay?"

"Oh! yes; you see; I'm a-sort of grown used to it, and—"

"You will become used to a better place and more comfortable things, Moggs. You will have them all. A good house, some good land, fifty acres or more, a horse, cow, and all that's necessary for Ephraim as a farmer."

"But you know, your honor, Ephraim's not the man for work, you know."

"Well, if hanging suits him better—"

"Oh! sir, don't say it."

"Enough; he will do, or he will not do. You will try to make him do as he should. I have done for him, and for you, all that is necessary for your comfort and his success. He must do the rest.

He has made me his promise—has *sworn* to me; and you are both quite old enough to do for yourselves—to go alone! You will not have me much longer to help you. I expect, in less than a month from this, to be in Europe; to cross the great seas, and be gone more than three thousand miles from Carolina, to be absent for many years—perhaps forever! Meanwhile, I have saved your son from the consequences of his own folly. He is now free. I have given him a sufficient start, and you—you, too, have money—"

"Oh! your honor,—but a very little—I am so wretched poor—"

"Silence, woman! no lying! If you are so wretched poor, then there must be another owner—who must have forgotten it,—for the pile hidden away in the hollows, down below the horse-pool!"

"O Lord! O Lord!" with a shriek of terror. "He knows everything. Oh! your honor, don't you tell! It's all mine, and I'll move it this very night. It's not that I fear *your* taking it, your honor, but—"

He interrupted her dryly:

"I think there must be at least one hundred dollars in that one pile—"

"Oh! Lord, your honor, not half of it."

"Pshaw, woman, why will you lie to me! And do you mean to say that you have no other pile hidden away?"

"Not a copper, you honor."

"Ah, well, I must then be the owner of what lies under yonder stone, Moggs," pointing, as he spoke, to a small boulder in a corner of the wall.

"What stone, your honor?"

"Give me your knife, Moggs, or take it yourself, and cut away the soap, which has been stuck around the edges of yonder stone, and see what we shall find!"

"But I don't see any stone, your honor."

"Give me the knife, woman."

"Oh! your honor, I'll tell the truth! I see the stone, now. It's thar! It's mine; Lord love me, you knows everything, your honor."

"Then why try to deceive me? Why lie to no profit? Enough of this! There will be no need of lying hereafter, either to me or anybody else. When you and your son are settled on a farm all your own and his, with your own horse and cow, raising your own pigs and poultry, and with so much money, you must get rid of all your bad habits. You must help cure Ephraim of his. He will not need your money, if you can make him take care of his own. Keep him from bad company, from sots and gamblers—"

"Ah! thar's the trouble, your honor; old Swipes is too cunning for Ephraim, and ef 'twan't for me, and the fear of me, that Brown Peters would beat him to death!"

"*They* will be gone, too, Moggs, very shortly. You will see no more of them, after a few days. Let me repeat to you, now, that you must be gone also from this place, else Ephraim and yourself will be in danger. Five days from this, he should have you in your new home. Gather up your money, from all your hiding-places, and begone! Should these fellows *suspect* all that I *know*, you would be robbed of it all, and have your throat cut in the bargain. You will take heed that they do not suspect; and Ephraim has my instructions not to suffer them to know whither he goes. Keep your own secrets from your son, Moll."

"And whar is it, your honor? Is the place far off?"

"For safety, far enough! But your son knows it and likes it. You will like it, too. I can tell you nothing more to-night. You will see me once more before you depart!"

And, with no more words, the master was about to take his own departure, when the woman suddenly caught his hand, with the earnest, eager manner of one who suffered somewhat from compunctious visitings, and wringing it earnestly, exclaimed:

"Oh! your honor, don't think me sassy, now, but I must tell you—thanking you first for what you've done for Ephraim, and what you're a-doing for the two on us—I must tell you—yes—but I'm so scareful—"

"Well, speak quickly!"

"Well, you see, your honor, I'm a-thinking that thar's a watch set upon you! Brown Peters is a-spying, ef he can, whar you go, and what's about you. He's cur'ous—"

"Well?"

"And Swipes always shied off ontill now; but now that you've gin 'em up, and told 'em to be off, down to the Massissipp, they says it's a sign you has no further use for 'em; and so Swipes gives in to Brown Peters, and they're a-hanging about, keeping hawk eyes how you ride, and whar you burrow."

"Well!" as she paused. "Go on!"

"And, I'm not so sure but that Dick Gorham's as deep in the mud as they're in the mire. He watches you. But he's on the sly, all the time. But I knows he's a-watching you. And I do think, your honor, that, no matter all you've done for them, they'd be jist as willing to put a bullet into you and rob you, as iver they would into the strangest pusson in the world. They're all on em cur'ous to find you out."

"I know it, Moggs!"

"Lord! Lord! what don't you know?"

"My good Moggs, the fool who thrusts his fingers into a hollow, in search of a rabbit, will be just as apt to waken up a snake. Men pay for their curiosity just like women. They're all fools together. You had better not say to them what you have said to me—"

"Look you, master, they're on your track this very night; and I'll tell you where they're watching—"

"Well?"

"Down by the floored piece of road, where the broad flat of the stone faces clean across the road. It's what they call the grave-stone, or the Devil's Slide."

"I know it, Moggs. But there's one thing, woman, that you can't say of Gorham."

"Eh?"

"He don't hunt in couples, either with Swipes or Peters."

"No! that's true! He's by his own self; but he watches *them;* and when they gits on your trail, he gits on *theirs.* I've seed him; and when they talked over the business, he jest made believe to sleep, and he overhearn all they had to tell. He's as sly and soft o' foot as any mountain painther (panther.)"

"You've told me nothing, Moggs, that I don't know; but I thank you nevertheless. Now, let me caution you that you do not let them know what you have said to me. In a couple of hours you will probably have them here. In less time than that, your son will be here also, or should be here. Now, woman, tell me honestly, for your son's sake and for your own, without any lying, have you any whisky in the den?"

"Only jest a leetle, for sickness, and for the stomach's sake."

"Bring it forth! let me see it! These fellows have no more stomach than conscience, and will no more need whisky than they desire virtue. Bring it out,—let me see it; but before you do so, let me tell you only '*jest a leetle*' is a demijohn of three gallons nearly full!"

"Lord! Lord! there's no use! He knows it all."

"Bring it forth, Moggs," was the peremptory order, and it was brought.

"Now, get five quart bottles and fill them."

It was done, however reluctantly.

"I suppose, Moggs, the whisky is yours! You love it just as well as your son."

The woman bowed her head in silence, as she filled the five bottles.

"Put these five bottles away; hide them; and when required to find the liquor, produce bottle by bottle. I save you these bottles that you may be able to pacify these fellows in some degree. You will have them here in a few hours more. Let your son, if he comes, as I think he will, beware! see you that he does not drink freely, and do *you* not taste a drop! You will need all your senses. Give me the demijohn."

She did so. He raised it to an overhanging shelf, then adroitly tilted it over, and it came down on the rocky floor with a crash. In a moment after, the strong fumes of the wasted liquor filled the chamber. The woman wrung her hands in despair.

"Sich waste! sich waste!" she exclaimed; "all the good whisky!"

"Hush! the loss of that liquor probably saved your own life and that of your son! See that you give out the bottle sparingly. Let them all see the broken demijohn where it lies. See that you leave it there."

"Well, 'tain't my loss!" cried the woman. "Brown Peters, hisself, brought it here last night."

The old man left her, not well knowing whether to bless or curse!

Chapter XXI

ESPIONAGE

Into the night, over the hills, in the deep dark, silent and thoughtful, the old man rode, giving free reins to his steed, and seeming to leave to him all choice of route and pathway.

But not so; the rider was cool, calm, stern, and well-observant of things. He rode musingly, but not heedless. He was *the* master; and, if ever, in the eyes of his subordinates, a man ever loomed out before them, a superior being, endowed almost with the gifts of a god, then it was the old man that rode that night.

But there was a questioning devil in each of their bosoms, that rendered them all curious. When you once admit subordinates to the degree, even of occasional equality, you overthrow all veneration. A full, free coöperation in crime reduces all parties, ultimately, to the one level equality. There is no other equality which society can legitimately recognize, save that of crime.

The old man sped upon his steed. He had now reached the grave-stones, known as the "Devil's Slide."

Just above it, in the great hollow between two rocks, but looking down upon the pathway, only indistinctly perceptible by the gray whiteness of the flat masses of stone, crouched two men, whom, by their speech, we know to be the two subordinates—Swipes and Brown Peters.

Their purpose was not robbery, perhaps—only watch. Their relations with their late leader and master, were, as Moggs had suggested, pretty nearly, if not entirely, closed. They had come to the conclusion that they had survived their uses, and that the man, hitherto the commanding genius of their company, was preparing to get rid of them. They did not thus far feel the degree of their dependence upon him—knew not, therefore, the extent of their loss, and had, as yet, given no expression to their discontent.

At a later day, they would, probably, desire to rob even him, and to extort from him that share of plunder, which, in their own cases, they had not been willing to economize. He had not wronged them—had not endeavored in any way, under their miserable laws, to defraud them of the proper share of their spoils, in their long partnership of crime. But there is an impatient desire, in all human bosoms, to fathom a mystery. He had held himself aloof from them. He saw them only when he thought proper. He knew all *their* secrets; they possessed none of his. If, as yet, they did not conceive how necessary he was to them, they yet felt, by infallible instincts, that they had no power to command and control him. This was the secret stimulus to the curiosity which they felt.

Now, a secret, once known to exist, is already half discovered. Human ingenuity, in the making and the evading of law, is always met by human ingenuity in turn, and, in society, that of the felon has always shown itself quite equal to that of the law-giver. Enough, here, that Brown Peters had inspired his comrade, if not with his own mere "cur'osity," at least with the desire to obtain some degree of power over the master who had so long ruled themselves, and who, they now felt, was disposed to shake them off.

The solution of a mystery, of itself, might be a sufficient charm and motive to human espionage. Such is the case—a vanity, an appetite, a lust, a mere whim, a caprice, a miserable impulse of the blood, will move to enterprise—good or bad—where wisdom would counsel a patient waiting upon God, and nature, and time, and opportunity.

Well, these two subordinates, governed each, perhaps, by different, but, in both cases, by mean and base, if not murderous motives, lay in watch along the side of the mountain, comforting themselves in an impatient espionage, by an occasional sup of whisky from a copious flagon.

At length the keen ears of both, almost at the same moment, discerned the distant echoes of a horse's tread upon the solid masses of the mountain.

"He's a-coming. That's him. Now, you be all eyes, Swipes. Look over the cliff close, for hyar's the very place, jest along the Devil's Slide, where I always loses him. Now, you've got the eyes of a very night-owl in the dark. See what you can see, and let's diskiver him."

"He's a-turning Hell-Hole hollow now."

"He's at the bend. Click, click, you kin a'most count the steps of the horse."

"He's a-drawing nigher and nigher. He'll be hyar in a minute."

"Why, Gimini, he's a-running a race, I'm a-thinking. He's got to a gallop. Sight him, ef you kin, Swipes. I reckon his wallet's full of gould and silver. Sight him, Swipes, as he comes down the Slide."

"What! shoot!"

"In course. Ef we're to split, why, thar's no tarms a-tween us, and we mout jest as well git his money as any other man's."

Thundering downward came the steed. Thundering along, he went round the mountain, down the Slide. A shot rang from the top of the rocks, but idly. Steed and rider rode by unharmed.

"You've missed! You were too dern'd slow!"

"And how could a man sight a rifle at a flash, in a twink of time, and hyar in this allfired darkness?"

"Hush! he don't stop!"

"No; he's a-gwine a-head as fast as iver."

"He's on the grave-stone, now, jest thar; he always stopt afore, and that's whar I always lost him."

"But you kin hyar. He's gone—jest like a bullet from the gun. He don't make a stop thar this time."

"Well, we'll git down now, and look a leetle more about us. Ef we gits on them flat stones we kin see a bit, though I'm a-thinking either it's not 'Old Grizzly,' or he's taking another road to-night. It's mighty cur'ous how he kin dodge us so etarnally."

We need not follow them in their search. Enough that it was made in vain. They reascended the heights, stole back a hundred yards to where their horses were fastened to saplings in a hollow, and, mounting, made their way, at their leisure, to the obscure recesses of the "Wolf's-Den."

When they had gone from sight, another party rose up from out the darkness—a dim figure, which had been "squat, like a toad," watching also, from a contiguous rock. This was Gorham.

"The miserable fools!" he exclaimed, "to shoot; as if that would do any good. Had they hit him, what would have been the use? That would only cover up his tracks. He's too sharp for such as them. But it's jest here—just where they watched, that he swings round, somehow, and gets out of sight and hearing, and you lose him in the darkness; and lose him from all hearing besides. It'll take time, and I'm not in a hurry. I must make the search in broad daylight. I'm not so willing to break off from the contract. He has taught me some lessons. He has helped to make me what I am. I'm not going to let him off so easily. He's rich; *that* I'm sure of. I want much that I can get from riches only. He shall find the capital. He may send these hounds down to the Mississippi, but he shall not send me."

He made his way to where his horse was hidden. "Well, what now? I'll find them at the 'den', and it's just possible they'll have something to say that'll give me another opening for a start. I'll go!"

He newly primed his pistols, and adjusting his bowie knife, he went.

The horseman, the object of all these acts, meanwhile proceeded on his route. He had heard the shot, and the bullet whistling by him.

"Well," he said, muttering between his teeth; "I had to give them this chance. I know them fully now. But I will watch them. The fools! Did they suppose that I had left myself no second outlet?"

In a brief mile above, he checked his speed, turned into the woods, rode along the side of a precipice; again, at a certain point, wheeled about, and made his way by a new route, which hitherto was unknown to us, to the cavern, where he found his ancient and German confederate, the artist; where we propose to leave him for a space.

Chapter XXII

CONSPIRACY

"What's this?" said Brown Peters, sniffing with his nose, as he entered the "Den."

"Why, Moggs—woman—what hev you been doing with the vartuous whisky? It smells strong everywhar!"

She pointed to the demijohn, which still lay where "Old Grizzly" had shattered it upon the floor. One stupid moment, motionless, he stood, as he beheld the wreck.

"What the ——, woman! Hev you broke it, and spilled all the beautiful sperrits?"

"'Twas HE, did it—"

"Who, 'Old Grizzly'?"

"Yes, *him!* He was s'arching on the shelf for something, and knocked it over somehow."

"Dern his buttons! so *he's* been here to-night? You see, Swipes, *'twas him.*"

The other assented with a grunt.

"And how the ———, woman, air we to git on to-night without the liquor? Look you, Moggs, you've got some of your own put away somewhar, you old beauty. You loves a kiss of the bottle as well as the best of us."

And he began wheedling her.

"You don't reckon on me to giv' you *my* liquor, does you?" was the reply, in savage tones, and with savage manner.

"*Give*, my Queen of Clubs? no! Dern the word! I never says '*give*' when my pockets can say '*pay*'. I pays as I goes, in shining gould, or purty bank paper. Let's hev a bottle, now, Old Beauty, and you shall hev the clinkers, and the shiners, or the rumplers— don't matter which."

"On the nail—down!" said the woman, producing a bottle, and receiving a bank-note, which Peters thrust into her hand without looking at the denomination.

Clapping the mouth of the bottle to his own, he gulped down a large potation of the fiery mountain beverage, then wiped his moustached lip with his sleeve, and, shaking his fist at the woman, cried out fiercely:——

"You old hag! I've a great mind to smash your muzzle! It's my own liquor, that I brung all the way from Clough's, and he brung it all the way from Asheville! I'll swear to the liquor! It's been dript through the charcoal! Oh! you old heifer! I'll be the death of you yit. To sell a man his own liquor!"

"As ef I couldn't buy *good* liquor as well as you! Don't you lift your hands at me, Brown Peters. You knows what I kin do ef you riles me. Stand off now, ef you're sensible!"

"Why, yes, you skileton-wolf; you kin show your knife, but mighty little would that do for you, ef 'twan't that you're a woman; though how you ever did grow into a woman, thar's no telling. You was cut out for a wolf at first, or mout be, a painter. But don't you go too fur with me, I tell you! Some day I'll forget that you passes for a woman, and I'll wipe you out with a hickory towel."

The woman did not reply—prudence, perhaps, getting the better of her temper; but she turned away with a very savage countenance, which had no little malice in it; and had she been observed, Peters would have been somewhat more prudent himself, at the determined gripe which she took of the great butcher's knife which lay convenient to her grasp, on a contiguous shelf.

There was a bright fire burning in the huge chimney of the "den," and Swipes had already taken his seat beside it, and was mixing sugar with the whisky in his pewter mug, when Peters, waving his own mug in hand, made a motion with it to the inner door, leading to the sanctum of their superior.

"Let's take possession of the old Satan's room to-night, Swipes. We've got to talk private, you know, and I reckon we'll not hyar of him ag'in to-night."

"What! You think that, Brown? Thar!"

"I does! The very thing!" and he moved towards the cell.

"Better don't!" interposed the woman. "He won't like it, I reckon."

"Why, Moggs, he ain't hyar now, and who's to tell him when he comes?"

"Why, *I'll* tell him, sure, ef he axes me."

"You will, will you? you infarnal old ———!" Here a brutal imprecation of Peters, and another threatening gesture, which the woman promptly met, by taking position and brandishing her knife directly in his face.

"Stand off, or I'll hack your throat for you, you ———!"

And she, too, had her oath.

"I'd give a pretty pansy of gould, you old hag, ef you was only a man!"

"Lord, ef I was! I wish I was! I'd ha' licked the life out of your witals long afore this, you crooked sarcumstance of a man!"

"Come on," said Swipes, interposing; "you two fools kain't meet without a quarrel, and it's only between the Devil and the Snake."

"*She's* the snake—the *wiper*—that's setting as a spy upon us, when we air a paying her for everything she does!"

"Come on—come in! I reckon there'll be no harm done, even if she does tell. Ef we've got to talk secret, thar's the best place."

And Swipes now leading the way, in they went, the key being left within the lock, which its owner employed only when seeking privacy for himself.

There was still a *debris* of coals and embers, remaining from his own recent fire. The dry wood was contiguous, and the two robbers soon rekindled the flames brightly, until they lighted up the whole gloomy apartment. Then, with their bottle of whisky, already half emptied of its contents, and their pewter mugs beside them, on the table, they addressed themselves to the work of conspiracy against their superior.

But, scarcely had they begun, when their attention was drawn to a paper which they had not before seen, marked with certain characters which they seemed to comprehend instantly, but for which we lack the proper key. The paper lay before them, on the table, and between their mugs of liquor.

"How did it come thar, Swipes? I wants to know. When did you see it?"

"'Twan't thar, I'm a-thinking, when we fust sot down to the table."

"I didn't see it."

"And that old hag, she hain't been in, that I've seed, sence we come in, hev she?"

"No! I don't think."

"Well, now! that old Satan must hev know'd that we'd be hyar to-night."

"Yes; and what's more, he must hev guessed that we'd make free with his room."

"*Guessed!*—Blast him, but he *know'd* it! I'm almost afraid of him! I'm jubious he suspicions everything. I rather think, Brown, that we'd better give up this business of yourn, and jest do what he tells us—make clean tracks for the Mississippi country, as soon as we kin!"

"I'm too cur'ous, Swipes, to give it up; and, I'm a-thinkin' I'm nearing the very edge of the diskivery! You see it's cl'ar to me that he's got another hiding-place, down among the rocks, close on to the river. We knows he comes and goes it in three hours."

"He's got a mighty fast and powerful horse in that black, Brown."

"Yes, and ef I'm to go down to the Mississippi, I'd like to do it on the back of that same beast."

"I wouldn't cross the critter for all the gould in the country. Do you know, Brown, I sometimes think"—here the speaker looked stealthily and timidly around him, and lowered his voice to a whisper—"I sometimes think he's the very old Satan himself, under the disguisement of a harmless animal."

"Ha, ha, ha!—ho, ho, ho!—I do think, Swipes, for a strong, full-grown man, and as cunning a rogue as goes on two legs, you're about as scary in some things as a child or a chicken. You believes in ghosts, and sich things, made out of the night air and a white sheet. I'll lay you a *ten* to a *five* that you wouldn't walk through a church-yard after night-fall."

"I don't care to do it in broad daylight. I've *seed* sperrits, Brown! Don't you laugh, now; but it's a mortal sartainty that I've met a ghost, all in white, coming down this very mountain."

"Oh, shet up, and take another swig! The only sperrits I ever seed, and the only sperrits I believe in, are made out of good old corn and good old rye, and peach and apple, and they calls them by the respectable names of whisky and brandy. Take a fresh pull, old fellow, and keep your sperrits up by pouring sperrits down, the only kind of sperrits in country or in town."

Here Brown subsided into drink and doggerel at the same moment, the latter, most probably, being borrowed from some backwoods dithyrambic.

Swipes was easily persuaded, and Brown resumed his persuasions.

"You see, Swipes, when I sets out on a journew of diskivery, I never likes to turn back with nothing done. I gits cur'ous and always pushes on. Now, I've been pushing a'ter the tracks of Old Grizzly for more than six months, ontill I thinks I got pretty close on to his hiding-place, and to my diskivery—"

"Yes, and you got knocked over, as you says yourself, by an inwisible hand, that went all over your body, yet struck you in no place in partic'lar."

"That's true; and I'm cur'ous to find out all about *that;*—but, look you, Swipes, did you ever calkilate how much good money 'Old Grizzly' must have put away in all the times he's been at this business? Now he's a pusson to put away his money. He's not like you and me, you see, that drinks and gambles, and makes it fly that way jest as fast as we gits it. Hyar, you've helped me to make a big hole a'ready, in that big pile we all had t'other night. Now, he don't drink, and I reckon he don't gamble—"

"About the gambling, I kain't say! I never seed him gamble—but I hev seed him drink."

"To be sure, he does, a little; jist by way of being respectable to his company; and if he didn't begin the drinking himself, when he axes us, I'd be thinking he hed put some p'ison in the liquor! Well, I consider that *he* don't *waste his* money. Ef so, he must hev it; and I'm pretty sart'in he's got some hiding-place, close along the river, where he goes and gits it when he wants it; and, perhaps—who knows—he lives somewhar about thar, and has a wife and children and family, perhaps, and all that sort of sarcumstances. Now, you see, if we're to go down to the Mississippi country, I wants to go with heavy pockets; and I tell you, Swipes, I considers that the pile that 'Old Grizzly' has got hid away among them river rocks, must be a good million of dollars—"

"A million! Oh, Lord, Brown!—a million!" quoth Swipes, opening his eyes wide.

"Yes! a good million, in gould and silver and paper, to say nothing of the *blink*—"

"A million!" Swipes could say no more. The magnitude of the suggested spoil completely seized upon and spelled his imagination.

"You don't mean a *million*, Brown?"

"A million! Not a copper less! I won't believe in one copper less than a round million! And we kin git it all, Swipes—all; and not leave the old Satan a single dollar!" And to give due emphasis to his asseveration, he brought his fist down upon the table with a thundering blow, which set the bottle and the cups to dancing.

Swipes rose up, swung his hands in the air, grasped the bottle, poured out a full brimmer, and swallowed it at a gulp.

In the effort to say "a million" before the liquor had been fairly disposed of, he was seized with a convulsive hiccough, which required several other draughts to allay.

"Yes, a million! And we'll hev it all! Ef he's willing to shake us off, we'll shake him off, too; and shake out his bags before we be off, Swipes. Ef he's so ongrateful as to shake off them as has sarved him, day and night, for sich a long time, then he desarves to lose all his airnings, ef they was a dozen millions! Now, what says you, Swipes? We wants *two* for this business, and no more; one to watch, while t'other trails; and you see a million of dollars, in gould and silver, kain't be well toted off by one pusson; and, anyhow, we'd hev to make a good many trips, back and fora'd, before we could git it all away. Is't a bargain, Swipes?"

The hiccough of Swipes prevented his speech; but he grappled the outstretched hand of Peters, and wrung it with a shake that spoke eagerness as well as assent. The pledge was sealed by a renewed draught together from the bottle, which was emptied by the operation.

It could only be replenished from the stores of Mother Moggs. When, with this object, Peters burst into the outer chamber, he found the woman seated, with her arms affectionately thrown around the neck of a man who sate beside her.

Chapter XXIII

ALL THE DOGS AFOOT

"Hello, woman! who've you got thar, hugging as close as the devil does his dam?—as he'll hug you some day!"

"It's me, Brown," said the stranger, rising, and coming forward, and offering his hand.

"What, Ephraim! Glad to see you back, old fellow! You've jest come in time for a sup! Come, Moggs, git us another bottle. That's a beauty, and thar's your change."

The woman was in better humor than usual, possibly from the prompt payment,—probably from the coming of her son; and proceeded to bring forth the second bottle, without waiting the second requisition. Then, seeing that the note thrust into her hand, inadvertently, perhaps, by the half-drunken man, was five dollars, she brought forth two bottles, which she carried herself into the cell where Swipes was still sitting, and where, at intervals, between his hiccoughs, he continued to ejaculate—"*A million!*"

"Here's two bottles, Swipes," said Moggs.

"Two millions!" quoth he.

"Two bottles, I say! Where should I get two millions? He's drunk a'ready," *(sotto voce)* as she departed. Reëntering the outer room, where her son and Brown were talking together, she said, hastily:

"The sperrits is on the table, Brown Peters, *two* bottles."

"*Two* bottles! why, Moggs, ef you goes on at this rate, you'll frow into the very yaller flower of the forest! Come in, Ephraim Moggs, and take a pull of your mammy's milk. You're only a suckling yit, you know."

"Let Ephraim be, Brown Peters. Kain't you leave him to his mother for a bit, what hasn't sot eyes on him for more'n two months, and he jist got out of jail?"

"Well, old boy, when you're done with the old woman hyar, come into the young fellows thar. But don't you put it off too long, or we'll be sending the sheriff a'ter you ag'in."

We are sorry to say that Ephraim Moggs exhibited a rather too great yearning in the direction to which he was invited; but the imperative voice and hand of the mother, and possibly some latent sense of filial duty, prevailed with him, for the present, to forego the invitation.

"You knows what you air, when you're a-drinking, Ephraim, and it won't do *now*. You've hearn all that 'Old Grizzly' said, I know, and what he said to me, over all, was *this:* don't you let him git at the liquor with these fellows, or he'll come to no good ending! Ef all he's told me is true, and I reckon it is, he's done handsome for both on us."

"Mighty handsome."

"Well, I've got a good chaince of money, myself, and—but you jist up now and tell me about the fairm, and whar it is, and what you calkilate on."

We leave the two to their confidential communications. These do not concern us. In the other chamber, the drinking and the discussion were resumed together.

"Who do you think's come, Swipes?"

"A million, I reckon!"

"Drunk a'ready, old boy! It's cur'ous. It's not upon the whisky. It's the idea of the million! Well, Ephraim Moggs is back;—Old Grizzly said he'd git him out o' jail by an allaboy; and he's done it. That old satan kin do a'most anything. You see, Swipes, ef he hadn't that million of money, he could do jist nothing—nothing more than me or you. He kin *buy* justice and law, and larning and religion, all with money!"

"A million!"

"Yes; a million! But, blast your buttons, kin you say nothing else but that?"

"Yes, Brown! You say Ephraim Moggs is here? Is he to go along with us?"

"What do we want with him, I wonder? What's the good of him? What kin he do? He's a good sneak enough, but he's too cowardly in his conscience. He won't stand up to the rack when the trouble comes; and then we don't want him for this business. We two kin manage it all; and ef we took in any other hand, 'twould be so much lost, you know—"

"Of the million! But I was thinking, Brown—"

"Well, what?"

"What about Gorham?"

"Oh! blast him, for a snake in the grass! He's as sly as a brown sarpent under a green bush."

"But he's devilish sharp, Brown."

"Yes, so sharp, that he'll git our throats cut when we're a-drinking, and work his own from under the knife. He'll use our fingers to git the bait out of the trap. What we've got to do, we kin do by our own two selves. We don't want anybody to help. They would only cut into our shares."

"Yes, yes! That's true, and we goes for the whole million atween us two? Half a million apiece! Is that the figure, Brown?"

"Half-and-half of what we gits! Let Gorham go to ———. We've done with him, I reckon, now that we're about to be done with 'Old Grizzly.' Let's liquor!"

And they drank! The talk was resumed over the bottle. It became spasmodic—Peters declaiming, and Swipes occasionally lapsing into song. The senses of both were somewhat obfuscated. Peters then said:

"Somehow, Swipes, I think you're taking a sort of liking to that fellow, Gorham. Now, he's always on the sly. He never drinks. He never lost a picayinne, at dice or cards, to either on us. *He* hides away his money, too! Lord, ef I could only find whar he hides it!"

"He's mighty sharp, Brown."

"So's a knife, sometimes, and, in good hands, it kin do sharp work. But he's all knife, and won't let our hands use him. He uses us, when he kin. I think he's a derned coward, that will no more fight than he will drink or play, but expects to do everything by cunning, on the sly."

Swipes suffered from that sort of mental subjugation—an instrument only—that he felt at sea, without rudder or compass, unless under the guidance of a superior. Brown, with more will, more bold and insolent, had no such consciousness, and was rather (when drunk) restive under any authority. The former had implicitly obeyed the old man, their common superior, and, next to him, had learned to look on Gorham as the wisest person to follow. Half-fuddled, greatly excited, yet powerless to reason, he could now only mutter his half-fledged conclusions.

"Brown," quoth he, "you're a good fellow, and a bold fellow, but you ain't the master! You kain't fix it! You kin drive, but you kain't make the plan for the drive! Now, if 'Old Grizzly' shakes us off, and we shakes off Gorham—who is dern'd sharp—who's to manage the business?"

"Oh, dern the business, Swipes. What the devil do we want with business, when we've got a million to divide?"

"A million! To be sure, a million! Well, I say, too, dern the business! But, what a'ter that? What'll we do, and whar will we go?"

"Anything! anywhar! Everything! everywhar! We kin live like fighting-cocks, old fellow! We kin take the town at New Orleans. We kin ride the elephant in New York. We kin buy up all them people and sell them out—and you heard what 'Old Grizzly' said he would do—we kin do like him—we kin go to Europe, over the big waters, and see t'other world! How 'Old Grizzly' kin do it, a'ter all his money's gone, I'm slow to see."

"A whole million! a whole million!"

"Yes, a million, Swipes! Think of it! Hafe to you, hafe to me! Ef we meets 'Old Grizzly' in Europe, we kin make his acquaintance ef we please, or we kin look at him with one of them dern'd little eye-glasses that some of them people carries at Flatrock, and jest spile him out of all ricollection! As for Gorham, we must get shet of him! He's jest the sneak to spile our chainces, ef he should get wind of 'em."

At that moment the door opened, and Gorham quietly walked in.

"Who the devil's that! Who the devil air you?" cried the now half-drunken Peters, as, rising up, he seized Gorham by the throat.

"Take off your hands, Brown Peters, or I shall hurt you!" was the quiet remonstrance.

"Hurt h—l! Who air you, I ax!" without releasing his grasp upon the other.

Gorham simply drew a pistol from his pocket, held it to the assailant's head, and deliberately cocked it.

Though very nearly as drunk as Peters, Swipes now started up, caught Peters by the body, and pulled him away, Gorham seeming quite willing that he should owe his own extrication to this process.

"You're a dern'd fool, Brown Peters! It's Gorham!"

"Gorham, is it? but why the devil does he come in upon gentlemen, busy at their secret arrangements, without axing first? Why didn't he give the signal?"

"I did," said Gorham, still quietly, and taking his seat, but not putting aside his weapon, "but I suppose you were too drunk, both of you, to hear."

"Whar's Moggs and Ephraim?" cried Brown.

"Off somewhere, for there is no one in the front, and the door opened at a push."

"The ——— you say!" was the response of Peters, as, rushing to the outer door, he gave the signal—the wailing cry of the panther. He was answered from the rocks above, from which the woman, Moggs, presently descended.

"Whar's that whelp of yourn, Moggs? Where's Ephraim?"

"Gone!"

"Gone—whar!"

"A'ter his own business!"

"And hyar you've left the door open, jest as ef it never had a bolt!"

"I watched it."

"You did, did you?—yet you never seed Gorham get in."

"Yes, I did! I know'd his signal, and I seed him when he come down from the rocks."

"You old tom-cat, I'll be the death of you yet!" were the amiable words with which he parted from her to return to the "Den." She followed him, but not without her imprecations.

"Lord send that I may hev the spinning of the cord that you will hang by some day,—oh, Lord! some day,—only let it be soon!"

"Well, what have you come for, Dick Gorham?"

"I came to see Bierstadt."

"Bierstadt! Why do you call him by that name, instead of 'Old Grizzly'?"

"Why, that *is* his name."

"Ef it ain't Satan himself! Well, you see he isn't hyar to-night."

"Yes! but he has been here to-night. Have you seen this paper?"

And Gorham lifted the paper from the table, which the two had discovered at their entrance, but which, in their potations and discussions, they had temporarily forgotten.

"Well, what about it? It only tells us that he will meet us again—once more—and on a Friday."

"Well, that's enough! We shall meet him again."

Saying this, Gorham departed, quietly, even as he had entered.

"I'm a'most as cur'ous about that fellow as I am about 'Old Grizzly.' I kin tell nothing about him. He used to stay at Mother Canter's; but whar he stays now, who knows? He's so sarpent sly! I reckon he's got a pretty penny laid up, too. I'd like to find the nest whar he keeps his birds."

"He's sharp, Brown!"

"Oh, blast his sharpness! Look you, Swipes, ef you should blab only to the rocks and winds what we're a'ter, his sharpness might lose us—"

"Don't you say it, Brown! A million! I won't speak above my breath ag'in till we've got that money."

"And then, Lord love you, you can sing out, loud as you please, like any night-hawk a'ter a good supper!"

The night was finished only with the whisky, of which a fourth bottle had to be provided from the stores of Mother Moggs. Meanwhile, the sly Gorham stole away along the heights, then down the slopes, and through the gorges, until he stood beside the river, and hearkened to its numerous voices. Gazing thus, he said—

"To-morrow—no! One day of rest! To-morrow I must sleep; but this is the track which I next shall follow. It is the silent hound that is surest on the trail!"

Chapter XXIV

"MICHEN-MALICO"

While these events are in progress, and while these parties are severally working, each at his own scheme, and after his own habits and fashion, it may be well to report that Fergus Wallace was steadily recovering from his hurts, and, on his last visit, "Voltmeier" said to his patient, encouragingly,—

"In a week or two, at farthest, you will be quite fit for travel."

"I hope so," answered the other, languidly; "I hope so, for I am weary of this sort of bondage, and impatient to resume my journey in quest of the party to whom my letter was addressed. You tell me, sir, that you have my packets safe in your possession?"

"They are safe! Let them give you no farther concern. I pledge myself, my young friend, that you shall meet with the person you seek as soon as you are able to travel a day's journey."

"You know him, then?"

"I do; but deem it only proper to say nothing about him, or your own progress, while we are in this region. When you shall have overpassed the boundaries of this range of mountains, you shall have all your desires gratified. Meanwhile, restrain your impatience, which may retard your recovery. It is possible, indeed, that in a week's time you will be able to mount your horse, and just as soon as you can endure the fatigue of a three days' progress, making short stages each day, we will journey together. Make yourself quite easy, meanwhile, under the assurance which I give you, that I have your business in my hands, and, to use the phrase of the country, will see you safely through the mountain."

"Ah! sir; you are too good! I owe you my life."

The other smiled, somewhat sadly, as he said,

"No more of that, Fergus."

"What! you know me, sir—my name?"

"Yes; I know more about you than you think for. You will remember that your name is endorsed upon the packet. But I know

138

more—a great deal more; but you must not be impatient for the revelation. Nothing more must be uttered in this precinct. When we are beyond this range, Fergus, you shall know everything, and I promise you that your quest shall be fully satisfied."

"The young men here tell me that my horse is here also."

"Found near your body—yes!"

"And you it was who made the discovery."

"Yes, it was a lucky chance that I did so."

"God's hand was in it, sir," devoutly.

"Yes, perhaps!"

The youth fancied that there was a latent sneer in the tones of the speaker, and the smile that played for a moment about his mouth; but this passed off, as Voltmeier continued—

"Yes, God's hand, no doubt; but man's too, and possibly the Devil's! In an affair like yours, it is probable that more hands than one were at work. But enough now. I must leave you for a while. In a few days I trust to see you again, and to find your improvement such as to justify my present hope that you will be soon ready to take the saddle."

"God grant it, sir."

"These boys, the Harnesses, and the old woman—they treat you well?"

"No one better, sir. The old lady sits and talks with me, and the young men, though less communicative, are uniformly kind and considerate."

"That is as it should be. They are good people, the very best in all this range, which, as by this time you must have conjectured, is none of the most safe or civilized."

"Yes, indeed, sir,—I find that I have been robbed of all my money. How I shall requite these kind people—"

"Let not that concern you. You shall be provided. Do not forget that I have taken your case in hand. I will carry you through."

And he took the hand of the youth and pressed it affectionately. Their eyes met; those of the former expressive of a loving gratitude, while a sad intensity of gaze in those of Voltmeier seemed, to the youth, to be strangely stern; and of singular contrast with the feeling which the warm grasp and pressure of his hand seemed to declare. The hand, indeed, was wrung for a moment, then released, and

Voltmeier, still unknown to Fergus by name, hurried quickly out of the chamber.

"There is something strange about it all, which I can not comprehend," murmured the youth to himself. "I seem to be in a dream."

Then, as if to shut out his perplexity, he closed his eyes, and yielded himself up without further speech to the meditations which he found it so difficult to order into shape. Voltmeier had his murmured utterances also.

"How like! how like! Even as she looked that night!—*that* night —when I flung from my heart the treasure which my hand had sought to spoil!"

He was gone! gone into the thick darkness, and lost to sight!

In a few hours "Old Grizzly" appeared once more in the recesses of the cavern, in earnest conversation with his German art professor. We condense briefly the dialogue between them.

"I have altered our plan somewhat, Gellert. It now seems to me better that you should take the gap down for Spartanburg, from thence take stage for Columbia, and again proceed by stage to Raleigh. Carry with you nothing but a small valise, with a few changes of linen. You will find everything prepared for you at Raleigh, with the necessary drafts on New York. Then all the rest is easy. You are an old voyager, and know what is to be done. The first packet, you know. Exchange on London or Paris can be had, and is safer than gold. You shall have the black horse for the trip to Spartanburg, and I shall give you instructions how to dispose of him there."

"What! you part with the black, Mein Herr? The best horse in all the mountains!"

"Except the white, Gellert."

"Well, I never thought, Mein Herr, that you would sell the black, though you do prefer the white."

"I shall not *sell* him, Gellert. He will pass into the hands of one who has done me good service in times past, and whom I have never yet been able quite to repay."

"Dat is good—to remember the friend! Ah! well, and so it is all settle for me? We have to part! I shall be very miserable, I know! But we shall see you soon in Jarmany?"

"Yes, I think so. I long to go over the old ground in Germany and Italy."

"And I will go with you, Mein Herr. I have a dream about Italy, myself, and yet, Mein Herr, I had great thoughts in this old cavern here, of the French Broad! It is beautiful as the Rhine, though it have not the castles or the antiquity. Here I have had the visions of art. Here it was that I first caught the first glimpse of my beautiful invention, my inspiration, my grand conception, the—"

"You shall perfect it in Germany, Gellert; and I, probably, unless you work too fast, will be there in time to help you."

"Ah! yes, Mein Herr! You, too, have the art, the invention, the genius! You are a great master! What pity you was born in this savage country, where dere is no two tousand years of civilization. What would you not have been, in all tings, if you had been born in Jarmany or Italy, and never left it when you was there?"

"Ah! Gellert, but where, unless in America,—here—could you have found the money for the grand invention? You have now the means to perfect it in Europe."

"Dat is my hope, now, Mein Herr. I shall go! Well! You know much! You know my secret—the grand conception of my life—my great invention! If it shall so happen dat someting shall happen to me,—ah! Mein Herr, will you not bring my discovery to the world? You are artist, man of genius, man of science—you are everyting, if you please; you will do for the old man's memory in art—make it known to the world, so that the world shall say: 'Gellert, too, is a master.'"

The other simply wrung his hand. Then he said:

"It is now time to finish the work of destruction, Gellert. We must leave no traces behind us;" and, with that prompt energy which marked all his actions, "Old Grizzly" proceeded to lift and bear tables, and benches, and bedding—with the exception of a single mattress—to the center of the cavern. The walls were searched for boxes, bundles, all manner of furniture, all of which were piled up in one undistinguishable mass. Gellert could only look on with a pitiful aspect, and sigh and murmur.

"Ach! it is all to burn! and I have live here so long, and hear the singing of the waters, and have the vision of the beautiful inventions! Ach, but it is very miserable to see!"

The flame was applied, and leaving it in full blast, the dry piles burning furiously, the two left the cavern, and proceeded under the sad starlight, to muse beside the hoarsely-moaning surges of the ever-chafing river.

And all that little world into which we have introduced our readers has been alike busy as these two. The conspirators of "Wolf's Den" have been active in equal degree. The *cur'ous* in the nature of Brown Peters; the avarice in the breast of Swipes; the mercenary and the brutal appetites of both—once set upon a favorite plan for the gratification of their passions, left themselves no time for play or rest. The debauch which succeeds the toils of the day had never rest nor play in it. From their first waking, the day after they had agreed upon their object, and conceived its plans, they proceeded to work, on that business of exploration, which was to bring them upon the tracks of their master, and possess themselves, if possible, of that "million" of treasure, which had taken such fast hold upon the imagination of the avaricious Swipes. They were in the field early. They had hidden their horses away in the well-known gorges, and, rifle in hand, made their way on foot, down to the broad plains of flat rock, which had hitherto been the terminus of their search, and where they had hitherto always lost the tracks which they had followed.

Gorham pursued his discoveries alone. He has tried the pathway along the ledge of the river as he had proposed to do, and found them impassable, not simply to all horsemanship, but to any progress on foot. Bold rocks rose and thrust themselves into the river—huge billows rolled over them, casting great sheets of spray into his face. Little gulfs opened beneath his feet, where the waters boiled as in a maelstrom. He gave up the search, which had lost him a day, in this direction. He paused; and, covered from sight by overhanging crags, he watched the road through their crevices, while giving himself up to meditation.

While thus covered and thus employed, two men became visible below him. These he soon ascertained to be Peters and Swipes. He followed them as long as possible, with his eyes, then, winding his way through dells and hollows, to slopes and overhanging rocks, he moved along in parallel lines, following their footsteps also.

"I must take their tracks," said he, to himself, "if only to keep them from taking mine. They shall be my scouts, my sleuth-hounds, so long as they are good for anything. If they find the lair, I shall bag the game. If they fail, it will be quite time enough for me to take up the trail, and see if I can do better. We can not hunt together."

More was said in detail; but such, in brief, was the policy which he proposed to himself.

There were other policies and other parties at work, each in his small game of "*michen-malico*". Even the miserable old woman, Moggs, had her "cur'osity." We have seen the espionage which she exercised over "Old Grizzly," when he was working in the inner chamber of "Wolf's Den."

She had seen him bury something. She, too, had golden visions like Swipes. The moment she could command the opportunity, and feel herself alone, she proceeded to ferret out the secret. For some days, Gorham, Swipes, and Brown Peters, being in pursuit of the chase, afforded her an excellent chance of search. Taking due care to bolt and secure the outer fastenings of the "den," she went to work vigorously to see what "Old Grizzly" had buried. With knife and fingers, she dug along the walls, amidst the *debris* of fractured stone, until she found the deposit in a keg. A further scrutiny discovered the keg to contain gunpowder, and further, that it was connected with a long train of seeming rope, which she soon discovered to be a fuse of gunpowder.

"Lord deliver us!" she exclaimed. "He means to blow up the whole consarn. The sooner we're off, the better!"

She followed the fuse, until it found its outlet in the wall. Then leaving the "den," she traced where it issued from the wall. She tracked its windings, till it led her to the terminus, between two rocks, below, near the spring, and at the very foot of the mountain. It had been carefully covered from any chance wayfarer. It could not, however, escape the search of one, once in possession of the clue.

"Oh, Gimini!" she cried. "The sooner we're off the better! I don't want to be blowed up! Oh, Jericho! and oh, Jerusalem! and oh, Jemima and Jehosaphat! What a man! what a man!"

Though panic-stricken, she carefully covered up her own tracks, restoring the *debris*, so as to leave the mine and its train precisely as she found it. Hardly had she done so, when the panther-signal was sounded from the rocks above, and her son, Ephraim, came down to her.

She knew his weakness. She did not tell him of her discoveries; but, acting upon them, she grasped his wrist eagerly, at his approach, and said to him hurriedly—

"I'm glad you've come to help me! Hev' you got the cart? We've not got one minute to lose."

"No, I hain't! Why, what's the matter?"

"Why not? We must be off this very night! we kain't stay! You 'member what the master said—them last words—"

"No! what did he say in preticklar?"

"Lord love me! Oh, Lord! You'd stay and poke here to be slaughtered! What air you good for, Ephraim Moggs? You've been a drinking somewhar, and hain't got no sense in your body! Ain't we to be off from this place to-night?"

"To-night? Was it to-night?"

"Yes! this very night! Ain't this Tuesday? I thought you knowed it; that you was to hev the cart and mule, and everything ready for a start to-night. We hain't got no time to lose! I tell you we're a hanging on the very varge of etarnity! What did 'Old Grizzly' say—'Don't let Ephraim stay with them fellows. They'll be the death of him! Don't you stay hyar a'ter Tuesday night. Ef you does, I kain't answer for the safety of your souls and bodies.' That's what he tell'd us both. Now, Ephraim, my darling, we've got a purty smart something here to lose; and you tells me you've got everything right and comfortable for you and meself, at the new home; and it's a purty long drive; and ef we stays hyar a'ter to-night, thar's no telling what'll be the eending."

"But you tell'd me that 'Old Grizzly' was to meet them boys a Friday night."

"Yes; but what's that to you?—that's not to meet *you!*"

"But I wants to see him fust, afore we goes."

"But that's not the same as ef he wanted to see you! Ef he tells us to go, we'd better go. What do you want to see him about?"

"Well! there's a heap of things—"

"Look you, Ephraim Moggs, you don't want to see him at all! You only wants to stay and be with them fellows, a-drinkin' whisky, tell all your sense is swallowed up, and all your money clean gone! Now, I'm not agwine to resk all my haird airnings with them fellows. You go and git the cart and mule, and hev it here ready this very night, a'ter the moon goes down. You fool!"—here the voice was smothered

—"I've got hundreds of dollars hid away in the 'den,' and among the rocks; and I tell you, what I've got in the 'den' must be taken out to-night, and we must hide it away among the rocks. This very night, I say! and do you now go, and keep watch on the Panther Rock, 'tell I kin git everything ready for a move. I'm not gwine to let you resk soul and body; and I'm not gwine to resk my own soul and body, and my gould, and my silver, my own haird airnings,— and paper money too,—all good, and no *blink*—to be etarnally blowed up and burned up, and lost forever and forever! Git you up, now, and keep close watch, and don't let them bloody varmints come upon us. A'ter that, and when we've got everything of vally hid away among the rocks, whar we knows whar to find them, then do you start off and git the cart, and hev it here to-night, by the time the moon goes down, and see that you don't hev nothing to do with them fellows. Keep from the whisky, honey, 'till we kin git cl'ar of them, and then you shall hev the whole jimmyjohn to your one self!"

Chapter xxv

THE VISION

While Gellert lay sleeping, for the last time, in the cavern of the river—one mattress having been spared from the sacrifice of fire, for this temporary use—his more sleepless companion, or superior, sate upon the rocks beside the tumbling waters, and meditated the several steps in the doubtful future, which he was required to take. He had plans and purposes now to order into symmetrical relation.

"To-morrow," said he, "finds Gellert on his way to Spartanburg, and, as soon as possible, to Europe. These men, Gorham, Peters, Swipes, all have had their warning to quit, and go hence! Moggs and his mother are provided for, and, in two days, will quit also. The former are to meet me on *Friday*, as they think, but I shall fail them! Once assured that they are gone, I will apply the match to the 'den', and destroy that link in the chain of evidence. With these all disposed of—all so many links—I shall sunder every connection—obliterate all foot-traces of *that* past *with them*—and, hereafter, even should these men ever appear, they shall see me, if we should meet, in no single respect as they have seen and known me.

"That they have their suspicions—that they pursue me in their curious search, even as the old woman reports, I well know; but, as yet, they have been baffled; and, with the destruction of all proofs, even should they discover the cavern, it will no longer be occupied by its former master.

"I shall then be free; turn over the new leaf; begin the new life; and lose, if I can, the sense of that haunting dread of discovery, which, in the terrible unrest of my nature, I have braved so long! I shall live then for my Mignon, my bright spirit—live to make her happy, if I fail of happiness myself.

"Ah! that burden of atonement! What mockery to dream of its satisfaction, when I still cling to the profits of the crime, while lamenting the crime itself! There lies the difficulty, my dear Goethe! How solve me that! Shall I command the courage for that last and greatest virtue—for the sacrifice of all for which I have sought and striven—to attain that ideal of the great brave man—the courage of utter self-sacrifice, which alone constitutes the required atonement? As I ask myself the question, the image of my child—my beautiful Mignon, rises up before me, and I feel that I can sacrifice myself *only* for her!"

It is difficult to say whether the speaker slept that night—whether, indeed, he ever slept! a terrible earnestness of temperament—a will sternly concentrative as death; an intellect forever active, in the play of numerous and sometimes conflicting faculties of mind—which did not always play harmoniously together—and, in some degree an uneasy conscience, beginning for the first time to be troublesomely suggestive; these, combined, had made his life a sleepless one! and —he had begun to long for sleep—a dangerous symptom; yet this is now his frequent prayer. And, sitting still upon the naked rock, his head sank forward upon his palms, and he seemed at once to sleep! But, suddenly, after an interval of a few minutes, he seemed to start, as from a dream, with a sort of cry, gazing wildly about him! and, before his eyes, rising as it were from a bald rock, in the very middle of the river, over which the perpetual billows combed in volumes of snow-white foam, rose gradually and gently a soft purple cloud, which as gradually swelled into a fine oval, and, parting in the middle, unvailed a beautiful girl, just emerging from childhood, with rich auburn locks that streamed down over white shoulders, contrasting exquisitely with the pure white flowing garments, simple as the Greek, in which her form was habited. She smiled upon him— her white arms were stretched out towards him, and, starting to his feet, his own arms were outstretched in return, as if he were about to plunge into the water in pursuit of the beautiful phantom. A single word escaped him—

"Mignon!"

And with that word, the vision was gone from sight, vanishing into thin air almost in an instant.

Was it, indeed, a phantom?—

Had he beheld the specter of his child? Had he slept—had he dreamed—or, had his eyes actually beheld a vision, vouchsafed to soothe the troubles of his mind? Was it the vision which beguiles, or the ominous aspect of a Fate?

And now, surely he hears a voice of singing. He hears the words—they are his own—paraphrased from the German of his friend, Goethe. The song floated around and above him in the air, in the zephyr, and in the gurgling of the waters, and he clasped his hands about his head, and listened with amazed and trembling attention, to the well known choral chant of the pure angels to the soul struggling in the deep waters.

I.

"Wo to us and to thee,
Star most beloved;
Thy world and ours,
Trembles and falls abroad
Thou, in thy weakness,
Brother, most erring—
Thou in thy loneliness,
Thou hast destroyed it!

II.

They bear away—
They, the dark spirits,
Whose pleasure is ruin;
They bear away
The hope and the harmony,
Wrecked into nothingness,
While *we* weep over
The beauty that's lost!

III.

Mighty among the stars,
Bright one, rebuild it;
In thy own bosom,
Rebuild it again!
Begin the new structure
With spirit unshaken;
Then shall new music
Unite the now sundered!"

Was he still dreaming? was it madness? Did he indeed hear that mournful chant of tender pity and angelic sympathy, as if good spirits were really hovering about him, conducted by his angel child, and striving to strengthen that new feeling in his bosom—that reviving conscience, working equally in heart and brain? Or,—and here the philosopher prevailed over the poet, as, recovering himself, when all the echoes of the music seemed to have died away, he sighed and smote his head, exclaiming—

"Something is wrong here! there is a pressure of blood upon the brain! it is disease—and yet—I must take physic—blood must be let, or—"

He was silent—still looked out eagerly towards the rock of his vision, over which there hung now no purple cloud; no beautiful damsel; the black billows alone rolling over, with all their crests boiling in white foam.

He listened, bent forward his head, but there was no longer a singing in the air. He glided down to one of the pools at his feet, and buried his head in the cool waters; then rose and tottered, rather than walked, to the recesses of the cavern; for a new and terrible fancy now possessed him, embodied in a single sentence thrice repeated—

"Oh, God! should anything have happened to my child—my beautiful Mignon!"

Chapter XXVI

COLD TRAIL—THROWN OFF

When Gellert arose the next morning, he found his superior already risen, and showing no traces of those exciting emotions with which he had retired the night before. These, Gellert had not witnessed. The strong will of the strong man reasserted itself; and with the argument which he was pleased to consider philosophical, the master persuaded himself that he had been dreaming; that song and vision were only the creatures of his imagination in a dream; or that, as he had said the night before, there was disease somewhere. At all events, nothing was said to Gellert of his nocturnal experience. But to himself he said:

"The moral, nevertheless, is in the dream; no matter whence it comes, it speaks for our necessity—whether it represents the diseased mind or body, the troubled conscience or the apprehensive heart. Dreams frequently constitute themselves a judicial court, in which the conscience is constrained to come in and make confession."

Gellert ate his breakfast: biscuit, smoked venison, and——cold water! There had been coffee among his stores; but the coffee-pot had perished in the flames. The superior took a biscuit and a few morsels of the venison. When the repast, such as it was, had ended, and the artist seemed to be satisfied, and was lighting his meerschaum, the other spoke:

"You understand, my good Gellert, all my explanations touching your route?"

"Every word, Mein Herr;" and he sent forth a cloud of smoke from his pipe with true German phlegm perhaps, or—to hide his emotion.

"I mean to see you through the gap, Gellert."

"Ah! dat is so good! I am so happy!"

"We will separate only when we have reached the plain country."

"Good! good!"—a puff of smoke as from a cannon.

"But we will not ride together in passing through the gap, Gellert. You shall ride half a mile or so in advance of me. I will follow you at a short distance, and try always to keep you in sight."

"Ah! my good friend, dat is good! But—is there any danger from dese—"

"There may be, and I will be nigh enough to succor you. At all events, I shall keep you full in sight, until the doubtful gorges have been overpassed. When I feel that you are safe, we will ride together some miles farther. I shall not return upon this route."

"Ah! you will go to———?"

"Perhaps!"

"And you will never come back *here*—no more—never again?"

"It may be! On Saturday or Sunday I will return to the den. These people will then be gone, and I have prepared to destroy it!"

"Ah! good! Dat shall make more safe!"

"Enough! all's understood between us. Let us now put fire to all that remains here."

This was quickly done—mattress and blanket—clothing of various sorts—all were soon in a blaze, such articles only excepted as seemed to be necessary for change of habit.

"We will now get our horses ready, Gellert. You, as I said, will ride the black. Here are your pistols and belt. Buckle them on; and, the better to hide them, you shall wear my cloak. Now for the horses."

These were soon in harness. Then the superior returned to the cavern, threw his own cloak over the shoulders of the German, and bade him ride.

"You have only to look about you, at every straight tract of road, and you will see the white behind the black."

There was a gripe of hands, and a few parting words in German between them, and while a big tear was trickling down the nose of the artist, he leapt into the saddle with something of the agility of youth. His superior waved him on his way, which seemed to be equally well known to both.

When he had gone from sight, his companion reëntered the cavern, and proceeded to change his costume entirely, from head to foot. He was no longer the same man. The clothes which he cast off were all committed to the flames. Then, tall, erect, as if suddenly endowed with youth, he vaulted into the saddle, and the white horse followed upon the traces of the black—making a wide circuit of the rocks, and emerging finally into the great road, from a seemingly impervious tangle of mountain laurel, in which the bear and panther alone were supposed to find harborage.

The German, when he had gained sufficient elevation upon the main gap road, looked back, and the white steed was visible behind him, and so the two rode, maintaining the same relative distance.

They did not ride unobserved. Crouched upon a rock, the two outlaws, Swipes and Peters, were preparing to descend to the gorges; on another projection of the mountain, with his keen eyes following *their* every movement, stood Gorham, concealed from their observation behind a mountain pine which grew from a crevice in the rock. With the tread of the approaching horse, each squatted under cover; all of the three were armed with rifles, in the usual fashion of the professional hunters. Brown Peters was the first to exclaim—

"I'll be dern'd, Swipes, ef thar ain't 'Old Grizzly'! Wonder whar he's gwine now. Kain't be the 'den,' or he's gwine to make a sarcumbendibus, and he ain't to come until to-morrow. To-day aint Friday, Swipes, is it?"

"No, to-morrow."

"Thar he goes, for sartain. I reckon he'll bring some grits to our mill, a'ter all! He's a'ter some beautiful business, now. He's not agwine to stop business, I reckon, so suddenly. Whence once a pusson gits his hand in at a business and the trade's profitable, it's mighty hard to leave it off."

"Mighty hard,—and I ain't gwine to leave it off either, Brown! I reckon you're right. He'll be bringing us a fat job to-morrow night. Lord, what a man he is! I reckon he knows everything, Brown."

"Knows! No, I reckon he don't know that we're here a watching him, and twouldn't be hard to draw a dead sight bead on every button of his coat! See whar he rides, the same black coat, black cap, black horse! Lord, how I longs for that horse! I could drop 'Old Grizzly' now, Swipes, so that he wouldn't know what hurt him"— and the fellow involuntarily raised his rifle to his eye. But Swipes quickly caught his arm and pulled him down.

"What air you about, Brown? You're a dern'd sight too quick to shoot. And hyar, we don't know but he's gwine to bring grits to the mill to-morrow. Let him ride."

"Hah! what's that? Look, Swipes! Another man a horseback. And if t'other horse was a dead black, this is a dead white, and a beautiful critter, too. I wonder who's he? He's rounding the hill at a smart canter."

"And jest like his horse; he's in white, too!"

"Gray, I reckon! The horse is milk-white. He's a tall fellow, and rides as ef he had money in his pocket. Suppose we feels him!"

And the rifle was again uplifted, and again pulled down by Swipes.

"You're about the greatest fool, Brown, with a rifle, that I ever seed! What do we know about this pusson? Now, 'Old Grizzly' always found out the valley of a prisoner before he sot us on. That's whar we shall lose, ef we gits separate from him. And wouldn't he hear the crack of the rifle, hardly a quarter ahead? No! it's a fool's game to spill blood for small stakes. I'm a-considering the million, Brown, all the time."

The black and the white had both rounded the hill which the two occupied. It was hardly possible for the rifle to reach either of them now. Soon they passed beneath the ledges of the second height, where Gorham was in ambush; and he, too, had his meditations.

"Where can he be going now! He's to meet us to-morrow night. It's a wonder that fellow Peters suffered him to pass! I could drop the old rascal myself; but, in doing so, the chance is I shall lose his tracks. No! no! He must live, were it only that I shall be able to follow and find him out."

The black horse passed from sight. The white horse, again at a smart canter, came thundering along in the rear.

"Ha! who can he be? He rides well. A big fellow, who looks up as he goes, as if he knew that some one is here upon the watch. Can he be in pursuit of 'Old Grizzly'? He's a stranger in these parts, and rides like an officer. Ha! can it be that this last affair has got down to the settlements? That man may be the sheriff! If I thought so"—and he too raised his rifle—"but no! twon't do just now, and my game must be a quiet one—no noise—no burning of powder, if I can help it! Nothing but silent scouting, never breaking a twig or leaving a footmark!"

And the two horsemen sped along in safety.

And, Brown Peters leading, he and Swipes stole down the hillside; and, even as they moved, Gorham stole forth also, following all their movements, and so regulating all his own.

"They shall do my *hounding*," quoth he, "and where they blunder, I shall be able to find the scent!"

And so all the several parties passed from sight.

Chapter XXVII

FRIDAY NIGHT

The dawn of Friday, that most ominous of all days in the calendar, according to the superstitions of former days, prolonged even to the present, found the old woman, Moggs, still an inmate of the den, and feverish, almost furious, with her disappointments.

Her hopeful son had disappeared, avowedly to procure horse and cart, and remove her and her valuables by midnight of Thursday, in anticipation of this fatal day.

But Ephraim, whom we have reason to regard as a weak and empty vessel, peculiarly susceptible to temptations of the spirit, the flesh, and the devil, failed to return that night.

The interval during his absence, however, was actively employed by the old woman in the removal of her stores from that precinct, which she expected to see blown into the air at any moment. She watched well, and, with due precautions, carried forth her treasures, partly by day and partly by night,—secreting them under great boulders, and in hollows of the rocks, in spots which had been carefully selected for the purpose.

In the grand solitudes of that mountain range, so little known, and so little likely to be explored, which the wayfarer did not care to seek, and where the only parties likely to penetrate were few in number, and with their appointed times and seasons for coming and going—her opportunities were quite sufficient for her objects, and her *caches* were not liable to be disturbed.

She had thought them entirely secure, until startled from her propriety by the discovery, made by "Old Grizzly," of one of her hiding-places. But that *he* should make the discovery was by no means wonderful, considering his assumed connection with the devil. Briefly, then, the old woman had transferred all her possessions, worth removal, from the interior of the "den" to the sides of the contiguous mountains. All was in readiness for the transportation,

155

to be procured by her son Ephraim. Her "gould and silver, and paper money, too,"—to say nothing of the "blink," or counterfeit money, was all now in places of supposed safety without. Nothing of hers remained within the "den;" and she had even cast her eyes upon the pewter mugs for drinking, and the kettle for boiling water, and certain other small matters of household stuff, but these she did not dare to remove, lest she should provoke the wrath of the bacchanalians at their midnight orgies.

Day passed, and the weary woman, hands folded in her lap, sat restive in the "den," watching the door, hearkening to every sound from without, and gratefully employed in nursing her wrath to keep it warm, for the coming of her son.

The fatal night came at length and found her thus occupied, with her occupation nearly over. Hardly had the night set in when she heard the tramp of horses' feet, and, almost at the same moment, the usual panther-cry,—the signal from without, thrice repeated, in the well-known tongue of Brown Peters.

Opening the door, she discovered not only Peters and Swipes, but her hopeful son at the entrance—all of them evidently touched, if not saturated, with liquor.

Ephraim was decidedly the worst case of the three. Where the others had picked him up was not said, but he had brought no cart, nor was there any horse visible which he could properly claim. The party had evidently been drinking and gaming together, and whatever money might have been assigned to Ephraim, for the purchase of horse and cart, had no doubt been lost.

The old woman savagely seized the arm of her son, with the grip of a tigress.

"Oh, you bloody sneak of an etarnal fool! Is you never to get right sense, and know when you're in the hands of the old satan? Where have you been all this time?—tell me that!"

"Oh, let go, old woman!" was the reply, as, with a lurch, Ephraim reeled out of her grasp.

"Old woman! you onconscionable scamp! Who do you call an old woman?"

"Well, ain't you an old woman?"

"Lawd! Lawd! and my own son, too!"

"Let the boy be, Moggs," said Brown;—"Ephraim's a mighty

good fellow, ef you only let him hev' his own way! Come in, fellows, it's Friday night, you know."

"Yes, Brown! and we'd better keep sober ef we're to hyar from 'Old Grizzly' to-night. I'm a-hoping he'll give us a fresh job to-night to help swell the pile."

"Well, perhaps he will. I'm consenting!"

"A million, Brown! a million!"

"I reckon that's enough by itself—ef we kin only find it!"

"A million!" cried Ephraim, reeling towards the two, with outstretched arms as if to embrace them.

"Well, what's it to you, young one! Your mammy don't want it! So, old woman, you air to have a farm, air you, and go to farming? And 'Old Grizzly's' to set you up in a vartuous ockipation, raising corn and hoeing 'taters and milking cows, eh?"

"Lawd! Lawd! that a son of mine should be sich a fool! So, Ephraim, you've up in your liquor and blabbed out everything to these bloody varmints! Oh, Lawd! Oh, Lawd! preserve us from all fools gwine on two legs and conseating themselves to be humans!"

"Oh, git out, old woman, and don't be bothering about nothing!"

"Oh, I hate a pusson that kain't keep a still tongue in his head!"

"Then, by the hokey-pokey, you kain't be loving yourself too much, mother Moggs," chuckled Brown, interposing to release Ephraim from the grasp which she had again taken upon his arm. Ephraim was only too glad to be released.

"Come out with me, Ephraim! Don't you stay with the drinking varmints."

"Kain't be did, old lady, for you see, I'm to hev' a right onderstanding with 'Old Grizzly' to-night. I'll make him settle up, you see!"

"Oh, the fool! Oh, Lawd! oh, Lawd! and we're to resk everything on a fool without a head, and that kain't keep his two legs steady under him. Come out, Ephraim, and leave these varmints to themselves."

But Ephraim sided over to his two more congenial companions. Brown was busy in drawing the stopper from a fresh demijohn which he had brought with him.

"Time for a drink, boys," said he—"come up to the rack, Ephraim, fodder or no fodder."

"He shan't drink any more, I tell you," cried the woman.

"And I say he shill ef he wants to! The liquor's free! It's *my* treat, woman. You smashed and drunk up my best liquor, but you shan't drink this."

"You're a born liar, Brown Peters."

"Look you, woman! I never lets a man give me the lie without putting my hammer into his muzzle. But when it's a woman, like you, an etarnal ugly old black hag of Satan, I jest wheels her about and uses my foot, and she goes forward by a sort of back-motion—so!" And, suiting the action to the word, promptly, and before the old woman could prepare for it, he took her by the shoulders, wheeled her about, and with a kick of no moderate force, fairly precipitated her to the opposite end of the apartment.

Then rose the storm. She was quickly on her feet, and rushing upon her assailant, knife in hand. But he was prepared for her, and grasping her wrist, disarmed her.

"Gi' me my knife, I say, you bloody varmint! Oh, Ephraim! that I hev' a son that stands by quiet, and sees a bloody beast kick his mother before his very eyes, and he never to lift a we'pon for her satisfaction."

"Look you, Brown, don't you be kicking my mother! I kain't stand *that*! Ef you tries it ag'in, let me tell you—"

"Well!" said Brown, suddenly confronting him.

"Well, then, I won't stay any longer in your company!"

"Ha! ha! ha!—that's the right determination! That shows you to be the right sort of man. You *hyar* that, mother Moggs!"

The woman only groaned, looking all possible scorn at the miserable son.

"Hyar! let's drink, and be done with this foolish business," quoth Swipes. "Come up, Ephraim, and liquor. And you, mother Moggs, take a pull, too. It's foolish of you and Brown to be quarreling always; but he means no harm."

"No harm! and what does kicking a pusson mean,—and that pusson an old woman what's got no son of the right sperrit to take her part."

"Oh! he's gitting the right sperrit mighty fast," with a laugh, as he pointed to Ephraim, busied with the pewter mug at his mouth, bottom upward, while his head was thrown back for the better facilitating the descent of the liquor down his capacious gorge.

The old woman could only groan bitterly, and, after renewed efforts to drag or persuade her son out of the pernicious companionship, she hurried to the entrance and sate down beside it, rocking her body to and fro, wringing her hands, and muttering ever and anon:

"Oh! Ef Old Grizzly would but come!"

"Look you, boys," said Brown, "let's git in thar," pointing to the inner room. "It's better thar for comforting the body and infectorating the soul!"

"Well, but ef he comes," said Swipes.

"What then? Let him come! What kin he do? Ain't thar three on us?"

And he looked significantly round as he put this question, and lifted his brawny arms with the manner of a man who was anxious that his muscle should be tried.

"I ain't afeared! Pick up the jimmyjohn, Swipes. Don't let Ephraim handle it. He'll smash it to a sartainty."

They all followed him in. When seated, the mugs were newly filled, and at the elbow of each, sitting around the table.

"Yes," continued Brown, "I've been a-considerin' about this very night, and about this very thing, and about what might happen. Thar's three on us, you see! Three on us!"

"Yes, Brown, that's true; but—what?"

"Well, you see, ef we air to be throwd off, you see—"

"Yes, ef we air to be throwd off—that's it—that's true."

"To be sure! That's true."

"Ephraim's not good for much, Swipes, at any time, but you air a strong man, and you can dig into a pusson's ribs as well a'most as myself. And I reckon I needn't tell you what I'm good for, when the word goes round to knock down and drag out."

"I knows it, Brown; and so—"

"And so, you see, ef thar ain't *three* on us, thar's *two* that we kin count upon in a skrimmage; and I've been a-considerin' and a-calkilating, for this very night;—and, you see, ef we're to be throwd off,—and turned loose,—and to hev' no more business,—

why then let Old Grizzly show himself hyar to-night. Thar's two on us, you see, Swipes—"

"Two on us—sure! and Ephraim—"

"He! Oh! Well, I reckon he's got feeling enough to stop a bullet that's meant for another pusson. What do you say, Ephraim? Ain't there three on us?"

"Three blind mice—" *(sings.)*

"Three what?"

"See how they drink—" *(sings.)*

"Oh, your mug's empty."

He filled the vessel while Ephraim quavered out an old catch well known among drinking men.

"He's onsensible to what we says."

"Don't matter! Thar's *two* on us! And when *he* comes—eh?—ef we are to be throwd off, you know—what do you say to that?—you say 'good,' do you?"

"Good! Ef we air to be throwd off—"

"Your hand upon it, Swipes!"

And the grip was taken.

At that moment, Gorham, with his usual stealthy, cat-like tread, entered the room.

He was received with a scowling look by Peters, with an evasive one by Swipes; but he noticed neither, and was regarded by all in profound silence. He himself was the first to speak, which he did quietly, but abruptly:

"Well, you expect to meet *him*, to-night."

"Yes; he 'p'inted to-night—Friday."

"He'll not be here."

"How do you know?"

"It's impossible! He went down the gap yesterday."

"Ah! How do you know that?"

"I saw him!"

"Saw him?" demanded Peters. "From whar did you see him?" And he looked significantly round to Swipes.

"From the cedar tree by the long bend."

"What time?"

"Some five hours by sun."

"Ah!" said Brown, with something of a sigh of relief.

Gorham had simply lied to them. It was only about three hours by the sun when he saw the two speeding horsemen, and at a point fully eight miles nearer to themselves, in the position which they occupied, than the place, which he designated, and which they well knew.

"But that don't prevent him from being hyar to-night—late, perhaps."

"Impossible! He's gone beyond, down, I think, into South Carolina."

"And what the hokey kin carry him thar!"

"Two things, I'm thinking! When I saw him he was going at a smart gallop; and he didn't pull in even when he had to turn the sharp corners; and there was another man in full chase of him!"

"And who's he?"

"My notion is that he's the high sheriff of the county, or some officer of the United States, that's got on the track of 'Old Grizzly' at last. The man was a large, tall man, in gray clothes, and he rode like an officer—like a military man. He rode a beautiful horse—milk-white—and I'm pretty sure he carried holsters."

"And you think it's the sheriff?"

"Or some officer of the government."

"And he's smelling out, you think, about that last business—the Cherokee money."

"Possibly! I hear there's a good deal of stir about the transaction at Asheville, and some soldiers are there—cavalry, come up from Augusta."

"The —— you say! That looks squally, Swipes. But you had another idee, you said, Gorham."

"Well, either that man in chase of 'Old Grizzly' is the sheriff, or, an officer of the United States, or—they've nothing to do with each other—jist happening to be traveling at the same time; and 'Old Grizzly' is making off out of the country, as he told us he meant to do. At all events, I feel sure that he won't be at the 'den' to-night; and, between us, I'm not so sure that he ever meant to come back!"

"By the hokies!" cried Peters, bringing his fist furiously down upon the table, "I've had that *idee* myself!" And then, after a pause, with a significant look at Gorham:

"Look you, Gorham, why do you think he didn't mean to come back? He's gi'n orders for it, you know, to-night."

"Yes; but I think only to throw us off guard."

"And why should he try the sly on us?"

"Well," with a quiet smile, "for the simple reason that he apprehended, perhaps, that some one of us would try the sly on him. He thought, no doubt, that you were cooking for him such a pot of gruel as wouldn't sit well on his stomach."

"And why *us*, more than *you*, I wants to know?"

"Because you *were* cooking the gruel and I was not. Look you, now, you sit drinking here and telling over your plans with big voices, and don't know what ears are fastened on your tongue. You thought yourself more safe here than without, or among the hills, and you never thought of old Moggs in the other room; and you never once caught sight of that little glimmer—there! Do you see it in the wall beside the door—look, where the light comes from?"

Swipes and Peters were both on their feet at once, and, examining the wall, under guidance, they found that Dionysian "ear," which mother Moggs had contrived for obtaining all the secrets of the prison-house.

"The blasted old hag! I'll be the death of her yit! You Ephraim, you blasted sneak! I reckon you're only pretending drunk, now, to find out our secrets—you and your cussed old mammy."

And he seized the drunken fellow by the throat. Gorham rose, but without interfering, said—

"And now, gentlemen, I bid you good night, and good-by, too! I shall not stay long in this region. It's getting too hot for me, and for the whole of us, I reckon. I'll take 'Old Grizzly's' advice, and work my way down to the Mississippi. I think it likely that I shall find the old fellow there, if he does not go to Europe. He will have money—"

"A good million!" cried Swipes.

"We shall probably be as good friends there as here. Good night!" —and without waiting for any answer, he stole out of the apartment, passing Mother Moggs without speaking, and emerging from the "den" into the open starlight of the hills. He smiled in his sardonic fashion as he clambered up the rocks, and muttered a soliloquy quite in character.

"I've put a spoke betwixt their wheels, I reckon. I've thrown them off the scent. I need them no longer, if I ever did need them, and can certainly do without them now! And now for the secret! That secret track, even if I never find out 'Old Grizzly,' is worth a fortune to me. But, I must watch those fellows for a while longer,—watch them till I fairly get them off the ground, and out of sight; at least, they must not watch *me!* I must cover all *my* tracks as I go!"

CHAPTER XXVIII

CATASTROPHE

Meanwhile, the drunken and drinking scene within the "den" continued in its original vigor. There had been at no time any love between Brown Peters and Gorham, and the former listened to the last speech of the latter with coldness, if not indifference, still keeping firmly the hold which he had taken upon the throat of Ephraim Moggs.

"Who cares?" said he, as Gorham passed out. "Let him go. I reckon we'll meet him, Swipes, long before we wants him. Time enough for that. As for this worthless hound of a white man—ef I kain't whip the mammy, seeing she's a sort of a woman, I kin and will whip the son, though he is so mighty leetle of a man."

"Let go, Brown; you're a-choking me to death."

"And I means to do it, you hound, and something better. Dern you for a bloody spy. Hyar you've been a-pertending to be 'how-come-you-so,' and all the time you've been drinking in our liquor and our secrets together. I'll thrash the villain out of you!"

He dragged the fellow, while speaking, to a corner of the room, where a horsewhip hung suspended. The half-choked and half-drunken man struggled in vain against the superior strength of Peters, who, by the way, was terribly warmed by his passion and by the liquor which he had himself drunken.

Swipes expostulated in vain.

Holding his victim off at arm's length, Peters began to administer the lash.

At first Ephraim Moggs simply winced, and renewed his entreaties, but as the lash continued to descend, he howled and writhed; finally, with increase of the torture, he shrieked wildly, broke away from the grasp which held him, retreated till the wall arrested him, then, with another yell, most like the *cri de guerre* of the red man, he bounded like a tiger-cat full at the throat of Peters, and clung

164

about his neck, using his teeth and nails in a wild-beast effort to bite and tear.

It was with no small effort that Peters threw him down flat upon the floor, and renewed the scourging. The prostrate wretch howled and shrieked, but made no further effort; till, suddenly, with a wild howl like his own, the woman Moggs dashed into the chamber, and, before Swipes could interpose, struck her knife into the shoulder of the assailing ruffian. It was his turn to howl.

"Swipes, she's dug into me this time."

The interposition of Swipes alone arrested the second, which might have been the fatal blow, aimed directly at the ruffian's back.

Meanwhile, Ephraim was again upon his feet, and grappling with Peters, and he now exhibited so much cat-like agility as to justify the suspicion of the latter that he had been only shamming drunkenness.

But he was in error. The poor wretch *had* been drunk, but was suddenly sobered, or partly so. With his back to the wall—retreat cut off—he was no longer the mere sot and imbecile. You must not press even the coward too closely. He felt his stripes, and showed himself now as savage and vindictive as before he had been timid and subservient; and it needed the joint efforts of the two outlaws to fling him and the woman off together, and expel them from the room, and finally, altogether from the "den," which they did with strong hands, blow upon blow and kick upon kick.

"Bolt the door, Swipes, and come and see to my shoulder! That old hag has given me a wipe as broad as the Devil's paving-stone, and as deep as dernation. I do think she's slashed into my very liver. Oh, ef 'Old Grizzly' was here now, he could dress it up! But there's a bottle of balsam somewhar about. Look for it!"

While Swipes was binding up the hurt of Peters, which was neither so wide nor so deep as he fancied, cutting really only into the fleshy parts of his shoulder, and letting blood freely, the woman Moggs, raging like a tigress, foaming, indeed, with passion, was dragging her son away from the "den"—he still showing some reluctance to go with her, and struggling all the while, but yielding to her superior will.

In the open air he seemed to grow feebler. The cool night acted upon his excited brain unfavorably, and the sudden rage and agility of the catamount, which he had shown towards the last in the *melée,* seemed to depart from him full as rapidly as they came, and he tottered rather than walked, as she hurried him down the hill.

"Whar would you carry me, mother? I'm all in a trimble."

"Whar would you go, you poor fool! Back to them varmints?"

"I'll sink my tooth into that fellow's heart!" was the vindictive reply.

"Why, so you shall, my honey; and I'll show you how to do it. Come!"

She dragged him down the rocks, never once releasing her hold—down, with the ground constantly subsiding beneath their feet, till they reached a hollow, where a basin received the waters of a mountain runnel.

"Drink, Ephraim," she said, "and wash your face and head in the cool water. Drink!"

"I don't want it! Ef I had a leetle drop of whisky now!"

"Water! water! nothing but water. They'd make you a dog on whisky—a dog to be managed by the lash."

Ephraim groaned as he rolled upon the ground.

But the woman seemed to exult. Her whole countenance was aflame. Her eyes glittered with the subtle fires which fill those of the snake when about to dart out his venomous fangs—of the panther when about to make his final spring. Her voice was hoarse and thick and broken, as if embarrassed by the foam which continued to accumulate about her mouth, and trickled down or crusted itself upon her withered and yellow cheeks and skin. Huskily speaking, she said—

"Whar's your steel and flint? Feel in your pocket, and give 'em to me."

Then, as he moved slowly and feebly, she thrust her own hand into his pockets and drew forth the desired articles.

"What air you gwine to do?"

"Never you mind! You'll see! Ah! I could bless 'Old Grizzly' for it! and how lucky that I watched and made the diskivery! It's a long account to settle, and has a mighty eending! The bloody brute varmint! He kin kick, kin he? Ha! ha! He won't kick much longer."

"What's it, mother? What's it you're gwine to do?"

"Lie close; lie flat to the ground! Don't you stir till I tells you. Lie down—flat—I say."

"But what's it you're about? Ef you makes the fire it'll jest be telling them whar we air a hiding."

"Only you be quiet—close—I tell you—down, and never you lift a head tell I comes back!"

She disappeared. Ephraim could see only a twinkle of light—a faint gleam for a moment, like that of a fire-fly, on a contiguous edge of the hill, leading up to the "den," some fifty yards distant; this was followed by a bright flash; and suddenly, a fiery serpent, all wings, and all aglow, and hissing as it went, seemed to be darting up the slope.

"Well, I do think," said he, "that she *is* something of a witch, a'ter all! What kin it be she's a'ter?"

His farther conjectures were soon silenced. Suddenly the mountain reeled beneath him; a thunderous explosion followed. It was a convulsion of the earth—an earthquake, and the terrible echoes roared back hoarse thunders from all the hills.

"It's the eending of the world!" he cried; "Lord Jesus Christ have marcy on my soul!"

The woman came to him at this moment. She was now speechless! She shivered in her terror, and the old teeth rattled in her jaws. Her eyes were wild with fright, her voice feeble and broken. She grasped her son by the arm, and cried—gasping out the syllables—

"Come! come!" which was all she could say, as she dragged him down the hillslope—both crawling, rather than walking—down, down, into the deep thickets of the laurel range, in which they hid themselves from the sight of the very stars!

Gorham had reached one of the topmost crags, looking down upon the gorge in which the "wolf-den" stood, when the explosion took place. He at once conjectured the catastrophe.

"'Old Grizzly' has made the gruel for them this time, and I reckon they've had to swallow it! How lucky I left them! He thinks to put a wall behind him, does he? We shall see! I knew he was too much for *them*! I must take care that he's not too much for *me!* It's *him* now against *me*, only!" and as he spoke, he seemed to brace himself up against the rock, as for further effort, and a more determined will. He will curiously survey the scene to-morrow.

Chapter XXIX

FREEDOM, SUNSHINE, AND THE MOUNTAINS

In the broad, generous air; upon the mountain top; with the sun glorious in his ascending march, and you have that perfect sense of freedom which exhilarates, almost intoxicates, as with a draught from some celestial fountain.

Once more released from the bondage of a bed of inability and pain, Fergus Wallace found himself again on horseback, and rode forth, jocund and bright, to the great peaks of the Apalachian. He had bade adieu to the Harness family, having expressed his gratitude to all its members, with the frankness of a noble heart, which feels no sense of mortified pride or vanity, in acknowledging an obligation incurred. He had commended himself gratefully to the widow and her sons, as he became able to commune with them, during his recovery, by his quiet, simple, genial manners, his grateful and sensible conversation, the modesty of his pretensions, and a certain easy and elegant vivacity, such as we have not hitherto been permitted to behold in him, and hardly supposed him to possess.

It seemed, in this new world, and under this fresh emancipation from restraints, that he had shaken off a former nature, and acquired one as dissimilar as new. We have seen him as a clerk, treated somewhat as a menial, under the check and control of a narrow-souled shopkeeper. And in all this time, there had been hanging over his heart and home an incumbent care and anxiety, making a perpetual dread to thought, in the long struggle of his mother with disease, and the final close of that struggle in death. Almost prostrated himself, by this event, it seemed to himself, for a certain period, that, beyond the absolute duties of life, and such as had been assigned him by the solemn requisitions of his dying mother, he had little else for which to live.

But nature is wonderfully recuperative with youth; and, with his

168

safe passage through the perilous adventure of the Gap, and the ordeal of physical suffering through which he had gone, he seemed to have sloughed off all the cares and anxieties which had threatened to become chronic about his heart. He was, indeed, a new man; glowing, as it would appear for the first time, with that generous ardor—that fine flush in the temperament—which provides the impulse equally to thought and action, and makes every taste and faculty susceptible to enjoyment.

Emerging from the cottage of the Harness family, for the journey before him, of the destination of which he himself was still ignorant, Fergus Wallace was accompanied by the stalwart sons of the widow, two tall hunters, in their hunting-shirts of blue homespun, thickly fringed with falling capes. Each of them carried the familiar long rifle in his grasp.

Voltmeier was present also. He had come, the previous day, to the cottage, and slept there the preceding night; and he was to conduct the youth to that home of which, as yet, the latter was suffered to know nothing. The Harness boys were to accompany the two over one range of the mountains for a few miles, rather in courtesy and kindness, than because of any necessity for such an escort.

The eyes of Voltmeier followed the movements of Fergus Wallace with an evident expression of satisfaction, as he declined all help in mounting his horse, and showed his full sense of recovering strength, by vaulting into the saddle with some of the agility of the practiced cavalier. That he was a good rider was evident; but that accomplishment might safely be assumed, on behalf of most men trained in the hardy exercises of forest and mountain life in the south, where long distances between the several settlements made the horse a necessity, and good riding a matter of course.

Voltmeier uttered some words of caution, as he beheld the young man thus quickly asserting his independence; but the anxiety in his countenance was blended with an expression of satisfaction. The figure of Fergus was that of finely developed youth, while his grace and ease of carriage indicated that knowledge of society, which refines and dignifies the possession of mere strength into elegance.

He, himself—Voltmeier—now, in the eyes of Fergus, seemed a very noble-looking personage. The tall form, muscular, without an ounce of unnecessary flesh, was erect, and his carriage was that of the strong man, of strong will, and conscious of position. The face was of marble whiteness, in wonderful contrast with that Indian brownness, that coppery hue, which was that of the aged man, the "Old Grizzly" of the Wolf-Den. Very keen and piercing was the glance of his eye, which seemed to dart through you as he gazed, giving you a somewhat annoying sense of a scrutiny which was resolved to allow you to have no secrets. Something about the mouth of this man was expressive of cynicism, until he smiled, and then it wore a character of sweetness, even of playfulness, that was apt, however, to pass into the satirical.

The conversation was general as the party rode on their way. The young mountaineers, both of whom had taken a strong liking to Fergus, related their adventures of the hunt; the frequent encounter with bear and panther; and their simple narrations were alive with the picturesque to the imagination of Fergus, who had enjoyed no such sylvan experiences.

At mid-day the party separated, having reached a certain designated point, where, passing over the valley which divided one range of mountains from another, they were about to enter upon a new tract of country. The leave-taking of the young men was quite affectionate. In their comparatively brief association, they had learned to call each other by their Christian names, and Fergus, and Jake, and Benjie, were now their equal words of salutation and of farewell.

"You mustn't forget us, Fergus. You knows *we'll* always be glad to see you; and the old lady, you know, a'most considers you one of the family now. The Colonel, I reckon, will bring you out hyar sometimes, on a great hunt, and we'll go and camp out for a week at a time, somewhar along the great laurel ranges, whar the b'ar sucks his paws all the winter, with the recollection of the bee-trees he's been into the season before. You'll bring Fergus, won't you, Colonel, some time when you gits a chaince?"

"Yes, Jake, to be sure; and we'll all go on a hunt together. But you are to visit us, boys, you know, when you can, and, you remember, Jake, our trade about the cattle. Don't think of taking your stock down to Spartanburg, when you can get as good a market so much nearer home. I'll buy all that you want to sell."

"I'll remember, Colonel, and you'll see me, and perhaps Benjie, or some other boy that I kin trust, coming along your way, at the right season. And now, good-by, Colonel—good-by, Fergus! We hev' to put out, Benjie—the sun's jist overhead."

And the good-byes were freely exchanged; and the young men squeezed each other's hands, and made mutual pledges, in all the confiding spirits of simple youth, not yet tainted with selfish cares and vain and idle aspirations.

Voltmeier was also kind of manner, at parting; but it appeared to Fergus that he was somewhat impatient of the long delay, and the many repetitions and promises, queries and assurances, which preceded the final words of separation.

Parting is usually a sadness, even where we separate from those whom we have only briefly known. Fergus looked back once at the retiring forms of the young mountaineers, and found that both of them had paused upon the summit of the hill, and were giving him a last gaze also. Then they waved their hands simultaneously, in adieu, and Fergus followed Voltmeier slowly down the hill-side.

The two rode on in silence for a while; Fergus, with a slight sinking of the spirits, and Voltmeier apparently absorbed in thought. As the latter rode forward on that splendid white charger—a beast as strong as an elephant, yet light of foot, and easy and graceful of motion as a doe, Fergus thought of the rider as an embodiment of the single idea of *power*—so erect was he; so easy; seemingly so calm; pressing forward resolutely; swerving neither to the right nor to the left; but, as grasping some one leading purpose of the mind, and going forward under its coercive impulse, even as the hero goes into battle.

But now the voice of Voltmeier summoned him forward, and arrested his meditations.

"Ride up, Fergus, close. We can ride together."

"Your steed outwalks mine, sir. He is a great walker. I do not think I ever saw his match."

"He has the legs, certainly, and can walk his six miles an hour with ease, and keep at that gait all day. I will try to accommodate his paces to those of your beast. We must now talk together, as we have not spoken hitherto; and it is due to you that I now make myself known. That I have not done so before, was due to some precautions, the reason for which you will comprehend hereafter. But one of these reasons may be told you now. I was desirous that you should know *me* simply as a *man*, apart from any knowledge of my name, or of the close relationship that exists between us."

"Relationship, sir—except that of—"

"I have no purpose to surprise you, yet must do so now. You would say that the only tie between us is due, perhaps, to the service which I have rendered you."

"That was my thought, sir."

"The tie is a much stronger one than that. It is the tie of *blood*— the bond of kindred—and blood is strong, and has its claim acknowledged as earnestly in *my* bosom as I trust it does in yours. Fergus Wallace, I am Leonard Voltmeier, your father's half-brother: I am your uncle!"

Fergus was speechless for a moment, and his whole frame in that moment was shaken by a tremor that almost threatened to unhorse him, when at length he spoke:

"Good God, sir—is it possible—my uncle!"

"Yes, Fergus, and I fear that I do not commend myself greatly to your sympathies when I declare myself to you. It was that you should *know* me simply as a stranger at first, and that you should gradually come to know me as a man—not prejudiced in your judgment by anything that you may have heard before—in brief, that I should have a chance to win your sympathies before I made myself known to you as a kinsman of whom, perhaps, you have been taught to think unfavorably, and with hostility."

"Oh, no, sir; not with hostility! My poor mother, sir, on the contrary, sir—all her last words—"

"Ah! tell me of *them!*"

And the strong man, crouching in his saddle, with face averted from the speaker, listened to those mournful revelations which his mother had made upon her death-bed, touching his father's and her own previous history; and, as he listened, it was Voltmeier's turn to shiver and to shudder. He too felt the tremor of a vexing thought and a bitter memory; but he was better able to subdue or suppress their expression. The youth concluded thus:

"No, sir; though I tell you frankly that my mother did have her reproaches, she yet spoke of you tenderly—even with affection, in those last moments of her life, when, I am sure, there was not a word that fell from her lips that did not speak for the most thorough convictions of her mind, and the true feelings of her heart; and these were in your favor."

"Ah!" with a long-drawn sigh, as it were a relief. Then a pause, and an involuntary spurring forward of his horse, which he checked a moment after, and curbed back to the spot where Fergus stood. Both riders, a moment before, had come to a full stop upon the highway.

"Go on! go on!" said Voltmeier.

"I think, sir—my uncle—that I have said all that I can say, or have need to say. But I bore a packet to your address, which, if I rightly understood you, has been saved, and is now in your possession. That packet, sir—my uncle—was penned painfully by my poor mother in the last hours of her illness, and without my knowledge. Had I known how she was engaged in those hours of pain and exhaustion— I should have—"

"No! no! boy! Had you stayed her hand, I should never have forgiven you. In this packet, Fergus—my dear nephew—nay, my son—lies your uncle's salvation! Look! I have it here—next my heart! Here is the record of your mother's forgiveness—signed, sealed, and witnessed before high heaven, by death himself! would you have robbed me of such a document?" He showed the packet.

Here was the white heat of passion—a sudden burst, a blaze, soon extinguished, but leaving the metal as fiery hot to the touch as if the flames were still raging insurmountably. It was passion sublimed by thought, and undergoing the purification of conscience.

"Poor Catharine!" was his next exclamation. Then, after a pause:

"Fergus, do you know what has been written here?"

"No, sir, I have never read the paper. It was sealed when given me. But, I tell you frankly, my mother told me much of your relations with my father—"

"And herself?"

"No, sir."

"Ah, well! Great God! and to think that *it might have been!*"

"What, sir, what might have been?"

"No matter; and yet—hark you, Fergus Wallace, my nephew— nay, you shall be *my* son. She—your mother—has given me the right to call you so. I will tell you all. I was a great criminal to your mother and father. I loved them; yet I wronged them. In the passionate perversity of a youthful heart, a proud, rebellious spirit, impatient of control, moved by passion, I did them wrong, and did *you* wrong, though then only in your cradle. She gives me the *opportunity*—I use her own language—*to atone;* and on her death-bed, and in the sacred language of this last writing from her hand, she gives me *her* forgiveness. Fergus, my son, do you give me yours?"

The strong man trembled like a child. Great big tears gathered heavily in his eyes, and found their way slowly down his cheeks. He stretched his hand over to the youth, who grasped it with fervor, but could say no word in reply.

It is a somewhat terrible spectacle to behold the great tears gathering in the strong man's eyes. The youth was awed, amid all his sympathies, and, unconsciously to himself, the big drops trickled from his own eyes.

"Enough! enough!" cried Voltmeier, with a strong effort of the will. "Enough, Fergus, my son. But know why it was that I became criminal—why it was that I did wrong to you, and to your sainted mother! Alas! Catharine, she hears us now, *if all be true!* These rocks, these mountains, the skies, the sun—all hear and bear me witness, when I tell you *I loved your mother.* And my brother won her. This maddened me, and defeated passion depraved and degraded my heart, warped conscience, baffled justice, and made the misery of years to them, and—*to me!* And, when I think of what *might have been,* but for the violent and vexing passions of my nature then, I could fling myself down upon these hills and pray to them to cover me. In this packet, so strangely brought to me—"

"It was a Providence, my uncle."

"A Providence? Ah, well, we will call it so. In *this* packet lies *my salvation.* It affords me the *opportunity*—mark the word—the most precious to life, to make *atonement* for wrong doing. It is *the* great privilege, so the great master, Goethe, said to me years ago, which enables us to put ourselves at peace with ourselves—"

"And—*at one* with God. Is't not so, sir?" interposed the young man.

"Perhaps, perhaps," somewhat impatiently, as he proceeded rapidly. "And, as if there were some law ruling in this, I begin the work of atonement by being permitted, the humble instrument, to rescue you from death. Fergus, my son, you will forgive me for your mother's sake, and in obedience to her wish. And you will try to love me for her sake also, for, as I live, my son, I loved your mother beyond all other women—beyond all other loves."

Chapter xxx

WITH WHAT OBJECT?

"Yes! it might have been! It might have been!" was the repeated exclamation of Voltmeier.

These words were murmured unconsciously, rather than addressed to the ears of his young companion; and, in the same moment, Voltmeier drove his spurs into the sides of his horse and went forward with a bound, which left Fergus far behind him. The latter followed at an increased pace, but without seeking to gain the side of his uncle. He, too, had need to think to himself and muse mournfully of many things.

It is needless to say that he was greatly impressed by what he had heard, quite as much by the manner as by the language of Voltmeier. It opened to him long vistas in the domain of memory and thought, and led his mind into wandering speculations as to what *had* been, and what *might* have been; and he began slowly to conceive the clues, which, as his uncle no doubt had designed, were to account for that course of conduct, on his part, which had outraged the sensibilities of his mother, and led to the privation of his father's rights.

Upon these subjects, however, he did not dwell with feelings of bitterness or resentment. The revelations of his uncle, given with such evident proofs of feeling and of passionate self-reproach, had disarmed him, and he was prepared fully to accept that atonement, which had been so effectually embodied in the affectionate and even tender approaches of Voltmeier.

Yes! Even as a son, as his uncle had styled him, he was willing to be, and to be considered; and this spontaneous growth of sympathetic relationship seemed to him to be nothing more than his mother had expected and desired.

Nay, was it not in continued evidence of that guiding and ruling Providence, which, as he thought, had so directly shown itself, in those events which had brought him so soon to his uncle's knowledge?

of course, he only knew him as the benevolent stranger who had found him bleeding upon the highway, and had saved his life.

It required but a few moments of time and a single effort of the will to restore Voltmeier to that calm and equable mood, which seemed the normal condition of his mind. He curbed his horse and waited for Fergus to come up with him; and when the latter rode again alongside of him he spoke, but without making any reference to the subjects of the previous dialogue.

"Have you no curiosity, Fergus, to know whither you are going?"

"Now that you ask the question of me, Uncle, you arouse the feeling. But, till this moment, I confess that I had so completely surrendered myself to your discretion, and so fully relied upon that and your own generous feeling, I had really never thought to ask. As a matter of course, I am now curious."

"Well, you shall be satisfied as we proceed. You will go with me to my home. You shall make it yours, always, however, with reference to your future plans. If I understand rightly you are a student of law, and desire to pursue that profession."

"True, sir; and that reminds me to ask you whether there were not some other papers left upon my person by the robbers, besides the packet of my mother's?"

"I am in possession of the one paper only."

"There is a very dear friend of mine, a lawyer of Spartanburg, and quite a distinguished citizen of South Carolina, Major Henry, who gave me a curious document, along with an ivory tablet marked with letters and characters, which I did not comprehend, but which he assured me would prove eminently useful to me in my journey, especially if I should fall into difficulties. I am sorry if they are lost."

"Yes, if they had any value—"

"Oh! they must have had some value. Major Henry attached no little importance to them. He called the tablet an amulet, and told me some curious particulars in regard to the unknown person—quite a mysterious person—from whom he received it."

"Ah, yes!—who was the person?"

"He could tell me nothing really, except that he had served a North Carolinian, a person guilty of some great crime, and, as a lawyer, had saved him, at some peril to his own life. This was all. He thought it possible that I might meet this person."

"At all events, it will not be necessary that you should *look* after him. Now,—look around you, Fergus!" and, stopping his horse on one of the commanding eminences of the mountains, he waved his hand with a great sweep at the grand amphitheatre which opened before their eyes, and exclaimed:

"Here, Fergus, you behold an imperial group,—world giants—each a crowned head, such as the world rarely beholds; stationed, as it were, as guardians over the loveliest empire of vale and dale, grove, thicket, and waterfall, that was ever sung by the poet, or accorded to the dreams and fancies of art or fiction. At the same moment you behold no less than five beautiful cascades glittering in the sun, and each wearing its rainbow crown, trembling with its weight of gems; diamonds encrusted with all the beautiful and various dyes that sunbeam ever manufactured from the clouds in heaven. Look, my son— gaze your fill, and if you feel with a poet's feeling, your raptures will keep you dumb!"

And while Fergus gazed with delighted amazement and in deep silence on the grand amphitheatre around him, Voltmeier was gazing *on him,* with a keen, earnest scrutiny, which the youth did not perceive. The uncle broke the silence.

"These mountains," said he, "constitute the Helvetia of our country. They are the loftiest elevations this side of the Rocky Mountains; not only grand in their stupendous summits, but beautiful in their thousand varieties of aspect which never stale upon the eye; with the great height of these ranges, stretching far beyond all grasp of vision; with the wondrous rivers which seem to have torn their way through the rocks, overthrowing all impediments, and making a way for themselves through vast gorges, which are plowed out of the rocks to depths of fifteen hundred feet or more—rivers of continual rapids for many miles;—with the vast number of beautiful cascades, leaping in successive bounds hundreds of feet in the air, and subsiding to perpetual murmurous songs, in the sweetest lakes that ever harbored in hidden glens of fairy-land; you have here the elements of a thousand pictures which might well persuade the painter to perpetual studies of his art, here, in the primitive abode of nature. But art is not here yet. There will come a time when these valleys shall have their palaces. These heights will some day be crowned with castles, and the beautiful in art will come to the relief of nature, and extricate her charms from their present sterility of wilderness. Art, my dear Fergus, is the true province of man; and until we shall attain the use of that wand of Prospero, man himself will be little above the level of the Caliban—humanity in subordination to the beast. Do you read Shakspeare, Fergus?"

"Oh, yes, sir; it is one of my favorite studies."

"*Studies* is the right word in respect to Shakspeare. Merely to *read* him is not to *know* him; and you can never *see* him on the stage. No actor, however greatly endowed, has ever conceived his characters, embodying, as they do, all the types and ideals of human perfection; nor has any philosopher yet fathomed, with any plummet of thought, his wondrous depths. He is a thousand years beyond them all. I sometimes doubt if my own favorite master, Goethe, comprehended more than a tithe of his genius. He was not, himself, sufficiently the *natural* man for that. *His* art predominated too greatly in his mental constitution for his humanity; and he sought too much for the natural in the metaphysical, which is only the natural with a select and greatly endowed few. Schiller *felt* Shakspeare, rather than *knew* him; and this because of sympathies which Goethe seemed perpetually striving to subdue under the dominion of art. But let us ride forward."

In this manner, thus communing together, like father and son, the two rode on, along the great ranges; from spur to spur; pausing at every fine prospect as it opened upon them at each ascent; each receiving its comment from Voltmeier, whose long experience and knowledge of the country enabled him to discourse freely of scene and situation.

The ingenuous nature of Fergus was a grateful study to Voltmeier, who watched all his answers and impulses, and, in brief, made *him* a subject of study.

But this Fergus did not perceive or suspect. He had no notion of the keen inquiry harboring in those searching glances of the eye which scrutinized every answer from his lips. From the general tenor of Voltmeier's conversation, it would seem that he had two objects of study in this: the moral character of Fergus, in the first place, and, in the next, the degree of mental endowment which he possessed, and of mental acquisition which he had made.

Of the former, he was soon satisfied. No spirit could be clearer, no moral seemingly more pure, no temperament more simple and femininely ingenuous. The heart embodying these qualities seemed to be in the right place, richly gifted with the best virtues of humanity, while the mind showed itself just, logical, expansively capable, and rising, at times, to the utterance of large views and a comprehensive grasp of topics; showing the original capital to be considerable, and the acquisitions which it had made to be of a nature well calculated to confirm those impressions of Major Henry which Voltmeier had not known.

One whole week was given up to these wanderings of the two, uncle and nephew, as father and son, among the Apalachian ranges. Their routes were desultory of direction. The purpose of Voltmeier *seemed to be to gain time,* and, as we may reasonably assume, solely for the purpose of that close study of the young man which he religiously pursued. But why? He had an ulterior object, which will probably develop itself as we proceed.

In this progress, they visited the most conspicuous of the grand points in the mountain scenery, and at all these points the senior challenged the attention of the young man to all the most salient in the picturesque realms which they traversed. The more eminent features of the grand domain of the Cherokee, in two States, were displayed before him. One day found them on the Table Rock of South Carolina, looking down on the great plains lying in beautiful verdure below. There was the Sassafras Mountain; there was the Saluda, with the lovely Indian stream of Oolenoe, gliding to its own sweet music on to an embrace with the river in which it was to be lost forever. Cæsar's Head, Dismal Mountain, the Saluda range, the Panther's Knob, and the Hogback, were all traversed; and from these, stretching eastward, they distinguished King's Mountain, in York, seventy miles distant, and famous for the defeat of the British Ferguson, by the mountaineers of the country. From the Oconee Mountain, they looked over into the Cherokee ranges of Georgia, and grasped, in long vision, the blue tops of the Curachee. The transition to the Whitesides, the Balsam, and the Black Mountains of North Carolina, still more enlarged the province of vision, and was easy—the latter being supposed to be the loftiest of all the summits in the South.

By night they lodged in cabins of the hunters, or snug farmsteads of a thrifty people, isolated too much for much culture, perhaps, and unlettered, but frank, cordial, and hospitable. From this mountain progress, finally, they descended to inferior, but still noble heights, where, if less grand and imposing of outline, the scenery was more beautiful, more attractive, and more susceptible of cultivation, as well by agriculture as by fine art and the highest civilization. In this descent, they visited some of the pleasantest and most picturesquely-situated of all the mountain settlements of the Old North State. They lingered beside the plashing, bright, and bounding waters of the Swananoa, and there found welcome in dwellings where the refinements of society united their attractions with those of nature. Asheville, Henderson, Flat Rock, and other precincts, gave them grateful welcome; and, in all this progress, Fergus Wallace observed that Voltmeier was well known to the best people, and was received with a deference well calculated to increase the respect, if not veneration, which he already felt for his uncle. He was introduced to professional men, to the leaders of society, to distinguished officials, the politicians and the statesmen of the land, at a preiod when statesmanship had not yet given place to roguery and fraud.

In all these progresses, from day to day, the watch of Voltmeier was unrelaxing, yet so circumspect, that Fergus never once suspected it. The eyes of the former met his own with an expression as clear and frank as affectionate. *How* he looked, when the other spoke, with an oblique glance which searched the speaker through, was never permitted to be seen by himself.

But the smile in the *eyes* of Voltmeier never quite satisfied the youth. It was too intense for sympathy, and there was a something, as he thought, satirical or cynical, in the expression, which declared for a circumspect and suspicious nature. But the *smile* of his *mouth* was irresistibly sweet, and following, as it usually did, his most grave expression of look or utterance, it carried with it a charm which made its way at once to the young man's heart. He thought to himself that he had never seen anything in man more beautiful. Voltmeier's teeth were singularly white and uniform. The poor boy did not dream that the entire set was false. Voltmeier now wore neither beard nor whiskers. He made his toilet with great care, and shaved regularly every morning. In every respect he was singularly unlike the "Old Grizzly" of our former acquaintance, who had no teeth, and whose lips sank inwards every time he spoke. The teeth of Voltmeier made him almost youthful to the eye.

At Asheville, when the two met at sunrise, on the eighth day of their rambles, Fergus was pleased to hear the words, most affectionately spoken—

"And now, my son, for home. You shall see my little family. It consists only of my dear little *Mignon,* my daughter and only child, and her aunt, Miss Gertrude Leyfenholdt. You shall be one of us henceforth, if you desire it."

The heart of Fergus leapt wildly at these words, but with vague emotions. Why, he knew not. Voltmeier seemed in an excellent humor. We know—what Fergus did not—*that he was satisfied;* that his study of his nephew had been satisfactory; and that, whatever his objects, his calculations, his hopes, or his fears, he was now at his ease. He seemed to be in superior spirits. Always placid, cool, meditative, he was now in a joyous state, almost of ecstasy, and whistled, and snapped his fingers, with a sort of exultation, as they went forth from their lodgings, to take their horses.

"My Mignon! my Mignon!" he murmured, as they mounted their steeds for their closing progress.

Chapter XXXI

THE NEW MASTER

L eaving these two to continue their progress to the habitation of
Voltmeier, wherever that might be, we will return to the scene
of the catastrophe at "Wolf's Den," taking up our narrative at that
point of time, in which Gorham, standing upon a contiguous peak,
beheld the explosion, and shrewdly conjectured the occasion of it.

He did "Old Grizzly" injustice, however, if he thought the mine
had been set by him with the view to the destruction of his former
associates. He was more nearly correct when he assumed one of
the purposes of the chief outlaw, to be the annihilation of all the
clues leading to the life which he had so lately led.

"But he shall not escape me," muttered Gorham to himself. "He
will not throw me off the track so easily! As for this old hag, and
her beast of a son, they shall not escape me either. I must find out
what she knows, and what he knows. *He* must know something. How
it was that 'Old Grizzly' got him out of jail; by what lawyer-trick,
and by what lawyer. If Ephraim Moggs knows anything he ought to
know that. He must have seen and heard the lawyer in court, if
nowhere else, when he appeared in his defense. As for the woman,
she must have seen 'Old Grizzly' set the mine. He never would have
told her; and, if she could see him at that work, she must have
made other discoveries in the same way. I'll have all out of them.
They are now in *my* power. I have their secret; and if Peters and
Swipes are killed in this explosion, it is by their act, no matter who
prepared the powder."

He glided down the hillside, carefully keeping in shadow as much
as possible, and avoiding all exposure of his person to the starlight.
He approached stealthily the site of the late "Wolf Den," and, as
he expected, found it a mass of ruins, all in a heap; stones, and
earth, and clay, blended together in a great heap of *debris,* in which
nothing beyond could be distinguished in the darkness of night. He
listened silently for sounds from the ruins.

"If," said he, in underbreath, "there is anybody still living, after such a blow, there will be groans, and I can hear them."

And he stooped his ear towards the pile and walked around it. Everything was silent to his ears, save his own footfalls and thick breathing.

"All's still," said he. "I can hear nothing. They are dead! Dead at the same minute, without a minute's warning! Well, if there be a devil, they've made his acquaintance before this! and I wish them much pleasure of it!"

He stole away from the pile, to a little distance, covering himself in the shade of a great boulder, from which he could overlook the scene.

"Now," said he, "for the old hag and her hound of a son! This is a good place to watch for them. They have hid themselves away in the hollows, down among the laurels. But they must come out, and they must come this way. Even if they were not compelled to come out *here*, they *would* come from very fright and curiosity together; a sort of magic which draws down the bird from the tree into the open mouth of the snake."

Gorham was not without his philosophy; and, with a full faith in it he lurked in waiting, like the snake, for the coming of *his* prey.

There is, in truth, a fearful fascination in the consciousness of a great crime, or terrible event, in which one shares, which exercises a demonic sort of attraction, and so spells the imagination as to drag, however unwillingly, the criminal to the scene of terror. And, of this nature, is that sort of fascination which flows from an intense and morbid curiosity. Such was the spell that exercised the mind of Gorham, himself, in the pursuit of the secret of "Old Grizzly," his late superior. But, he did not associate the one idea with the other, nor see the presence of that demonic passion in both, which might well be supposed to be occasioned by demonic inspiration.

For hours he watched and waited, neither restless nor impatient, being one of those cold hounds for scent, which, slow to get upon the scent, are dogged in hold of it, and make up in stubborn endurance, for the lack of speed and headlong activity of spirit. He was slow in progress, but wonderfully tenacious of purpose; and, while waiting for his prey behind the great boulder, with sleepless eyes, he meditated his secret purpose; turned over, in his mind, the several steps he had taken; reviewed the value of the clues which he had already found, and felt himself more than ever confident of success.

"I'll have 'em all in a net!" said he, exultingly. "I feel myself on the trail, though I don't see it yet! Something tells me so! And it's a pleasant thing to have such a beautiful game to play. It's just like some Indian hunt, as they tell us, where the hunter goes for months, and even years, in search of his revenge, till he gets on the right track and finds the scent, and comes up with the game at last, and strikes him down with a tomahawk, or with a bullet, or arrow, from behind a bush."

And so he cheered his lonely watch by meditations, such as hound or panther or red man might be supposed to feel—a cold head, stimulated by a vague appetite and a morbid want, which is at once human and wolfish.

And the cold stars twirled in their orbs above him, in melancholy troops and groups, waxing paler and paler, as Lucifer gained upon their pathway, bearing a torch which took from all the luster in their lights!

The same glorious stars now looked down into the laurel hollow, where the woman Moggs lay crouching with her son, and startled her into activity. She had not closed her eyes during the live-long night. But her miserable son, overcome by drunkenness, pain, and exhaustion, had long before sunk into a deep sleep, almost coma, in which nature found relief from suffering. With difficulty she aroused him, and, when but half awake, he started up and grappled with her, crying out:

"Take your hands off from my throat, Brown Peters, or I'll knife you!"

"Hush, you fool! It's me, your mammy. Come to your senses, Ephraim, and be a man for once."

"I am a man! I'm Ephraim Moggs, I tell you!"

"Well, git up! Wake up! We must be moving."

He had sunk back again, after a spasmodic effort to rise, growling:

"Let me be! I must sleep, I tell you. I'm sore all over. I'm jest like a bile and a blister. Oh, that lash!"

"What! you feels it, do you? Well, wake up, Ephraim, and onderstand. The hand that laid them lashes upon you will never handle whip again, I reckon! Wake up—git up—and I'll tell you all."

"I must sleep! Hands off, Brown!"

"You must wake, or I'll put the lash on you, myself. It's a'most daylight; and we must be off, or the sheriff and all the constables will be upon us."

The threat had some effect. The besotted wretch, still stupid from drink and sleep, though writhing with pain at every movement, contrived, with the old woman's goading and assistance, to stagger to his feet; but only to fall back again. Picking up his hat from the ground, she hurried to the basin of the spring, filled the hat with water, and dashed it fiercely into his face. Then, with another effort, she helped him from the ground, and, still half tugging, and half supporting, she continued to make him stagger forward.

"Oh! Lord!" he cried, "where will you be dragging me now, when I'm almost dead with the misery?"

"Come away, quick, Ephraim, my son, or they'll be catching and hanging us both."

"Who'll be catching and be hanging—what's the trouble now?"

"The Sheriff, I tell you! the law—the Jack Ketch and all the constables."

"Why, what's happened? What hev' we been doing now?"

"Come and see, and that'll open your eyes wide enough!"

She continued to get him forward, slowly enough, till he stood beside the massed ruins of what had been so properly styled the "Wolf's-Den."

"Look thar, and tell me what you sees!"

"Lord ha' marcy! What has done it?"

"The airthquake!"

"The airthquake? I did dream something about an airthquake, mammy."

"It warn't a dream! 'Twas an airthquake, and all the mountains trembled! and you see, it blowed up the 'Den.' "

"And whar's Brown Peters and Swipes?"

"Thar'!—under thar! Call to 'em! They won't answer! They'll never cut skin of any son of mine never more!"

"Lord ha' marcy! Let's git away from this, mammy! In my dream I thought the world was coming to an *eend*. Let's go, for it's sartain to come!"

"Come along, and be spry, now, Ephraim, my boy. Day's breaking, and before the sun gits up we must be down the mountain, and cl'ar away from this."

"Stop!" cried a stern voice in their very ears. "Stop!" and at the single word, a heavy hand was laid upon a shoulder of each.

"Oh! Lord!" was the cry of the mother, and "Oh! Lord" was the echo from the throat of Ephraim; and they shrank beneath the grasp; both trembling with newly-awakened terrors of the sheriff and the gallows! They turned, and, in the dim light of dawning, distinguished the harsh features of Gorham, with a cold smile upon them which seemed to be full of devilish malice.

"Oh! Lord—the Lord be praised, it's only Gorham!"

"Yes! Oh! I'm so glad," cried the son, gasping—"it's only Gorham."

"Only Gorham," responded the latter. "*Only* Gorham! But Gorham's the man to hang you both!—woman, what have you done?"

"Me! I've done nothing! I didn't do it! It was the airthquake."

"Earthquake! Yes, indeed, it was an earthquake, but your hand made it! Tell me no lies—I know all! 'Old Grizzly' set the mine. You watched him. You knew all about it. You fired the mine, and sent those two poor devils, Brown Peters and Swipes, to hell, in the twinkling of an eye. I know all; but you shall tell me all! I know more than you think for. You are to have house and farm, eh? Well, it's very well! We'll go and look at the farm together, and you'll mind me, Richard Gorham, hark you, just as you did 'Old Grizzly.' I'm your master, now! Come, I know all your plans. I know where you've hidden everything about among the rocks. I know that you were to have a cart to run them off to-night! *I'll* get the cart! I'll have all brought away in the next three nights. I'll not touch your things; not a stiver of them will I take from you. *But you two shall be mine!* Body and soul, you shall be mine, or I'll see you both swinging on the same gallows!—march! You must be three miles from here by sunrise; so, move briskly, Ephraim Moggs, as if the whisky were as fresh and as full in you this morning, as it was last night!"

Droopingly, the two sped away under the guidance of Gorham; groaning and moaning as they went, but otherwise silent. They spoke not even to each other.

They had found a new master, in one quite as wicked, but even more terrible than the old.

Chapter XXXII

MIGNON

The two, Voltmeier and Fergus Wallace, now stood upon the last barrier range of mountains between them and the river. The elevations had gradually lessened. The heights which they occupied were very noble and very beautiful, but as mere pigmies in contrast with the gigantic masses from which they had descended. No river was yet perceptible; but the air trembled with faint murmurs, mournful echoes, from the perpetual roar of its trembling waters.

The travelers looked down upon the beautiful slopes of a valley which bore its undulations also; but these were hardly distinguishable from the height upon which they stood.

Through the valley stole, or leapt, a little streamlet, which looked like a silvery serpent in the afternoon sun. It wound its way through green banks of verdure, dotted with varieties of wild flowers of all colors, that sprinkled it with a gay and beautiful regularity, almost like that of a carpet fashioned in the loom.

These aspects were confined, however, to the margin of the streamlet. Farther removed, they beheld a tract of an almost perfect green, while, more remotely, spread another tract—the herbage of which, stretching away in the distance, and rising up along the hill-slopes on either hand, was as exquisitely blue as the ether, and appeared to lose itself and blend with the horizon. A grateful breath from odoriferous shrub-trees, brought on the breezes, through the mountain gorges, reached the wayfarers, and fanned them with a delicious coolness.

Along these gorges and valleys the soil is exceedingly fertile, producing great forest-trees, and dense groves of calycanthus, and other odoriferous varieties.

Down the valley, but yet distant, the eye of Fergus could distinguish great corn-fields, maize, and a more beaten pathway, which crossed the little streamlet over a rocky bed, and just on the edge of a little precipice, over which the waters tumbled in an even sheet of foam. Cultivation here began to give proof that they were approaching a settlement of wealth and refinement.

"Was this the habitation of Voltmeier?" so Fergus asked himself. The former said nothing, but led the way across the stream, into a sudden gorge of the hills—the crags beetling over like a tunneled passage, and darkening all the route, until, suddenly, they burst forth into the broad sunshine, and another valley spread below them, stretching far, with all the varieties of hill and dale; the widened streamlet reappearing along the meadows; green fields enlarging to the eye; slope upon slope seemingly in highest cultivation, the whole rounded at a point, where the hills seemed to grow and accumulate, in a beautiful avenue of forest-trees; from a gorgeous clump of which, in the rear, rose a stately mansion, with a mountain for its back-ground on the north and east, and the whole beautiful amphitheatre between the closing hills, on the two sides, and rear, opening only on the south, southwest, and west.

"Keovala!" said Voltmeier, riding forward.

"Your place, uncle?" inquired Fergus, spurring after him.

"Yours, Fergus, if you please," replied the other, turning round upon his horse, and looking, with his sweet smile of mouth and eyes, full into the eyes of the youth. The moment after he rode forward, saying no more.

What did he mean by this speech? Fergus did not comprehend him. But for the pleasant smile which accompanied it, the youth might have held it to be a sneer, or a jesting allusion to the well-known superlative of Spanish compliment.

He was confused for the moment, and, in that moment, Voltmeier had disappeared behind a rock.

The route was changed. On a sudden Fergus found himself within another gorge—a dark fissure in the mountain, which had been disparted by some convulsion of nature. The beautiful amphitheatre of plain, valley, verdure, green fields, and grand dwelling, had gone suddenly from sight, as if it had been a vision in a dream.

The road now wound among a continuous chain of peaks, passing between them, in a series of little gorges or passages, which were rarely wider than an ordinary carriage-track.

But Fergus noted that the descent was continued and regular. For another brief moment they emerged from these gorges, rounding an eminence, and once more the grand valley appeared in sight, broad in the beautiful sunset, with all its appurtenances of cultured field and lovely streamlet, grand trees and noble dwelling.

But only for a few moments did it appear. Again it passed from sight, swift as before; the great sides of another elevation rising up between their eyes and the prospect.

Voltmeier curbed his horse till Fergus came up beside him.

"This," said he, pointing to a circular mound in front, "this, Fergus, is artificial. It is one of those mounds, so frequently found in our country, which, in the common ignorance and want of thought, have been called Indian mounds or tumuli. They were never raised by any red men, or any nomadic people. The red men do not claim them. Their traditions all ascribe them to a superior and civilized race of white people, whom their ancestors, coming from the great West, overrun, overthrew, and destroyed. When we shall round this eminence, you will have 'Keovala' immediately at your feet, and from that point your eye may take in the whole valley at a glance."

Then they rode forward, Fergus following, and preparing, with all eyes, to survey once more the beautiful vision which had tranced his sight before, when the thought of it was all driven from his brain by another vision, more surprising, more sweet than all, in which all others were forgotten.

They had nearly circled the mound, and Voltmeier had stopped his horse at the point whence the survey was to be made, Fergus still following, when a wild cry of pleasure, from a full, sweet voice, sounded in his ears, and the moment after his eyes were dazzled by a flash, as it were—that of a light figure—a girl in white costume, with a rich green bodice, who darted suddenly from the side of the mound, and with admirable dexterity planted herself on the back of Voltmeier's horse, and grasped the rider about the waist, with the words:

"Ah, papa! I've caught you at last!"

"My Mignon!" exclaimed the father, with a slight tremor in his voice. "My Mignon!"

Fergus Wallace now saw no valley, and Voltmeier forgot to remind him that the beautiful amphitheatre lay fairly beneath his feet.

The two riders wound their way below, Fergus slowly following, and noticing only that the girl ever and anon cast a stealthy glance behind her, from the ticklish seat which she still maintained, with the grace and ease of one who had long since become familiar with all sorts of horsemanship.

Chapter XXXIII

AT KEOVALA

"Papa, who is the man behind us?" was the whispered inquiry of the girl to her father, looking round at Fergus, even as she spoke.

"What man, Mignon?"

"Why, the man riding behind us!"

"Man! That's not a man, pet."

"Not a man, papa? What are you saying? Haven't I eyes?"

"They are of very little use to you, baby, if you call that a man. Why, child, that's a strange creature—not yet described by the naturalists. I caught him in the mountains. He does look something like a human being, it is true, but upon closer examination you will see that he is a nondescript."

"A what? Come! come! papa. No more of your nonsense. Tell me who he is and what he comes here for!"

"Come, come, baby, and be patient! You will hear all in time."

"But why not tell me at once, papa; now, as we ride?"

"For the best of reasons. It's a long story, and I'm quite tired already, in running down the animal—"

"Oh! foolish, obstinate papa!"

"Oh! curious, pettish puppee!"

"Can't you now, dear papa, satisfy my curiosity?"

"Not, baby, while I exercise you in that beautiful virtue which men call patience, and which women so rarely practice."

"And which you make a torture, papa, sometimes, instead of a virtue. Now, only tell me his name, papa?"

"His name?—oh, yes! His name, or rather that of the species in which I rank him, is, 'Iliacus-Troijanus-Hellanus—'"

"Oh, pshaw! papa! You wicked papa!" And she began pummeling him with one of her pretty little hands, until she was near falling off from the horse.

"Have done, you monkey, and hold on, or I'll make the animal devour you. He has terrible teeth, and such claws!—"

"You provoking papa!"

This little dialogue, which served only to show in what excellent spirits Voltmeier reached his home, and that his daughter was sufficiently the woman to be impatient in her curiosity, was entirely lost to Fergus, in the space which he had suffered to divide him from his uncle. But his eyes had been doing double duty in surveying the bright creature whose introduction had been so unceremonious. That bound from the tumulus to the back of the horse, seemed to show, along with her graceful agility, that she was largely free from city sophistications, and the rigid conventionalities of fashionable society. But so graceful had been the movement, and so lovely seemed the form and features of the actor, that Fergus saw no want of propriety in the action, and the fair face—Mignon was a perfect blonde—the golden hair, which streamed loosely and long from under the chinchilli boy-cap which she wore, falling down and literally overspreading her shoulders, riveted his gaze, while the oblique glance which she sometimes cast behind her, showed him a large full eye, which as yet he could only conjecture was of a sweet cerulean blue.

These fettered him in a long muse of reverie and watch together, from which he was only aroused by the voice of his uncle, calling to him to ride up, when he himself had stopped his horse in front of the dwelling.

The girl at the same moment leapt lightly to the ground, leaving Voltmeier to make a more deliberate descent. Two negro servants, in a modest livery, showed themselves promptly to take the horses; and ere Fergus had ridden up, a tall, elderly lady made her appearance on the piazza, where she was joined immediately by Mignon.

Both came forward to meet Voltmeier, who, taking the arm of Fergus within his own, ascended the steps to meet them.

"Gertrude," he said, addressing the elder lady, "I have found a kinsman. For you, Mignon, I have brought a cousin. This is my nephew, Fergus Wallace."

"My cousin!" exclaimed Mignon, as she gave her hand, and then ingenuously enough she exclaimed:

"Oh! I'm so glad, papa!"

Miss Gertrude was kind and cordial, but undemonstrative. The two young people gazed on each other in silence for a while. Voltmeier said, quietly enough:

"I will tell you about it hereafter, and explain all. Enough now that I tell you that the finding of my nephew was one of the most remarkable incidents of my life, and possibly of his also."

Here he seemed disposed to pause; but Mignon exclaimed:

"Oh! tell us all about it, papa. Tell us at once, papa."

"To-night—some other time—that is, if you do not show yourself too impatient, Mignon."

"Oh, papa! You are so provoking with your mysteries. But *you* will tell me, Cousin Fergus, won't you?"

And the ingenuous frankness and simplicity with which she caught his hand, and the sweet entreaty which spoke in her large and soft blue eyes, were irresistible with the young man, though without moving him to the desired revelation. He was able, however, to reply, though his heart beat rapidly as he felt himself called upon to use his tongue.

"Your father can better tell you than I. He found me senseless, and I knew nothing for some time after. To his surgical care and attendance, perhaps, I owe it now that I am living and here."

"Oh! how was it, papa?"

"Not now, baby. To-night."

"Yes, you put me off as if I *were* a baby. And you were not here on my birthday, papa. How was that? Thursday last, papa, you know, and I was seventeen! Aunty and myself both thought of you. But you did not think of us. Why did you not bring Cousin Fergus in time, and where are my birthday presents?"

"Seventeen!" said the father. "Impossible! You are a mere child yet—hardly more than fourteen or fifteen at farthest. It is monstrous that a little thing like you should presume to be seventeen."

"Little?" said the girl, looking askant at Fergus, and raising herself to her full height. "Little! Well, I confess that I am not a giantess—not a great tall masculine creature—but neither is Aunty—and—but I won't let you worry me, papa."

"That's a good puppee! Only be you so amiable as not to suffer yourself to worry papa. There, go with your Cousin Fergus, into the piazza, and into the garden, and show him 'Keovala,' and all its pretty things. He will tell you all he knows of his adventures, and you will tell him all you know about—the kittens!"

"Come, Cousin Fergus. Papa is forever trying to make fun of me.

Kittens, indeed! That's his fine humor, Cousin Fergus, and I've no doubt he thinks it wit. Come with me, and I will show you the garden, and you shall tell me everything you know."

Fergus was not unwilling, and the two went forth together.

Voltmeier watched their figures as they passed from the parlor with much of that sort of anxious scrutiny with which he had noticed the look and words of his nephew during their late progress. It seemed, for the time, that he forgot the presence of Miss Leyfen-holdt, for he murmured:

"It is well! And yet—it might have been!"

"What is well, Leonard? What might have been?" asked Miss Gertrude.

He looked at her with a stern sadness of gaze as he replied:

"We are still children, Gertrude, and the saddest of all children, when age is creeping upon us, since then, unlike the wisdom of children, we are perpetually looking back upon the past! The true wisdom now is to bury memory, and live only with thought."

"But is this true, Leonard?"

"What is true?"

"This story of your nephew? You never told me that you had a nephew."

"No! and it is to my shame that I did not know it myself till accident—you will call it Providence—threw the boy in my way, with all the credentials on his person establishing the fact. He is the son of my half-brother, Fergus Wallace, from whom he takes his name. But give me time, Gertrude. You are almost as curious as Mignon."

"He is quite a handsome young man, Leonard."

"Ah! woman-like. You see only the physical charms—the animal perfection. I tell you, Gertrude, that young man has in him the best elements of manhood. Give him time and opportunity only, and you will see."

"And give *me* time and opportunity, brother Leonard, and I will *judge*, as you have done, and I trust come to a like conclusion."

This was said with some little air of pique.

Miss Gertrude Leyfenholdt was not a beauty—something of an antique, indeed, without having become a gem—to the eye at least. But she wore her maiden honors and advantages with due meekness, and it is doubtful if she ever thought even of leap-year as a period when she might assert some grateful privileges. She was calm of manner, gentle of temper, with something of phlegm in her constitution, though it may be that her undemonstrative carriage might be due to the fact that she too had suffered losses, as well as from the world's denial.

Chapter xxxiv

STUDIES OF THE BEAUTIFUL

"And so," said Mignon Voltmeier, as the two young people went forth together, "and so you are my cousin, Fergus Wallace! I like the name, Cousin Fergus; and I like you, too, Cousin Fergus, already. We must be good friends, you know, as we are cousins. Shan't we, Cousin?"

"To be sure we shall, my fair Cousin Mignon," replied the youth, catching freedom from the young girl's frankness, which was evidently the most perfect artlessness, and yet worthy to be the perfection of art. He, too, had hitherto lived an unsophisticated life, comparatively in the solitude, with an experience of society quite too small to have developed any rule of forms, in conflict with, or for the restraint of, the natural man. "So we shall, Cousin Mignon. I am sure I shall be very happy while I am here with you. You shall show me all the beauties and wonders of 'Keovala.' "

"And so I will; but, Cousin Fergus, you must begin to win my favor, first, by telling me all about your coming, and your hurts on the road, and papa helping you; and where you came from, and how it is that papa and none of us ever heard of you till now, Cousin Fergus."

"Why, Cousin Mignon, it would take a month to answer all these questions."

"The very reason why you should begin to answer them at once."

"The very reason I should not attempt to answer them at all."

"Now, look you, Cousin Fergus, don't you be imitating papa, already, in that mocking and worrying temper which he has, of trying to put off and baffle my curiosity under pretense of teaching me patience. Papa's a sad mocker, and so provokes me that I sometimes call him Mephistopheles—"

"Mephi—what?"

"Why, Mephistopheles."

"And who's 'Mephistopheles'?"

"What! have you never read the 'Faust' of Goethe?"

"Never!"

"Oh! how charming! You ignorant cousin! Well, I will teach you. We shall read 'Faust' together. It is *the* grand metaphysical drama, and all sorts of a mystery; and Mephistopheles is a form of the old Satan himself, and he buys up the soul of Faust, you see—but we'll read it together, Cousin, or I'll get papa to read it for us at night. He reads it beautifully."

"Yes, that *will* be charming. But, Cousin Mignon, I'd rather hear *you* read it."

"Would you? Well, I will! But now for your story. Tell me all. Here—let us go to the grove yonder. That's *my* thicket, Cousin Fergus. I read there. I have nice benches, and—but begin, Cousin. You can tell me as we go."

"But, Cousin Mignon, you have told me nothing of 'Keovala.' Be generous, now, and tell me all of this beautiful little world which you inhabit."

"You think it beautiful, Cousin?"

"Very beautiful," and his eyes scanned closely every feature of the sweet, innocent face under his gaze. In that, rather than in Keovala, did he behold the beauties of Keovala. The exquisitely fair skin, which, exposed to mountain air, and the free glances of the mountain sun, was yet free of spot or freckle. Never was skin more fair, pure, and soft, and delicate. She was as perfect a blonde as ever blossomed in the cold regions of the north. The golden hair floated free, like fine-spun silk, long, flowing, and beautifully fine. A delicately wrought nose, an exquisitely chiseled mouth, with lips neither large nor thin, but of a certain indescribable pulpy ripeness, chin finely rounded and well developed, and eyes that could dilate with every emotion, large and full, and arched with brows of a darker hue than her hair—these constituted the *ensemble* of charms, such as Fergus had never before beheld in woman. No wonder that he found all the beauties and wonders of "Keovala" in the miniature creation of loveliness immediately under his eye. His eye and mind were equally absorbed and lost in the study.

Poor Fergus! little did he dream that the eyes of another were watching his, with the intensity of a passionate interest, from the heights above; that Voltmeier, the uncle, stood in the obscure shadows of tree and boulder, and beheld every movement of the pair below. No word could he hear, but the distance was hardly too great to prevent his detection of each emotion. What purpose had Voltmeier in this espionage, which would seem to be ignoble, we shall learn hereafter.

Chapter xxxv

THE WATCH

"I thought to find you here, and at this hour," said the voice of Voltmeier, suddenly surprising them, and startling Fergus Wallace from his propriety.

"This is one of Mignon's favorite studies," continued the father; "and here she sings her vesper song. Are we to have it now, Baby?"

"Not this evening, Papa. I don't feel like singing now. I'm not in the humor, Papa."

The father, in a fatherly, yet authoritative manner, led the way back to the house, Mignon clasping his hand closely and chattering to him like a bird, and Fergus silent, abstracted, on the other side.

Regaining the piazza, Mignon retired to the interior, while Voltmeier and Fergus took their seats, and the former began somewhat abruptly, as follows:

"You mentioned, Fergus, a certain Major Henry, of Spartanburg, who had been your friend; and expressed a purpose to write to him promptly. Suppose you do so to-night. Take your seat at the library table, and pen your letter, and it shall be dispatched in the morning. Leave it, properly addressed, on the table. You will find there all the necessary materials. I could wish that you would say no more in that letter, than simply to advise him that you are here, in safety, with your relatives. You should, of course, report to him your adventures, your mishap, your fortunate escape and recovery, and promise a further communication, at an early opportunity, when you will be more explicit as to your future. From something that dropped from you in our mountain progress, I gather that you contemplated a connection with Major Henry in the practice of the law. While, of course, very grateful to that gentleman, I would beg you not to commit yourself. There may be good reasons why you should *not* return to Spartanburg; and it may be your policy to commence your profession here, in our county town, and in the other contiguous county towns, where there is now, as I happen to know, a good field, and a good prospect of a successful practice. I beg you, my dear Fergus, to convey to your friend *my* assurance that you will not only have my assistance—which is not inconsiderable—but that you are advised of superior advantages here, in your profession. You will believe me, when I tell you that I am prepared and resolved to work in your behalf, as if you were my own son. At our leisure we can go into details, when I will give you a complete chart of the prospect, and the superior advantages which will await you here. At all events, I *require* of you, responding to the last appeals of your mother, at least a few months trial with *me*. You must, in accordance with her wish, afford me the opportunity in your own legal phrase, to put myself *rectus in curia*. I shall never be too grateful to your dear mother—very dear to me, Fergus—for affording me this opportunity to do that justice to her son, which was probably denied to herself. Can you comply with my wishes in these respects, Fergus?"

The young man was not wanting in proper acknowledgments. Voltmeier had been growing upon his regards as well as his esteem. He promised. The other resumed:

"You will need some additions to your wardrobe. You will need various supplies, which I can not decide upon. You will suffer me to be your cashier. You have been robbed of all your money. You can return mine, if you think proper, from your first fee in a land case. My sister and daughter will cheerfully accompany you to the county town of ——, where you will procure anything you need. I shall be absent for a few days from Keovala, but you will say nothing of my intention at present."

Here he put a pocket-book, well-filled, into the hands of the young man. The wardrobe deficiencies of Fergus had been pressing upon him, so as to occasion some anxiety. Youth, in the presence of beauty, is necessarily somewhat anxious, clad in a coat soiled by travel, and in trowsers of too doubtful integrity to permit of such mountain clambering as was likely to be undertaken under the auspices of a girl of the mountains, so wild of mood as Mignon Voltmeier.

Fergus felt oppressed at taking the money. But so graciously was it offered, with so little ostentation, and his necessities were so great, that he soon overcame his very natural scruples. And there were his mother's injunctions and her avowed expectations. He murmured his thanks.

"One thing more," said Voltmeier. "It is curious to know that, in robbing you, the robbers overlooked one relic of value, which you had in your bosom, and which I have saved. That relic was, in fact, the safety of your life. It is the watch of my brother—of your father."

"Good God, sir! Is it possible? My poor mother gave it me on her death-bed. She had parted, in her poverty, with every valuable, every jewel, but she still clung to that, and bade me always wear it."

"Poor Catharine!" exclaimed Voltmeier, in such tones as filled the young man's eyes with tears; but struggling through them, he continued:

"She made me put it on at once and wear it, and required me to preserve it sacredly as the only memorial—that, and my poor father's desk—which she had to leave me."

"Poor, poor Catharine!"

And Voltmeier's head drooped upon his palms, while his elbows rested upon his knees. Then, uplifting himself, he drew the maimed watch from his pocket, still keeping it covered in his hands.

"The watch saved your life, Fergus. It received the first bolt of the bullet which struck you down. Hit obliquely, the ball glanced from the watch, shattering it as you see. I have preserved it, that you might see how narrow was your escape, and how much you owe to this last gift of your blessed mother."

He gave to Fergus the watch as he spoke. At that moment, and while the latter was curiously surveying it, Mignon reappeared, and seeing the battered toy, she conceived the facts in an instant.

"Oh, let me see it, Cousin Fergus!—How it is shattered!"

"It saved his life, Mignon."

"He was shot, then?"

Voltmeier only nodded.

"Now, now, papa! You *must* tell me all. I can't be patient any longer."

And she seated herself on his knee, watch in hand, and her finger pointed to the blood-stains still striping the gold. Miss Gertrude made her appearance at this moment, and Voltmeier could no longer resist their joint and clamorous demands for the whole story. Fergus retired to his room; and we who have witnessed the scenes need not now listen to the narrative, which, of course, began only with Voltmeier's discovery of the body of Fergus in front of the Harness cottage. Night closed in upon the group still in the piazza, and Fergus only rejoined it to be summoned in to supper.

*　*　*　*　*

The next morning, when Fergus arose, Voltmeier was gone.

Having, in this chapter, again introduced, passingly, *our* friend, and Fergus Wallace's friend, Major Henry, of Spartanburg, it is, perhaps, proper, in this place, to mention that the Major was one day—some weeks before this scene—surprised by the visit of a stranger, who brought him a splendid black horse, as a present, with an accompanying letter, from the unknown and mysterious source from which he had been in the habit of receiving annually a gift, acknowledging a previous service. By the northern papers, about the same time, advices were had of the sailing of the German artist, Gellert, for Europe.

Chapter XXXVI

A NEW TEACHER AND
OTHER LESSONS

For six days Voltmeier did not reappear. Whither had he gone? Hereafter, we may hear from himself, or find means for conjecture. Meanwhile, the two young people were hardly conscious of his absence. They had music and study, conversation, pleasant rambles in grove and garden, up the sides of rocky heights, whence they looked down upon leaping waterfalls, and hearkened to the wedded music of breezes gliding through long avenues of shadow, seeking the cool grottos which harbor murmuring fountains. And they had youth, and a nature each which had never suffered from any warping of convention. Under the teachings of Mignon, Fergus began the study of the German. She taught him orally, and the German tongue, rugged to his ear at first, became so much music when falling from her lips—not that he made any very rapid progress. He was too much absorbed in the melody to memorize the language. Still, he picked up words, here and there, and caught meanings from her lips far other than the words conveyed. His studies were slow enough, but never tedious.

But soon Aunt Gertrude became a party to these rambles, songs, and studies. The good lady seemed now to show some anxiety; but, to these young people, what could occasion this anxiety? She had never shown any like anxiety before. Was it because of Voltmeier's absence? She had been long accustomed to his frequent departures from home, and his long delays to return.

Mignon at first welcomed her aunt's presence at their studies, and challenged her praises at the progress of her pupil. But at length it occurred to her that the good aunt might interfere with, and somewhat embarrass, Fergus in his lessons.

The truth is, Miss Gertrude indiscreetly suffered her anxiety to be seen, in the fact that, when she joined them, it was always suddenly, and operated like a surprise. It suddenly occurred to Mignon that they were watched.

This discovery, perhaps, argued a growing consciousness in her own bosom, which somewhat disquieted her. She noted that Fergus showed himself uneasy at the presence of her aunt. She felt that, on such occasions, there was a constraint upon his conversation; and she also herself felt a sympathy with this feeling of constraint. But, before this discovery, she had said to her aunt, in her usual simple abruptness of style and manner:

"What do you want here, Aunt Gertrude, with that solemn face of yours? Don't you see that you put Cousin Fergus out in his lessons? He don't recite half so well when you are here watching him."

"I am not *watching* him, Mignon, my dear," was the reply, while the cheeks of the aunt were suddenly flushed up to the very eyes; "but can't you conceive that I am as curious as yourself to see what progress he is making? Give me credit for some interest in his studies. And can't you conceive, my dear, that I have as much pleasure in walks in the grove as you can have? You surely know how fond I am of a ramble in the open air, and I prefer to take it in company, you know."

Why should Miss Gertrude be at such pains to account for her presence? That was the question of Mignon—to herself; and why that sudden flush of the cheeks of the aunt in making her apologetic reply? In putting these questions to herself, Mignon suddenly opened clues of thought, which as suddenly sent the warm blood redly into her own cheeks, and kept her silent. She closed the book in which she and Fergus had been reading—closed it with the softest, slowest possible movement of her fingers; rose from the rustic bench upon which they had been setting, and, without a word to either party, moved away in the direction of the dwelling.

"Why, Mignon," said the aunt, "where are you going so suddenly?"

But Mignon did not seem to hear her, and continued moving on in silence. Miss Gertrude felt some vexation, as she said:

"I am afraid, Fergus, I *have* marred your lessons for the day. That child is so willful, so capricious, there's no understanding her."

Fergus was fully conscious that *his* studies had, indeed, been marred for the time, and his pleasures too, but he said, evasively:

"We had nearly got through the lesson, Aunt Gertrude."

"And so you have begun 'Marie Stuart'? I am only afraid that Mignon has been hurrying you on too fast. She is quite too impetuous to be a good teacher."

Fergus thought her the best he had ever known, but he said nothing. The aunt continued:

"The German, Fergus, is not to be acquired in a day. You must take time for it, and to learn it thoroughly, you will need several hours of daily study *by yourself,* and with the grammar in hand."

The lady had shot her bolt, but, as yet, the consciousness of Fergus was not sufficiently demonstrative to comprehend the occult purpose of the shaft. He saw nothing latent in what was spoken, but received it dully, and with no other than its surface meaning. Then the two walked on together, following the steps of Mignon. But she was already out of sight, and was nowhere to be seen by Fergus, when he had reached the dwelling.

After a few brief sentences of a languid conversation, Miss Gertrude also disappeared, to attend to those household duties which she may be supposed to have somewhat neglected in the new *rôle,* which she had assumed, of the circumspect matron, watchful and solicitous of the progress of the young people in the pursuit of knowledge through a German medium.

Fergus sate silent for a while, brooding vaguely over delicious, but disordered fancies, which, as yet, he did not seek to fathom, or to define for himself. At length he suffered from a feeling of vacancy and listlessness. He walked the piazza. He wandered into the flower-garden, in the rear of the dwelling, where he found himself girt by an exquisite variety of shrubs and flowers, native and of foreign origin. But the idiot beauties around him scarcely fixed his eye, and did not kindle his fancies; and, strolling about with a strange feeling of discontent, he finally returned to the dwelling, and sought the library.

It was tenantless, except by himself. He took up a volume of Schiller, but the German characters seemed to swim into mystical mazes before his eyes; and, though he resolved, with the aid of the dictionary, to work out a verse of the great balladist and dramatist of Germany, he found it in vain. He seemed, of a sudden, to have lost every word and phrase that he had already acquired. Was

it because he had lost his teacher? That question suggested itself to
him.

"What a strange girl!" he thought. "Capricious!"

That was the word of Miss Gertrude. What did this caprice
mean? and why should it be any concern of his? Yet, it *did* concern
him. He *felt that;* and then he found himself meditating the thousand charms and fascinations that seemed to be embodied and imbedded in this very caprice. And as he thus meditated, her beauties
arose before his mental vision, the picture of the perfect woman,
most perfect of loveliness, in spite of all caprice; and a delightful
dream possessed his fancy, seeming, indeed, to fill his eyes—a vision
of a sylph-like form, with golden hair floating free in billowy sweeps
and tresses, so silken-fine that the zephyrs flung them out, toying
with them at their own free will. Then those great dewy, bright
blue eyes lighted up the whole face with a sudden dawn, even as the
meteor, born with a flash, makes a sudden glory of all the sky. Yes,
as the meteor. But how beautiful!

And, lost in these delicious reveries, sleep came to him, as if to
give rest to fancies that might have become too acute for a too long
endurance. He lay upon the sofa in a slumber that had no dream,—
nor knew that, while he thus lay unconscious, a fairy-like creature
glided into the room, and stood over him for a moment. A merry
smile was upon her mouth at first, and she was just about to clap
her little hands, and shriek playfully in his ears; but suddenly she
arrested herself. A grave expression passed over her features, and she
withdrew in perfect silence.

Had the lesson of Aunt Gertrude already produced its effect? But
a day before, and she would certainly have roused the sleeper by a
wild laughter and clapping of hands. And now, she stole away to her
own chamber, possibly to sleep also, while some suggestive fancies
should make of her dreams a premonition, seconding that of Aunt
Gertrude.

That day they read no more. That night, in spite of all the entreaties of her aunt, who felt that she might possibly have done some
mischief, Mignon resolutely refused to sing and play. And Fergus
went to bed, musing sadly, having had no music in any form.

Chapter xxxvii

AN EVENING AT KEOVALA

At the beginning of the sixth day, Voltmeier suddenly showed himself at the breakfast table. He had returned to Keovala some time in the night; none but the servants knew at what hour, and neither Miss Gertrude nor Mignon were accustomed to inquire as to his movements.

Voltmeier was affectionate and kind as usual; was quite as cordial to Fergus as ever, and asked pleasantly after his occupations during his absence. Mignon was silent as well as her aunt, leaving Fergus to make his own answer, which he did with the utmost frankness.

"And so you have commenced with the German. And how does he get on, Baby?"

Miss Gertrude here interposed.

"I am afraid that Mignon is hardly the teacher for Fergus. She is too impatient, and is hurrying him a little too fast for thoroughness. She has commenced with reading 'Marie Stuart.' "

Voltmeier fixed a steady glance on the speaker, looking curiously and inquiringly into her face, and there was a slight expression of sternness in his gaze, and in the grave tones of his reply:

"And not an unwise selection, Gertrude. 'Marie Stuart' is a good play for the beginner. But *I* will help Mignon, Fergus, in your studies."

The eyes of the aunt sank under his gaze.

It seemed to Fergus that the face of Voltmeier was unusually wan; that it had grown older, indeed, and that there was a certain sadness and haggardness in his very smile, which argued the presence of some secret care, or some oppressive thought.

But the ladies did not seem to notice this change, and did not express any anxiety. They had evidently been as little accustomed to study his looks and habits as to note his movements to and fro. Voltmeier had taught them, indeed, by a simple process of training, that he was not a person to be watched or studied.

Soon, however, as with an effort of will, the clouds cleared off from the countenance of the uncle, and he assumed once more his sportiveness of mood and language; but the instincts of the nephew were quite too quick and shrewd not to see that the change was the result of effort; that the present aspect was a forced one, in conflict with his mood; that propriety demanded of him a more scrupulous method of looking his uncle in the face.

There was no change during the day to indicate any subject of disquiet in any of the household. The young people strolled or read as usual; and, with the night, they had music, both Voltmeier and Mignon playing and singing, without ostentation, and simply, as it seemed to Fergus, in compliance with a long-established habit.

The hours went by unconsciously to the little circle; and even Miss Gertrude forgot their progress till the sudden strokes of the clock, beating twelve, prompted her to rise and give the signal of departure to Mignon.

When the ladies were gone, Voltmeier also paced the room, but now in silence; in which, as he seemed disposed to persevere, Fergus took it as a hint that his uncle held the *evening* to be legitimately at an end. The young man was not himself disposed to sleep. His imagination had been too much exhilarated by what he had heard during the evening's communion and discourse. He did not know that Voltmeier was slow to sleep, and prompt to wake, and for years had given himself but few hours for repose. The "good-nights" were exchanged affectionately between them, Voltmeier's being that of a father—"Good-night, Fergus! good-night, my son!"

How the tones and words sank into the heart of the young man—thrilling it to the core with a like tenderness. Voltmeier was left alone; and in an instant after—what a change!

As soon as the sound of the retiring footsteps of Fergus Wallace had ceased, Voltmeier rose from his seat, passed to the door of entrance and locked it carefully. The house was silent. He returned to the chair where he had been sitting, resumed the seat, but only for a moment; then paced the apartment for the space of several minutes, during which progress he took a little silver box from his pocket, from which he detached a single small dark pill, which he hastily swallowed. His face, meanwhile, seemed to have lost all its animation. The vitality of eye and muscle seemed wholly gone; the skin was of a corpse-like complexion; all the features seemed to have suffered collapse; and, as if incapable of farther use of his limbs, he suddenly sank into the seat beside the center-table, and covered his face with his hands. And such, for a space of twenty minutes, was his posture. Another change of look and posture as suddenly as before. He kept his seat beside the table, his left elbow now resting upon it, and his left hand supporting his cheek. His eye grow brighter; his lips were closely compressed together; his head was thrown forward; his legs drawn up, and his feet drawn in beneath the chair. His whole frame was contracted suddenly, as if with spasm, but his attitude was crouching, as if in act to spring. Every muscle now seemed rigidly set, as with a desperate purpose, while his eyes glared out, brightening momently more and more, with a savage sort of intensity, as if seeking a victim or an enemy. Wonderful, these changes. He who, but an hour before, had seemed to his happy family but a mild and blessing patriarch, seemed now to chafe beneath the goadings of some remorseless passion which possessed every avenue of his nature.

And thus for a while he sat, silent, crouching, with his eyes dilating, looking out on vacancy! It was quite evident that his glance took in none of the objects which were yet within their scope. There was no rich carpet beneath his feet; no piano within reach of his arm; no harp in the corner; no pictures on the walls; no grand curtains to the great windows which reflected the big light of the grand astral lamp which still burned before him, as little seen as all the rest.

What then did he behold in that world of vacancy, from which deep, and perhaps dreadful thoughts and fancies had shut out each material object? It was a terrible spectacle, when we remember the wise and thoughtful teacher of that happy, unconscious little family, but one hour before.

Chapter xxxviii

SHADOWS

Thus, for two mortal hours! Fixed statue-like, motionless, he sate, but not all the while silent; nor were the features of his face unmovable. They now expressed the various moods, passions, or feelings, which were the inspiration of his language. He spoke, after a while, in low, subdued tones, as if he were unwilling to hear his own voice—a broken monologue; and, as we listen, we may extract a meaning, here and there, which may possibly illustrate, in some degree, that history of which something is already written, but of which we have yet much more to learn.

"Somehow, a clue has escaped me! I had shaped it all for security! I had prepared all things to break the links which should connect my future with my past. But there is a fate in it! It is one of the damnable characteristics of guilt and sin, that we know not where they are to end. There is no limit set to the consequences. We plant the seed, but who shall answer for the bearing of the tree? What ashes shall there be in these beautiful apples of Sodom? What poison in the vine which bears such gorgeous flowers? Who shall say that our very whispers shall not be borne by the winds, and be written upon the face of the firmament? What wisdom shall provide that the worm shall not undermine the tower? What are all human precautions or securities? And shall I not now be permitted to begin that new life? —to acquire those securities, from conduct in the future, which had been temporarily forfeited by conduct in the past?" Here a pause.

"Ha! who spoke?"

He looked about him. Save by himself, the room was vacant as before, and, but for his own voice, all was silent.

"Surely, I heard a voice!" Another pause.

"If ever ear ever heard, mine did!" and he seemed to listen, while his eyes roved the apartment.

"Speak again!" he cried, still keeping his position.

"Speak again, whoever thou art! I have no fears!"

But there was no answer to the challenge.

"Surely, it said: 'What, claim the securities of heaven, while in hourly enjoyment of the wages of hell?'

"So it spake!—short, sharp, keen, satirical, like the mocking fiend of Faust. Demon or Deity, speak again!"

A long pause, and utter silence. Then, suddenly:

"It is the voice in my own soul, if soul there be! It is what men call the voice of conscience, and surely the voice of conscience is now sustained by that of reason. Shall I hope escape from the penalties of crime, while enjoying all its pleasant fruits? Atonement for crime means something other than mere forbearance from crime. To say that I will sin no more, is not enough. Atonement means *restoration*, as well as repentance.

"How can I restore? Have I the courage for *that*, even if that be possible? What, sacrifice *all* for which I have striven? Make this dear child a beggar? Make pangs and trials of the very tastes I have tutored in her, so that she shall curse the very memory of her father? Impossible, my Mignon! Though I perish, *thou*, at least, shalt be safe. I must still toil for this and for thee. Toil! and—*endure!*

"And yet, God or devil! what have I not endured already? What a horrible spectacle! They are before me now. The two miserable, mangled wretches. I see the shattered skull beneath the rocks; the broken arms, putrid and fragmented, splintered, shooting through the dismembered masses of clay and stone! I hear their shrieks, in the sudden moment of their doom! My brain whirls as I remember! I wonder I do not madden! Yet, *this* was not *my* crime! I dreamed not of this. I meditated it not. I but sought to destroy one of the material links that bound me to the past, but sought not *their* destruction. I counseled their flight. Why, why did they not depart? I would have saved them, as I would save myself, for another start in life."

Again, after a pause, he spake, as if another voice had sounded in his ears:

"Ha! you tell me that Fate is not to be so baffled—that human reason and calculation can not provide against the evidences of crime; that we can not break the links between past, present, and future;

and that all records of human performance are records written—
even as the deeds are done—in the archives of eternity!

"Be it so! I have the strength to endure. I *have* endured! Great
God, what a night! That I should have had the strength for that
horrid task; that I should have struggled through that loathsome
scene, yet held my brain in check from madness. To hide away in
the earth at midnight the putrid carcases of the two miserable
wretches who had followed me so long, while great wings of blackness overshadowed me as I strove, and these terrible voices out of
the blackness cried to me in audible sounds:

" 'We are the hounds of Fate, following at your heels, even as the
Furies tracked the footsteps of Orestes!' "

And then, after a pause, as if some other voice had spoken:

"Aye, I hear you! jeer, jibe, threaten—I fear not! I have still
my mind—my mind! Yet, how could it happen? Was it the miserable
woman, or her more worthless son, or both? Or was it that serpent
creature—Gorham? Yet, how could he, or they, see or suspect? Yet,
some one *must* have seen! It was the woman! Yet, why should
she—"

The question was unspoken. The voice of Voltmeier suddenly
ceased. His head was bent farther forward. He seemed to listen.
Then his eyes, staring wide, followed some object around the apartment, as, unconsciously, he murmured:

"It is lambent—a flame! How beautiful! It is as if the electric
fluid had illuminated a cloud, and bedded itself within it—a little
lakelet of lightning, so subtle, so exquisitely pure, so bright, so
unspeakably beyond light of sun, moon, and stars!

"It is gone! Sounds have been in my ears such as no mortal could
have made; sights have passed before my vision such as no mortal
could imagine."

Then, after a pause:

"Ha, ha, ha! what a fool am I! Hardly stronger than the poor
rustic, who starts back at his own shadow against the wall! It is
here," touching his head; "it is blood upon the brain. I must see to
this. I must take medicine. I must have blood let. There is either
apoplexy or madness here. I must guard against both. *I still command my mind—my mind! There, I am still the master!*"

And, so speaking, he arose from that crouching attitude he had so long maintained, while seated and speaking. He stood erect, arms folded upon his breast, head uplifted, and eyes steadily fixed across the apartment, as if following some spectral Presence.

"Ye wave me on, but I defy you! I have still *my mind*. Over *that* ye have no power. *There*, I am still sovereign. *There*, I defy ye; and, no matter what the fate, I am still its master. Ye may crush, but ye can not subdue. I defy and baffle you."

And he strode forth into the floor, and with clenched hands he struck at vacancy; and, standing erect as an athlete, he seemed to challenge all the Fates at once, while following some visionary object with his eyes around the room.

"Gone! baffled! I have still my mind!"

He took the silver box again from his vest, and swallowed another of the little dark pills.

"I must sleep now," he murmured, rather than spoke. So speaking, he strode, with even steps, towards the lamp, extinguished it, and, amidst the darkness, felt his way toward the grand passage leading to his chamber opposite. He knew it well—but he muttered as he went:

"The soul must brave the dark, even as it faces the light!"

Chapter xxxix

SOMETHING OF THE PROBLEM
SOLVED

How Voltmeier slept, if he slept at all, may not be said; but the next morning he appeared at the breakfast-table as usual; calm, sedate, graceful and easy of manner, kind of remark, and genial with all around him. He had wonderful strength of will so to subdue that demon to his den, who had so fearfully striven with his soul the night before.

But, to the eyes of Fergus, the greater wanness of his cheek was apparent still. There was a hollowness about the eyes that hitherto had not been evident to his own, and, ever and anon, the young man fancied that there was a wandering in the mood and manner of Voltmeier, which argued the presence of some great anxiety. He was prudent, however, and forbore to scrutinize too closely, or to show himself in any degree more conscious, when meeting the gaze of his uncle. But he remarked that he ate but little. He drank his coffee as usual, nibbled at a biscuit, and rose from the table before the family repast was ended. His movements occasioned no remark or observation either from Mignon or Miss Gertrude. Custom seemed to have staled these things to their eyes, which obtruded themselves upon those of Fergus Wallace.

Voltmeier was gazing from one of the windows upon the lawn, when the other parties rose from the table. Soon Mignon gathered up her books, and said to Fergus:

"Come, Cousin Fergus, now for Schiller and Marie Stuart. Let us go study in the grove."

Fergus was prompt in obedience, and, with an armful of books, the two went forth together.

Voltmeier watched them from the window.

It was a beautiful day in spring, all verdancy and sunshine, and the two young people, walking side by side, seemed to be imbued with all its harmonies. Mignon might be seen opening one of her volumes, and pointing to a passage in it as they walked, possibly one of those deep and tender passages in which Marie Stuart gives full play to all that is feminine in her character in the favoring portraiture of Schiller. But in doing so, the books became disordered under her arm, and tumbled to the ground. Fergus hastily gathered them up, and was endeavoring to secure them under his own arm, when, in the effort of Mignon to repossess them, and his struggle to withhold them, they again came to the ground. Then the two strove to gather them, and Mignon, in a fit of laughter, was seen playfully to slap her companion on his shoulder. All this was witnessed from the windows by Voltmeier and Miss Gertrude. A smile might be seen, faint, but grateful, on the face of the former. Miss Gertrude laid her hand on his shoulder.

"Do you see that, Voltmeier?"

"Yes, Gertrude, I see."

"Well?"

"Well, what would you say, Gertrude?"

"Do you understand what it means, Voltmeier?"

"I think I do. The books have fallen. There is an amicable contest between the two cousins as to who shall pick them up. It is so much child's play; the natural exuberance of good spirits in an innocent frame of mind. What more?"

"Play, indeed, Leonard Voltmeier! You are not usually so obtuse. Do you not know what such play will end in?"

"In no quarrel, I hope," was the quiet answer.

"Really, Voltmeier, there is no understanding you. Can it be possible that you are reconciled to those young people falling in love with each other? For that is the end which I see to all this child's play."

"Very likely," was the phlegmatic reply.

"And you are prepared for this?"

"Why not?"

"You are willing, then, to give your daughter to this young man, this stranger, poor, obscure, of whom, as yet, you can know but little?"

"I know everything, Gertrude—everything that has need to be known."

"Oh, that self-esteem, Voltmeier! How should you know, in the brief period in which you have known him."

"To the student of men, Gertrude, it does not need much time to acquire a knowledge of men. There are some natures which lie open, clear as the sunshine, open as the green fields and the blue heavens, to him who has the eyes to see. I persuade myself that this young man is one of them. I persuade myself that I am one of those men who do not need the necessary eye-sight for study. I know this young man just as well as if we had been together a thousand years. There are instincts which, in some men, supply the place of ordinary reason and long experience in others. I never have needed much time to arrive at my conclusions as to the persons whom I meet."

"Ah!—Lavater!—and you are frequently deceived, Leonard."

"Not frequently, I think, Gertrude," was the quiet answer.

"Well, even suppose yourself right in the present instance, Leonard; allow that this young man is honorable and ingenuous; still, you desire something better for your daughter—"

"Nothing can be *better*, Gertrude."

"Something *more*, then, Leonard—something besides—rank, birth —not an obscure—"

"He is my nephew, Gertrude—the son of as noble a woman as ever breathed the air of heaven, and seemed to gather the airs of heaven around her where she came."

He paced the room as he spoke.

"You speak, Leonard, with all the warmth of a lover."

"You force me to a painful confession, Gertrude." He paused in his walk and confronted her. "I *was* her lover, and an unworthy one—"

"Ah!"

"And an unsuccessful one, as I deserved to be. I loved her with all the ardency of a boy's passion."

"And were unsuccessful?"

"I have said it. My elder brother, and my better, won the precious prize, and then I went to Germany."

"I know the rest, Leonard—spare yourself."

"You know nothing, Gertrude. Now that I have begun this dreary history, you shall know the rest. My father wronged the father of this young man, wronged him of his rights and inheritance—and I, Gertrude, in an evil hour, goaded by disappointed passions, I seconded the wrong—I was a party to the act that deprived my half-brother of his marital rights. Should I not rejoice in the opportunity which this boy affords me, to make such atonement as I can? I tell you, Gertrude Leyfenholdt, that I have no dearer hope in the world than to see these young people united. In this way can I make some atonement to the woman whom I loved unwisely, and to that luckless brother whom I did not love too well. Alas! it is my great misfortune that I can not atone, in like measure, for all my offenses."

"Still, Leonard—"

"Still—no more, Gertrude. Let me tell you further. I am not altogether unselfish in this matter. I need not tell you how dearly I love my Mignon. She is the one best treasure in the few affections left me. She is the redeeming sweet in a great cup of bitter which I have yet to drink. It is because I so much love her that I would have her wed this young man. Marriage is a valuable consideration to all women. She is born to look up to a superior, and like a delicate tendril of grace and beauty, to require the steadfast support of a manly breast, a noble heart, and a gifted head. It is not so easy to find men endowed with all these qualifications."

"And you think that you have found them in this young man?"

"I *know* it! I have no question. With these endowments, you will be secure of fidelity in man—that perfection of the virtues, whether in man or woman. I would give to Mignon a husband upon whose bosom she can lean with full faith, assured that every beat of the heart beneath her head is an utterance of truth and love and protection."

Miss Gertrude Leyfenholdt sighed, as with the touch of a painful memory, and sank into a chair, with head resting on her hand, and eyes bent upon the floor. Voltmeier looked upon her tenderly, as if he understood the sigh, and the old memories that occasioned it, brought into activity by something which he had said. He approached her, and laid his hand gently upon her shoulder.

"You, Gertrude," he said, "have had some reason to question that virtue of fidelity in man."

"Do not, Leonard—"

"Nay, fear not, my sister. I would simply say that, as a general rule, you are apt to do injustice to men in your estimate—to be suspicious—jealous—"

"For Mignon's sake, only, Voltmeier."

"I know it. But, be sure of this, that if ever I felt secure of the good faith and the virtues of mortal, I do so feel in the case of this young man. You tell me of his obscurity. He will not remain obscure very long. You allege his poverty. I have shown you that my wealth has been somewhat based upon the wrong done to his father by mine; and, Mignon will need no wealth that he can bring. I tell you, Gertrude Leyfenholdt, that a generous and noble manhood is worth a thousand fortunes. Wealth may take wings, but the qualities of manhood are not only imperishable in this life, but, if we are to believe in the soul existence, as a thing apart, then we must regard them as constituting the capital of the individual, in determining his immortal *status,* and the new point of departure in any future progress he may take."

Such was Voltmeier's philosophy. Miss Gertrude listened in silence; till, rising at last, when the former had ceased to speak, she said:

"God grant it be for the best, Leonard. But I have my misgivings —my doubts."

"Dismiss them. There is a Fate at work which you may not oppose —which I may no longer oppose. Submit."

"And give these children perfect freedom?"

"Ay! Have faith!—children!—Gertrude, have you forgotten that, in another week, Mignon will be eighteen?"

"Yet what a child!"

"Child! In that week she will be a woman. She will love! Love will endow her with a soul. No woman ever has a soul till she loves! This is the mystery of mysteries. Love is the wand of the prophet, to make the rock give forth its waters."

"Oh, what nonsense! Then I have no soul, I suppose."

"You can not lie to me, my poor sister! You *have* loved—you still love! What matters it if you have loved unwisely and in vain? The rock gives forth its waters, though no one may seek them in the wilderness. It is not in vain that we love, not in vain that we toil, though it seems to profit us nothing of the ends proposed. To have developed the woman sensibility and susceptibility is to live. It is mere stolidity, the existence which develops neither. The profit and the loss are nothing. The development is everything. You may not reach the goal for which you set out; but the march is sufficient. Moses was not the less the prophet, not the less worthy, because, while pointing out Canaan to his people, he was unable to reach it himself."

Chapter XL

TRAILING

With the morning, Voltmeier had again disappeared. His sudden and unannounced absenses seemed to occasion no surprise to any of the household, but Fergus, who spoke of it at the breakfast-table. Mignon promptly replied:

"It's the way with papa. One hardly knows anything of his movements; when he will go and when he will come. He says that parting, for however brief a time, is always a sadness and sometimes a pain, and a sudden, unlooked-for return, is always a pleasant surprise where one is beloved, as papa knows he is. Sometimes, he has gone in this manner, and been absent for ten days, and even two weeks, and he will always return by night, when everybody is abed. We only know that he has come by seeing him at breakfast in the morning."

"That should make you sometimes very anxious about his safety, traveling alone among these mountains, where, as I happen to know, there are robbers perpetually wolving about for prey."

"Oh! papa fears nothing! He knows the mountain paths so well; knows all the short cuts; and he always goes armed, and is quick to see and to hear. He has the finest eye for sight, and he's so quick of hearing, that the robber must be a very sharp one indeed, who takes him by surprise."

Somewhat curiously, but innocently — incautiously, perhaps, Fergus insinuated a question.

"But his business, whatever it is, must be a very fatiguing one!"

He was answered quite as innocently:

"So we sometimes think, and chide him for his long, hard rides, but these, he says, are unavoidable. You must know that papa owns large herds of cattle upon his mountains; horses, mules, sheep, and other cattle; and the mountain range is very long; and he has several herdsmen scattered all along, whom he has to see frequently.

Sometimes he buys a herd, and sometimes sells one, and so he makes all his money. He does all this sort of business whenever he disappears from Keovala; and we know nothing about it. Papa loves this sort of life, and he is such a great rider, that he prefers horseback exercise to every other, as, indeed, we all do. He has trained us to it. But, the truth is, as I tell him, he suffers from a sort of Demon of Unrest! He is never satisfied unless he's doing something, and he never likes to stick to one thing long."

Miss Gertrude now said quietly to Fergus:

"I half suspected that Voltmeier would be off this morning, from his giving me a commission respecting you for to-day. He says we must take you to town, if you desire it, as you may wish to make some purchases. Now, if it suits you, the carriage will be at the door soon after breakfast."

"It will suit me, Miss Gertrude—"

"Call her aunt, cousin Fergus, as I do; you have almost as much right. Hasn't he, Aunt Gertrude, and won't you let him?"

The aunt smiled, as she answered, good-naturedly:

"To be sure, Mignon; and to make the effort easier to him, I shall drop all prefix in addressing *him*. He shall be Fergus to me hereafter, and I will be Aunt Gertrude, if he so pleases, to him."

"There, Cousin Fergus; be a good boy, and don't you take your aunt's name in vain!—well, what do you say? Are you for a ride to the village?"

"Oh, certainly—you will both go with me."

"Oh, we never lose a chance to go everywhere. Life sometimes gets to be very humdrum here, at Keovala, though we *do* love it so much; and I have some shopping to do in the village myself. What are you going to buy, Cousin Fergus?"

"Mignon, my dear!" said Aunt Gertrude, rebukingly, with uplifted finger.

"Now, Cousin Fergus, where's the harm in my asking you what you mean to buy? I'd willingly tell you of what I want. There's—now—"

"Really, Mignon!—"

"Oh, Aunt Gertrude! You are such a fault-finder!"

"And you are such a silly child! But go, Mignon, and get yourself ready. There's no time to lose, and I shall order the carriage at once."

Having seen the party off for the country town, let us change the scene, and, without farther seeking to discover whither Voltmeier had gone, we may yet chance to follow in his tracks.

At the foot of that long range of the Apalachia, looking over into South Carolina, of which Mount Tryon is one of the monarchs, a substantial frame cottage, a single story, with shed-rooms attached, and a low piazza in front, stood at a little distance from one of the roads leading southward. Here, about noonday, were grouped together three persons in close consultation. These are all old acquaintances, to whom we need no other introduction than their names.

At the head of a table, with writing materials before him, sate Richard Gorham; opposite him, seated also, was Ephraim Moggs, over whose shoulder leaned his amiable mother. We happen upon them at the moment when Gorham smote the table with his heavy fist, exclaiming—

"None of your dodging, now, Ephraim Moggs! I tell you, the whole truth must come out, or you shall hang, both of you. You shall tell the truth, the whole truth, and nothing but the truth; just as they make you swear in court-houses! *I'd* make you swear it here, if we had a Bible, and if I believed the swearing would bring out the truth sooner than the sight of the gallows. Answer squarely, now, when I ask the question, and don't dodge anything."

Richard Gorham was already playing the master!

Ephraim Moggs looked equally scared and sullen, and answered, doggedly:

"I don't mean to dodge anything. I'll tell you all I know; ax what you pleases."

The mother here interposed. She had been watching Gorham with a savage gaze, that seemed to threaten a burst of violence.

"And what's the right you has, Dick Gorham, to be making Ephraim answer to you, jist as if you was a judge and jury, all in one, I'd like to know? You ain't *my* master, and I reckon you ain't his'n!"

"You'll find that I *am* his master, and yours, too. But your time will come next, old woman. As for my right, it comes from your blowing up them two poor devils, Peters and Swipes, and sending them to Kingdom Come without a moment's warning. Either you both answer *me*, or you answer court and jury, and my evidence will hang you both!"

Here a pause, and his eyes were fastened upon the two with the intense gaze of the serpent, while his expression of countenance was that of a vindictive will, under which, for the moment, the pair quailed in terror. They had known enough of the man to fear his capacity.

"Ax away!" said Ephraim.

"Who was this man, Franz Gellert, that signed this title for the house we're in, and this farm we're on?"

"I don't know! I never seed him but once."

"Where was that?"

"In the lawyer's office."

"What lawyer?"

"Squire Tom Brownlow."

Gorham wrote down the several answers as they were given, and continued:

"Was this man, Gellert, a Jew?"

"Don't know. He looked like a furriner. He was a little old man. That's all I know about him."

"Did you *see* him sign the deed, with his *own* hand?"

"Yes; and two other men seed him, too. They put their hands to the paper jist after him."

"Was 'Old Grizzly' present?"

"No."

"The paper says that, in consideration of three hundred dollars, to him paid by you, he had sold the property to your mother. Did you pay him one copper of money?"

"Not a copper; but I reckon 'Old Grizzly' did."

"And I tell you, Richard Gorham, the property belongs to *me*; it's in my name, ef you kin read the paper."

"And what good turn was it that you did for 'Old Grizzly,' to make him set you up with a farm?"

"Well, I sarved him a matter of seven years, me and Ephraim; and you knows *how*, for two years of that time; and *you* got rich on it, Dick Gorham, ef ever man did; and you've got a plenty of money, of your own, not to *invie* me what's give to me! 'Old Grizzly' said I hed sarved him faithful, and he'd make me comfortable in my old age, jist through nat'ral love and affection."

"Affectionate Grizzly!"

Here we read Gorham's memoranda, as he writes:

["*Mem.*—See after Franz Gellert, Lawyer Brownlow, and the two witnesses, Peter Eckles and Silas Gouge."]

"Did you know Peter Eckles and Silas Gouge, Ephraim Moggs?"

"Never seed them but that one time. Squire Brown called 'em in from the road, jist to sign."

"Now, Ephraim Moggs, about your trial. I wish to know who was the lawyer that got you out of jail by an 'allaboy'?"—*alibi* being understood.

"Squire Brownlow."

"And what do you know about it?"

"I don't know nothing, only he got me cl'ar!"

"No dodging, Ephraim, or no 'allaboy' shall save you another time! Who was the man that swore in court that you slept with him that very night, twelve miles away from Hoppins, when the house was broken into and robbed of all the silver?"

"His name was Furze, or something like it."

"Did you know him?"

"Never seed him till he come to me in jail, and had a talk with me, and told me what I hed to say, and what *he'd* swear to."

"Who sent him to you?—'Old Grizzly?' "

"I reckon—I don't know; 'cept what 'Old Grizzly' telled me himself, a'terwards, and gi'n me warning."

"Who employed the lawyer?"

"Furze brought the lawyer to the jail; that's all I know. The lawyer tell'd me that a friend of mine had got him to git me cl'ar, and sent Furze to him to prove the 'allaboy.' "

Here Gorham made his memoranda.

But the examination ceased, as the gallop of a horse was heard, and a stranger appeared at the entrance, suddenly throwing open the door, while Gorham was most busily employed in making his notes.

The stranger was Voltmeier.

His eye took in the group at a glance; the papers and the title-deed, which lay spread beside Gorham on the table; and, in that glance, and from a previous knowledge of Gorham, Voltmeier readily conceived what mischief was on foot. A pleasant smile, however, played over his features, as he said:

"Good morning, my good people! I am sorry to disturb you, and only called to ask you how far it is to Dr. Columbus Mills' farm, and whether there is any road to put me out?"

He was answered by Ephraim Moggs, while Gorham busied himself in putting the papers out of sight. The stranger thanked him, bade the company "good morning," and, mounting his horse, sped away at a canter. The trio were at the windows, watching with eager eyes.

"Who's that man?" asked Gorham. "I've seen him before, somewhere."

"He looks like a Gineral or a High Sheriff," said Moggs.

"Sheriff, very like! and now I think—he looks for all the world like the man on the white horse that followed close after 'Old Grizzly' *that* day,—you know when; that Friday! What a splendid horse for a charger! Now, Ephraim, if we could only *head* him, at rifle shot, by the next hollow, what a chance! Did you see the gold watch and chain that he carried?"

"I seed the gould chain, but didn't see no watch."

"And what a charger! what a beauty of a horse! Ephraim Moggs, we're getting cold and slow at the business. That man, like as not, has his wallet full of Uncle Sam's paper."

"We lost the *head*, Dick Gorham, when 'Old Grizzly' went off," said Mother Moggs, with something like a sneer, in look, tone, and manner.

"You shall have the head yet," was the self-complacent answer of Gorham. "There's much to be done yet, in these parts. But I'm sorry to lose *this* chance. Why, Ephraim, coward as you are, *you* might have filled your pockets at the next turn of the road by a single rifle shot."

"Look you, Gorham, ef you'd ever been so nigh the gallows as me, you'd fight shy of shooting a Sheriff. As for coward—well, it's no matter jist now."

"Well, he may be the Sheriff, for anything I know. But I don't care to know that cattle any more than you. Still, one *ought* to know, even if only to keep out of their way."

The stranger, meanwhile, rode upon *his* route, and with an energy that prompted the free use of his spurs.

"The old group," he murmured as he rode, "but not a *family* group. I know that subtle villain—Gorham. He tracks me, does he?

Well, we all have our fates, and he seems disposed to fancy that he is mine. But I have throttled more than one fate already, and—let him find the slot if he can."

Meanwhile, Voltmeier rode below, but not in the direction for which he had inquired at the cottage of Moggs. He knew his whereabouts quite as well as Moggs. But he had his purpose in seeing into the condition and associations of the hopeful son and amiable mother; and that he made some discoveries, which he had somehow anticipated, may be gathered from his soliloquy, when he had ridden out of sight of the house.

"So that cunning scoundrel has established himself with those poor devils? He will rule them while he remains. He is pursuing his inquiries; looking into the title, and cross-examining Ephraim. Well, I see his game. But he will make nothing of that blackguard. I guarded all that matter too well. He will fail to follow a single clue, even though he should make his way to the court house, and peer into the privacy of the worthy lawyer Brownlow, who is as great a rascal as himself, and would like just as much as he to make discoveries. But Gellert is in Europe, and as for the John Does and the Richard Roes, who were the witnesses, let them find them if they can. Even should they happen upon Furze, what does he know? Gellert managed *him.* And Gellert is gone. I am safe on these tracks. Still, I must, in turn, watch after this fellow. He is a cold dog, and slow, but cunning as a fox. What does he aim at? Simply to find out a secret—having found one of its clues? Perhaps. He has that sort of curiosity which ingenuity itself will always prompt. But he aims at money also. He shall have none of mine. I am safe. Yet, the wretch annoys me. Somehow there is an instinct that warns me of this man. I must beware of him. If it comes to the worst, why—"

Here he paused, looked behind him, and clutched the butt of the pistol under his belt. He carried a pair of beautiful European weapons, which had been made to order—single barrels; Colt's day had not then come.

"But for *that,*" he continued, "there will be time enough. It may come to that yet, and if so, it will be life against life."

And so he rode, taking a route obliquely off from that which he had hitherto pursued.

That night found him at the house of the Harness family. The brothers seemed to have expected him. The old lady received him with smiles of welcome, especially holding up to his sight the pair of gold spectacles, which he had promised and taken care to send her.

"I sees through them beautiful," said she. "My eyes now air young as ever, when I gits on the specks."

He remained there that night, and until noon the next day— arranging with the Harness brothers touching the purchase of a herd of cattle. This was the ostensible business, but casually, and in a careless manner, he insinuated sundry inquiries in respect to the neighborhood, and learned that there had been less robbery of late along the roads, and but little horse stealing from the mountains.

"The rogues seem to have gone off to furrin parts," said one of the brothers, "but they're not *all* gone, as we hear now and then of a traveler being waylaid and robbed. But there's not so much of it now, specially as we've got up a 'regulator' company, which makes the robbers lie low, and keep dark for the present. There's a chap named Gorham about, from Connecticut, whom the boys suspicions, but we hain't been able to fasten anything upon him. But we're a-keeping a sharp look-out on him."

"*Rid me of him,*" was the mental wish of Voltmeier, as he heard. He rode away at noon, having arranged with the brothers for a business visit to Keovala.

Somehow, as he rode, a sudden notion seized him to visit the mysterious cavern in which "Old Grizzly" and Gellert had so long carried on their secret occupations. It was hardly a purpose in his mind, but an involuntary movement of his impulse or instinct, which led him to turn his horse out of the main road, and seek the successive coverts, by which, in former times, "Old Grizzly" had traveled; not the rude precipitous path coming *from* the "Wolf's Den," but the one, almost equally obscure, but less difficult, by which he had made his way *from* the cavern to the Harness habitation.

The distance was a few miles only, but through dense thickets and broken grounds, over which Voltmeier traveled slowly. He reached, at length, that group of separate boulders which had been so fashioned by nature, and so adapted by art, as to serve the purpose of a stable. Into this he rode, dismounted, and tethered his steed.

Proceeding then towards the cavern, he was somewhat surprised to find a bright glare of light issuing from the otherwise gloomy jaws of the vaulted chamber. Pausing at the entrance for a moment, he peered cautiously into its recesses, and discovered the figure of a man bearing a torch, which he waved along the floor of the cavern, as if in search or examination. A sudden change of position in torch and man revealed the features of the latter, and it was with a momentary feeling of misgiving, apprehension, and irresolution, that Voltmeier discovered the face of Richard Gorham.

Was there a fate in this? Whatever might be the degree of skepticism in the mind of Voltmeier, he was yet superstitiously impressed by the discovery.

"Surely," said he, "this is not a thing of chance! Are the hounds of fate then certainly at my heels? This fellow is making his way, step by step!"

He paused for a moment, irresolute. Then, drawing a pill from his box, he hastily swallowed it, and seeming to brace himself up for the encounter, he strode fearlessly into the cavern, exclaiming loudly:

"Halloa, stranger! what den of devils have you here?"

The torch of Gorham fell from his hands, and his feet hastily trod out the fire. For a moment the transition from the glare of the flame left the cavern in darkness.

Chapter XLI

COVERING THE TRAIL

The moment after, Gorham grasped his rifle, which he had leaned against the side of the cavern, and retreated into its darker recesses—maintaining perfect silence.

"Halloa, my good friend, whoever you are!" said Voltmeier, in his most cheery tones, "what are you afraid of? What have you got to rob in this dismal den of yours? Come out, and let's have a look at you! I'm but a man, like yourself—that is, supposing you to be a man, and not a devil, living in such a dismal den as this of yours!"

"No den of mine," answered Gorham, now coming forward, but with his rifle at *the present,* and his finger on the trigger. He came forward warily, and the smoke having lifted in the cave, and their eyes now equally accustomed to the dim light of the vault, they were enabled to behold each other, though still imperfectly.

"What place is this?" asked Voltmeier, looking about him curiously. "Kindle your torch again, my friend, and let us see the whole of it. You have a match-box, flint and steel, I suppose?"

"Something better," said Gorham, now a little more at ease, and pulling forth one of the old-fashioned pewter vials of phosphorus. The Lucifer match had not yet been kindled for the world's illumination.

Soon the dried sticks were in a blaze on the pavement of the vault, and, with torches in their hands, the two went about the great hall in equally curious contemplation.

"The place has been inhabited," said Voltmeier. "Here fires have blazed before."

"And here is an old knife," said Gorham, displaying it.

"And here is a chisel," quoth Voltmeier. "There has been a lodger here, certainly, at one time or other. What a perfect habitation this for a hermit—for one who had quarreled with the world!"

"Yes, indeed. It might be made very comfortable for a family that wanted to keep dark."

"How long since you discovered it?" asked Voltmeier.

"Hardly an hour ago. I was hunting cattle."

"So was I," was the prompt echo of Voltmeier. "Are you in that line of business?"

"Sometimes; and you?"

"Well, yes; but I'm for *buying* for a dealer in South Carolina. Have you any to sell?"

"I may have in a month's time."

"Where shall I find you then?"

"Down at the foot of Tryon, a little off the Mills' Gap road, at the farm of one Ephraim Moggs."

"Why, I was down in that very neighborhood only two days ago, and, now I look at you, didn't I see you at a house where I called to ask about the way to Columbus Mills'?"

"I was there at Moggs'. But you didn't reach Mills', I reckon?" curiously.

"Not quite. I changed my mind. I'll take him as I go back homewards. But let's look about us a little farther. We may make some curious discoveries, for it is very clear that some poor devil has dwelt here, and not very long ago, I should say. You see the chisel is hardly rusted. How's the knife?"

"It's rusty enough. 'Twon't open."

"Now, who knows what miserable wretch ended his days here. What if we should happen upon a skeleton? It's very chilly and damp here. Throw some more of those sticks on the fire. Heh! what's this? It looks like a regularly spread bed of moss."

And thus exploring and wandering, Voltmeier led the way for a goodly hour of seemingly curious scrutiny, when, declaring himself tired, he said:

"I doubt if we shall make any further discoveries. I will travel. Do you ride?"

"No. I'm afoot."

"Well, you will be found, you say, at the foot of Mills' Gap? What do you say is the name of the farmer?"

"Ephraim Moggs."

"And what may be *your* name?"

"Samuel Martin; and yours?"

"George Clinton. You may see me—in a month, you say?"

"About that time. Well, good-day. We may trade together yet."

"I'm willing."

By this time the two had reached the entrance of the cavern, and, bowing his adieu, Voltmeier proceeded to the stable of boulders, where he had left his horse.

"He didn't offer me his hand for a shake," muttered Gorham, as the other went, and he followed him with his eyes; and after Voltmeier had ridden off, he sauntered around, and finally reached the rocky stable.

"It's a regular stable," said he, "with two stalls and a basin of spring water. Now, how did *he* happen to know about that stable, and to find it at the first jump? That man has been here before, I reckon. It does look so! and yet, he may have happened upon it *first*, before finding the cave! It's curious."

The manner of Voltmeier had been so frank and seemingly artless, and his researches had been prosecuted with such an air of innocent curiosity, that, in spite of Gorham's conjecture touching the stranger's previous knowledge of the stable, he felt himself somewhat bewildered. Still, his cunning did not desert him.

"But I'll take the track of his horse," said he, "and see how he gets out of this wilderness."

"The hunt gets warmer," said Voltmeier, as he rode; but, swallowing a second of his brown pills, he added: "I'll throw him off the scent, yet," and, sending his horse forward with the spur, he kept the track, until it wound off from the river, when, passing over a huge flat boulder, he turned aside, and made his way into the stream itself, at a point called "the shallows." He knew every foot of the way, and emerged into a foot-path, a few hundred yards above, which traversed a rocky ledge. When he had reached this ledge, he turned in the saddle, and, looking back, shook his fist in the direction of the cavern, which yet he could not see.

"Ah! villain! I shall baffle you yet! I know that he will take the track of my horse as far as he can. But he will lose it in a single mile, and keep the path which leads to the Harness farm. Now, if those boys and the Regulators should take him off my hands, I shall be well satisfied. The wretch annoys me.

"But how should I suffer him or any man to annoy me, when it is so easy to crush him in his tracks? I might have done it this very day, and yet I would not. I would slough off my former self if possible; *forbear*, if I can not *atone*. Forbear! forbear! for the sake of Catharine! And yet, there is still so much of the demon within me that I can not *long* forbear! He may force me to it yet!"

Chapter XLII

THE NEW MAN

It was at breakfast table, as usual after any return from his wanderings, that Voltmeier first showed himself. He had been absent now four days. He appeared as usual—calm, gentle, even playful, and when breakfast was over, he said to Fergus:

"If you will ride with me to the court-house to-day, Fergus, we will see Col. Graham. You are anxious to begin your profession, and he will examine you and prepare you, if necessary. If satisfied of your acquisitions, he will cheerfully give you a certificate. The examination of the Courts, he tells me, is usually very slight, and I take for granted that, after the instructions of your friend, Major Henry, you will scarcely suffer from apprehension or embarrassment."

So, accordingly, they went, and Col. Graham was pleased, after a certain amount of "quizzing," to give the certificate. In a few days after, the examination took place, and Voltmeier was delighted to hear that Fergus was not only admitted to the practice of law, in the Courts of North Carolina, but that the Judges complimented him, especially, among a crowd of youthful candidates, on his very superior proficiency.

Voltmeier was not present on the occasion, as he feared that his presence might possibly exercise an unfavorable influence on the nervous system of his nephew. They returned home together that afternoon, discussing by the way the future course and prospects of the young lawyer. Of the details of this discussion we need not speak at present. Enough, that Fergus desired to begin the practice as soon as possible, and that Voltmeier approved of this desire.

"Some few weeks first, Fergus, that we may feel our way. I have spoken to Col. Graham, who will advise us of a proper opening. He will probably afford you, from his own docket, an opportunity to make your *debut*, and give you the subject-matter of the case in season, that you may work it out at your leisure."

And so the affair rested for the time.

Mignon was delighted at the beginning of Fergus, and his prospect for the future, as depicted in warm colors by Voltmeier, but she said:

"Ah, Cousin Fergus, I fear that your law-studies will spoil you for the German! You will forget all that I have taught you."

It was by an irresistible impulse that Fergus exclaimed, passionately:

"Nothing, Cousin Mignon, that *you* have ever taught me shall my heart ever forget."

And then he blushed after he had spoken, and looked to Voltmeier. So did Aunt Gertrude, and Voltmeier smiled pleasantly and looked to Mignon; and Mignon did not smile, but looked down upon the carpet, which suddenly seemed everywhere sprinkled with eyes and hearts set in laurel wreaths; a sudden and strange illusion of the senses, surely, but one that was no doubt perfectly natural.

After a while a case was provided for Fergus, upon which to prepare himself—trespass to try title—a land-case of endless complications. In this case he was to be associated with Col. Graham, and to open it. In the study of the case he found his advantage in the thorough training of his early guide and teacher—Major Henry, of Spartanburg.

The cause at length was tried, and again Fergus was singularly successful. He received the highest compliments of the Bar.

He was soon to distinguish himself in another field in the criminal courts—a case of the deepest dye of murder, in which he was employed for the defense.

The great case of "The State against Abner Twaits" will long be remembered in the annals of the mountain courts of North Carolina, for the interest and variety of its details, involving forgery and murder; the contradictory character of the testimony, the vigorous and savage energy of the attorney-general in the prosecution on the one hand, and the nice sifting of the testimony by our young friend, and his admirable speech in reply. It was a great triumph, and at once established his reputation as an able jury-pleader. A conviction, it is true, followed, but for manslaughter only. It was conceded that, but for the dexterity and skill of Fergus in rendering doubtful that which at first had seemed to all parties a most heinous, designed, and deliberate murder, the convicted party must have suffered the most extreme penalties of the law.

At this trial Voltmeier permitted himself to be present. The case employed three days, during all which time the two were absent from Keovala. At its close they returned home together.

The news of the great success of Fergus had reached Keovala before they came; and, full of eagerness, Mignon rushed forth to meet and congratulate her cousin the moment he came in sight. She was quite in ecstasies. Even Aunt Gertrude expressed her satisfaction in no measured terms of pleasure—Fergus having grown upon her regards very greatly during the increased knowledge and experience of his character in the two months passed in the family.

"Did I not tell you so, Gertrude?" said Voltmeier, triumphantly, to the ancient maiden. "I knew I could not be mistaken in the man, Gertrude. *I* had studied *him,* and could not be deceived as to his qualities—and we have seen the beginning only. Fergus Wallace is destined to be a great man! I have a prophetic instinct—an insight— which can not be deceived."

Somewhat of egotism in this speech, no doubt. So thought the aunt; but egotism did not sit ungracefully in the case of powers like those of Voltmeier.

"Saul among the prophets," said Miss Gertrude, with a good-natured sneer. "I shall not gainsay you, brother Leonard, in *my* opinion, and I shall certainly sustain you and Fergus by my prayers and wishes."

This was all said when the two were alone together. Fergus and Mignon had already strolled forth for an afternoon ramble, to behold the favorite sunset. Mignon's old enthusiasm, at this grand panorama of the sky, which usually, among these mountains, closed the drama of the day—a wondrous spectacle of golden clouds, and orange and purple vapors, islands in seas of green and azure—was singularly blended with that with which she again and again hailed the young conqueror in the courts of law; the rising of *his* sun seeming to partake of the grand glories of that of the natural world, now setting beneath their eyes.

And, as she pointed to the scenic splendor of the heavens, she looked up into his face with all the bright enthusiasm of her southern nature beaming in her eyes; and, still pointing to the scene in the west, she spoke only of *his* triumphs, and the grand prospect before him; and she cried out, with the tears filling her beautiful eyes, while she clasped one of his hands in her own—

"Oh, cousin Fergus! I am so glad, so happy! It is just what papa said of you!"

Carried away by what she said and looked—carried away by his own exulting sense of success—so great, so unanticipated, Fergus was no longer the subdued and shrinking youth who had hitherto striven to subdue, in his own heart, every exhibition of pride and vanity. By a sudden impulse he caught her in his arms, drew her close to his bosom, and while she trembled in his embrace like a young lily shaken by the loving billows of the lakelet, lifting her eyes, with timid inquiry, to his face, he pressed his burning lips down upon her own! Her eyes closed, and her head sunk upon his breast.

Rapture was born dumb! Neither spoke!—neither could speak, until, as she lifted her head again, looking up with the wild, dilating eyes of a startled fawn of the wilderness, he again fastened his passionate lips upon her mouth.

Releasing herself at length from his embrace, with eyes drooping and downcast, she murmured faintly—

"Oh, Cousin Fergus! can it be love?"

And he answered her first with another fond embrace, and said in low, but passionate tones, "It is love, my Mignon, if it be not madness!"

Chapter XLIII

MIGNON IS ENDOWED
WITH A SOUL

Oh, that first kiss, that passionate embrace, where love, no longer bound by false constraint, asserts itself all soul; and, with a fire that rages, but hath never power of harm—so long as blent with truth and chastity—what like hath it in nature for delight? what sweeter boon for poor humanity? what charm to soothe the darkness into smiles and make the soul, though in all else denied, far happier in its singleness of boon than with all other blessings, *that* withheld.

The first sweet rose of dawn; dew on the flower; down on the peach, and odor in the breeze; light on the waters; glory in the sky; song in the zephyr, and all earth made heaven by that first birth of love within the soul—which makes two souls, without design or aim, glide eagerly together, lost in one; even as two little mountain streamlets gladly leap from opposite summits down the precipice to meet in air, and, in the embracing lake, subside to one—a glad sun over all, making the bridal-bed a bliss in nature.

That first sweet kiss! It well might make them dumb, those two young creatures, 'neath that evening light!

They sat together upon a boulder in a sweet muse of delicious reverie, such as lovers so deeply feel, but such as no language can describe; and little did they speak. The sudden, strange consciousness of a new being was present in both souls, for which neither could find adequate words. Feeling absorbed thought as well as speech, and consciousness had become too acute for utterance. The arm of Fergus was wrapt around the waist of the maiden, and her head was leant upon his shoulder. And thus they sat; the murmurs which occasionally broke from their lips declaring as well for the novelty of their consciousness as for its absorbing influence.

"And oh, Fergus, do you really love me as I love you?"

"Are you sure, Mignon, that it *is* love that you feel for me?"

"What should it be, Fergus? It is a strangely sweet feeling, that I can lie thus upon your bosom. What is this faith that I now feel, if it be not love?"

"True! I believe it is—it must be love, Mignon! It is certain that I feel nothing but love for you."

"I could die so, Fergus, for I feel now, as papa said it, that love only endows with a soul; and I now am possessed of a soul!"

"You are possessed of mine, Mignon."

"And your heart too, Fergus?"

"Yes, and my heart too, if there be any difference between them."

And so, murmuring together, they saw not that the sun had gone down in a blaze of glory. They saw no more—looked no more for the sun that day! What was the glory in the sky to the gladness in their hearts?

"Papa was surely right, Fergus, when he said that love endowed the woman with a soul. I feel such a new birth in my bosom that I am sure it must be a soul—it can be nothing else!"

That second allusion to her father awakened a new and painful consciousness in the mind of Fergus.

"Ah, Mignon, I fear that we have done wrong—that *I* have done wrong! What will *he* say to this? He has trusted me; favored me with his confidence; treated me with the affection of a father for a son; and I have abused his trust and love by presuming to win the affections of his daughter."

"Oh, never fear! You know not papa. He does love, and he will welcome you as a son. He loves *me*, and he wishes to see and make me happy. I do not fear him, Fergus. I do not doubt that he will 'smile upon and bless us. I will tell him all, and he will put his hands upon my head, and kiss me on the mouth, and bless me!"

"No, Mignon, it must be *my* task to tell him," answered Fergus, somewhat sadly. "I am not so hopeful as you, but I *will* hope. It is from my own lips that he must hear me honestly confess my fault."

"What fault? Are you not worthy, Fergus, my own cousin? And does not papa speak of you and of your talents with the pride of a father as well as an uncle? Don't you doubt; don't you fear from papa. I have no sort of fear, Fergus."

"But I have yet to work my way. I have no fortune, and you have; and to seem to seek a wife for her fortune, Mignon—"

"Oh, hush, Fergus! hush! Is it not enough that I love *you* and that papa loves *me?* I do not think of wealth when I love, and papa will think I have wealth enough when I have won a soul for myself out of a brave soul like yours! Yes, Fergus, I feel that it is love, and nothing but love, which makes me so bold to lean upon your bosom now—now, with such a faith that you love me, too."

"And will never cease to love you! But I must go at once to your father; I must tell him all. See, dearest, the sun is gone, and the darkness grows upon us. I must go to him now while the sense of error is upon me, and tell him all as soon as I reach the house. It may be, Mignon, that he will expel me from it, and then, Mignon?—"

"We will be expelled together! What nonsense, Fergus! Papa expel *me,* and expel *you* because you love *me.* Were you to *hate* me now, Fergus, he'd do it fast enough. But I know papa, and you don't. So go to him, Fergus, and tell him. I know what he will say."

The poor children! Little did they dream that the father already knew their secret—that he had watched the scene between them from his frequent place of perch, where, hidden by a convenient boulder, he could behold the region all around. He had beheld that first fond impulsive meeting of their lips; had witnessed that first unpremeditated fond embrace; had seen the arms of Fergus entwine her waist closely, as they sat side by side, while her head reclined upon the shoulder of her lover; and he had said to himself, even as he beheld it—

"It is well! It is as I could wish! Now, Catharine, your son is mine also!"

Then, as if Catharine Wallace were listening at hand, he murmured:

"Shall this not be something, Catharine, towards atonement?"

Voltmeier was prepared for the coming of his nephew, and for his revelations. He had himself reached the dwelling by a shorter route, and had passed at once into the library. There, when Fergus made his appearance, and, with resolved mind, but trembling heart, began his confessions, the uncle gently silenced him.

"I know what you would say, Fergus. I know all. I hold *my* daughter to be worthy of the noblest gentleman of the country, and I regard you, Fergus, as worthy of *my* daughter! Leave me now! Go and be happy."

When Fergus had disappeared, Voltmeier musingly said:

"The course of true love shall run smoothly for them, so far as I have the power to control its currents. Yet, somehow, there is a shadow upon my mind—a cloud is athwart my vision. There is a doubt which I can not pierce or fathom, and from the shadow of which I try vainly to escape. But, whatever *my* fate, it shall never mar the beauty or the bliss of theirs. I am prepared for any trial, any fate, any sacrifice, that they may be happy. Yes; I have lived long enough; but, save with regard to these children, I have lived in vain. My life has been one long mistake—one prolonged guilt, if not misery. Ah, Catharine, how far otherwise might it have been, had *our* hearts ran together, like those of our children! Well, it is my happiness at last, if they may be made happy!"

Spite of these sad musings, when Voltmeier appeared at supper he was cheerful and pleasant as ever. Fergus and Mignon both sate silent, eating nothing, and snatching, at every moment, hasty and furtive glances at each other. As yet, Aunt Gertrude *knew* nothing, but she observed the change in the deportment of Mignon, if not of Wallace, and she half conjectured that, in the language of Voltmeier, Mignon had been "endowed with a soul." The dear old maid sighed, and thought upon her own.

Chapter XLIV

ADVENTURE IN THE
MOUNTAINS

It had been arranged, a day or two before, for an expedition the next day to the great gorge of the Tselica, commonly called the Hickory Nut Gap. All the family but Fergus had seen and well knew the beauties and wonders of the grand scenery of this place; and it had been decided by Mignon that his initiation into the new world which he at present inhabited would be incomplete, unless he could behold the spectacle with his own eyes, and under their guidance.

As it was several miles distant, it was resolved to make a day of the excursion, and, for the creature exigencies of the day, cold meats and breadstuffs were provided. Sandwiches of ham and steaks of venison, eggs and cakes and pasties, were got in readiness the day before, and Voltmeier added to the materials for the *picnic* a few bottles of old Madeira.

After an early breakfast, the party set off, the ladies traveling in a light carriage, and the gentlemen on horseback. These carried their rifles, as was very much the custom of the country; the probabilities of encountering buck and bear being considerable in so wild a region. Besides this, their weapons were naturally carried as a measure of precaution against marauders, quite as frequent, and even more to be apprehended than buck or bear.

Voltmeier had his pistols also, without which he rarely went from home; but they were concealed—strapped by a belt about the waist, and covered by the flowing hunting-shirt of the professional hunter; a costume in which Fergus Wallace had also newly garbed himself for the occasion.

The party was all in excellent spirits; even Voltmeier, whatever his secret fears or feelings, showing a cheerful and buoyant mood, which, at times, seemed more natural to him than any other. He was a man of wonderful elasticity, and was so much at home on horseback that his flow of spirits was never greater than when he rode through the mountain ranges, his imagination being always lifted by rapid motion, and in the survey of grand and varied scenery.

At this time he was especially moved to cheerfulness and buoyancy of spirit; for, had he not fully succeeded in his object of bringing the two young hearts together, in whom he took such profound interest?

He had, besides, worked out, as he thought, successfully, a social and heart-problem which had been a favorite conception of his mind. Had he not provided for his daughter a husband who realized his best ideal of a noble, unselfish gentleman; strong of soul, firm of will, highly endowed with intellect, and pure in spirit as a virgin?

Such was his estimate of Fergus Wallace—the son of the woman whom he had loved best of all, and wronged worst because of his own jealous nature and perverse passions.

For the time, therefore, he was all animation. His cares seemed to be forgotten, and he breathed freely of the lively mountain airs, and drank in the generous sunshine which crowned skies and earth with wedded glories, that made all the gracious elements tributary to the inspiration of the scene.

As they rode together, he pointed out all the objects of interest to Fergus in the progress; named height and rock and valley and stream; for many of which, in addition, he could provide some history or tradition, some wild legend, some tale of elf or gnome, satyr or wood-demon. These stories he told with the air of one who in part believed them, and he told them well, succeeding, frequently, in inspiring a certain degree of faith in the mind of his hearer. Strange incongruity, indeed, that he, who was so skeptical in regard to humanity in general, and so imperfectly persuaded, if at all, of his own soul and its immortality, should yet prove susceptible of such beliefs, and yield any degree of faith to the suggestion of his merest fancies! Yet he greatly insisted with Fergus that all nature was occupied by beings, differing from man and beast and bird, yet partaking of some of their properties and qualities, with whom man might occasionally hold communion, and, through certain innate sympathies, possess curious affinities.

The party now crossed one of the arms of the magnificent Tselica, or French Broad River, at one of its most placid points, and, riding beside the carriage, Fergus received from Mignon a description of the two branches, the one beautiful, the other grand and terrible; the one wandering through a fertile, though undulating country, the other tearing its way through the rocks; a river of perpetual strifes and rapids, roaming over its shattered boulders, riven by volcanic fires, and raging along its way like the ocean in a stormy night, beating wild against the barriers which earth hath set to its domain.

They reached, at length, the grand gorge of Tselica, where the mighty masses of the mountain were abruptly rent in twain; the great walls towering on each hand, leaving between a magnificent avenue, which, in the imperfect light of moon and stars, would make the illusion perfect, to the eye of a stranger, of some enormous thoroughfare, the main street through a great Cyclopean city, reared by immortal art, when the land was inhabited by giants. There stood the walls of temples and towers, perpendicularly straight as high; pinnacles, buttressed with wonderful order, and for the proper support of the incumbent masses, covered with ivy and wild shrubs and lichens of various hues and colors, the fantastic drapery with which Gothic art, in its almost sublime audacity, lifted vast monuments to hang in air, the wonder and the mockery of modern civilization. And, here and there, from buttressed corner and overhanging terrace, the unleashed winds toss the slender cataracts across the avenue, and they grow, as they go, into prismatic arches, under the rich coloring of the noonday sun.

Fergus wondered in silence, as he beheld, while Mignon led him to numerous points of view, at every change of position developing some new miracle of Nature in her seemingly fond ambition to emulate all the capricious audacities of Art.

Voltmeier, cup in hand, and bottle, led the way to *one* fountain, and then to another, within a brief space from each other; and, filling the cup partly from each, he said to Fergus:

"Drink, Fergus! It is one of the laws of the Genii of this place, that every visitor shall quaff the blended waters of these two fountains. They are grand eyes that possess a history of their own."

Fergus drank, and Voltmeier continued:

"These fountains wander off, after marriage, like divorced parties, each seeking a new abode—each taking a separate course, never again to unite. The waters from this fountain descend the Atlantic slopes, and seek escape to the sea, pursuing an easterly progress, while, from this fountain, the stream glides down the western declivities, and loses itself finally in the Gulf of Mexico. So men part, so women, to lose one another forever, swallowed up in one or other of the great gulfs of human life and society—in realms far distant from, and hostile to each other."

But now, Aunt Gertrude summoned them to their repast, which she had spread on a great flat boulder, convenient as a table, while all around it, similarly convenient, were so many little rocks affording comfortable seats. The bracing airs of the mountains, and the long ride, had sharpened appetite, the Madeira stimulated while refreshing it, and the whole party ate, not even omitting Mignon and Fergus, as if Love were preparing to prove itself quite as mortal as any other, the most vulgar of human passions!

When the appetites of all were fairly pacified, and a quarter of an hour had been passed in that quiescent, half-drowsy manner which usually prevails with virtuous people, after having done full justice to their viands, Fergus and Mignon wandered off in exploration, under the lead of the latter, who had too often sought the spot to need any guide in finding out the most imposing points of view.

How they prattled together, freed from the presence of aunt and uncle, need not here be reported. What heed need we give to that idle, silly, disjointed, but sweet discourse with which young lovers delight each other, after the fashion of Romeo and Juliet—that great love-drama of the great master—without summoning Reason to resolve the why and wherefore of each child sentiment and bodiless fancy which may prompt their happy hearts and licensed tongues.

They wandered on, till suddenly surprised, at the foot of one of the cliffs, by the rolling of a great boulder from its higher ledge, the mass which, a little further on, might have crushed them both, tumbling with a great crash, towards their feet!

Recoiling, they looked—Mignon with a little scream—and discovered the figure of a man, peering over the cliff, and seemingly about to descend its rugged ledges, approaching in their direction.

He carried a rifle in his grasp, and it seemed to Fergus that he meant mischief. Inferring this, under a sudden impulse of indignation, he cried out loudly to the stranger, in words of rather harsh import:

"How now, fellow! What do you there? What do you mean?"

The speech reached the ears of the other, who replied in like manner:

"No more fellow than yourself! I've as much right to be here as you!"

The tone and manner of the new comer were insolent and defiant, and as he now came more rapidly down the rocks, towards them, Fergus, assuming a hostile purpose, hurried Mignon back, towards the boulder where Voltmeier and Aunt Gertrude were still sitting, and followed, himself, but more slowly, towards a buttress of a neighboring rock, against which he had leaned his rifle. Of this, in a few moments, he had repossessed himself, and, turning promptly about, met the intruder, who had by this time just reached the level upon which the former stood, having his rifle ready at the *present,* and still bearing towards him.

"Stand back!" cried Fergus, lifting the rifle.

The stranger answered as promptly:

"I can shoot, I reckon, as well as you!"

At that moment Mignon darted between them, and cried:

"Oh! don't shoot! don't shoot! Fergus, stop! The man meant no harm. It was surely an accident!"

"To be sure it was an accident!" said the stranger; "'twas all an accident! The rock hung upon the very edge of the cliff, and I only brushed it, and down it went! I didn't mean to hurt you, young lady! I wouldn't hurt you for the world!"

And certainly, the expression of his countenance underwent a vast change, from sullenness and defiance, to civility, as he gazed upon the beautiful girl, who still confronted him, standing between him and her lover, with her arms still outstretched, and hands and eyes pleading equally with her voice, to prevent violence.

By this time Voltmeier made his appearance, rifle in hand, exclaiming, as he hurried forward:

"There are two of us now!"

But, as his eyes rested upon the person of the stranger, a strange expression of disgust and loathing filled their glances. His face became discolored, almost jaundiced, and, instead of dropping his weapon, he presented it, raised it to his eye, and seemed about to take deadly and deliberate aim.

"Stop, sir," interposed Fergus, catching his arm. "There is no difficulty. The man has apologized. It was all an accident!"

"It is well!" said Voltmeier, coldly. "It is well!" and so speaking, he drew away from the scene, and slowly walked back, followed in a few moments by Fergus and Mignon, all eager to quiet the apprehensions of Aunt Gertrude.

"It is well!" muttered Voltmeier, as he went; "and yet!—a single shot would have done it!"

The stranger was Richard Gorham!

Chapter XLV

THE SHADOW THAT
WOULD NOT FLEE

"If I said anything hastily to you, my good fellow," said Fergus to the stranger, "it was under momentary excitement. If I had reflected, I must have seen that you could have no motive to hurl a rock upon us, when you might have sent a bullet more surely to the mark!"

"That's true, young man," was the answer. "But I would no more send rock or bullet against the young woman, than I would against my own mother."

And he gazed full in the face of Mignon, with eyes of such undisguised admiration, that she averted her face, and, slightly bowing, walked away, while a feeling of intense disgust pervaded the bosom of Fergus, who, bidding the stranger a cold "good morning," followed in the footsteps of Mignon.

The party were now all again together, and making their preparations to set off homewards. The Jehu had already got the carriage in readiness. Aunt Gertrude had recovered in a great degree from a fit of nervous agitation, and the whole exciting affair was briefly discussed among them.

Voltmeier alone remained silent. The cloud had not wholly passed from his brow, nor the intense fire from his glance, nor the jaundice from his complexion. He rode with Fergus, in the rear of the carriage, occasionally looking behind him. Could we look into his thoughts, or hear those internal soliloquies which he did not utter, they would show him to be much more disturbed by the adventure than were either of the two immediate actors in it. The idea of a fate at work against him, its hounds dogging at his heels, was ever uppermost in his thoughts.

"Can it be," he mused to himself, "that these frequent meetings should be the result simply of chance? Are all my plans, so deliberately calculated to throw this sleuth-hound off the scent, to be baffled by the merest accident? Surely, there is a fate in it—such fate as Jove himself could not escape! The Greeks were right! There is no such thing as chance! There are greater gods than Jupiter! This Black Dog of mine is making progress! But, what should I fear? What clues hath he? He may discover the abode of Voltmeier, but how shall he find that of Bierstadt? How find Gellert, or any of the seven? I defy him, but he vexes me, nevertheless—he worries me. I could have shot him down like a dog, as he is,—and perhaps— but no! For the sake of *these* children—for the memory of Catharine, I will forbear to add to the long catalogue of crime which is written down against me. I will forbear when I can no longer atone! Forbear,—if the Fates will suffer me!"

Such, in substance, were his musings, unexpressed, but still working, like so many vultures in his bosom. Gorham had his musings also. Before the party of Voltmeier had left the ground, he had disappeared behind the rocks, and was slowly moving off to the hollow in which his horse was hidden. As he went he soliloquized in this fashion:

"What a beautiful young woman it is! Now could I marry such a woman for love, and never ask for any portion with her? How she looks with her eyes. Such eyes I never saw set in a woman's head before; and when she came between us, and lifted up her hands, and didn't seem afraid though both rifles were p'inted against her; and spoke with that sweet voice, and said 'Don't shoot!' my heart fairly jumped towards her! Yet, she's proud—proud as the devil!

"But who was the young fellow? Her brother, perhaps; or may be, he's courting of her. He's a good-looking fellow enough, but somehow I don't like him! The other tall man is the same one—let me see—what's his name? Oh! Clinton—George Clinton—that I seen first down at Moggs', and met afterwards in the cave. If he had given me a chance, I'd have asked him about that trade in cattle. I don't forget he had his horse fastened in the rock stable at the cave, as if he know'd all about it. That was curious! There's something strange about that man; and, so far from remembering me, and behaving civil, he looked, for all nature, as if he wished for nothing better than to shoot me! His eye had the very devil in it! I must find out who he is. If he's her father, I'll think no harm of it. But I must find out about 'em all. Lucky for me they've come in a carriage, some of 'em, and I can easily follow that track. I wonder if he rides that famous white horse. I must look."

Here, turning aside, he hurried up to the top of one of the cliffs, which gave him a view of the whole valley. He arrived just in time to see the party moving off.

"Yes; there's the white horse! How he rides! Like a General, or like the Sheriff! What if he should be the County Sheriff now? I must fight shy of *him* as long as I can. They're off now, and now I'll find out where they are going to burrow to-night, if there's any virtue in a good horse and a good eyesight!"

He was soon following upon the track of the carriage, some half a mile in the rear. He, too, rode a fine horse, fleet and strong, but not the steed to keep up with that of Voltmeier. Had the latter been alone, the pursuer would have been very soon thrown off.

Keovala was reached in safety by the party. Did Gorham succeed in following the tracks of the carriage? Perhaps! It traveled slowly enough for the pursuit, and the pursuer was one of those hounds tenacious of the trail, and not to be diverted from the deer on the track of the rabbit.

It did occur to Voltmeier at one moment that they would be tracked, and for a brief space he thought to send Fergus with the ladies forward, while he turned off on another route; but he soon abandoned the idea with the gloomy, but unuttered reflection,—

"If there be a fate in it, it must come! There's no escaping fate, and I begin to get tired of the effort! If I must face it, be it so! There is always time for that. And if this be a mere thing of coincidence, I have surely guarded my secret sufficiently for its safety."

Chapter XLVI

THE HOUND!

Though somewhat graver in deportment than usual, Voltmeier maintained the same gentle and amiable carriage towards his family. He was the same affectionate and indulgent father; calm, pleasant, free from any expression of that irascibility which might be expected of one, uneasy, if not greatly anxious, about the progress of events, such as his instincts moved him to feel and fear, in defiance of all thoughts and reasonings.

That night he retired, not to sleep, but to study. He sought the library rather than his chamber. This apartment was on the lower story of the house, and joined his sleeping-room, having an entrance from the one directly into the other.

Fergus had a room, convenient to the library also, but within a section which protruded from the body of the dwelling, having roof and entrance of its own. The library separated him from the chamber of Voltmeier. A noble piazza extended along the south front of both; the doors of the library opened upon the piazza, and were glassed and latticed to the floor.

Entering this apartment, which was also his study, having writing-table and escritoir, with writing materials always convenient, Voltmeier extinguished his light, and walked out in the darkness, or rather into the bright starlight; while, over the eastern peak of a neighboring mountain, the moon was sending her own bright harbingers, in the shape of long stripes of fleecy clouds, the edges of which she had begun to silver with her sweetest smiling.

But Voltmeier was not engaged in the contemplation of the scene. He was given up to that mastication of the cud of sweet or bitter thought, which was too absorbing to permit of any exercise of the mere senses. He paced the piazza in deep silence for a full hour; then, as if he had reached a definite conclusion, and formed a resolution, he reëntered the library, swallowed one of his Lethean pills, drew forth his writing materials, and proceeded to work with all the rapidity of one who knew what had to be written, and was at home in this sort of exercise.

He covered sheet after sheet, great sheets, such as lawyers employ for records; filled up sundry legal blanks, which he signed; and, after consuming much ink and paper, and some three hours of time in this employment, he placed the documents in his secretary, and, extinguishing the light, withdrew to his own chamber.

Here, swallowing another pill, he addressed himself to slumber.

The morning found him at breakfast-table with the rest, and his conversation was marked by a degree of vivacity and spirit, which showed him to have found some relief from his anxieties of the preceding day. It seemed as if his labors of the night had taken the burden from his mind.

But, the breakfast over, his labors in the library were resumed, and so earnestly, that Fergus failed, when he went thither, to attract his attention—Mignon was equally unsuccessful; at which she seemed somewhat surprised. When she spoke to him, he answered only with a nod; and the two young people went forth together, to the groves, but no longer to read in Schiller.

The next night, cards and music till ten o'clock, when Voltmeier again left the company, retired to the library, thence to the piazza, which he paced for an hour, as on the preceding night; then, swallowing his usual pill, he resumed his labors at the desk, which were continued as before, until near three in the morning.

The day after he had his horse saddled, the famous white, and started, immediately after breakfast, for the Court and county town, carrying his papers with him. Here he sought the office of Colonel Graham, and submitted certain documents for his examination. Graham, after reading them, expressed his surprise.

"Is it possible, Voltmeier? You convey Keovala, with all its possessions to Wallace, in trust for Mignon Voltmeier?"

"That is my purpose."

"Well, the young fellow seems a gentleman, and, whether honest or otherwise, is no doubt a splendid fellow, and will make a great lawyer. But, it is a vast property—an important trust—full of temptations."

"I have perfect faith in Fergus Wallace. Besides, Graham, I need not keep it from you. He is to marry Mignon."

"Ah! that alters the case. I congratulate you. But, my dear Voltmeier, what have you left for yourself, and how have you provided for your sister, Miss Leyfenholdt?"

"At sixty years of age, my dear Graham, a man really needs very little, and even if I lacked in means, I could safely rely upon my daughter and her husband—"

"And so thought old Lear!" was the interruption—"though, God forbid that I should suspect my lovely little friend, Mignon, of any features in common with those accursed jades Goneril and Regan. No! I do not doubt that she will prove as devoted to you in your old age, as ever was the exquisite Cordelia. Still, I do not like to see a man strip himself utterly in his old age, to become a dependent, as it were, upon his children. I am for the patriarch holding the wand of rule to the last."

"I do not strip myself, Graham. I have other and adequate resources, as well in Germany as in this country. I meditate a trip to Germany as soon as the young people are married, and it is a part of my plan to take them with me."

"But, how about Miss Gertrude?"

"You will see, by this paper, that I have made adequate provision for her, securing to her, in her own right, the estate called Tremont, with all its possessions, including some fifteen hundred acres, a good house, with all the stock and appurtenances upon it, consisting of several hands, mules, horses, and cattle. There is money besides; and she will go with us to Germany."

"A goodly little fortune of itself! Why, my dear fellow, all this might have been done by will, to take effect upon your death."

Voltmeier shook his head, saying:

"It is a vicious policy to keep your children dependent upon you to the last. It makes them live in a long and painful state of suspense; is apt to make them worthless; and, but too frequently makes them wonder why the veteran lingers so long upon the stage! My notion is to start your children as soon as they become able to manage, and throw the responsibilities of life upon them just as soon as they have reached maturity. The marriage of Mignon, with Fergus

Wallace, will, I think, secure for her the proper administration of her property, and I have no longer any of that miserable self-esteem —vanity, rather,—which makes one jealous of his own children, which makes him fear, lest, in stripping himself of property, he loses consequence and power. My whole ambition now lies in and for those young people."

"Well, these are not the notions of our people generally."

"The more's the pity. We should have a more noble and generous manhood among us, were it otherwise."

"I do not deny that your views have reason in them. What do you wish me to do in the matter?"

"First, are the papers drawn fully, in proper legal fashion, to carry out and sustain my wishes?"

"I could not have drawn them more skillfully myself. I have always told you, Voltmeier, that you were born to be a lawyer."

Voltmeier smiled, as he replied—

"And I have always told you, Graham, that you were born to be a statesman."

"Had you said politician, I should have said that I have not sufficient glibness in lying, sufficient dexterity in thieving, and a conscience sufficiently flexible for the desertion of my friends! Shall I have these papers put on record?"

"If you please; then take them all into your own keeping—for the present at least. Call in some good witnesses, that I may acknowledge my signature; and, I shall be obliged to you, if you will sign with them also. You can explain all, as you fully comprehend all my plans and purposes."

The deeds were duly executed and left with Graham. Their conversation was somewhat prolonged after this, but, as it helps us nothing in the business of our narrative, we need make no report of it.

Graham accompanied Voltmeier to the door of the office. At that moment, who should pass but Richard Gorham, in company with Lawyer Brownlow, who, in the county town of ———— occupied the rank of an "old Bailey" lawyer in London, a "Tombs" lawyer in New York, a pettifogger in the Carolinas, and a "Jack Legged" lawyer in Georgia.

The brow of Voltmeier involuntarily contracted as he beheld his black dog; his cheeks assumed a swarthy and turbid complexion;

his lips were sternly compressed; but he neither started, nor showed to Graham any signs of emotion. He had detected Gorham at a glance, and turned immediately about, and spoke to Graham as coolly as if he felt totally unmoved. Gorham, in turn, discovered Voltmeier, but not till the latter had seen him, and he fancied himself unseen. After they had passed, he said, with the slightest possible air of interest, to his companion—

"Who is that gentleman?"

"Which?"

"The one in the hunting-shirt."

"That is the rich Colonel Voltmeier. He owns a thousand hills, and thousands of cattle upon them. He owns perhaps one-tenth of the whole county."

"A—h!—and the other?"

"Colonel Graham, one of our most eminent lawyers, and one of the oldest families. He, too, is a very rich man, but nothing like Colonel Voltmeier."

"The Hound of Hell!" muttered Voltmeier to himself, as he mounted his horse and rode away. "He is with that scoundrel, Brownlow! I see his game! But he will gain nothing from Moggs' or Brownlow's revelations. The game is blocked in that quarter!"

Chapter XLVII

THE SERPENT

It was a royal game of Fox between the two parties, Gorham on the one hand, and Brownlow, the "old Bailey" lawyer, on the other. They had entered the office of the latter together, that den in which all iniquities are manufactured in the name of equity and justice. The place was worthy of its uses; a mere cabin, cribb'd, confined; innocent of all cleanliness, a court of *pil poudre* literally, the fine dust overlaying floor and tables, books and shelves, in liberal quantities. A small collection of books, an old table, covered with mouldy papers, a row of pine shelves, and, in one corner, a washstand with broken basin, and pitcher *minus* the handle; these, with a clumsy escritoir, comprised all the furniture of this rude office, not forgetting a single pair of chairs, upon one of which, without scruple, Gorham deposited his person.

"Not *that* chair, my good fellow," said Brownlow. "I never suffer any one to sit in that chair but myself. That is the chair of authority, and when I sit in it, all my senses grow into full activity. My memory comes fully to me, and my judgments become perfect. I then know the law thoroughly, and deliver it wisely. I then fully comprehend the case and counsel advisedly. It is not so if I sit in any other; so, if your purpose is to consult me, it is your policy to allow me to sit in my own judicial chair. Please take the other. To you it will prove quite as comfortable."

Gorham obeyed. He saw no difference in the chairs, and began to fancy that the lawyer was something of a fool; for how should a wise man find such a difference in two chairs, both of the same pattern? He did not, with all his cunning, understand how much the wits of men depended upon their humors.

"And now, my friend, what can I do for you? What's your hobble?"

The experience of Brownlow led him naturally to assume that

every client was a criminal, and that his business was to extricate him from the meshes of the law at all hazards—for a becoming consideration!

"Well, I'm in no hobble myself, but I think I see a way of hobbling somebody else."

"Ah! ha! that's the humor of it, eh? Well, you wish my advice?"

"Well, not exactly, lawyer. I want to get some information first."

"Information, my friend, is the fruit of study and observation. It takes a long life to acquire the means of giving information. One must study a great deal—must lose a great deal of brain-sweat; must pay for his education; and when he gives advice or information, he expects the *quid pro quo*. You ask a doctor for a prescription, and he expects you to pay for it. You get a parson to marry you, and he expects something more than a bit of cake and a glass of wine and a 'thank you.' His empty pockets admonish him of to-morrow, and he would fain pocket a fee. The lawyer has similar expectations, and if you desire my advice, or even my information, you must needs down with your dust. You understand me?"

"I guess I do. If 'twas your advice as a lawyer that I was wanting, squire, I'd see the sense in what you say; but you see the information that I wants, if I can get it, is to lead to the advice, and perhaps a great deal more."

"Oh! It is not a professional matter?"

"Not exactly. 'Tis to know—"

"It is simply a desire on your part to obtain some information, which, as a lawyer, I happen to possess?"

"Exactly that."

"It's to be a friendly act?"

"Y-e-s! But it may lead to something—"

"My good fellow, possibilities are to be paid for. Here you, a man whom I never beheld with my legal or mortal eyes before, have suddenly and graciously appointed yourself my friend; and, as such, you claim the privilege to take up my time, and to extract from me that knowledge in my profession which has cost me years of experience and thought and study, and a confounded sight of trouble and expense. Can't afford it, my friend. What may be your name?"

"Richard Gorham, at your service."

"By Jove, you are disposed to read it, 'Lawyer Brownlow, at the service of Richard Gorham!' That cock won't fight, Richard Gorham. Why, Mr. Richard Gorham, where were you brought up, that you should conceive such strange ideas? Your education in the law certainly has been strangely neglected. You could have had but little experience among my learned brothers at the bar. No, Richard Gorham, we don't do business on the score of friendship for everybody who appoints himself our friend. We choose our friends and waste much time upon them through love, and ask no fee. But time is money, Mr. Gorham; and he who consumes my time, whether I am to advise him, or simply to inform him, must pay for it. *That*, Mr. Gorham, is the law—and all the *profits!*"

Gorham heard him patiently, preserving all his coolness, and inly saying to himself all the while—"For all that he gets not a copper of my money till I sees the profits of it. I'm not going to buy a pig in a poke."

After a few moments of seeming deliberation he answered, quietly:

"I know all that, Lawyer Brownlow, and I understand the good sense and the reason of it; but you see the matter that's on my hands is very different from the sort of business generally, and before I put any money out of my pocket, I must first see that there's a chance of getting it back again, with a good chance of profits, too. Now, you see, though time's a vallyable thing to you, as to everybody else, yet it's a truth that, in every business, everybody must take some risk, jist as the farmer risks his seed corn, at the proper season, in expectation of a good crop at harvest time. I'm risking *my* time and my experience, too; and when I ax you to risk your'n, it's but fair, particularly as I expects to make fair share with my lawyer if the thing turns out any profits at all. Now there's an old say that I learn'd when I was a boy, that says—'Penny wise and pound foolish.' Here you, now, for a little bit of a fee, ten or twenty dollars, may lose a chance of making jist as many thousand. Just consider, now."

"There is sense and shrewdness in what you say, Master Gorham," answered the lawyer, whose cupidity was suddenly stimulated by the high sum held up to him as a lure by the cunning fellow. "Ten or twenty thousand dollars is certainly an amount not to be periled for a trifling fee in hand. Now if, instead of asking me questions you would suffer me to question you, that would be much more in the proper order of things."

"I don't altogether see it in that p'int of view," was the reply. "I'm no fool, lawyer, and when I came to you on this business I knowed what I was about, and how the thing was to be worked out, and saw, at the jump, what was needful to get the proper evidence; all I wanted was help to do this, and a smart lawyer to manage the thing, in case it should have to come before the courts. But my notion is that we may make the money, and the thing need never to come before the courts."

"There is a secret, then?"

"There is a precious big secret."

"Well, ask your questions, Mr. Gorham."

"Well, sir, in the first place, you was employed to get out of jail, and I reckon out of the gallows, a certain person named Ephraim Moggs. He was up for burglary and robbery, and mayhap other matters."

"I remember something about the case. I have some notes upon it, made at the time."

"Well, sir, if you can only remember who employed you to do the business for Ephraim, you got him off by what the lawyers call an allaboy."

"Alibi, Master Richard."

"Well,—al—i—bi—if that's it!"

"I did."

"Well, and who came to you to get him off, and who swore him off and al—i—bide him?"

"I will just look at my note-book, Mr. Gorham."

"If you please."

After a search, Brownlow exclaimed:

"Here I have it!—'Retained by Simon Furze—cash one hundred dollars. Alibi established by Furze, Moggs being his guest, and sleeping with him in the same room the very night when Squire Clayton's house was robbed and burned.'"

"Now then, Lawyer, who is Simon Furze, and where can he be found?"

"Devil take me if I know. I never saw the fellow before or since, and shouldn't know him were I to see him again. But I can find out, if any man can, if he be living in this county."

Gorham's lower jaw dropped. He was disappointed; and muttered to himself:

"It's deep! Furze must be one of the *seven*. I only knowed *four!*"

"What's it, Mr. Gorham?"

A few of the words spoken were sufficiently audible to reach the keen ears of the lawyer.

"Nothing of no consequence."

"You spoke of seven of them?"

"Days in the week, Lawyer. I was just counting up what time I had. But, considering what's to be got out of this business, Lawyer—"

"Twenty to thirty thousand dollars, you mentioned," said Brownlow.

"No! say ten to twenty thousand, though it may turn out a good deal more—and you'll see how needful it is to get at this Simon Furze—"

"That I do not yet see, Mr. Gorham. What will that prove? only that he gave me one hundred dollars to defend Moggs, and that he proved the alibi on his own oath."

"Well, sir, you see, I'm thinking that Furze was made use of for that business by a bigger man than himself—a man I guess, that's rich enough to pay for all our time, and give us profits enough. You see, Lawyer, I've been putting several things together, and making them fit; and there's a great deal more to tell you when the proper time comes. In the meantime, if you could only find out this Simon Furze—"

"I will make a memorandum of it, and put some sharp dogs on the track. I know half the county myself."

"Well, there's another person that, perhaps, you may know. Did you ever hear of one Leopold Bierstadt?"

"Never!"

"An old man, over sixty, I guess, with his mouth all caved in from want of teeth, and a great big bushy head of reddish brown hair, bushy on the sides, and bald atop. He stoops in his walk, and looks weak, but he's strong as a horse, and rides famous. Do you know him?"

"Don't know that I ever saw any person answering this description."

"But you've heard of the man by name."

"Never that I recollect. I don't know that any such person lives in the county."

"Oh! that he does, I'm certain. Well, it's these two persons that I want to find. If we can fix upon Furze, we can fix the other, I guess; and if we can find and fix the other, Bierstadt, wherever he is, we can bleed him, I guess, to the tune of twenty thousand dollars, if not more."

The avarice of the lawyer was growing active. He wrote the name of Bierstadt in his memorandum-book, and copied literally the description given of his person.

The dialogue was continued for some time longer between the two, Brownlow subjecting Gorham to a subtle cross-examination, which the other dexterously baffled and evaded. They were well matched; and, at the close, beyond what we have already shown, neither had gained of the *profits*, however much they might have been enlightened in the law.

That day Gorham pursued his way to "Keovala," or its precincts, rather, hovering about on foot, from hill to hill, and from valley to valley; circling the establishment, and gradually contracting the circle, until, at sunset, he looked down from an eminence upon the grand dwelling, the beautiful gardens, the glorious shrubbery, the noble avenues of trees, the slopes, exquisitely lawned or terraced, and the whole domain of wealth and peace and beauty, even while Fergus Wallace and Mignon, from their favorite height, were communing of love together, little dreaming, in the midst of all their dreams of happiness, that the serpent had already found his way into their Eden; and that, even then, he was watching them with feelings of hate and envy, not unlike those with which Satan regarded the happy couple in the Garden of their Paradise!

Chapter XLVIII

PRESENTIMENTS

What object did Gorham propose to himself by establishing a plan of espionage on Voltmeier and his dwelling? He had established no shadow of connection between this personage and those whom he sought—Bierstadt and Furze; nor was there, in his mind, a single thought suggestive of a connection between these parties. That Voltmeier should have stabled his horse in the stone cavity near the great cave was curious, as he professed to be a stranger to the place; but that might be accidental, and it was, at best, a mere coincidence, upon which he did not lay any emphasis. To himself, he spoke only of the beautiful girl whom he had encountered at the gap of the "Hickory Nut," and he entertained a sort of curiosity to see her again. He had tracked the family carriage to the great avenue leading to Keovala, and, taking lodgings that night with a grazier, some four miles off, named Watson, who occupied a farm on Voltmeier's land, and found occasional employment with him as a cattle drover, he obtained certain clues to the family of Voltmeier.

With his usual cunning he had thoroughly sifted Watson, and obtained from him all he could relate touching the household; but the distance between the aristocracy of the country and its poorer classes was too wide and deep to permit Watson to know much; and, beyond the mere facts that Voltmeier, with a single maiden sister and an only daughter, were the sole occupants of the premises, and that they lived in great splendor, and that Voltmeier was as rich as a baron, and had larger possessions than a German prince, was pretty much the amount of his acquisitions from this source.

"But he has people living with him—gentlemen?" insinuated Gorham.

Watson did not know—had never seen them. He had visitors at times, and sometimes there were great occasions—dinner-parties and dances, but only when great people came to visit them from Asheville, Flat Rock, and other places.

"Did you never see or hear of a Mr. George Clinton there?"

"Never haird the name."

"There's another—a tall young fellow, who seems to be quite sweet upon the young lady—what's her name?"

"They call her Mignon—a sort of outlandish furrin name that don't seem to me to have any meanin' in it. 'Tain't American, I know."

"Mignon! But the young fellow?"

"I've hairn tell of him, but never seed him. He comes from somewhar' in South Carolina, and I've hearn tell how he got shot on the road somewhar', and how Colonel Voltmeier came across him in the night time, and tuk him up, and tuk him home and doctored him; but I never seed the pusson or haird his name."

"A-h!" was all that Gorham said; but the fact struck him as another coincidence. He had, of course, heard, while one of the band with Bierstadt, or "Old Grizzly," Peters, and Swipes, of the adventure in which Fergus Wallace had been wounded; but he had not been one of the party on that particular occasion. Still, the fact became intimately associated with the other facts which he had gathered, and as he had a habit, to use his own phrase, of "putting things together," he stored this away in memory, to be brooded over in their connection. But after all the revelations of Watson, his mind recurred, at length, only to the vision of female beauty in Mignon, which, for the first time in his life, seemed to kindle a soul within his bosom. Her exquisite loveliness, grace, sweetness of voice, earnestness of speech, action and manner, as shown in the moment when, with outstretched arms, she darted between the muzzles of the two rifles, and arrested the hands of the combatants; these rose before him with the vividness and reality of an ever-present drama; and, had he been asked to say what motive led him aside to Keovala, perhaps he would have answered—but only to himself—only to behold once more that vision of beauty which had inspired a new emotion in his breast.

But Voltmeier would have come to a different conclusion. He had. His instincts, if not his philosophy, found in all the events in connection with Gorham, the presence and agency of a pursuing Fate! That there was something in the instincts of Gorham, also, which, as yet, he himself had failed to comprehend, may be assumed as probable; and Voltmeier may have been quite right in regarding the ruffian as simply a blind agency, under the guidance of a power which did not permit itself to be seen. The "still small voice" was speaking to both souls; one as the destined victim, the other as the hound of Fate, with nothing but the nose of instinct to direct him in the chase.

Contracting his circle so as gradually to approach the dwelling, Gorham, at length, reached the shrubbery which formed the margin around the immediate court, extending from front to rear, and making a dense hedge which enclosed the flower garden—a garden fully an acre in extent, and filled with the choicest exotics which could survive the winter in that mountain region. There was a spacious conservatory, also, full of delicate shrubs and flowers, which rose on the side of a gentle swell of land on the west; and, near this, was a sort of ledge, devoted to the gardener. On the same line was a row of small buildings, employed for various uses; the dairy, store-house, and houses for grain and provisions. Further off, but within sight of the dwelling, were the stables, in the rear of which was a well-fenced cow-pasture, where a score or two of choice milch cattle might be seen throughout the day, lazily feeding, or resting their fat sides upon the long grasses in profoundest rumination.

Gorham made a complete survey of the precincts—took in everything with his eye, and cautiously pursuing his way, found himself about to enter the enclosure, when the sullen growl of a watch-dog cautioned him against farther advance. He saw the dog, in the dim starlight, strolling across the court, coming from beneath the shelter of the piazza, where he usually harbored. The dog was a famous Newfoundland slut—a beautiful animal, powerful as beautiful, and capable of dragging a drowning man out of the water.

Now a dog was one of Gorham's aversions, as it was one of his greatest fears; and, as the animal walked in the direction whence her keen ears had caught the sounds of approaching footsteps, the intruder beat a hasty retreat; and, after a few moments, found himself upon the height from which Fergus and Mignon were wont to take their views of the sunset.

He had accomplished all that he proposed for that night, and proceeding to the hollow where he had hidden his horse, he rode off, and soon disappeared within the shadows of the mountain.

In blissful ignorance of this intrusion, or of any danger that might arise from it, the family of Voltmeier enjoyed their music and their cards as usual. The young people were quite happy, with not a cloud on their horizon. Good Aunt Gertrude was sedate as usual, and quite reconciled to that selfishness of the young folks, which prompted them to prefer their own to her companionship. When not hearkening to the music, or playing whist, or talking Goethe and Schiller, Voltmeier conversed with the aunt upon family affairs, and discussed the project of a visit to Germany as soon as Mignon should be married. This event he proposed should take place without any unnecessary delay.

"But there is no necessity for haste, Leonard. It will require a great many preparations for such an event, and Mignon is so young!"

"My dear Gertrude," was the sportive reply, "Mignon is now possessed of a soul, you know."

"Pshaw!"

"As for preparations, the more simple the better. As for any ostentatious wedding, I am utterly opposed to it. The more private the better. The family and a few friends will be quite enough. When the marriage is fairly over, the young people may do what they please, as respects dinners and evening parties. I mean to resign everything into their hands and yours. And, by the way, I'll tell you what I have done to-day."

He apprised her of the settlements he had made, as well on herself as the young couple.

"I thank you, Leonard; but as I expect to live and die in the family of Mignon, no matter whom she marries, special provision need not be made for me."

"It must be as I have said, Gertrude; but the possession of the little estate which I have given you, need, by no means, interfere with your desire to remain with Mignon. You know *her* by this time, and I trust you feel sure of the good heart and the generous nature of Fergus. You will, in fact, be necessary to the young people. They will feel *that*, as I do."

"But, in this disposition of 'Keovala,' and the homestead for me, Leonard, you have left nothing for yourself."

"Have I not, when I shall have you all to the last? I shall need but little, and shall not need it long. I have my presentiments, Gertrude, and feel that my tenure of life is destined to be short."

"How you talk, Leonard! It is wonderful that a strong man like yourself should be troubled with such superstitions."

"It is because I *am* strong!"

"No, Leonard, it is because you are, in one essential respect, so very weak! You are at once credulous and skeptical, and accord a faith to the merest fancies, to what you call the spiritual, which, I am sorry to think, you are reluctant to yield to a God and a Savior."

"Do not believe so hardly of me, Gertrude. I believe in both, but not as you do! But enough of this. One more word. I am conscious of very peculiar changes going on in my nature; in thought, feeling, and a rapidly-growing consciousness of hitherto unknown things. I begin to see many things more clearly than before, and the light grows within me. I now see the vanities of things. Thus it is, that, if we grow at all, we grow into a new consciousness, with every decade. My consciousness is coupled with certain presentiments of evil, of which I can not shake myself free; and by these I feel that my career, for good or evil, is very nearly run! This is one reason why I have made all these provisions seasonably, and it is because of this that I have resolved that Fergus and Mignon shall marry as soon as possible. With these matters off my mind, I shall sleep more soundly by night, and be better prepared for that long sleep which may, in my case, have no waking."

"Leonard, you are sick! Your head is wrong! Take something and go to bed! You need sleep! You overwork yourself, and recuperation of tone, body, and spirit, is difficult. If you go on so, it will soon be impossible!"

"Sleep! sleep! 'But in that sleep what dreams do come?' My labors are now nearly over, Gertrude. Do you not see that I propose devolving them upon you and the children? I am stripping myself of all *impedimenta*, as one who prepares for a long journey and shall need nothing by the way."

Meanwhile, the voice of Mignon, that was laughter a moment before, now broke out in song; the "Song of the Spirits," from Faust, which she sang in the original. When the strain closed, Voltmeier, who had been pacing up and down the room, and listening the while, murmured broken passages from that vague spiritual and passionate lyric.

"Yes!" quoth he; " 'Thy world and ours tumbles and falls abroad!'

'Thou! Thou! in thy weakness'—it was madness surely—'Thou hast destroyed it!'—For me, yes!—'They bear away,—they, the Dark Spirits,—they bear away, wrecked into nothingness—all the hope and the harmony; while we weep over the beauty that's lost!' Alas! alas! the terrible truth! But the hope—if there be hope—ay, Gertrude, if what we *hope* be a *belief*—and if the belief be *true*—what remains? We shall not substantially differ, my sister, in the faith that is ours, though we may differently construe its tenor. Allow for the phraseology of the Poet, and, substantially, I believe that we may be 'mighty among the stars'; that 'the world which we have destroyed' may be rebuilt! What is the adjuration?

> 'In thy *own bosom*
> Rebuild it again!'

Ay, there's the rub. Submission—repentance—atonement—these are the grand architects, no matter whether you or I be right in any single article of Faith.

> 'With that new being
> The discord shall vanish,
> And the true music
> Unite the now sundered.' "

With this close of the quotation, Voltmeier abruptly left the apartment. Aunt Gertrude followed him with her eyes for a moment, laid down her work, and folding her hands in her lap, forgot herself in brooding; while still the song of Mignon, at intervals, thrilled throughout the dwelling. Happy children! They beheld no Fate. No dark shadow as yet overcast their young and ardent souls. Their consciousness, being all purity, was all peace.

Chapter XLIX

THE FACE AT THE WINDOW

We will suppose three days to have elapsed. In the meantime, the hours were not left unemployed by the several parties most interested in their profitable use—profitable according to their several tastes, ideas, and propensities. Voltmeier was frequently busied, day and night, in the library. He was clearing his decks, as it were, preparing for action in some way, destroying papers, and writing them as fast. In those three days he covered a vast bulk of foolscap with ink; and when he spoke with the family, it was of Germany and Italy, and of the pleasant memories of those lands, entertained in his youth. With these ideas and desires Mignon was already inoculated. Aunt Gertrude looked forward eagerly to Fatherland, and her hope to revisit it grew stronger day by day, as the language of Voltmeier appealed to her own memories. It need hardly be said that Fergus Wallace, young, ardent, curious, of literary tastes, and as yet wholly untraveled, found the suggestion one of rarely-exciting interest.

"In six weeks after your marriage, Fergus," said Voltmeier, "we can be in Europe, in Italy, on the Rhine—everywhere!"

In six weeks!

It was appointed that the marriage should take place in three weeks from date! What a world of happiness did the prospect open to Fergus, and how sweetly did Mignon discourse to him of the wonders that they should see—that she should show him! She should be the cicerone everywhere, and boasted of the memories of her childhood, as if the things in that grand old world beyond the seas should ever remain the same.

But while all things and thoughts sang happily together at Keovala, there was a silent speech in the face of Voltmeier, which caused some uneasiness to Aunt Gertrude. She could see what the young people did not see or heed. The secret anxieties of Voltmeier were telling upon his person. He now stooped in his walk. His face had grown cadaverous, with a somewhat jaundiced hue; his step was occasionally uncertain; his movements spasmodic and capricious, and he now suffered the aunt to see, what he had hitherto with care concealed from all eyes, his frequent resort to the little pellets from his opium-box. He seemed to swallow these unconsciously, even as the habitual drinker or smoker drinks and smokes when under anxiety or deeply immersed in thought. His mind, however, never seemed more elevated, more audacious, and even grand in his imaginations. He spoke loftily, communed with high and deep philosophies; was mystical, far-reaching, and eloquent of utterance; so as to compel the eyes of Mignon to dilate as she heard him, while Fergus listened with wonder, and thought:

"What a wonderful man is this. And yet to be nothing. Neither lawyer, nor statesman, nor politician; yet seemingly endowed as a prophet."

And Voltmeier was frequently oracular, in all the higher senses of the word. Fluent, elegant, bold, the words flowed from him as from a stream issuing from the smitten rock, and giving forth all the waters, pent up for ages, when the world's gray fathers stood upon the heights and delivered or received the law.

Thus was it at Keovala.

Gorham, the Black Dog, the Fate of its master, was, in the meantime, far from idle. He, too, could travel and toil, day and night, having an object. In the three days thus employed at Keovala, he had made a visit to the farmstead of Mother Moggs, at the foot of Mount Tryon. He had made that place, will he nill he, in spite of mother and son, his head-quarters; had possessed himself of a room, which he held the key of, and there he had stored away an enormous chest. This chest, in especial, seemed to be the object of his visit on the present occasion. He searched its contents, and drew forth a variety of objects, for which, in our inexperience, it would be difficult to decide the uses. There were various files, nippers, screw-drivers, and other tools, which we can only conceive of as implements of the burglar. Gorham, by the way, as we happen to know, had neglected none of the arts which belong to his profession as rogue and thief in general. He had bunches of skeleton keys, and pick-locks, adapted to almost universal use for the entrance to fastnesses of thrifty house-keepers. Shylock's treasure chests could hardly have been security against his ingenuity. All these things he gathered up in a compact form, in a convenient sack, which he bound fast about his person, to be concealed beneath his hunting-shirt. There was also one other article which he had found particularly useful on sundry important occasions of his adventurous life. This was a dark lantern, small enough to be hidden within the folds of his coat or vest. It was glassed only on one side, closed up and quite dark on three others. Add to these a small vial of corrosive sublimate, a deadly poison.

Looking over him as he examines his chest, we note the presence of rouleaux, uniform of size, which may contain gold; little leathern bags, which seem to be heavy, and which, we may assume, contain the same metal, or, perhaps, silver.

Gorham has been no profligate of his gains. He did not game; did not drink of those fierce potations which usurped the brains of his late associates to madness. He hoarded his spoils, and was comparatively rich. Among his possessions were two great packages of what seemed to be bank-notes. These were separately bundled and marked. One of these he drew forth and examined, if he did not count. There was a huge sum of it—several thousand dollars. From this pile he detached bills to the amount of five hundred dollars, then folded up the residue, and dropped it out of sight, into a capacious side pocket. He then emerged from his chamber, and reappeared in the hall in front, where Mother Moggs and her hopeful son seemed to be awaiting him—perhaps watching him also.

"Well," said Ephraim, "what's the *lay* (scheme) now."

"One in which you can do no service. But there is something that you *can* do. Take these bills, Ephraim. There are five hundred dollars. Get down to Greenville, or Spartanburg—but the farther off the better—and buy yourself a couple of horses, one for yourself, one for me. You want one on your farm; your horse won't work, I see."

"It's queer-kone (counterfeit), I reckon," said the other. "All *flam?*"

"Well, you're only good now, as a shovel-pitcher (passer of counterfeits.) It's just as good as the bank, where I send you. It will pass through a hundred hands, before you ever see it again."

Ephraim took the money, and Gorham rode off with his bundles, but not before the old woman had spied the sack containing his burglar implements.

"He's got his 'round robins' with him," said she. "He always carries them in that bag. He's after a 'dub-lay' " (burglary).

"He's on the 'sly' for the small hours. He's got his 'shady glim' (dark lantern). It sticks out square in his buzzom pocket. Why the diccaner don't he want me?"

"Keep cl'ar of him, Ephraim. Now this money—it's all 'nums' (sham). But, far off at Greenville, or some of them low-down towns in South Carolina, 'twill go like hot cakes. They won't know any better.

"You take care of what you does! Git off pretty fur before you offer to trade. We does want the horse, and two of 'em too, ef we could git 'em. What does he want with another horse, I wonder."

"For work. I'd better git a mule."

"Git a horse, Ephraim; an easy-going one, that I kin travel on. I'd like sometimes to git down to Greenville and Spartanburg myself; and thar's no riding your horse for me. He'd shake my poor bones to pieces!"

"Ah! mammy, we'd git everything we want, ef we could only git into Gorham's chist."

"Thar's a way, I reckon, whar thar's a will."

"Yes, by knocking it to pieces with an axe."

"You hev fust to knock the head off his shoulders! How I do hate the sight of him! and to think thet he hes the power to bring us both to a dance upon nothing. Oh, ef you was the right sort of a man, Ephraim! But you never had the hairt for a bold thing yit."

"Let me alone, mother, and jist you give me time. I feels it as much as you, the hate I has for him."

"To keep us al'ays afeard of him! To hev him always a-picturing the gallows before us, as he does at a'most every meal, and to know that he's jest as bad, and jest as desarving of the gallows as the worst one among us. Oh! ef I was only a man; or ef I hed only that strength I hed when I was a young woman,—Lord! wouldn't he ha' got it, long afore this. I'd ha' laid sich a trap for him, riding up them long narrow ranges of the mountains, with a sudden bend in the road at every quarter, as would stop his tongue from singing gallows in my lugs every hour."

"We'll do it, yit, mother. You'll see! We'll hev that chist and what's in it yit. He'll get his salt before long. You'll see."

"Ef I was only a man!"

The woman did not repose much faith in the bully-brave words of her hopeful son. Still he could be dangerous at times, as the wild cat is dangerous when driven into close quarters, and with no outlet for escape.

Gorham made his way back to the precincts of "Keovala." In that grand establishment he beheld the means to add to his accumulations, and all his instincts, appetites, and habits were revived, in full force, as he meditated avariciously the great increase of his gains from an establishment that promised so amply of resource. What precious plate, what jewels, what money, perhaps, were all to be found in so showy a household! The rich planters of the country were notorious for their rare collections of silver plate, and for this commodity Gorham had a special passion.

He hid away his implements of burglary in a convenient gorge of the mountains, selecting some great boulders, in an obscure hollow, for his *cache*. This done, he made his way to the wigwam of Watson, the grazier, where he spent the night. Before dawn, Watson was up, engaged in killing a beef which he prepared to drive to the market town, bright and early, that morning. He had hardly shot the bullock, which he did with his rifle, the bullet being planted between the eyes of the beast, when he found Gorham standing beside him.

"What! you're up," said Watson, "bright and airly."

"Yes, I'm a peep-o'-day boy as well as yourself. That was a pretty shot, I guess."

"Yes, indeed, I reckon 'twas. I never misses to plant the bullet jist whar I wants to!"

"And you're going to market?"

"Yes; jist as soon as I'm done with the butchering."

"Well, as I'm staying with you now, for a few days, off and on, going and coming, I'll want some of that meat. Bacon don't suit me, every day. Leave a quarter here for me, and here's your money."

"Well, your money's jist as good, I reckon, as I kin git in town; and I'll leave a quarter at the house afore I starts."

"Very good!"

"You'll be home all the day?"

"I'll be about; though I may start off before night."

"Well, I'll be back in time to see you. The old woman will see to what you wants."

Leaving the butcher, Gorham returned to the house, and when the beef was brought up, he called to the negress for a knife, and cut off several steaks from it, some of which he ordered for breakfast.

"Set about it at once, old woman," said Gorham; "I like my breakfast as soon as I get up."

Watson had eaten his by torch-light before going forth to butcher. He had left the quarter of beef for Gorham, and moved off at once for the county town.

When the negress had gone off to prepare the breakfast, Gorham seized the opportunity to cut from the beef a monstrous collop, which he seasoned dextrously, here and there, from his vial of corrosive sublimate. This he carefully rolled up in one of the coarse cotton towels of the establishment, and hid away for the present. The residue of the beef he hung up from one of the rafters.

When he rode off, as he did during the morning, he carried the poisoned beef along with him. He was at home again when Watson returned in the afternoon, but stayed only till near sunset, when he again took his departure.

The night found him once more circling the domain of "Keovala," gradually nearing it as the darkness grew more dense; finally, reaching the shrubbery immediately girdling the dwelling, he threw the mass of beef over it, into the area beyond; then sped back to his hiding-place in the hollows of the mountain.

The next day found him again at Watson's, at early dawn, once more slicing his steaks for breakfast, and with the evening he had gone again.

It was night at "Keovala," and the lamps were lighted in parlor and library. Voltmeier paced the piazza. Fergus and Mignon had just returned from their evening ramble, which was now rarely terminated by the sunset.

The evening had been so mild, so sweet, that they lingered till the heavens had become so thickly sown with eyes, that even love became admonished that they were so many watchers; and as "the chariest maid is prodigal enough, if she unvails her beauty to the moon," so is she apt to fancy that even starry eyes must not behold the liberties which loving lips are yet authorized to take.

They joined Voltmeier in the piazza. He said:

"I have been waiting and wishing for you, Fergus, but it will do after supper. That, too, is waiting for us, I fancy."

At the same moment the little silver bell of Aunt Gertrude gave the anticipated signal, when they all proceeded to the supper room. The meal ended, after a moderate time, they retired to the parlor, whence Voltmeier withdrew Fergus into the library, while Mignon placed herself at the piano. In a little while after, she was joined by Aunt Gertrude, and they sat together, both delivered to an atmosphere all music.

Voltmeier held Fergus in long, protracted, but interesting conference, touching his own affairs, and the future of the young couple. He gave him a full account of his possessions, his lands and houses, his herds of horses, mules, and other cattle; the bonds due him; his stocks, etc., all in detail. For all of these the evidence had been prepared, and a full inventory made out; severally, in respect to each, each class of property having its own catalogue in ample detail. Then, there was a list of the several graziers and herdsmen in his employ, the terms of their service, and all necessary particulars. In short, Fergus Wallace was put in possession of all the knowledge requisite for asserting the rights of the estate, and of conducting its affairs.

This done, Voltmeier told him of the settlements which he had made upon Fergus, himself, Mignon, and Miss Gertrude Leyfenholdt; copies of each instrument being placed within his hands, with a memorandum, referring to Col. Graham as the custodian of the deeds fully executed. All these details, blended, as was Voltmeier's manner, with frequent episodes, in which he always contrived to rise above and relieve the more tedious parts of business, occupied considerable time. Towards the close, Voltmeier handed Fergus an envelope, saying:

"I wish you to attend to a piece of business which I can not attend to myself, as I shall be away in another direction at the time. Here are three thousand dollars—count them—take charge of this money, and to-morrow attend the sale of Houscal's property—"

"To-morrow is Sunday, sir."

"Is it possible! I have lost a day! It will be on Monday, then. Old Houscal possessed some of the finest cattle in all this country, and I have long been desirous of having his stock. His children sell for a division. I will see the Harness boys, and get Benjie, or, perhaps, both of them, to attend the sale, when I wish you to buy to the full extent of this money. Benjie Harness is a first-rate judge of cattle, and is to be fully trusted. He will have an eye to the finest lots, and you will act upon his judgment and suggestions. Have you counted the bills?"

"They are right—as you say—three thousand dollars."

"Very good! Put them up in the escritoir, with these papers, until Monday; and now let us to the parlor and get some of Mignon's music."

Never was melody more sweetly made! Never did Mignon sing more ravishingly in the ears of her betrothed, or more soothingly in the ears of her father. The one had his eyes only for her; the other leaned back in his chair, closed his eyes, and yielded himself to that delicious reverie, which seems rather to entreat the affections than to exercise the mind. But, in the midst of the strain, and when it was at the sweetest, there was a sudden crash, and Mignon suddenly started up with a cry, exclaiming:

"Oh! papa! Fergus! There's a strange man in the piazza! I saw his face at the window!"

In a moment both the gentlemen were on their feet, and darting for the casements, which were of glass, paneled below, to the floor. These were soon thrown open, and the gentlemen in the piazza.

The piazza was empty, and they descended to the shrubbery about it; thence into the garden; but with vain search. However bright the starlight, they could follow no tracks. They heard no sound. Whoever might be the intruder, he was evidently fleet of foot, as well as cunning of discovery. It was clear that he had made himself familiar with all the passages of the precinct. The two returned to the house after the fruitless search. Of course there was much speculation and conjecture upon the event.

"It is strange," said Voltmeier, "that we have not heard 'Jessica.' She was wont to resent the slightest intrusion of this sort."

"I forgot to mention, Leonard," said Miss Gertrude, in her quietest manner, "that Jessica is dead!"

"Dead!" exclaimed Voltmeier. "Jessica dead! Why, I played with her only yesterday!"

"Dead!" cried Mignon; "the poor old slut! and, Aunt Gertrude, you never told me!"

"Was anything the matter with her that you know of?" demanded Voltmeier—"she seemed quite well but yesterday."

"We found her dead this morning at the well!"

"Was she swollen?"

"Very much!"

Voltmeier, on receiving this answer, left the room abruptly, murmuring as he went:

"Poisoned, by heaven! And by this stranger! I must see to this! The hounds are pressing too closely upon me! I shall need to show *my* teeth!"

After a while he called Fergus from the library. When the latter came to him, he said:

"You have the key of the escritoir, Fergus; see if the packet of money be there as you left it."

The answer was satisfactory.

"It is here, sir;" lifting up and showing the envelope containing the money; the packet, being unsealed, displayed the pile of banknotes.

"It is well! Lock the escritoir and keep the key yourself! We must be watchful! There are rogues about! Such an intrusion has very rarely occurred at Keovala, save by some traveler who had lost his way. The poor old slut! I feel as if I had lost one of my oldest friends."

And Gorham, having made his escape, chuckled in security on the side of the mountain, looking back on Keovala with all the satisfaction of a conqueror. They little suspect at Keovala how much reason he has for satisfaction!

Chapter L

"LOOK FOR BLOOD, FERGUS!"

A few days of calm. In the meantime, Fergus Wallace has bought three thousand dollars' worth of the finest stock of cattle on the Houscal estate. A day was assigned for driving them to the vast mountain pastures contiguous to "Keovala," and the whole family on horseback, including even Aunt Gertrude, rode forth to witness the reception.

The herds driven by the two brothers Harness, and two or three others, graziers employed upon the estate, made a highly picturesque display, as, driven through the gorges, and up the sides of the mountains, they rushed amain, headlong, seeming to seek out, and to find by instinct, the salt which was spread for them here and there, on the great flat boulders along the summits.

In the contemplation of this sight, the vast array of cattle, his own former stocks now blending with the newly-bought, Voltmeier seemed, for the time, to be forgetful of all cares and anxieties. His was a swelling nature, and his mind luxuriated in the possession of large ideas, and in the idea of large possessions. He was quite exultant as he thought of the little principality which he had secured to his posterity. And, with Fergus and Mignon riding beside him, he seemed to have taken a bond from Fate; the youth and beauty of the pair, their sympathetic natures and active intelligences, all seemed to assure him; and with a natural pride, he exclaimed, as his hand swept over the scene:—

"These are all yours, my children!"

Gorham also beheld the fine spectacle, as the cattle were driven along in front of the house of Watson, the grazier. But he himself kept unseen. He could fire the match, but was not the person to await the explosion. He was well aware how the cattle had been bought, and as he mused upon the event, he chuckled to himself, and muttered:—

"I know who has got the best of that bargain!"

Since his nocturnal visit to the house of Voltmeier, he had ridden down to that of Mother Moggs, and had deposited there a packet of bank-notes, of the genuineness of which he had no question. This done, he returned to the precincts of "Keovala," having further designs on the peace and prosperity of that household.

The next day, Voltmeier, riding forth, very nearly encountered him. Gorham had barely time to put himself under cover till the other had passed by. Had the eyes of the latter happened upon him, it would not be difficult to say what would have been the consequence. Voltmeier went always armed, was quick as lightning in the use of his weapons, and, regarding Gorham, by this time, as an enemy, the subtle creature of the Fates, and bent on his destruction, he had more than once said to himself:—

"Why *did* I not shoot him when I met him in the cave?"

The instincts of Gorham also taught him all that he had to fear from the man whose life he haunted from day to day, with a persecution, which, up to this time, seemed to have hardly a motive beyond the gratification of a mere morbid curiosity. The desire for plunder, it is true, now that he had seen and conjectured the wealth of "Keovala," was opening momently a new and hopeful vista to the avarice in his soul. It will be found that his first visit to "Keovala" had resulted to him in large and unexpected money profits; but of this hereafter. His heart of greed, with hourly-increasing appetite, was set upon still further acquisitions.

Meanwhile, Fergus Wallace resumed his labors at the law. He had some important cases to study, in which he was still further to distinguish himself. For three days he was absent from "Keovala," lodging with Col. Graham.

Mignon pined in solitude. Wrestling with study, Fergus continued to endure the separation much better, but still he felt very desolate. Mignon could no longer follow in the footsteps of Schiller, and drink in the lessons of his genial humanity; nor could she pursue the wanderings of Goethe's muse, and discern the spiritual graces in his art.

Even Aunt Gertrude missed the frank and highly endowed youth, who had, long ere this, begun to give to the family a taste of those intellectual resources which had made his friends prophesy greatness for his name.

Voltmeier would have felt his absence as keenly as the rest, but that he kept on horseback during these days; riding forth, none knew whither, and coming home weary, fagged, and with that air of distress and anxiety on his visage, which none but Aunt Gertrude had discovered. His thoughts were vague and wandering, but his instincts were busy. He murmured to himself, as he walked or rode, as if striving to reassure himself:

"Why should I fear from such a source? I am guarded at all points against him! Yet it is enough to know that he is busy, and that he has the cold, malignant cunning of the Devil! Now, if Fate would afford me but a moment's opportunity!"

And his eyes glared as he spoke, and feeling the butt of his pistol under his belt, he clenched his teeth together with the manner of one resolute on desperate measures.

And, in this mood, he rode to the cave once more, and traversed its recesses, and sate upon the crags which overhung the boiling waters, and murmured, looking forth eagerly and listening:

"Were the scoundrel now to appear! Necessity shapes the wisdom, and compels the will! My thoughts have not kept their usual pace with Fate. I have been slow. But it is not too late to repair the error. I would have foreborne for all the future, for these children, if not for myself. Yes! for myself even; and those dear memories which, so lately, have sprung up so freshly in my heart. But I struggle in vain against the Fates. There is a law in all this, though we may not fathom it, and the atonement may be made—though I see not how—yet only with the last sacrifice!"

He gazed down upon the boiling cauldron of ever restless waters, plunging over in huge billows, and rearing upward, then subsiding in the gulf below; and, strangely enough, he murmured:

"They speak to me of peace! That is now my only prayer! With all human desires gratified, with the prospect fair on every side, why this torment? This Demon of Unrest is born of my own soul! We create all our devils! They are all personal! I have made mine—have conjured them up from the depths of my own soul, and can not lay the fiend I have created! He will not down at my bidding, any more than the ghastly Banquo, at the imperial summons of Macbeth. Peace! Peace! and to secure this peace,—to find security from this demon, I must give him farther employment!"

Voltmeier returned home at evening, writhing under disappointment, yet, subduing himself, as of old, to those gentle household influences which befitted the pure feminine atmosphere of Keovala.

Three days had he consumed in these restless ridings, having but one object in his aim. The close of the third day found him, just after dark, alighting at the door of his dwelling. Fergus Wallace had ridden up but a moment before, and he and Mignon had received him at the threshold.

For a moment their speaking faces, all delight and rapture, made him oblivious of his soul's discomforts. He embraced them both, and the little silver bell of Aunt Gertrude tingling just then, they went into the supper-room together.

After supper, in the parlor, Fergus delivered his budget of village news, and went over the case to Voltmeier, upon which Col. Graham and himself had been studying closely for several days. He reported his conception of the treatment of the case, after the narration of the facts—being particularly happy, inasmuch as Col. Graham had paid him some high compliments in respect to it. The sense of Voltmeier readily took in the argument, and he made some comments upon it, but with an air of languor and effort, which Fergus could not help but remark. Unconsciously, too, as it would seem, Voltmeier more than once detached one of the little pellets from his opium-box, and swallowed it in open presence of the company. It was only with an evident effort that he kept up, and it was possibly to avoid further speech that he called upon Mignon for music.

Mignon was too full of happiness to be perverse. This night she rose to the harp. Fergus drew it out from the wall, and she took her position before that classical, but much overrated instrument. Still, hers was a hand that could draw much from it—of its peculiar virtues. Her *petite*, slight figure, did not furnish a good subject for a picture, before such an instrument; but you forgot her figure in her play, and, accompanied by the voice, as harp-music should always be, she soothed Voltmeier of some of his troublous thoughts, while Fergus hung over her delighted—at every moment doubting of that good fortune, which found him in such pleasant places, and with prospects of such rapture so near at hand.

It lacked but two weeks of the period appointed for their marriage.

In the very midst of the music, Voltmeier rose abruptly, pushed back his chair with unwonted noise, and made several hasty strides across the apartment; then, wheeling suddenly about, he left the room. The music stopped. Mignon looked up, and rose.

"What's the matter with papa?"

"I will see, Mignon. He seems more wearied than usual. That is all."

Mignon would have accompanied her aunt, but the latter pushed her back.

"You will only distress him by your show of anxiety. Stay here with Fergus. I will come and tell you."

She followed Voltmeier to the chamber.

"What's the matter, Leonard? Can I do anything for you?"

"Nothing, Gertrude, only do not trouble me or yourselves. Go back to the children. I am simply wearied. I have ridden too far, and my head troubles me. Go, now."

"If I can do anything, Leonard—"

"Give me peace!" he said, impatiently. "Let me rest. I must sleep if I can. Go."

She was about to go, when he arrested her.

"You should know enough of me by this time, Gertrude, to realize that nothing pains or vexes me more than this sort of solicitude. I am old enough to know what to do, without counsel or assistance, and when I suffer, I prefer to do so alone."

"Voltmeier, if I or your children *see* that you suffer, you can not expect us to be calm and quiescent. Enough; I will report you to be wearied and wanting sleep."

"Do so; yes, sleep! I must rest if I can."

Miss Gertrude disappeared.

When she had gone, Voltmeier strode the chamber.

"It is *rest*, not sleep! I know not how it is, but my brain is more than usually troubled. I do not know that there is any weariness of the body that now troubles me. I feel that I could mount my horse now, and canter over a score of mountains. But for these dogging

hounds of thought! There is a whirl within my brain, and I find it
hard to concentrate thought upon anything, even for a single moment! That law-case of Fergus—I know not what I said—but I
remember nothing of it! But for rest, I must try sleep! I must quiet
this presentiment of cloud—this great black-bat of speculation and
doubt that seems to close its wings over me!"

His resort the same instant was to his opium-box, from which he
swallowed two of the pellets, one immediately after the other. An
hour after, Aunt Gertrude passed quietly into the piazza, and discovered that the light was extinguished in the chamber of Voltmeier.
The night was warm and close, even to sultriness, and the latticed
doors, reaching to the floor, were not fastened, simply closed, and
admitting all the air. She would have fastened them, but, in his
moods, Voltmeier was apt to be imperious.

Fergus and Mignon had now separated for the night. Aunt
Gertrude followed the latter to her chamber.

Two hours had elapsed. It was now midnight. The house was
silent. All parties slept, or seemed to sleep, when suddenly the
silence was broken by a crash—a sound like thunder. Pistols were
fired, two in rapid succession, and apparently from the chamber of
Voltmeier.

Fergus was the first person to make his way into Voltmeier's
chamber. He found him in his night-dress, standing erect, the two
pistols in his grasp, and the doors of the chamber, opening upon the
piazza, wide open. To this Voltmeier pointed, and cried:

"Lights! get lights and see! There was a man in my room! Lights,
Fergus, lights and see!"

Fergus had brought his own lamp with him, but it gave forth
only a feeble gleam.

"Get to bed, Mr. Voltmeier," said Fergus, "the ladies are coming."

Voltmeier covered himself with the bedclothes.

A moment after, Aunt Gertrude appeared, followed by Mignon,
both bearing lights, and both in their night-dresses.

"What is the matter, Leonard?"

"There was a man in my chamber! He escaped through the sash
into the piazza. See if I have not made my mark upon him. Look for
blood, Fergus! look for blood!"

Search was made, and a single drop of blood was found upon the latticed-door.

"I think I could not wholly have missed him. I saw the dark outline distinctly. He is a bold burglar, whoever he is, for he carried a dark lantern."

"Shall I fasten these windows, now?" asked Fergus.

"No; throw them wider. I want air. He will hardly trouble me again to-night. Go to bed, women. Fergus, load those pistols. You will find the flask and the bullets together behind the glass. I should have killed the scoundrel, but I was so weary, and my brain seems so muddled. But search the garden. Follow the blood! Call up the servants! Get all the light you can. *Follow the blood.*"

Chapter LI

THE FLASH OF LIGHT!

For the fuller comprehension of the scene in the preceding chapter, and the discovery of its utmost scope, let us, for a few hours, retrace the steps of Time, and show more conspicuously the chief actor in this midnight disturbance at "Keovala."

Richard Gorham, for it was he, having duly planned his performance, and provided himself in all respects for his success in it, was, at an early hour of the night, in the immediate neighborhood of Keovala, and crouching among the boulders on an eminence by which it was immediately overlooked. Here he could see, the very moment when the lights were withdrawn from the parlor, and possibly even when they were extinguished in the chambers. He no longer ventured within the precincts until the evidence should prove conclusive that the family had retired for the night; for he had already discovered the frequent use to which the young lovers now put the piazza—their sympathies being well enlivened by the sweet spells of the starlight, and the gentle persuasions of the evening breeze.

His preparations for entering the house were those of an experienced burglar. He had practiced all branches of his art, in the great cities of the north, and had resources which enabled him to overcome all the obstructions and embarrassments of bar and bolt, and chain and key, such as the householder, Prosperity, usually employs for his protection against the housebreaker, Cunning. He had his files, his nippers, skeleton keys, and what not, all made in the best style of roguish art, adaptable to all conditions and circumstances, and every form of security. These he carried in a little bag dropped in a capacious pocket. In the same way did he carry a most admirable little dark lantern, known in the rogues' vocabulary, as a "shady glim," words which need but a little change to become very good and expressive English.

Thus fully prepared, he watched with the cool and almost phleg-matic patience of his nature, for the gradual disappearance of the lights of the dwelling. The night was warm and genial, and he suffered no discomfort, beyond the tedium of his watch, from his place of hiding upon the mountain. Nor were the myriads of pure bright eyes, looking down upon him, suggestive of any of those thoughts and fancies which might lead to compunctious visitings of any sort. They did not smile less upon a rogue, or speak more to his humanity, because of their purity and beauty.

At length he beheld from his perch, the lights severally go out from the parlor. Soon, he beheld them flash from the windows of the library, and anon from one or other of the chambers; and it was not very long before they disappeared from all. Still he waited. It was not enough that the parties should deliver themselves to sleep; time was to be allowed to that gentle minister to possess himself of their several senses.

This time allowed, and Gorham stole down from the mountain. It was now near midnight. He had made due allowance of time, and suffered not his avarice, in his eagerness, to mar the interests of his policy.

All his approaches were marked by caution. He wound about the shrubbery, then around the quarters assigned to the servants, before venturing to approach the dwelling. All was silent. The stillness, if not the peace of the grave, was over all the scene. He had dosed the watch-dog, the only one about the premises, and had no fear from this source.

And now he crouches beneath the piazza of the dwelling, crouches and listens. The breathless silence everywhere gives him welcome and encouragement. He ascends the steps to the piazza. The Vene-tian doors of lattice, opening upon it from the parlor and library, are closed and bolted. He tries the bolts, but has no need to employ his instruments upon them. The blinds which open to the chamber of Voltmeier himself are simply drawn to, not bolted, and already slightly parted by the breeze.

As yet he does not venture to touch them. He stoops almost to the floor and listens. His ear catches the distinct breathing of a sleeper, and notes from what quarter of the chamber the sound arises. This is one step gained.

He now slightly parts the light valves of the door. They creak slightly upon their hinges, and he pauses. He fancies that the breathing of the sleeper is arrested; but, after a few moments, he is reassured. The breathing is irregular, but deep. He glides into the chamber with naked feet. His shoes have been left below, beneath the piazza.

It is now for him to employ his "shady glim." This he produces, ready lighted, from his bosom, and from its front face only, he suffers a single flash to pass over the chamber.

This suffices to indicate the situation of the bed, the toilet table, and principal articles of furniture. This done, the "glim is doused" under his coat; and, seeing that no obstructions await him, he steals forward to the dressing table, which stands opposite the couch of the sleeper, and turns the face of the lantern upon the table, revealing all its contents.

Slowly his eyes take in the several objects which lie before him, and as he makes them out, he starts with something of amaze. He takes up article by article, and examines it, his surprise growing as he proceeds, and the look of amaze giving way at last to an absolute grin of delight. He can hardly restrain himself from crying out, and giving full expression to his astonishment, with the exultation of one who has made a wonderful discovery. But he subdues speech to a mere murmur, whisper, rather, as, taking up and examining the objects in his sight, he says:

"So! so! and this is the manner of it, eh? My God, how blind I was, not to see before! What a fool I was, not to think of it! and all so easy, and so natural."

He examines, with the interest of a naturalist who has found a specimen of some hitherto unknown bird or beast, a beautiful set of artificial teeth, admirably wrought and polished; set in silver, and calculated for the entire cavity of mouth and jaw.

Such a work of art was utterly unknown to that obscure region. Gorham, in all his experience of crime, had seen nothing like it. He knew that single teeth were occasionally supplied for the lost, but an entire mouthful was new to him, especially when wrought in so exquisite a fashion.

The beautifully prepared wig, which lay beside the teeth, was less a surprise, though it also contributed to his enlightenment; and there were pots of coloring matter, and dyestuffs, all of which he examined, by which all hues of the complexion might be simulated, and hair, and beard, and eyebrows, each be made to take, for the time, the black of the raven, or the red of the fox, or the brown of the deer.

"All a deceit!" was the whispered speech: "all a cheat! cheat in everything! Cunning! Lord God, how cunning! And so a man can make himself up so that his own wife who sleeps with him shan't know him, or any of his real virtues. Now who can this man be, if he be a man? But it may be a woman. The old lady of the house! These old women have wonderful tricks of contrivance for keeping themselves young to the eyesight. There's nothing so vexing to them as the idea of old age. It's a woman, I reckon, though these teeth are large enough for the jaws of any man; and this wig is meant for man's hair! I'll be sworn to that! Now, who the devil is he? Who can he be? This Col. Voltmeier, he's hardly to be counted an old man. He rides like a born soldier! I'll have a look at him, by the eternal Jupiter!"

Such were his whispered speculations and conjectures; then, as if doubt and anxiety could endure no more, he hastily seized the lantern, crossed to the bedside of the sleeper, and, for one long moment, flashed the full blaze of the light across his face.

We know that this is Voltmeier's chamber. We know that, to this chamber he retired, when leaving the parlor, and followed by Aunt Gertrude. Yet, can this be he who now lies before us, sleeping a deep but uneasy sleep? His skin cadaverous, his cheeks sunken; his lips, no longer borne out by the teeth—"caved in"—making, as it were, a hollow, and rendering more prominent the large nose and the massive chin! and the bald head, utterly bald, except for two thin scattered wisps of white hair above and behind the ears?

Our surprise is only surpassed by that of Gorham. For one blank moment, motionless he stood, stupid and staring wild; then, no longer able to restrain himself, he exclaimed aloud:—

"Great Jupiter! Bierstadt! 'Old Grizzly' himself!"

Whether it was the keen flash of the light across his eyes, or this unwary exclamation of Gorham, or both together, that aroused the sleeper to sudden, though imperfect consciousness, may not be said; but wake he did, and,

> "Like the tyrant roused to life,
>   By graze of ill-directed knife,"

he was at once prepared to act on the offensive.

In an instant he had raised himself in bed. In another, he had grasped the pistols from beneath his pillow, and as the light of the glim,—not "doused" too quickly—had shown him the dark outlines of Gorham's figure, he fired, quickly, one pistol immediately after the other, the shots ringing after the felon just as he was darting through the latticed doorway. Then, leaping up, Voltmeier prepared to pursue; when he heard the footfall of Gorham, as he leaped over the balusters of the piazza, to the ground. Not one moment after this did the fugitive delay in flight; and, before Voltmeier and Fergus, only half clad, could commence the search, he was making good his way up the sides of the mountain.

Chapter LII

A BLOW FROM AN
UNEXPECTED QUARTER

Gorham was something of a Puritan, virtuously abstaining from oaths, from drink, from all shows of levity; grave as an owl, solemn as a judge, and sententious as a master of ceremonies; but there was a point when exultation, an enormous self-esteem, and a greedy avarice, all excited, could make him cast aside every garment of hypocrisy. Safe on the mountain, crouched between two enormous boulders, he suffered himself to chuckle—nay, to roar and laugh, outright, and clap his hands. He did not ordinarily laugh like other men, but with a mental reservation. When he laughed, which was unfrequently, it was always with some doubt that his game was secure. Now, he laughed unreservedly. He had solved a profitable problem.

He gave full sway to his new *rôle* of merriment, which prompted him to sundry antics—rolled on the earth and chuckled; muttering to himself, the while, of his own success, and the glorious prospects laid open to him by his discoveries. When he recalled the details of these discoveries, his humor seemed to break through all restraints.

"Who would have thought it of old Grizzly! Beautiful young teeth, white as a virgin woman's, and sich a shock of fine hair—so glossy, in spite of the pepper and salt in it! And how nice the idea of pepper and salt hair for a man about forty-five—so natural for the rich and handsome Col. Voltmeier—just at that time of life! Oh! you cunning old Grizzly! But, I've found you out at last! I know'd there was a secret, and that there was money in it. I'll bleed you, old fellow! I'll milk you! You shall be my milch cow, old fellow, for a mighty long time to come. I've got my hand upon you, with such a grip, that you'll find it tighter than any blacksmith's vise; I've got my foot upon your neck, and you shall bleed or you shall hang. It is a question for you whether to bleed, or to hang, by a short cord, from the cross-timbers. And I'll hang you anyhow, when the time comes—when I've bled you and milked you till you can give no more; then, you old rascal, I'll hang you! Nothing less will do me; for you was always so grand in laying down the law, and saying to one 'go,' and to another 'go,' and putting never a word of civility in your talk—no matter what one did; I'll pay you off for all! You thought there was no finding you out. Ha! ha! 'Twas mighty clever—that's certain. But I worked it out handsome, and now I've got you; and now you shall sweat for the trouble you've gi'n me, in finding out your secrets. You must pay for all that, and for your conceit, too, and your pride. Oh! dod dern you! But I have you now!"

Here his countenance expressed the full feeling of malignant and vindictive hatred which his words expressed; and he shook his fist fiercely in the direction of "Keovala," chuckling horribly, even while the tiger passion spoke in all the lines of his face. He showed, in this speech, how much his self-esteem resented the reserve and authority of his former superior; how eagerly the same self-esteem had hungered for a confidence which was never given him; and how the lurking vanity in this feeling prompted him morbidly to seek after a discovery, which, only in some vague way, suggested itself to him as likely to be profitable. His ideas on this latter subject were only developing themselves fully to his avarice. But his vanity had awakened some other passions, and his desires momentarily expanded, more and more, as he continued to estimate the extent of his discovery.

"Yes! I have him, and I'll have his daughter, too! She's a very beauty, to my thinking—the most beautiful young woman I ever saw! I'll have her! I'll make it a law to his understanding, that I'm to have her, and plenty of money with her, to the bargain, or he tastes the rope! That's the first thing, and after that we'll consider how much more. I must study it all over. Not too fast, Richard Gorham. I must feel my way. It'll take some thinking, and I'm not going to risk all, by being in too great a hurry!"

Here he suddenly clapped his hand to the side of his head, and exclaimed—

"Bloody, by jiminey! If he han't shot me, I'll be hanged! He's made a hole in my ear, and I never felt the bullet. I heard it sing by my head mighty close, but didn't feel a scratch, and I'm dang'd if he hasn't regularly cropped me! I'll be marked for life, dod dern him! That's another account agin him. He shall sweat for all. Oh! how he shall sweat."

We need not, now that we see the train of his meditations, linger longer in his company. Enough that he feels the necessity of putting himself in present security.

"The old fox will be hunting all about these hills, soon as the day peeps in upon 'em. I'll be off, and just hide myself away, till 'I get a plaster on this ear; and the best thing I can do is to stow myself away secret, at Mother Moggs', for a few days. How that old hag and her beautiful son does hate me! They'd put p'ison into my soup if they durst; and anyhow I've got to watch 'em, close. Let me but fix this old rascal's flint for him, and set my trap for all the game, and I'll be off. I don't want his house and lands; but he shall give me the worth of 'em, and, with his daughter, I'll be off, and throw just as many hundred miles between me and these parts as there are days in a fortnight!"

Seeking his horse in the hollow where he had concealed him, he took the route for Mount Tryon and the Mills' Gap, a little before the dawn of day.

He was right in his apprehensions. While the east was just beginning to be streaked with the first rosy harbingers of light, Voltmeier was traversing the hills around Keovala, with all the ferocious, keen scent of a blood-hound. He had never shown himself so aroused before. Such a trespass, so bold an invasion of his premises, had never happened, except in that one approach to it, where the same trespasser had shown his face at the window. Though silent on the subject, Voltmeier naturally concluded the party on both occasions to be the same; and, by subtle instincts, his mind leapt to the conclusion that Gorham was the person. To find the trespasser—to happen upon him in some one of his hiding-places, and, if opportunity served, to wreak mortal punishment upon him, were motives which kept Voltmeier all day in the saddle. He found Watson's house at last, and ascertained that a person, whom Watson very well described, had sought lodgings with him on several occasions. He tested Watson closely in his examination, and the grazier, being simple and honest, readily told all he knew about the stranger, even to his purchase of a quarter of beef. Associating one thing with another, as the keen, quick wit of Voltmeier was apt to do, he readily conceived how his favorite slut, Jessica, had been got out of the way.

The conclusion he reached was that, for some motive, Gorham had made a dead-set at him. Was it plunder, or was he still simply indulging in that morbid curiosity, which Voltmeier had long since been aware possessed his mind in regard to himself? Was it, then, the quest of Gorham now, to identify Bierstadt with Voltmeier? Had he obtained any clues by which this could be done? And, these obtained, what would it profit him to make the revelation, when he himself had been a participator in all the crimes of Bierstadt? These were the questions which Voltmeier had now begun to ask of himself. They made him uneasy; but the influence upon his mind, beyond any appeal to his reason, lay in his instincts—shall we say superstitions? He recognized a dogging fiend in this fellow, and for some time, the image had been present to his imagination, of one of the hounds of fate, having found his tracks, and being ever in hot pursuit!

He returned to Keovala, vexed, wearied, but still impatient to resume his search after his victim. Here, he found that nothing had been stolen by the trespasser, nothing, at least, of such value as to tempt a thief. The shoes of the fugitive were discovered beneath the piazza, and a pair of burglar nippers which had dropped from his hands or bag, as he leapt over the balusters of the piazza. But these served no purpose. Of course, there was great wonderment and confusion at "Keovala." So daring an outrage confounded the family. Aunt Gertrude was earnest in her reproaches to Voltmeier about sleeping with all his doors and windows open. She had warned him of the habit frequently before, and was proceeding with the oft-repeated warning, when he silenced her abruptly:

"Oh, hush, Gertrude! You might as well attempt to bind the north wind with your ribbons, as undo the habits of a life! I must have air—will have it—and when did you know of Keovala being thus invaded before?"

For three days Voltmeier kept up the search—rode secretly to the cavern, and, indeed, to all the contiguous places where he thought it possible that Gorham might lurk: his whole soul being merged in the desperate purpose of doing murder upon him out-right! He did, more than once, meditate the journey to Moggs'; but he assumed that this place, where he was known to lodge, would be the last which he would seek as a hiding-place. His search was everywhere made in vain, and saving what he had picked up from Watson, the grazier, he had obtained no clues of his enemy.

Then his mind turned to the Jack-legged lawyer, Brownlow; but a moment's reflection satisfied him that he was not the person whom he should seek; and so, again, at the close of the third day, he returned to Keovala, a wearied, disappointed, and very anxious man! But he carried himself bravely before the family, and, though darker of brow, and sadder of spirit, and more taciturn than usual, he was yet the gentle father, and he listened that night to the music of Mignon, as quietly as if he had never known a care. He was soon to receive another shaft from the hands of Fate!

Fergus was absent; had been absent for two days, attending court. He was engaged in some case of old litigation, complicated and in-volving some ancient feuds in more than two families; such feuds as, where the property in dispute lies contiguous, are very apt to result in brawls, which are sometimes fatal. Col. Graham was particularly solicitous about this particular case, and both himself and Fergus had long been employed in its adjustment. By the lucky discovery of a clue, in an old title, which hitherto had escaped all notice, and by an admirable argument upon it, Fergus had added new laurels to his young legal reputation, and Col. Graham, with other lawyers, were in the very thick of their congratulations, at the door of the Court House, when the sheriff drew nigh, and, with as much courtesy as was consistent with firmness, laid his hand on the shoulder of the young lawyer, and announced his arrest for forgery—or, rather, for passing counterfeit money.

Fergus was overwhelmed with astonishment. Col. Graham was indignant.

"What does this mean, Mr. Sheriff?"

"I know nothing more, sir, than this; and this I have only heard: Mr. Wallace bought largely of cattle at the sale for the division of the Houscal property. He paid fully three thousand dollars in money, which, when offered for deposit at the bank, has all been refused as counterfeit; the officers of the bank have marked the bills over, crossed and recrossed them, and affidavits have been made against Mr. Wallace. I presume there will be no difficulty, however, as Mr. Wallace can easily tell from whom he got the bills."

By this time, Fergus had recovered himself, and declined saying a word on that subject.

"You can let this matter lie over till to-morrow, Mr. Sheriff, and we will get bail," said Graham.

"Impossible, sir; my orders are peremptory. The arrest must be made at once, and now that it has been made, it is impossible to release him."

"We will see the Judge at once," said Graham, and he hurried away.

But the Judge had taken his departure. He was nowhere to be found. Fergus, to his great mortification, was perforce an inmate of the common jail that night. He devoted it to writing to Voltmeier and Mignon. Graham sent off the letters by a special dispatch, and remained with the young man till a late hour. He keenly felt his situation, and left him with the full assurance that bail would be found and admitted the next morning.

Chapter LIII

CLOUDS

The dispatch of Col. Graham was brief, but sufficiently explicit. When Voltmeier read it, every feature became convulsed with agony. He writhed beneath the torture in his soul, and sunk into a chair in silence, covering his face with his hands. But the paralysis, or spasm, rather, wrought upon him for a few moments only, when he arose and spoke, pacing the library hurriedly, yet pausing almost at every sentence.

"Another bolt from this fated archer's quiver; the worst sent yet; and yet perhaps not the worst left to send! How could it be? I had none but good bills in the house! all the rest were destroyed! Yet the *whole* sum—three thousand dollars—counterfeit! How could it be? Ha! that villain, Gorham. 'Twas done that night when Mignon saw his accursed face at the window. I gave the packet of bills to Fergus. He lodged it in the bureau, and found the envelope afterwards, seemingly unchanged. The scoundrel had changed them all. 'Twas done while we had the music. All the devils take the music of that night! I see it all! Oh! blindness, dullness, damned stupidity, that left me witless. I should have seen it all before—in season—even as I see it now!

"What's to be done? The danger is but slight. He must come out on bail. I will avow the bills given by me to Fergus! The noble fellow! He has kept silence, and leaves it for me to speak. I will speak—declare the bills to have been mine, and account for them as I may. They will hardly question *me!* But much is to be done. I need a lawyer here—not Graham—no! no! *He* must know nothing. I will send express for Henry. He is Fergus's friend, and will work for him as fondly as ably! Ben Harness must go at full speed."

And he addressed himself to writing, hurriedly, but with that fiery energy which, on such occasions of necessity, he was apt to use. Scarcely had he begun writing, when Mignon burst in upon him with a wild cry, a paper shaking in her outstretched hands. It was the letter of Fergus written from his cell. It was brief, but calm and simple.

"DEAREST LOVE:—You will be surprised, but I trust not alarmed, to hear from me as a prisoner, charged with a grave offense against the laws of the country. I shall probably be released to-morrow. Your father will tell you all, and reassure you, should you feel any apprehensions. Meanwhile, give me your loving prayers, and believe me, whatever you may hear, your own faithful, and, I fondly think, not unworthy cousin,
FERGUS."

"What does it mean, papa? Fergus in prison! Oh! tell me, dear papa, that you will get him out!"

The tears stood big in her eyes; their orbs were dilated with the first grief and terror that had ever assailed her young heart and its innocent affection; and as she stood before her father, waving the little billet in her hand, the passionateness of her action, mixed apprehension and entreaty, was even more intensely expressive than her speech.

"So you have heard it?" he replied, affecting a calm which he did not feel.

"Yes; here. Here is Fergus's letter."

"He need not have written you. He need not have said anything about it, baby. It is a small matter, and is easily remedied. I will see to it directly."

"A small matter, papa! To be locked up in an odious prison—in a *jail*—with all sorts of wretches."

"Only for a night, Mignon."

"Only for a night! Oh! papa! a night in such a place is an eternity for Fergus. A common jail, foul and filthy, and filled with all sorts of criminals."

"Pshaw, my child; Graham has seen to this. Fergus has been made comfortable."

"Oh heavens! comfortable! And the shame—the disgrace, papa; to be arrested—seized by the common sheriff—dragged from the Court House—"

"Poo! poo! poo! baby, what horrible pictures does your imagination draw! The sheriff is an honorable gentleman. Fergus has been treated with every courtesy. The jail is really clean and comfortable, and Fergus has a cell to himself."

"A cell! oh, poor Fergus! a cell! The very name takes away my breath. Papa, when, when will you get him out?"

"To-day! to-day! Let me alone, now! As soon as I have done this writing, I will gallop to the village, and see to all matters. Don't be concerned, I tell you. It is only a brief annoyance. It is some miserable mistake."

"But what is the affair, Voltmeier?" asked Aunt Gertrude. "What are the particulars, and upon what absurd pretense can they have put Fergus in prison? There can be no debt that *he* owes, and if there were, why did you not pay it before?"

"Patience! patience! Gertrude! Give me time. The long and short of the matter is briefly this: that I gave a sum of money to Fergus to attend the sale of cattle at Houscal's estate, and some of the money proves to be counterfeit."

"And *you* gave him the money?"

"To be sure I did."

"Well, that's easy to say, Voltmeier. Fergus was simply your agent."

"Precisely; and I mean to say so. Will that content you? I am surprised, Gertrude, that you should contribute to alarm the fears of this child."

"I do not, Voltmeier. I have such confidence in you that I told her from the first, there was no danger—that you would see and settle the matter before another night. Fergus must not be suffered to lie in a dungeon a moment longer than we can help it."

"Oh, yes! papa! Go! go at once! and bring Fergus home with you."

"Leave me now, both of you. You mar my endeavors. Enough that I will start for the village in twenty minutes. Get hence, both of you, and let me write."

Voltmeier dispatched two letters in the same envelope, one to Harness, the elder, covering another to Major Henry, of Spartanburg.

Though speaking so confidently to the ladies, Voltmeier had still many misgivings. Not that he doubted, when he reasoned of it, that Fergus could be easily released on bail, especially as he had prepared to redeem the counterfeit bills with good notes, and avow the proceeding as his own; but his misgivings came from those secret mysterious instincts by which a man is taught to comprehend a hovering danger in the air; a lurking evil watchful for the moment when to spring upon the victim. As perfectly assured by his reasoning powers, as Macbeth had been assured by the witches' prophecy, he was yet weak as respects his faith, in what, when he *did* reason, he described to himself as the merest fancies of an excited brain. But the shaft, coming from a quarter where he had anticipated no danger; from a source of evil, suddenly showing itself in that which had hitherto only promised security; from the tenacious hanging about him of that black dog, Gorham; all combined to strengthen that superstition in his instincts, which, with a true German mysticism, he identified with a deliberate working of the Fates, seeking vengeance and compelling atonement!

Still he went forward to the county town, nothing doubting that Fergus would be easily released on bail. What he should do after that, or before it, by taking upon himself the whole responsibility of the affair, was yet hardly a subject of question in his mind. Fergus was to be released, as he had promised the ladies, and this, as he now thought, was simply a matter of course.

But, when he got to the court-house, he found this no easy matter. Great was the popular excitement about the so bold attempt to put in circulation so large a sum of counterfeit money. The report of Fergus's arrest had already spread through the contiguous country, and every small farmer who had been hoarding away his bank-notes as well as specie, for months, and, in some cases, for years, had become alarmed, and was crowding into the bank to deposit his money, or ascertain what he feared to find, its worthlessness.

And much of it was found to be counterfeit. The bank clerks were busy in the work of detection. Crowds hung about the porches listening to every report, and busily grouped in discussion of the affair. The popular excitement grew with every moment, and by noon the place was filled with a perfect mob of infuriated people. The jail seemed to be the only place of safety for Fergus Wallace. The mob wore a threatening aspect.

It was with a gloomy brow that Col. Graham received Voltmeier. When the latter spoke of bail, the former shook his head, and said:

"It is doubtful if bail will be taken. It is a capital offense, and one which has been so frequent, and of such mischievous effects, that the bank, as well as the populace, are strongly opposed to it. We shall try the question in an hour. The Judge is one who will be very much governed by the popular clamor. He is an old politician, and can not easily divest himself of the well-worn garments of the demagogue; and this fellow, Brownlow, has been busy making mischief among the people. He, like some others of our Jack-legged gentry, have been made jealous by the success of our young friend; and the fact that he is comparatively a stranger, seems to suggest him as a proper subject of sacrifice, *pro bono publico,* as an example to all future offenders. The fact, too, that he stubbornly refuses to say from whom he got the notes, is very much against him."

"Why, he got them from me, of course, and I am here prepared to avow it."

"That you must not do *now.*"

"Why not?"

"Because you will be more likely to be arrested as an accomplice yourself, than to acquit *him.* You will be charged, most probably, as *particeps criminis.* It is already said, by Brownlow and others, that Wallace had nothing when he came to the country; that he has been urged by some cunning accomplice of influence, who, fox-like, has employed him to pull his nuts out of the fire; and that the whole history of this counterfeit money among us proves the active connection of 'some of the big fish'—that was *his* phrase, and one which is frequently repeated among the populace. You are undoubtedly hinted at, if not pointed at, and your policy is to risk nothing, unless, indeed, you can show satisfactorily from whom you got the notes."

"That is impossible. They have been accumulating on my hands for more than a year, and, until I counted them the other day, I had no idea that I kept so large a sum in the house. I was just about to make the deposit in the bank, when the announcement of the stock-sale of the Houscal estate moved me to appropriate it in that purchase."

"It is greatly to be regretted that you had not made the deposit. You had better give me a check for the three thousand dollars, to satisfy the heirs of the estate. That will quiet some of them, and produce a good impression."

"I have brought it with me, drawn in your favor."

"It is well. It is now almost time for the case to commence, and I must see Wallace. You must keep silent—avow nothing; and, whether we get him out on bail or not, your policy is not to appear in the business—not yet, at least. If, now, upon avowing the purchase as yours, and the money as coming to you, from—whom?"

"The one I could do; but not the other. I have sold hundreds of heads of cattle, mules, and horses, and the money came to me through scores of agents, and in small sums, at different periods."

"It is unfortunate; but just now, in the temper of the public mind, *your* avowal, however clear and reasonable, would hardly suffice for *his* release, and would most certainly involve you in his predicament. It will be well for you, if Wallace shall still refuse to show whence he *got* the money, simply to state that that should all be shown on the trial. I still hope to obtain the order for bail, but, knowing the Judge as I do, I something doubt it. To serve Wallace properly in this business, you must keep wholly out of the proceedings, and keep out of the way. You will do him much more good by keeping on horseback, than by sharing his cell with him."

"Will you, my dear Graham, possess him of these facts and considerations?"

"Surely, it is what I design to do, even had you not told me anything. He is a noble fellow, and of first-rate talents; and, though he has made many good friends here, he has, I am sorry to say, provoked a good many jealousies. The curs of the law know, by infallible cur-instincts, when they encounter the lion, and Wallace is a very lion among them. He masters them at every stage of the game, though it be subtlety or strength!"

Voltmeier had to be contented. He rode off towards Keovala, sad of heart, vexed of mind, and altogether a disappointed man. He had hardly ridden off, when Gorham glided into the office of Lawyer Brownlow.

Chapter LIV

THE CRY OF THE CROWD

It was as Col. Graham had feared. In vain he argued the claims of Fergus Wallace, and made light of the imputation against his honor. The excitement of the multitude was too great for the combative power of the Judge, and the counsels for the State, or county, and bank, were strenuous in their efforts against him. Brownlow was particularly active, and had frequent resort to the *ad captandum vulgus,* dwelling especially on the cause and rights of the poor, as oppressed by the rich—a favorite subject with all demagogues, and one which always finds ready entrance to the ears and sympathies of the populace. Col. Graham had occasion, finally, to check him in the license which he gave his tongue.

"One moment, if you please, sir," he said. "I notice that, in the course of the learned gentleman's remarks, he has been pleased to hint at these forgeries as the acts of certain persons of this county or State, high in social or in official position. These he described as the nabobs of the country, the big fish, the big-bugs, the Christian Hebrews, the Jacob-cheating Labans, who carried high heads, yet were guilty of low deeds; I simply desire to ask if the honorable gentleman had any reference to myself in these remarks?"

To which Brownlow promptly replied:

"I might answer the honorable gentleman with the Latin proverb: *'Qui capit ille facit,'* but—"

"No, sir," said Graham, sternly. "No such answer could be made to me with impunity!" and he confronted Brownlow as he spoke.

The latter, in spite of his native impudence, was dashed, and answered hastily:

"I did not mean, your honor, to make that reply to the honorable gentleman. I only said it *might* be made—"

"And I repeat, sir, it could *not* be made by any man in this house, with impunity!"

"I was about to add, your honor, that I had not the most distant idea of referring to Col. Graham, individually, by anything I said. I have the greatest respect for that gentleman—"

Graham interrupted him—

"Your honor will please note all this. To disparage a lawyer is, in some degree, to discredit his client. No client shall suffer discredit through any *lachesse* of mine. The honorable gentleman has been pleased to speak here to-day, and in a matter of life and death, in a style of language which better becomes the stump than a court of justice. He has appealed from the court of justice, substantially, by appeals to the court of human and mercenary passions. But, speaking apologetically now to the court, for breaking the order of this trial, I must say that it was not so much what was spoken, that I felt free to resent, but the *manner* in which it was spoken. The gentleman was not simply pleased to *say* things which he meant offensively, whether to me or anybody else, or everybody else, but he accompanied these words by significant looks, and winks and nods and leers, and even finger-pointings, in the very direction in which I stand; and the eyes of this assembly, met here for justice, followed him in all his actions; and I have little doubt, that many weak, ignorant, and malignant persons, who delight to hearken to disparagement of those who happen to enjoy a high social position, were not only tickled with these indications, but, in some degree, prepared to give credit to the slanders which they conveyed. My profession is one, sir, which occupies the highest social position of any in this country, and I shall ever be the last man to suffer its disparagement in my hands or in my person. I leave it to birds of far different feather, to find satisfaction in fouling their own nests. This young man, my client, has distinguished himself in our profession, in the brief time in which he has been in the practice, among us, by talents and conduct which would do honor to any member of the Bar of North Carolina. His talents and acquisitions have won him the highest honors, and his uniform propriety of conduct, and modest, gentlemanly manners, should secure him the highest degree of social confidence. He has *mine*, to such a degree that I have assumed, and do hereby assume, to make good any bad money which he may be proved to have passed away. That he has done so ignorantly, *I know*. It is by my counsel that he remains silent as to all the facts in this case. They will be developed fully when it shall come to trial. Enough that I may here assert to the court, as I now do, as trusted counsel, that Mr. Wallace will, and can, at the proper time, show from whom he got the money which he paid to the executors of the Houscal estate. But, for special reasons, we are not disposed to anticipate that time, nor give way to any idle clamors of an excited multitude, or to the goadings of those who, for their own selfish purposes, or for mere popularity, would excite the multitude to violence. Enough, if I add, your honor, that though Mr. Wallace paid out *but* three thousand dollars, more than five thousand of money, received at this sale, has been declared counterfeit, at the banks! Yet, no person, so far as I have heard, has been fastened upon but him! *He* is selected as the victim. If the executors of Houscal had been so heedful of the moneys paid them, as to make Mr. Wallace responsible for three thousand dollars, known specifically to have been derived from him, they must surely have adopted similar means to identify all other paying parties. Why, then, is the rage of the community concentrated upon Mr. Wallace? Is it because he is a stranger, and is supposed to have few friends?—Is it because he hails from South Carolina, a sister State, which, I am sorry to say, finds very little favor in the opinions of many in ours. Whatever it be, your honor, it is enough for me to know his worth, his pure integrity of character, his personal innocence of all offense in this case, and I will be his friend, though it should cost me every other friend, and every dollar I have in the world. I saw him openly counting out the money which he has paid to the executors of Houscal. He did so without concealment, at my office desk, before he went to the sale. I did not examine the money closely; but, from what I saw, I had no sort of doubt that the money was good. I *know* that Mr. Wallace had no doubt of it; and I still doubt if *all* of the money he counted out before me was bad. There are some curious matters to be come at, which I will now mention, among those which we shall reserve for the trial. All of the notes of Mr. Wallace were tens and twenties; there was not a five among them. Yet there are no less than fifteen hundred dollars in fives, so adjudged by the banks to be counterfeit, besides other notes of smaller denominations, which are, seemingly, credited to him.

"But I do not purpose any longer to trespass upon the time of the court, by details which are unnecessary to the preliminary matter before it. I renew my motion that the prisoner be released, on proper bail. Let the sum be five or ten thousand dollars, or even more. I, and others of his friends, here, will become his surety!"

But the application was in vain. The learned Judge was too much under the promptings of that external pressure, which, as a politician, he had learned to reverence. He was, however, as smooth and courteous in denial, as he had ever been when suing for favor. He dwelt on the enormity of the crime, of the great extent of mischief done to the country, of the number of poor people, who could ill afford their losses, of the necessity of making the law felt in all its rigor, and of public and sharp examples for the prevention of the evil. The offense was capital, and should be. He expressed his great regret that Mr. Wallace, who had shown himself so able and full of promise, as a lawyer, should be placed in so painful a strait, and graciously declared his best wishes that he would be enabled to clear his skirts of all imputation of guilt; meanwhile, a painful sense of duty compelled him to remand him to prison, to await his trial at the Quarter Sessions—and so-forth!

The sheriff proceeded to remove the prisoner, and the court stood adjourned. The Judge hastily threw off his robe of office, and as hastily disappeared. The crowd broke away in confusion, and under great excitement. The passage from the court-chamber was obstructed, and the sheriff found it difficult to make his way through.

Loud cries from without encouraged the multitude within, and no sooner had the sheriff made his appearance, at the outer door, when the cries became significant of the intensity of the popular excitement. The shout went up, from a score of throats—

"Lynch him! lynch him."

Other throats cried—

"Hang him! hang him!" and there was a rush towards the officer and his prisoner, of sundry wild-looking mountaineers, hirsute of face and rude of garb, each of whom swung a monstrous club above his shoulders.

Chapter LV

THE SIMOON OF PASSION

The aspect of the crowd was ominous. It was rapidly growing
into a mob, under various exciting instrumentalities outside.
There were evidently parties at work to fire the popular passions,
which, within the court-house, were already glowing almost at white
heat. The stern aristocracy of sentiment and manner of Graham had
not tended, in the existing state of public feeling, to allay the mood
of the *hoi polloi*. And his speech, monstrously perverted, had been
conveyed from the one crowd to the other.

So, too, the course and language of Brownlow had been made
known, securing for him, which perhaps he aimed at most, a large
increase of popular favor. A shout welcomed his coming into the
area in front, while some groans and hisses went up in compliment
to Graham, on his appearance. But the brave man remained unmoved.
He calmly surveyed the scene, and said to the sheriff, whom he had
accompanied:

"You are going to have trouble. It will be necessary to use all
your firmness and discretion. Summon all your *posse* about you, and
be prepared to use your staff with vigor. Call upon the citizens. I
will stand beside you to the end."

The sheriff called up his deputies, and such of the constabulary as
were at hand. Col. Graham took his stand beside Fergus, a little
in advance. So did several professional gentlemen. The clamors continued. Roars and shouts rose from the mass on all sides, and the
fearful threats, "Lynch the villain! Hang him!" still broke forth
at intervals from groups of the excited multitude.

Endeavoring to push his way with the prisoner, the sheriff found
himself resisted and backed by the mere *vis inertia* of the increasing
crowd. It became forward; and the beleaguered party found itself
receding, perforce, inch by inch, till their backs rested against the
walls of the court-house. They could recede no farther.

The sheriff now, in vociferous accents, commanded the peace in the name of the State. His voice was drowned with shouts and screams of derision. One of the lawyers came forward, and, standing in front of the sheriff, prepared to read the Riot Act, but his voice was swallowed up in the universal hubbub and clamor which followed his attempt. The sheriff appealed to the citizens; so also, in tones of thunder, did Graham; but *he* was answered with yells and hisses, and cries of "Down with the big bugs!"—"Down with the nabobs!"

Several of the citizens now added themselves to the sheriff's party, but most of these were utterly unarmed, and they could all now perceive that a large proportion of these rioters were strangers to the place, and of a sort to strike terror into any quiet community of peaceful and law-abiding citizens.

Among these, few or none knew the cold-blooded and malignant creature, Gorham, who seemed to have newly clad himself for the occasion, in garments quite unlike those which he was wont to wear. A cap of coarse fur now surmounted his head; his person was wrapped in an overcoat of gray, reaching almost to his heels. Underneath this he carried a huge knife, and, in one hand, openly, his rifle.

He could be seen urging on other parties, and finally he appeared forced into the lead. None more vociferously shouted the popular cries for "Lynching and hanging;" none was more forward in urging, by voice and entreaty, to the assault.

The crowd thickened. The clamor increased, and three or four drunken men were thrust forward from the rear, as is apt to be the case in such commotions, evidently to bring on the struggle. These fellows, reeling towards the sheriff, struck boldly, but blindly, at the person of Wallace.

The staves of the *posse comitatus* warded off the attack, and Graham and other gentlemen threw themselves between, armed only with their walking-sticks. There were many drunken persons upon the ground, and these were chiefly put forward by Gorham. Had he drenched them for the purpose? He had some stimulating speech for each, chorussed by the cries of "Lynch" and "Hang."

In the background stood Brownlow, on a barrel, discoursing to the sullen circle around him, of the rights of the people; of the wrongs which they bore; of the nabobs who oppressed them, and of that patriotism which demanded redress! As they hearkened you could see the scowls gather upon their brows; see their lips compressed, and note them, one by one, turn away from the orator to lose themselves in the crowd, which gathered threatening to the front.

Suddenly the shrieks of women were heard. There were numbers of these upon the ground, as greatly excited as the men, and several of them with better reason. These poor, squalid, old, and wretched creatures, might be seen with dingy slips of condemned paper in their hands, the worthless, but long hoarded counterfeited notes which had been crossed and counter-crossed by the bank officers, as spurious. Bitter were their speeches, angry their complaints, and it was not difficult to persuade them that they owed the imposition wholly to the rich, the rulers of the people, those who rode in their carriages, and went clad in purple and fine linen, while they went in serge.

The exhibition of these spurious bills seemed to have an effect upon the multitude not dissimilar to that of Cæsar's bloody mantle on the passions of the Roman rabble. They were passed from hand to hand, and each had his comment of bitterness, and each turned his eyes of threat and hostility upon the professional men, the lawyers being generally objects of odium among the rustic population, which usually entertains large jealousies of the wealth and influence of the town, especially the court-house, which is commonly held to be hostile to the farming classes.

Still the passions of the multitude were simply apparent, and not as yet demonstrative of those violent extremes to which they can be driven. We say multitude, though the whole population of the county would hardly occasion an emotion of curiosity or fear, if assembled in any of the large cities. The term is of relative use. In the sparsely settled rural regions of the Southern States, a few hundred people suddenly thrown into one of the small streets of a country village may well occasion anxiety, if not alarm; and when so many of these showed themselves to be at once strangers, drunk, insolent, and reckless, the anxiety naturally became alarm.

But the waters are suddenly set in motion by the sharp cries of women, rising from the very center of the mass. A woman carrying an infant has been thrown down, and trampled under the hurrying footsteps of the crowd.

"Help! murder!" is the cry.

"Help! They have murdered a woman!" and upon this a hundred

confused and contradictory cries followed, each, by its very vagueness, stimulating the excitement.

"Come! let us push 'em to hell!" cried one furious fellow, goading on a couple of companions as wild of aspect, and uncouth as himself.

"Let's pull these fine nabobs to pieces."

"Let me get out, man," cried a young woman; "you'll kill me and my child."

"Give way there, fellows, and let the young woman out; it's bad enough to be robbed of everything, without being mashed to pieces, her and her child too! Heave aside, and let her out."

"What's she in for? What good kin she do hyar? Out, woman, as well as you kin; be off, and don't look behind you! There! heave ahead now, fellows, I long to brush the jacket of some of them nabobs! What kin they do?"

"Come on, then; break through! Dern these women, they're always in the way when they're not wanted. Whoo! whoo! whoop! Push in with a tiger!"

And the tiger was given, and close followed by the cry,

"Lynch the nabobs, boys! Lynch the counterfeiters and forgers!"

A chorus of feminine shrieks followed these cries; and the crowd came rushing up from the rear, some hot for the fray; others moved by curiosity, and the mass by a momentum given to it from impulses and influences too various to be described; but all with heated blood and disturbed faculties.

Blows were heard given in front. Clubs and staves were dashed together. And now there was a shout, as at some blow well delivered; and now there was a cry, as of some stroke painfully received. Anon, two or three men struggled to the rear with bloody sconces.

What, meanwhile, of the scene in front? The sheriff and posse, with a score of gentlemen, held their ground, presenting such an aspect, as, after a few blows exchanged, served to impress some of the rioters, and to discourage others. Some of the citizens had run home to procure firearms, and a few joined the ranks of the sheriff.

"If we can only keep our ground for twenty minutes," said the sheriff, "I will have force enough for these rascals."

"Had I but my pistols!" muttered Graham, between his teeth.

"Here are fellows I never saw before! what wild-looking scoundrels!"

Another rush from the rear silenced speculation. Another wave from the tumultuous sea drove the recoiling billows again forward, still forward; and blows were again given and taken more violently and numerously than before. One uncouth ruffian finally succeeded in felling the sheriff, by a blow from his club, while he was in the act of warding off the assaults of another.

Fergus Wallace immediately bestrode the prostrate officer, and, adroitly snatching from the assailant the club which he carried, felled him at a blow; then dashing forward, he smote right and left, making a formidable gap in the ranks of the enemy, but receiving a blow, himself, in the melee, which, for the moment, paralyzed his left arm, which he had thrown up to shelter his head from the stroke.

There was a momentary recoil of the rioters, especially as, by this time, Graham and others, following the example of Fergus, had, with like success, forced back their assailants also.

Several of them were prostrate. Gorham was busied drawing one man out from the mass, sorely battered and bruised, in whom we recognize the person of Ephraim Moggs! How came that miserable wretch into that business? Had Gorham beguiled him away from the watchful care of his miserable mother? What need to ask? Enough that Gorham had uses for him; and the poor wretch had been driven forward to the assault, saturated with whisky, and hardly conceiving that his leader had used him as his buckler. The blow which had been aimed at the head of the one had been received by the other.

There was a momentary lull. But, where a multitude shows itself of such a temper, blows and blood are quite as apt to stimulate to excess as to discourage action. The sight of broken heads, which makes tender hearts sick and faintish, only excites the fever in such as are of tiger character. It is then that the barriers of restraint, whether of prudence, fear, or law, are apt to be broken down; and it was so at the present moment.

The billows rolled upward once more, with a new roar of rage—a new swell of shout, and shriek, and hurrah; the cries equally from the throats of men and women. There was a great clamor for one Joe Sykes.

"Make way there, fellows, for Joe Sykes. He's the boy for 'em—give way; heave on, fellows; let Big Joe have a chaince!"

And the swell in front parted, and between two files marched up a huge fellow—a very giant, known as the mountain blacksmith, who presented himself in front, swarthy and savage, wielding a monstrous smith's hammer on his shoulder. The swell followed him—the crowd—as they looked for another sort of action now, from the presence of the well-known giant.

He confronted the sheriff boldly:

"Stop your howling, now, boys, while I speaks to the sheriff. We must first hev a little onderstanding. Look you, sheriff, I don't want to do you any harm, for you have a right, and I may say, you're a-bound to do what you're doing; and I don't want to do any of these *gentlemen* here, any harm, though some of them does deserve it, that's a God's truth—but I've come to take that young rascal out of your hands, that's been robbing and counterfeiting all the country. I'm a loser, myself, by that young rascal, of a mighty deal of money; all that I've been putting by for the last six months. When I got up this bright and blessed morning, I counted myself the owner of a hundred an sixty-six good dollars, which I sweated for; and when I heard the news, and brought my money to the bank, thar' 'tis—see what they've did with it! They've made the sign of the cross a hundred times on every bill in the bundle! And I'm not the only pusson that's been ruinated by that young nabob rascal. Jest see what fine clothes he's a-wearing—all come out of the pockets of honest, hard-working people, that he's robbed to fill his own. Now, sheriff, as I said, we don't want to hurt you or anybody 'long with you; but we'll have that young rascal, in spite of all the teeth in your head! And the question is, will you give him up quietly to Judge Lynch?—he's hyar and ready—or take your chaince for sich a fight as you never seed before, wrote down in cracked skulls and broken noses? Say the word, sheriff, and be quick about it."

"Beware of what you do, Joe Sykes. I warn you to depart, and not to lead these people to mischief. In the name of the State, I command you, and all of you people, to keep the peace of the State, and depart to your several homes. No man or men shall rescue prisoner of mine, unless you pass over my body."

"Oh, don't you fear! We don't mean any rest-cue. He'll not be the better for giving him to Judge Lynch—that I can tell you. So be easy about the rest-cue. I ax you, sheriff, will you give him peaceably, or must we fight for him?"

"You fight at your peril! If you strike, it will be the dearest blow you ever paid for!"

"That's my look-out! A hundred and sixty-six dollars is dearly paid and lost forever, and I'll have my satisfaction for it, whatever happens. Will you give up the villain?"

"Never, I tell you!"

"The Lord have mercy on your poor soul, Sheriff! Boys, right and left, spread, and when you sees me put in, do you put in, with head and hands, tooth and toe-nail, and I'll warrant you the swinging tree shall soon hev' its bearing fruit, and the devil git his due."

"That's the right thing!" cried Gorham. "That's the way to talk it! spread, fellows; spread and make ready!—what, Ephraim—is the head easy? Are you there again? Well! go it with a rush, as I do."

With a great yell, the front rank rushed on; the blacksmith wielded his hammer; and there was no heart in the sheriff's party that did not feel a thrill of disquiet as they beheld the giant, Sykes, deliberately advancing with the mighty weapon swung in air.

At that moment, Graham felt his arm pulled gently by some one through the Court House window, and as he turned, a female voice whispered him:

"Husband! here are your pistols!"

It was his wife—the slightest, frailest, palest, most delicate of her sex; but pale as was her cheek, it kindled under the bright fires burning in her eyes. Graham took the pistols as privately as possible, gave her a loving look, and whispered:

"Now, get home, Blanche, as rapidly and secretly as you can."

But she did not go. Sinking back from the window, she waited within the walls of the Court House, with a soul swelling into strength and courage, while her heart thrilled with a nameless dread and her knees trembled beneath her.

Chapter LVI

HOW VOLTMEIER RODE

Graham secretly slipt one of the pistols into the hands of the sheriff, who concealed it cleverly behind his back. And thus the parties stood, both better prepared for mischief, confronting each other during a brief pause, which, for a few moments, neither seemed quite willing to disturb.

Meanwhile, we have seen Voltmeier riding homeward to Keovala, under Col. Graham's counsel, just as the Court was about to go into session, for the express purpose of deciding upon the application for bail for Fergus Wallace. Graham's fear was, that something might leak out, on the examination, which should identify Voltmeier with the transaction, when he thought it possible that he too would be arrested, charged as *particeps criminis,* and both be placed in the same category, as criminals, thus neutralizing the saving evidence of both. Voltmeier was the more readily persuaded to take his suggestion, as his instincts persuaded him that one thing most essential for the safety of Fergus, was his own perfect freedom of movement. Though impressed by Graham's apprehension that bail would not be allowed, he at first scouted the idea, and persuaded himself that the matter was easy; but as he rode and thought, and duly weighed the successive events by which, in spite of all his precautions, he had been brought to a sense of insecurity, his mind misgave him, and he loitered along the road in a fit of moody musing, which made him wholly forgetful of the use of his spurs. His famous white charger had rarely been permitted to go so leisurely along.

It is with a painful sense of humiliation that a man, imperious of will, accustomed to indulge his moods, and exact submission, scarcely conscious of any limits to his authority, or any restraint upon his powers, suddenly finds himself fettered, cabin'd, cribb'd, confined, shorn of power, stript of authority, with embarrassments, if not enemies, accumulating around him, and with no resources in his own mind to decide in what manner wisely to exercise his energies. This was now the condition of the strong man, Voltmeier.

And when he thought of the agonies of that most precious child, Mignon, how could he return to Keovala, bringing no tidings of the situation of her lover, and utterly unable to convey to her mind that hope which did not now possess his own? He now dreaded to meet that child, the sight of whom was the greatest blessing to his eyes, whenever he returned home. And so, doubtful, indecisive, he loitered among the hills, rode to and fro, now alighted, and threw himself upon the rocks—then arose, in a few moments after, again remounted his horse, only to loiter again and dismount again; his mind teeming with all sorts of musings, wretched in degree with the consciousness of his own present feebleness. Gradually, thus, loitering on horseback, or pacing the rocks afoot, a fearful sort of fascination kept bringing him nearer and nearer to the town, and finally the whole area of streets and buildings was spread out beneath his gaze, seemingly at his very feet. From his perch, unseen, he could behold the crowds swaying to and fro, around the Court House; he could note parties descending the hills to the town, from the country places, and mingling, little by little, with the tides that kept in perpetual motion under the unusual agitation of the time; and faint sounds, like the distant murmurs of an increasing sea upon the beach, rolled up to his ears, arguing highly raised and excited voices. Nothing could be distinguished, and the sounds which reached him were those of shouts and hurrahs, and fierce cries, which, near at hand, shook the entire area. Voltmeier's own excitement grew momently, as he looked and listened. He knew enough of the populace, to comprehend, from these proofs, the degree of its excitement, and he chafed like the bear at the stake, at the sight of a conflict, possibly in which he could not fully comprehend, nor share.

Suddenly he sees a farmer wending his way up one of the contiguous hills, coming from the village, and evidently apprehensive of the tumult from which he desired to escape. Ever and anon the peasant stopped and looked behind him—then hurried forward with a fresh impulse.

Voltmeier jumped on his horse and rode to meet this man.

"What's the matter in town?"

"Hot times! There's old Scratch to pay, there. I reckon thar a fighting now. They was hot for it when I comed away. The people's in a mighty great stew, and it's just as like as not they'll tear everything to pieces. They's in a fury, now, I tell you!"

"What about?"

"Lord love you, don't you know? Whar could you ha' been keeping yourself? Everybody knows the whole country's in a stew, and h—l to pay and no pitch hot."

"What is the trouble, my friend?"

"Well, now, you see, the nabobs, as Lawyer Brownlow calls 'em, air trying to git a young rascal clar of the law, that's been a passing off bad money all over the country. He's a young rascal from South Carolina, and he's just as sharp at the business as a born Yankee. He's played old Smash with all the poor people of the county, and far beyond it, too, I reckon. There's no seeing the eend; and there's no eend to the weepings and wailings of the widows and the orphans, not to speak of the women and children that's been ruinated by the rapscallion. He's passed off, I reckon, more than a million of dollars of the rotten stuff; and thar's hardly an old woman that hain't got a pile of the rags that's of no more valley to her than so many dry leaves. Thar you sees the poor old women a-crying, and the men a cussing and swearing, with their bills a shaking, all scratched up, cross and file, contagiously condemned by the Bank. The officers of the Bank are all the time busy in scratching up the counterfeits, and everybody's in a rage agin the young rascal that tuk 'em in. They tried—the Big Bugs—to git him off; but the Jedge, he won't let him off, and nothing will sarve the people, but they must 'lynch him,' and hang him right away, and they're agwine to fight the sheriff, and the 'poseayou-come-and-take-us,' and a whole dozen of the nabobs, to get hold of the fellow. When I seed the fighting begin, I know'd some skulls would be crack'd—so I made off as fast as legs could carry me. Wouldn't I be a purty pictur to go home to Polly Scott, with a great hole in my head and an ugly slash of a knife, perhaps, over my very nose!"

Voltmeier waited to hear no more; but, snatching up a stick of hickory which lay at hand, he leaped upon his horse, and went, at full speed, down the hill towards the village.

"What! you're not gwine to whar thar a-fighting?" cried the

peasant. "What a fool of a pusson! He has no feeling for his own skull! But I reckon he's got no wife to look for him at home."

Voltmeier rode like one mad. The mountaineer looked at him with amazement.

"He goes headlong down the hill, as if it had no bottom. He's cracked, I reckon, and wants to git his skull cracked, in the bargain. I reckon I is no sich fool. Bob Scott remembers Polly Scott, and you don't catch him carrying home a cracked skull, to an unconsolate and weeping widow! Dern the money, and the counterfeiter! I haint got a darn'd dollar of it, thank the Hokies!"

Voltmeier relieved anxiety by excitement. He felt in his element, on horseback, and preferring to die game, in hot blood, sooner than confess defeat, and be incapable of reply to the dear child for whom he was ready to sacrifice life.

Chapter LVII

HOW VOLTMEIER SMOTE

The discretion which counseled the homeward movement of the mountaineer, Bob Scott, was by no means the general sentiment among the riotous populace at the Court House. What Bob Scott might have felt and thought, had he sustained such losses as the blacksmith, Joe Sykes, is a problem which it does not concern us to solve. A hundred and sixty-six dollars, suddenly cut off from a poor man's bank account, is calculated to render him something of a desperado; and had Bob Scott lost that money—who knows but that his losses might have made him the very hero of Crackskull Common? In such large degree doth the question of loss and gain affect the passions and humanity of men!

The stout, strong, and stubborn blacksmith, Joe Sykes, was differently circumstanced, and, accordingly, of a different mood of mind. He thought by different processes, and the mode of reasoning, in his case, had fairly turned all Bob Scott's prudence out of doors.

We left him confronting the sheriff, threatening him, and preparing for assault, with the aspect of determination which does not often deceive. The cries in the background stimulated his passions, and there was a constant and natural physical pressure from the rear, which impelled the more bold and daring of the rioters forward. Something of this pressure may have been the result of calculation and design; and with this the lawyer, Brownlow, and the subtle Gorham, now showing himself more daring as well as subtle, had something to do.

Brownlow maintained himself in the background, still busied in *talking* to the crowd. Gorham had brought forward numerous parties, and, without keeping himself wholly out of danger, was certainly more earnest in pressing others forward than advancing himself. Still, in the rush, he suddenly found himself near Sykes, the blacksmith, confronting the sheriff and his prisoner.

Gorham would willingly have shot Fergus Wallace where he stood; and no doubt his hope was, and hence his activity, that Wallace should perish in the *melee*; but, as he was one of the few who carried a rifle, and as it would be scarce possible to do the deed and escape detection, he was compelled to forbear a resort to this extreme measure.

Nevertheless, there he stood, side by side with the blacksmith, confronting Wallace, with none between, save the bull-headed and half-drunken Ephraim Moggs. Him he held by the shoulder; his head wrapped about with a handkerchief, and bloody from the effects of a previous blow.

We have taken some time to show the situation of the parties— much more time than was yielded by the rioters to the sheriff and his *posse*.

Still, there had been a pause, neither party being altogether willing to strike the first blow now, with the aspects of things looking so serious. The native population of the country is naturally pacific and slow to operate, in masses as a mob. There is great natural deference and respect to law, which would rarely be violated by the commonality, but for the influence of demagogues and professional rogues. Even Sykes, with all his bluster, was disposed to parley still longer; and perhaps might have been pacified by the sheriff, but for the cries and plaudits of the crowd in the rear, by which his vanity was stimulated beyond the control of his reason.

Still, it is possible that the collision might have been arrested, but for one of those unexpected incidents, not arranged in the programme, which seemed to set all the wheels in motion.

While Gorham was grasping the shoulder of Ephraim Moggs, as if to keep him to the front, he was suddenly darted upon by the old woman, Moggs, his mother, who, without a word, buffeted the ruffian soundly with one hand, while she dragged her hopeful son away with the other.

In this performance, the jostling crowd overthrew Ephraim, and his mother tumbled over him.

There was then a wild yell from the mass, and half a dozen stalwart fellows, taking advantage of the incident, rushed in, over their prostrate bodies, and made a resolute effort to seize Fergus Wallace. The blacksmith advanced at the same moment, wielding his sledge-hammer on high, aiming for the sheriff. The latter quickly raised his pistol, while dodging the blow, and pulled the trigger. The uplifted arm of the blacksmith fell, as he cried:

"He's hit me, by Jingo! He's broke my arm!"

"You've got another arm!" was the shout of one behind him.

"So I hev'! Here's at you, now, Sheriff! I've swore to hev' your man, and I'll keep my oath, ef I dies for it."

With the dexterity of an expert, he caught the hammer from the broken with the sound arm, and again renewed the attack.

Meanwhile, Graham and Wallace, with the few friends about them, after sundry blows, had baffled the attempt, in the rush, to seize the prisoner; and, though several of them had endured severe bruises, none as yet were disabled.

But, with the renewal of the blacksmith's assault, the rest of the assailants plucked up courage also, and made a second rush. The sheriff received a blow on his arm, defending his head, by which he was disabled. Wallace was pulled out of the ranks, and dragged a few paces, Gorham being now one of those who grasped his person.

It was not till this moment that Graham drew forth his pistol and fired! One of the assailants fell; the rest relaxed their hold, and gave back, and the blacksmith, bestriding the sheriff, and confronting the few remaining gentlemen, who stood by Graham, and assisted in drawing Fergus out from the *melee*, shouted for the renewal of the assault.

"I've downed the sheriff, and I reckon there's no more pistols in the crowd! Hyar's one, but it's empty," and so saying, he hurled the useless weapon over his shoulder.

"Now, put in, fellows, and crash 'em down; and we kin then take our time for trying the counterfeiter before Judge Lynch."

And the pell-mell again began; and, excited by example and event, new parties were showing themselves under old leadership; when, at the very moment of the crisis, and when the danger seemed most imminent, a horseman, at full charge, came rushing into the arena, directly between the two opposing parties.

So absorbed were the rioters, that the approach of the horseman was unheard, till he was actually among them, and smiting about him with a heavy hickory flail! He rode so recklessly, smote so fiercely, never once speaking, giving no warning, that the shock was almost as terrible, of the one horseman, as it would have been of the charge of a whole squadron of troopers.

The rider drew up his horse directly between the assailants and the assailed, the steed recoiling almost upon his haunches, so great had been his momentum, and so sudden had been its arrest.

The horseman was Voltmeier!

Gorham knew him at a glance; but, in the blind fury which seemed to impel the former to spur forward and smite, it is doubtful if he recognized the ruffian, especially in the new costume which he now wore.

Gorham knew *him*, and, with an ancient instinct, he recoiled, and shrunk back, and would have stolen away, but the blow descended ere he could do so. His efforts served, however, to lessen the force of the stroke, which barely grazed his cheek, and fell heavily upon his arm.

His rifle dropped from his grasp, and was instantly seized by one of the sheriff's party. The blacksmith next felt the weight of Voltmeier's flail, and was prostrated; and the sheriff, drawn out from beneath him, recovered his legs, not seriously injured, and, taking advantage of the diversion, and the momentary terror inspired by the wild rush of the steed, and the desperate efforts of all parties to get out of the way of his hoofs, he again vociferated his command to keep the peace, while the constables began to capture the persons who had been struck down.

From this danger Gorham was fortunate enough, by crawling between legs, and climbing where he could not crawl, to escape to the rear.

The blacksmith *hors-de-combat*, Gorham fled, the lawyer Brownlow no longer heard or seen, and some half a dozen of the rioters disabled and captured, the crowd seemed parting on every side. Luckily, there were but few firearms among the masses.

They yielded the contest. Beyond the pistols fired by the sheriff's party, there was but one shot sent from a rifle in the rear, which passed over the head of Fergus Wallace, and shattered one of the sashes of the Court House. It was mischievously aimed, but by whom was unknown.

Law began to assert itself. For the present, it was quite evident that no further assault would be made. The sheriff, with numbers of the villagers now gathered around him, some of whom appeared well armed, was now quite too strong of force to apprehend anything more from the rioters. Five of these were in custody, sore from bruises, and expressing themselves quite repentant. The mob was undergoing general dispersion, but still slowly and sullenly; and it was apparent that much excitement still prevailed, and that much bad blood was in agitation.

Voltmeier said to the sheriff:

"You are safe for the present. You are rescued!"

"You came not a moment too soon, Colonel Voltmeier. It is likely that we should all have been butchered. I thank you, Colonel."

"See to your prisoner to-night, Mr. Sheriff. Make his life safe at the peril of your own! I will be with you to guard the jail! Many of these rioters are mountaineers, and unknown here. They come from other parts! See to fires! Have out a patrol! These fellows mean plunder! Get up a strong force. I repeat, I will be with you to-night, and bring help."

Then to Fergus:—

"You are not forgotten, my son! Submit for the present. Fear nothing. This situation is for a brief time only. I shall tell Mignon that you are safe."

With a few whispered words to Colonel Graham, Voltmeier disappeared from the scene as suddenly and as rapidly as he had come upon it; and now he sped homeward.

But, how was he to meet Mignon? How tell her of the situation of her lover, the peril he had passed, and the doubtful ordeal which still awaited him?

He had not the courage for this. He shrank from the task, and did not return to Keovala that day. The night found him in the County Jail with the sheriff, Graham, and other persons, while a strong patrol scoured the streets. The night passed off without alarm, though many strange persons were seen about. Gorham, we may state, slept that night in Brownlow's office.

Chapter LVIII

GORHAM'S PROGRAMME

The next morning found Gorham in close conference with the Lawyer Brownlow. There was now an air of dogged determination about the ruffian, which impressed Brownlow. The face of the fellow, unwashed, was smeared with clotted blood, and marked with the bruises of the preceding day.

"Why don't you wash yourself?" asked Brownlow.

"Hain't got time for it! Didn't think about it! Don't care about it jest now! But, you see how 'tis! You see my face! I owe that bruise to *him!* a leetle more, and he'd ha' split my skull."

"Who?"

"Him you calls Voltmeier. But I knows him by another name."

"Ha! ah!—well!"

"Look at my ear. T'other side."

"That's the mark of a bullet, I reckon."

"I guess it is! Well, I owes that to him, too."

"How was that? What do you know about Colonel Voltmeier?"

"Colonel H—l! But, it'll *keep!* I'll tell you some other time. What I've got to say to you now, is, he's got to pay for that slash and that shot! and pay *high!* I own him, body and soul; he's my *property,* and, by the Powers, he shall pay well before he can get his freedom."

"Why, Mr. Gorham, you must be in possession of some great secret concerning Voltmeier."

"I guess I am. You'll think so when you come to hear it."

"Well, out with it. I'm your lawyer, you know, and never tell your lawyer only a part of the story. Tell him all; out with it; what's this matter that you know about Voltmeier?"

"It'll keep, squire. I mean that he shall pay for it—pay for my *keeping* it; but if I let my bird out of the cage, so that anybody can catch it as it flies, he'll hardly pay *me* for the keeping it."

"Well, if that's your game—"

"That's my game jist now, and it must be played out my way, and he mustn't think I've let on to anybody, you know."

"Well, I don't see how, in such a game as that, I am to serve you."

"I'll let you know afterwards. You must let me play the game after my own liking, as I knows the trump cards in my own hand, and you don't. But, I'll have a good deal for you to do that'll pay you well, 'specially if he comes to my terms. I tell you, Lawyer, I own his very body and soul, and he's got to sweat freely before he gits his freedom! He's got to pay for this shot here in my ear, and this bloody wipe across my cheek, besides paying for his soul. I've sworn it by all the devils in hell and out of it."

Here he smote the table with his fist so heavily as to make it dance again under the concussion.

"Well, he's rich enough to pay! If your secret is so important a one, you may get a few thousands out of him."

"A few thousands! I rather guess I will! The first thing I intends to have from him is his daughter for my wife."

"W-h-a-t!"

It was now the lawyer's turn to be aghast, as he rose from his seat, approached the ruffian, and with head stretched forward, and eyes staring, repeated his exclamation—

"W-h-a-t!"

"Well, what's there to wonder at? I want to know."

"Ha! ha! ha!" The lawyer was relieved of his surprise by a flood of laughter.

"Well, do tell! What's there to laugh at, Lawyer?"

"Why, man, Voltmeier will fling you out of the window the moment you name it."

"Don't think—don't mean, in the first place—to trust myself inside of his house. Next, I rather guess, when he knows all that I knows, he'll be only too glad to give me anything I ask for to stop my mouth. I must have that daughter of his—she's a beauty—I *must* have her; and he must give me, with her, to keep us comfortable and decent and respectable, wherever I carries her, the good round sum of thirty thousand dollars."

The lawyer drew a long breath, and fairly gasped with astonishment.

"Mr. Gorham, either you are crazy, or this secret of yours involves some most damnable crime."

"A damnable dozen of crimes, perhaps, Lawyer; but I'll keep the secret for *his* ears only, for the time present. I guess you'll find, Squire, that I'm not crazy; and I guess, moreover, that you'll have the drawing up of some law papers, and bonds, and mortgages, perhaps, and records, that'll put a few thousands into your pocket—defendant paying all lawyer expenses, you know."

"I know! I know! But I confess, Mr. Gorham, you so much astonish me that I can hardly believe my own senses, and certainly find it no easy matter to believe in the soundness of yours. This Colonel Voltmeier is a native of this county, I think. He has certainly been residing here long before I came into it; and though I never did cotton to the man, and confess I don't like him, I must say that his character stands as high in society as any man's in the State."

"That's the beauty of it, Squire. That's how I'll fix him! He's got to pay to keep up that character, since I guess, for the sake of his daughter only, he puts a very high vally on good character."

"Naturally enough! But you see further, Mr. Gorham, as far as anybody knows, he has always been a man of great wealth and substance, and, for the sake of money, certainly, had never any need to be guilty of any such great crime as you hint at."

"Look you, Squire Brownlow—what did you mean when you speechified in the court-room, and outside to the people, about them 'big fish' and 'nabobs' being at the bottom of all this forging and counterfeiting—"

"Ah! are you there, Mr. Gorham? Is that the secret?"

The ruffian had lost a point in the game, as he could perceive by the exulting manner and flashing eyes of the lawyer, taking the scent; but he replied coolly, and with apparent frankness—

"No, I'm not there. That's not it. I only put your own showing to the people, that plenty of money, and good character, and all that sort of thing, don't keep nabobs and big fish from robbing the people and doing other ugly things that you call crimes. Now, when you said them things in the court-house, you must have meant *somebody*. You didn't mean the lawyer you call Graham, for he brought you up with a short turn, and you 'spressly said you didn't mean *him*. Now who *did* you mean? I thought 'twas this very man, Voltmeier, that you was squinting at all the time."

"And are all your presumptions against Voltmeier based upon what *I said?*"

"The devil!—no! I had no guess of you or your speech in the business. What I knows about Voltmeier is jest as different as day from night, I guess; but that don't make the case any better for him. I only thought, from what you said, that you knowed something besides, which would make my showing a leetle stronger, though I guess it's strong enough for all I wants."

"For mere money's sake, then, I could not conceive of Colonel Voltmeier being the criminal you think him; and I still believe that you labor under some singular delusion. You have confounded two different men."

"I guess I have! That's one of the very p'ints in the case. But I'm not going to let you see the least bit of it until I wants you in the business. But, jist now, please you go on with what you was going to say."

"Briefly, then, this man, Voltmeier, is not only wealthy, but he is an accomplished gentleman—has received an European education, and is one of the most elegant men in the country. It is difficult to say what he might have been if he had not been above the necessity of labor of any kind. He would have made an excellent lawyer, I know, and I'd sooner have *his* opinion about the real merits of a case, than even Graham's, or any of the members of the bar here."

"I guess all that's true, about his education, and accomplishments, and talents; I don't deny it! But, after all, Lawyer Brownlow, you knows little about it, and I'm not going to let you know just yet; so you needn't worm into me any more. All I've got to say to you is, I'm not crazy, and know what I'm about. To-morrow, I mean to visit this Col. Voltmeier, as you calls him, and to ax for his daughter, and the money and property that's to support her in style, as a lady, and his own daughter, and my wife."

"Well, I confess, Mr. Gorham, I would not like to be in your shoes, when you make the proposition to him!"

"Never you fear! There will be no danger, if you'll give me the help I want."

"I don't wish to *appear* in this business, Mr. Gorham, in any way, if I'm to be kept in the dark as to the particulars."

"I don't mean to ax you to *appear* in the business, Squire, so long as I can do without you. If I can't make the bargain with Voltmeier, by smooth words, and showing him what I know, why, then, perhaps, you will hear the whole story. Now, I know that this person you calls Voltmeier would blow my brains out, or put a knife clean through my body, as soon as look at me, if he could do it with no eye looking on but his own and mine; but that's the very thing that I wants you to do for me. I wants you to git me at least two good pair of eyes, besides my own, to keep track with me, and do the watching, as I tells them; while I pays my visit to your Col. Voltmeier. They must be good strong fellows, with strong hearts, not easily scared, but up to everything—what do you call them—constables—detectives—such as you set to work when you've got to deal with bad customers. Kin you get me sich fellows?"

"Yes! But you'll need to pay them well."

"I kin do it!"

"They will require something in advance, if you expect them to do the work thoroughly and well."

"How much will do at first?"

"Oh, fifty or a hundred dollars a-piece. The more you give at first, the larger their expectations when the work is done. What will you wish them to do?"

"Never you mind to know. Only you jest tell them to take the word from me, and be quick to do the work when I call upon 'em to pitch in."

"You shall have the men. I have the very sort of fellows you seek—fellows who will ask no questions when the word is 'knock down and drag out!'"

"All right. I must have them at peep of day to-morrow. I must take to-day for cleaning up and getting my face a little decent; ann'inting my bruises, and dressing up handsome. As I'm to seek a wife, and sich a beauty too, I must get on my best Sunday clothes!"

"Do you know, Mr. Gorham, that this young lady, daughter of Col. Voltmeier, is said to be engaged in marriage to this young man, Wallace, who had so narrow a chance yesterday?"

"Wall, I guessed so from what I've seed myself, some time ago. But he'll hardly git her *now!* That game's up! If I could ha' got the chance yesterday, his game would have been up, too!"

"Ah, ha! you worked, then, for putting a rival out of the way?"

"Yes, and if I hadn't been a stupe, I could ha' done it easy. If I had only gone off to that leetle knob of the hill that looks down upon the square, I could ha' plumped him with my rifle, and got off among the hollows, into the mountains, and no man been the wiser."

"Wall, no matter what securities you provide for your own safety to-morrow, in your interview with Voltmeier, you will still have a perilous business, if you really mean to demand his daughter. He is a terrible man when roused to passion."

"Ha! *don't* I know him? I tell you, Lawyer, I knows every crook in his soul and body better than you does the nose on his face! Ha, ha, ha! yes! the devil help him! but I knows him now; and you says right—he's a most terrible person, if you let him sight you first."

"Great God! how he drove through the people yesterday, head-long—just like a madman rushing into the jaws of hell! What a splendid fellow to lead a charge of cavalry!"

"Yes! that's true! He's a terrible fellow. I confess he cowed me yesterday, when I seed his eye upon me, and sich a devil looking out through it, I felt myself shivering all over, and thought of nothing but getting out of his reach. But he won't scare me again! I'm death upon him next time! I feel that I've got a devil of my own to do my work, and I'm wound up so for business that my devil's eye shall look straight into his, till the work's done; and I'll do it without winking!"

Chapter LIX

FATE AT KEOVALA

It was with feelings little short of agony that Voltmeier returned to Keovala. What should he say—what report make, to Mignon, of the situation of Fergus, and of the peril of life which he had so narrowly escaped? That peril and escape argued fully the extent of the crime charged upon him, and of the deeply-seated feeling of the people whose losses were so heavily felt, and so angrily and bitterly resented. He could not keep the history of the affair from the family. It must reach them through some medium, and, possibly, with such exaggerations as would make the story of more mischievous effect upon their minds. He alone must make the cruel revelation, and, which his pride felt to be so much the worse, must confess his own present impotence for good.

It will be much easier to conceive than to describe his deep and keen sense of humiliation; and when he reached the last hill looking down from the road upon Keovala, and began the descent to the valley which he had persuaded himself that he had made an elysium into which no serpent could penetrate, he felt a sense of shame—a feeling most unwonted—of fear and trembling, and, but for a struggle on the part of self-esteem, he would have wheeled his steed about and fled from the necessity before him; and when he beheld Mignon coming towards him, and knew that she had been watching from the hills—how long!—for his coming;—with what fears, doubts, hopes and apprehensions—he could hardly suppress the scalding tear-drops which still gathered in his eyes.

He calmed himself as well as he might, making a great effort, and taxing his will to the uttermost to keep down all appearance of those emotions which made him writhe in his inmost soul. He leaped from his horse as she drew near, and took her in his arms.

"My Mignon! my child!"

She pushed him away from her, looking up in his face with

those great eyes which always dilated wondrously in her moments of excitement.

"Where is he? where is Fergus? why have you not brought him?"

"He will shortly come to you, my Mignon. I hope soon to see him here again and see you all happy."

"Hope! only hope, father! Is he not on the road even now, following close? But why not bring him with you—why leave him?"

"He can not come just now, my child. His case is not yet disposed of. He is still in the hands of the court, and the trial is not decided."

"Do you mean to tell me, my father, that Fergus is still a prisoner in that wretched jail—that you have come away and left him there to starve and perish? How could you do it? why do it? what is there against him? I do not understand it at all! Tell me all! Hide nothing, papa, if you would not drive me mad!"

Aunt Gertrude, by this time, sharing somewhat the anxieties of Mignon, had joined the two where Mignon had arrested Voltmeier in front of the piazza. She added her expostulations to those of Mignon.

"What is this mystery, Leonard? For God's sake clear it up, or this poor child will go distracted. She has scarcely slept or eaten since we first heard—"

"Heard what?"

"What you told us, of Fergus' imprisonment."

"Well, I can tell you little more now. He is still imprisoned, but we are busy in his behalf, and will try to have him released very shortly."

"Try! try! Is it a doubt, papa? speak! How—when will you get him out and bring him here—bring him home, and end this misery? Oh, father! I have such strange fears and fancies! and when *you* express yourself doubtfully, how should I hope? When will you bring him back?"

"In a few days, Mignon, I hope!"

"In a few days!"—with a scream; "and you only hope! and for days he is still in chains!—"

"Oh, no chains, Mignon."

"A prison is chains and tortures! I will go to him! take me to him! I will hear all from his own lips. I will share his bondage;

I will hold up his chains. I—I—oh, my father, tell me—tell me all, or my heart will break!"

"Here is a letter from Fergus, my Mignon. That will tell you."

"And why did you not give it to me before?"

She grasped the letter eagerly, kissed it passionately, then tore it wide and devoured its contents. It was a letter of soothing, and had been calculated to lessen her fears if not satisfy her affections. It made light of his prison restraints, and expressed a cool, calm, confident conviction of his early release. But, unhappily, some details were given—perhaps unavoidably—which gave to Mignon the first intelligence of his recent peril from the rioters. This opened a new vein of trouble. It saved Voltmeier, however, the necessity of making that revelation himself—of opening the subject, at least; for he was not suffered to keep silent in the anxious examination which followed.

"What is this?" she cried; "mob, riot, fighting in the town! Read it, aunty; I can not make it out. I can not understand it. The letters all dance before me. Read! read!"

The aunt took the letter, and as she read she too exclaimed— "What does it mean, Voltmeier? A riot, and fighting in the Court House and streets?"

Voltmeier had to tell them all. No—not all! He forebore to relate his own agency in the affair; modulated the extent of the riot; showed only how an effort had been made to resist the sheriff and take Fergus from his custody; then gave them to understand how the common people of the country had become infuriate from the counterfeit money in circulation, and had singled out Fergus as the chief offender upon whom to wreak their rages.

"And it was you, my father, who gave him that very money? and you were silent! You did not speak to the judge, and to the people, and say that the money was yours, and that Fergus had been your agent only. Oh, my father! how could you?"

For a moment the father hung his head. How could he meet those flashing eyes—behold those flushed cheeks, and read the indignation in her look, voice, and gesture, which was only subdued on her tongue by her sense of filial relation. The simple but pathetic remonstrance—"Oh, my father! how could you?" struck to his heart and conscience, and covered his sallow cheeks with the crimson evidence of shame.

At length, with something of his old pride of heart, he lifted his eyes and met her gaze without blanching. With hoarse and half-choking accents he exclaimed:

"You know not what you say, Mignon, or how your reproaches strike! Do you suppose that I will suffer Fergus Wallace to endure my penalties? I tell you, girl, that he is safe; that I will make him safe, though it drains the last drop of life from the living currents of my heart. Believe me, child! As I live and love you and him, it shall be so! All we need now is time—a brief delay; and Fergus is kept in prison now rather to secure his safety than to endure any punishment. It will be for a few days only—until the country is somewhat quieted, and the mountaineers shall retire to their homes. Now, it would be unsafe for him to venture abroad; and no words that I could say would be of any avail until the present excitement is over. Believe me, child, this is all! Have faith in your father's assurances, as you must have in his love."

"I must go to Fergus, papa! I must see him. I feel too wretched, papa, for the faith that you require. You promised me to bring him here. Instead of that, you tell me of his danger from the people. I must share his danger! I will! Oh! Fergus! that my father should bring you to this!"

"Mignon!" said the aunt, reproachfully.

"Let her speak! Let her speak!" Voltmeier gloomily responded, "it is a part of the doom, the penance! The Fates are not to be defrauded! It is, perhaps, but right that my own child should curse me ere I die!"

This was all spoken unconsciously, as if to himself.

"Curse you, my father!"—and the girl, suddenly stricken with a feeling of remorse, clung to her father, and sobbed wildly upon his bosom.

"Forgive me, oh! dear papa! I know not what I say; but I am so wretched! so very wretched."

And, no longer restrainable, the big hot tears swelled in the eyes of the strong man, and fell like rain-drops down upon her cheeks.

Then, as she felt them, she started from his embrace, with a cry of absolute terror!

She had never seen him weep before. She had been taught to regard him as so strong, so powerful, cast in such a mould of majesty and power, that tears from his eyes seemed to her as monstrous as unnatural. They did not befit his eyes! They seemed a very mockery of his manhood.

"Oh! papa! Do not! Do not!"

"Voltmeier, my brother!" cried Aunt Gertrude, seizing his arm; and now almost as much excited as Mignon, she too, clung to him wildly.

"Voltmeier, what is this?"

"Enough, Gertrude! Enough, my child, that your father is not a cast iron man; is not powerful for all things. These tears prove rather his sense of the decline of power to save those whom he loves, than of the love which made this power so precious in his eyes."

"Ha! papa! say you that? What! Can you no longer save? Ah! there is my fear come back again. You promised, and you failed to bring him back! And now you weep because you can not save! Let me go to Fergus, papa! I must go at once. I will save him, or die!"

"Stay! foolish child!" and he seized her arm, as she was going. "Stay! I command you! and do not misunderstand my language. I have promised you, and I *will* save him! Nay, you shall see him shortly. You must leave the time for me to decide; and you must not be permitted to meddle with the labors of those friends who are working for Fergus now. I am momently expecting the arrival here of his friend, Major Henry, one of the great lawyers of South Carolina."

"Father! every word you say adds to my fears! Why should you need a great lawyer from South Carolina, to help you in this matter? Why, if there were not dangers to Fergus, and if you did not yourself doubt"—

And she stood before him, erect, and looking into his eyes with a gaze which might be thought stern, but for the warm passion which infused and qualified the expression; and, for a moment, his eye quailed before the glance of the child. Then he spoke, and now his language became that of authority.

"You know not what you say, Mignon, and you will comprehend nothing that I say! Take her hence, Gertrude, and quiet her. There is nothing to fear, I tell you both, even if I can not now explain everything. To-morrow! to-morrow!—"

"It will not do, my father! Your eye quivers. You, yourself, fear, even while you counsel me to fear nothing! Oh! papa I never thought to see you afraid of mortal man."

"Nor am I, girl!" impatiently. "Go, leave me, and be assured that before a hair of the head of Fergus Wallace shall suffer, the head of your father shall be beyond all suffering! Go—I say; and let your *faith* in your father supply the place of your *love!*"

"You might have spared me *that*, my father! Go! you say! Well, I will go; but, mark me, father, I must see Fergus, and see him soon. Save him, I tell you, or you lose your daughter!"

And with face flushed to the very brows, her hair flowing wildly over her shoulders, her arm uplifted, and hand waving towards him, she gave him but one look—so proud, so resolute—so full of passionate tenderness, and an equally passionate reproach, that Voltmeier, as he gazed, thought involuntarily of the Cassandra of Eschylus, breathing some terrible prediction, and moaning over the dreadful necessity which rent equally the fibers of her brain and heart to deliver!

Voltmeier followed her with streaming eyes, as, never once looking back, Mignon retired within the house, slowly following her aunt.

Then the arms of Voltmeier dropped to his sides, and his chin sank upon his bosom, and he wandered away, seemingly without heed whither, and he muttered as he went:

"The Fate! The inevitable Fate! In what new shape is it yet to come? Great God, what agencies for torture dost thou not employ! My own child! That she should be gifted with the power, and goaded to its use, of driving the heaviest of all the darts of doom into the bosom of her father! And I have so loved her!"

Chapter LX

REUNION

Voltmeier made his way finally to his chamber, and busied himself by a stern exercise of will, in the prosecution of certain labors at the desk, of the objects of which we have no present knowledge. There was a settled resolve in his aspect and manner, which argued for him some fixed determination, upon a plan fully settled in his mind.

Miss Gertrude sought him, but he refused to see her. Mignon kept her own room, brooding over and nursing her anxieties. Her aunt wandered about the house with a vague sense of trouble and danger, and a more decided conviction of her own inability to encounter danger and difficulty of any nature; so peaceful had been "Keovala;" so sweet and calm its repose; hitherto so secure; and, hitherto, Voltmeier so strong—so equal to all things, that the good old maid was utterly bewildered at the change in him, and the prospect of change in all things around her.

She, too, had her instincts of evil, as the mere result of a change passing over her experience. Where now were the songs of Mignon? where the music? the happy *soirees,* in which reading, and conversation, and whist, and the arch, but innocent prattle of the dear child, precious to her affections as to those of Voltmeier, made life a succession of sweet dreams, and birdlike fancies, and the happiest communions from day to day.

For the first time Keovala was gloomy in her eyes, and exercised a saddening influence over her thoughts and feelings. Its bird sang no longer in its cage, which implied equal freedom of flight and song; and the Master Spirit, who had swayed all things with a spell like that of Prospero, seemed, on a sudden, to have had the wand of his power broken by some counter spell of a superior wizard.

But Voltmeier, that day, had his respite from one of the hounds of fate which had pursued him. The promised visit of Richard

Gorham was not made. The Jack-legged lawyer Brownlow had secured a couple of the best detectives in the county to second the objects of Gorham, and accompany him on his projected visit to Keovala. They appeared punctually, at the appointed hour, at Brownlow's office, where they were to await the appearance of Gorham. But the day waned, and, after several hours of weary waiting in vain, they became impatient; especially as they had not yet received their retaining fees; and the lawyer became apprehensive of the loss of that large compensation which had been held out before his hopes. His cupidity had been excited too greatly by the lures of Gorham—the thousands to be reaped from the one mysterious secret—and he was too keen of scent, after such a game, and too well experienced in it, to be altogether satisfied to forfeit a hope which had so gratefully possessed his fancy.

Having waited till noon, and the ruffian still making no appearance, he went in search of him, and, with some difficulty, found him at an obscure lodging-house, kept by a poor widow, in the suburbs of the town, and within easy reach of the mountain fastnesses. Gorham was a man of precautions, and always provided himself with a back-door means of escape when near the camp of the enemy.

Brownlow found Gorham sick with high fever, the result probably of exposure, bruises and excitement. He suffered from occasional delirium, and exhibited such an aspect as somewhat alarmed the lawyer. His bruised and bloated face, bloodshot eyes, wild looks and wilder expressions, seemed to indicate some considerable affection of the brain.

"He's too sick for any business, just now, Squire," was the remark of one of the detectives. "You'd better get a doctor to him."

Brownlow muttered, *sotto voce:*

"But who the devil is to pay the doctor? and how if the fellow never recovers?"

But the doctor was procured, and the patient confided to his hands.

Half-delirious, or so at intervals, the cunning of Gorham did not wholly desert him. After raving of unmentionable things—things equivocal and suspicious, to which Brownlow lent a more attentive ear than the physician, Gorham, with a grin of cunning, and a half-wild, half-wicked leer, said to the former:

"You may put your ears down, Lawyer, and you may think you've got it, but you hain't! Tain't time for that yit! Wait till I sees the vally of that soul I've got to sell, and gits my price for it! Then!"

But we leave him for a while, and return to Keovala.

That night, Major Henry, accompanying Ben Harness, arrived, and was gratefully welcomed by Voltmeier, with whom he was closeted for several goodly hours.

When they came forth, it was to a late supper, and both the ladies awaited them, both anxious, curious, and excited, and scarcely able to refrain till supper was over, from asking the questions which were evermore rising to their thoughts and tongues.

"What does Major Henry say, Leonard?" was, at length, the hurriedly whispered query of Miss Gertrude. A quiet nod of the head and a smile was the only answer.

But the moment supper was over, and the two gentlemen, rising from the table, seemed about to retire again to the library, Mignon, with a calm, but resolute manner—all woman and none of the girl about her—approached, and said, addressing her father, but looking towards Major Henry:

"Papa, what does Major Henry think of this case of Cousin Fergus?"

It was with a choking sensation that she was able to pronounce these few words. Voltmeier looked also to the lawyer, and the latter, a mild, amiable and graceful gentleman, with a lively expression of good-humor in his face, and no little upon his tongue, replied:

"I see no difficulty about the case, my dear young lady, beyond a little delay. You are aware that we lawyers find our profit in delay, and, like the doctors, the most profitable cases are those which we can make most tedious to our clients. I do not see that you have reason to fear for my young friend, Wallace; I will see my brother Graham to-morrow, and I trust we shall put things in proper order for procuring the release of Fergus from prison. Col. Voltmeier has told me all; and, though there are some complications in the affair, arising from the riotous conduct and excitement of the people, we, perhaps, shall only need to delay, in order that they shall cool off, when we lawyers shall grow warm."

Voltmeier had been very far from telling Henry all. That revelation, to be made in full, required the more coercive action of the Fates, upon the will or conscience of him, who now began to fear that he should fall their victim. But this aside.

With still a wondrous calm of manner, and appearance of a womanly strength of character which Mignon had not hitherto shown, she now said, to the equal surprise of Voltmeier and her aunt—

"Forgive my anxiety, Major Henry, which prompts me to ask these questions; but I am to be the wife of Cousin Fergus—"

"Ah!"

"And if he is in danger—if he is to be kept in prison, it is my duty to seek him, to see him, to be with him, and let him know that I truly love him, though I can do nothing for him!"

"Mignon!" exclaimed Aunt Gertrude, with prudish consternation.

"Mignon!" exclaimed her father, "better suffer me to communicate these family matters to the Major."

"No, papa! I am too much interested in this matter to be silent, and I fear you are too much interested to be a proper counselor. You feel too much for me, as well as for Fergus. I wish to know from Major Henry, if there would be anything improper in my seeing and seeking my affianced husband in his troubles, and in his prison?"

Henry looked at Voltmeier inquiringly. The latter nodded his head, as if affirmatively; then said Henry, taking her hand:

"There is no impropriety, my dear young lady, in any honest evidence which may be given, of a pure and true affection. You can securely visit Fergus, and your father will no doubt give you his full sanction; but, perhaps, it will be well to delay any movement, until I have seen my brother Graham, and been able to grasp the entire subject. Col. Graham is not only an able lawyer, but a high-minded and honorable gentleman. He will doubtless invite you to become the guest of his family, when your visits, should there be any prolonged detention of Fergus, will be easy. But I have no apprehension that he will be detained a longer time than will suffice to bring the case properly before the court, allowing a little space for the subsiding of that popular excitement which no doubt influenced the Judge in remanding him to prison. The case was, perhaps, prematurely brought forward. We shall now be better prepared for it; in fact, from the evidence put in my possession by your father, I think I am quite safe in assuring you that Fergus will soon be honorably discharged from custody. You will believe me when I say that I am almost as solicitous for him as yourself. He was a favorite of mine long before he became a favorite of yours."

What was the evidence furnished by Voltmeier, upon which Henry relied? It was simply the affidavit of the former, that he himself had furnished, though unknowingly at the time, the counterfeit money which Fergus had put in circulation. To this Voltmeier had solemnly sworn before the magistrate; yet, well knowing all the while that such was *not* the truth—well knowing that the money, when given to Wallace, was a proper and honest currency. But he well conceived by what means the counterfeit had been substituted for the good. This, however, he did not dare to declare, for it must then have fixed the whole responsibility of guilt upon the head of the innocent man. Voltmeier's hesitation to give this affidavit arose partly from a scruple to *swear* to a falsehood—a scruple which seems strange enough when we consider the life of falsehood which he had led. But, thousands will lie with little hesitation, having a selfish motive for it, who will yet, no matter how imperious the motive, hesitate at a solemn appeal to God as a witness to the lie!

The next day, accompanied by Benjie Harness, Major Henry proceeded to the Court House. He did not return that night, nor yet the next. He became the guest of Col. Graham, and we are to assume that the two lawyers discussed together the nature of the case, and the proper course to be pursued. A brief note from Graham apprised Voltmeier that there would be unavoidable delay, for some days, in consequence of the temporary absence of the Judge; and that, as there was still considerable excitement prevailing in the county, it was, perhaps, just as well that there should be some delay in their action, in order to avoid embarrassments.

Meanwhile, Major Henry embraced his pupil within the walls of the prison.

"I never thought to meet you here, Fergus," he said, as he took the young man in his arms.

"Nor did I ever think, my dear sir, to find myself here."

Fergus was very calm. How easy it is to endure trouble with an approving conscience! With a heart right, and a conscience at ease, the sense of fear and danger is feebly felt; and the calm of innocence becomes a courage which endures as firmly as it strikes bravely. When the friends of Socrates lamented that he should be doomed to perish, while innocent of offense, the grand old philosopher replied, with a deeper truth than even the wise man will usually acknowledge:

"Would you have me die *guilty!* Melitus and Anytus may *kill* me, but they can not *harm* me!"

Long did the senior and his pupil commune together that night, chewing the cud of sweet and bitter thought, which naturally grew from the stores of former memories. They spoke together of old friends.

"The mother of Wattie and little Flit is dead," said the Major. "We have been doing for the children; but when you are married to that beautiful creature, Mignon Voltmeier, my dear Fergus, you must take and train those children in your house. You were a great favorite with little Flit, and she asks after you whenever I see her."

Fergus thought of the long career of sickness and poverty, and the death-bed of his mother, and the big tears gathered in his eyes.

"You do not ask of your old employers, Brigham & Co. Well, you have not much reason to be curious, nor need you suffer from much sympathy in their fortunes. The firm is bankrupt, and Brigham is now clerking it with one who is likely to give him a taste of your experience while with him. And so, you see, Time brings about his great revenges."

Long into the night did they carry on this talk, which was grateful to both, until the jailer gave notice to Henry that he could allow him no more time that night; and, with an affectionate embrace, they parted; and while Fergus, with an easy conscience, slept soundly on his prison pallet, Voltmeier was pacing his luxurious library, swallowing, ever and anon, his pill of opium, and conjuring into sight a thousand specters that threatened him from wall and window!

Chapter LXI

A RUFFIAN'S WILL

Richard Gorham had suffered from a severe paroxysm of fever, during which Lawyer Brownlow watched him with the considerate care of one owning a golden goose, and anxious that it shall live as long as it shall be able to lay its daily egg. He was much more frequent in attendance than the physician, giving all ear to whatever the delirious man might utter in his paroxysms.

But the delirium was brief, and passed off as rapidly as it came on; and, though very feeble, and with still a low fever lurking in his veins, the spirit of the old ruffian resumed full possession, and, sustained by stimulants, he became all eagerness to be up and doing. He grew momently more and more impatient of bed and confinement. His nature, hitherto seemingly hard, cold, always calculating, and immovably calm, became suddenly irritable and excitable in the extreme; and, in frequent potations—having been very temperate before—he seemed to seek in alcohol for that quieting influence which Voltmeier sought in opium.

The impatience of Brownlow to get at his secret, and to secure the promised profits, made him contribute to the feverish irritability of the patient, by perpetually bringing up the one subject, over all, which occupied Gorham's thoughts and moved his passions, and when at length he came in one morning, and told him that Mignon Voltmeier was in town, a guest of Col. Graham, and that she had been to visit Fergus Wallace in his prison—when to this he added that the great lawyer, Major Henry, from Spartanburg, was also a guest of Graham, and that he had been brought to North Carolina to assist in procuring the release of Wallace from prison, the sick man leaped from his bed, swore a terrible oath, swallowed an enormous draught of peach brandy, and proceeded to put on his clothes.

"Come to clear him, ha? To git him out of jail, has he? That he shan't do! I tell you, Lawyer Brownlow, not all the lawyers in

North Carolina, and South Carolina to boot, kin git that fellow clear. He'll swing, and I'll see it. Either him or Voltmeier, or both of 'em, curse 'em! They shall both swing unless the man you calls Voltmeier comes down with the cash, thirty thousand dollars, I tell you, and even that won't do, ef his daughter don't go with it. Don't I own his very soul and body, man? Don't I? answer me that!"

Here he approached Brownlow, haggard with rage, with bloated red cheeks, disheveled hair, half-clad only, and with fists doubled, almost under the face of Brownlow, he seemed ready to strike, with his victim lying prostrate before him.

Brownlow was a little disquieted, and recoiled incontinently, apprehensive of the blow which seemed about to follow from the threatening attitude. He answered, as he retreated—

"I don't see it, myself, Mr. Gorham. I only hear you say it. What you know you do not let me know, and therefore I can't say that you are sure either of the bodies or souls of these men."

"You don't know, ha? and with all your cunning you ha'nt found out yit. But, you tried mighty hard, lawyer," with a grin and chuckle. "Well, I don't mean to let you know just yet. I tell you I must play out my game after my own fashion, because, you see, it's only I that knows what's in my hand. I tell you I've got all the trump cards, and the four honors, and it's I that's going to gather up the stakes. Ef I don't, why then, you see, I'll show *you*, and you shall help me to *try* the souls and bodies of these 'nabobs' and 'big fish' as you calls them! Your Col. Voltmeier won't be so willing to dance upon air, I guess, as to say 'No!' to anything I shall ax from him. The youngster must swing. He must be got out of the track!"

"Well, success to you, I say. Only, we are burning daylight just now. If you would but trust me with the whole business, I could bring it about much quicker than you, I think. You can do nothing while you are in this condition, and these men will have that young fellow out of prison before you can get out of your bed."

"Ain't I out of bed now?"

"Yes, but too feeble to leave the house, or do any business."

"Feeble!" he exclaimed, as he swallowed a potation of whisky. "Feeble!"—he laid down the glass, and approaching the small table which stood before the lawyer, he smote it heavily with his fist, and it crashed to pieces under the blow.

"What do you say to that?"

This unexpected demonstration of physical power, whether increased by the alcohol or stimulated by the fever, was so unexpected that the lawyer started up from his seat confounded and in silence.

"Talk of feeble!" exclaimed the ruffian. "Talk of feeble! Why, I feel strong as an ox, and if I had only had the same feeling when your Colonel Voltmeier rode down upon us there, like mad, I'd ha' crushed him like that table, and his horse too. No, lawyer, I feel strong enough for anything now. This sick has helped me. You will see what I can do! Only remember I wants them fellows bright and airly to-morrow. They must be ready for me by the very peep of day. By sunrise we must be off among the hills for—what do you call the name of the place?"

"Keovala!"

"An Ingin name, I reckon, and I'll play Ingin with the nabob when I gits there. Yes, I tell you, ef I can't sell *him* his soul, I'll sell the county his sculp!"

It will be seen that the *will* of Gorham was no less strong than that of Voltmeier. The question is whether *his* "Fate" was any more friendly. We shall see. It is certain that, whatever the influence which strengthened him, whether whisky or cupidity, or a brain which still lingered in the grasp of a subtle fire which might result in insanity or apoplexy, he was on the mountains at sunrise the next morning, accompanied by two able-bodied myrmidons of the law.

Chapter LXII

TO-MORROW!

It was even so, as Brownlow had said—Mignon Voltmeier had left Keovala, accompanied by her aunt. She was the guest of Col. Graham, as was Major Henry also. And she had visited Fergus Wallace in his prison. She was even then his visitor.

Who shall describe the first meeting between the lovers?

Mignon, our Juliet of the drama; a child of the sun; a petted, joyous, confiding creature; all emotion, all enthusiasm; bright with golden hopes; suffused with blended fancies and affections, that gave life and animation to each other, and made love, and a perfect faith in love, the enduring necessity of life, not feeding upon which, with hope and fidelity, she must die!

Juliet is in the arms of Fergus Wallace; his lips glued to hers, and she sinking upon his bosom, as if she were resigned to die there, if she can not live.

And he, not a whit less tender and truthful; not a whit less confiding and devoted; fond, fanciful in his fondness, as becomes the manhood of a pure heart and a clear conscience; and treasuring, as his most precious of all possessions, the fairy-like creature whom a gracious fortune had given to his love; yet, with calm nature and strong intellect; firm, fearless, brave; not insensible to care or danger; not unconscious of his painful situation, and feeling all its humiliation; yet stifling every exhibition of doubt, and yielding himself only to the one absorbing sense of a passion which seemed to give wings to his shoulders, and the imperial strength of heroism to his heart.

How describe the meeting of these two?

Knowing their relations, and, by this time, their respective characteristics and natures, it will be easier to conceive than to describe; easier to dream the details of love than to paint them; easier, in *your* fancies, to find the secret of *theirs*; and, in *your* sympathies, to read

340

of the sweet passions, warm, glowing, and glorious, in the equal sunlight of hope and faith, which enliven and enlighten all the warm currents flowing from and to their mutual hearts!

There is a moment of time when the wise painter drops the curtain over the beautiful tableau, in which he has brought together the ideals of his imagination; and we leave the young couple, as Aunt Gertrude most judiciously did, to the security and freedom which love demands, against prying eyes and cold spectators.

Meanwhile, the palace at Keovala has become the dungeon! and there alone, striding his chamber, as one fettered to its walls, and moving only the length of his chain, Voltmeier broods over the shadowy future, from which vague aspects pass before him. There are eyes that glare out suddenly from the cloud, and peer, with mocking glances, into his own. A voice of Fate seems ever tolling, like some old cathedral bell, within his ears; and he starts, in the intervals of its dreary clangors, to hear whispering tongues beside him, and to feel that he is girt in by shadows that speak.

"Why," he murmurs, "should these objects come to me now— why these sounds and aspects? I do not deceive myself. These are *not* the creatures of imagination; or, if they be so, why should they come, at this late season, to mock the present, reproach the past, and threaten for the future? Do we grow into new susceptibilities with increase of years, thoughts, and experiences? I have thought this! Can we, as Schiller taught, can we so train the soul as to make it the seer? Are all things becoming clear to me now, as they did to him, even in the moment when he passed from time to eternity? I am weary of the study, as of the struggle! Gather around me as ye will, ye scowling aspects of the grave; I defy ye! Ye mock, and I howl back your mockeries with scorn! Ye threaten! What? Fate! Death! Well, these are the inevitable; and whether I hear the summoning voice soon or late to-night—to-morrow!—

"To-morrow!

"Ha! Surely I heard a voice following close upon my own, that audibly said 'To-morrow!'

"Well! To-morrow! Be it so! Leonard Voltmeier will be no less himself *to-night*, though the morrow be the limit of his earthly life! Vague shadowy forms, vague whispering tongues—I defy ye! Back to your chaotic empire, and know that, even though I may hold your prophecy to be true, ye shake no sinew of this body; ye enfeeble no power in this soul!—I defy ye all!—

"Yet, ever and anon, there is one of your voices that I hear, that I would not have away—one soft, pleading voice, that seems to murmur to my ears in tones of equal love and pity! Oh! Catharine, is it not yours? If it be, linger with me yet. Forgive, if you have not yet forgiven; for of a truth, Catharine, best beloved even when most wronged, I have yielded all my treasures—my heart's best treasures —to your son; I have made him *mine,* as he is yours; and my blood shall be the sacrifice, if needful, to save him from harm, and make him at once happy and triumphant! I give him *all, my* all; my noble and beautiful, my pure and all-spiritual child; my life, my soul—my Mignon!

"Lo, Catharine! On my knees! If nigh—if thou behold it—if thou hear'st, and if it be possible for thee to pass into the heart and pierce the brain of mortal—thou, in thy immortal state, look into mine, and see there the living proof that I have purified myself to thee! Oh, whisper me, gracious spirit! whisper me! Tell me that my atonement has been made *to thee!*"

He had sunk upon his knees—that proud, strong man, and his hands were outstretched, pleading to the vacancy that filled the chamber. To him, there was *no* vacancy! Dim spectral forms passed before his vision, and, at the close of his apostrophe, he beheld, as it were, a cloud of amber—nay, not a cloud—an indescribable sort of transparent body of lambent flame, subtle and pure as the summer lightning, but soft, subdued, slow of movement, and gliding, in a twining motion, around the walls of the apartment.

He followed it with his eyes—he rose to his feet; he darted towards it with outstretched hands, grasping as if to embrace it; then, as it disappeared, he fell prostrate on his face.

Was this a fancy—the illusion of a diseased brain—of a disordered vision?

He no longer asked himself this question. He had ceased to ascribe to physical causes the various influences, seemingly spiritual, which for some time had been acting on his senses—influences which had acted, in turn, and sometimes all together, upon no less than three of his senses—feeling, seeing, and hearing.

"I have heard her voice; I have felt her touch; can it be that I have beheld her self in that subtle and wonderful flame? Is the soul, freed from the body, capable of this diffusion—capable of the fluid subtlety of the lightning, with its ineffable purity and loveliness of light, yet softened to the eyes which it would scorch to blindness under its vivid action and its fiery velocity? Oh, Catharine! best beloved—am I forgiven? I implore thee! I know that thou art here."

Whether it was that he still labored under the hallucinations of a diseased sense or not, he now heard, or seemed to hear, a soft murmuring song—that of the "Chorus of Spirits" in the "Faust" of Goethe—and he rose, bending forward with still outstretched hands, as if following the music, which seemed to pass out of the library, and into his chamber; when the last verses lingered on his ears, and found an echo from his own tongue, as, passing into the chamber, he murmured—

"Then shall new music
Unite the now sundered."

But, even as the melody closed, his ear was smitten by the more audible—the sterner voice—that only said—

"To-morrow!"

"Be it so! to-morrow!—I hear thee! But what care I for the morrow, or what it shall bring forth, if there be that hope beyond— if there shall be a new music to unite the now sundered?"

His form was again erect, as if endowed with a new security in life. Loftily he stood, in the dim midnight of his chamber, with no light burning, but one which seemed, mysteriously, to diffuse the whole apartment, soft, subtle, as of a thin haze penetrated by a cloudless moon; and he waved his hand scornfully in the direction of the ominous voice, as he said—"To-morrow! I defy thee!"

Chapter LXIII

THE ISSUE OF THE MORROW

"To-morrow!" was the exclamation of Voltmeier, as he rose from bed, and threw open the eastern windows.

It was a cloudless morning, and the grand sun, climbing the imperial mountain heights, was already gilding their hoary summits with his most ruddy glories.

"There is nothing ominous of evil in these aspects," said Voltmeier, as he looked forth. "Yet, 'to-morrow,' is 'to-day!' never day looked lovelier! what should I apprehend! Henry and Graham both assure me that my affidavit must certainly secure the release of Fergus; and what have *I* to fear! I frankly avow that I gave him the money; identify the counterfeits as coming from *my* hands; accumulated sums, gathered from all sources, within two years—from cattle sold by agents in Tennessee, South Carolina, Georgia, as well as here; the sources being now impossible to be reached or even found, who, then, shall hold me accountable—shall strike at me as a criminal?"

He paused—then proceeded:

"Yet would I have foreborne, had this been possible, that oath! It was this damnable necessity from which I shrank. I know that the money I gave Fergus was *good;* and readily conceive how it was changed, that night, by that subtle scoundrel, Gorham! That wretch haunts me like a loathsome specter, commissioned by the Fates! I have not had a moment's repose from apprehension since I met him at Moggs'; since I encountered him at the cave; since we met again at 'Hickory Nut Gap;' and since I know that he has found his way here! into my very castle. He is a hound, seemingly, which I can not shake off! I would that I had seen Fergus married a month ago; we might then, all of us, be safe now in Germany, and we *must* go thither. I must escape this hound of Fate, who haunts my heart, as well as my house. Yet, even from him I see no present danger! He has not a single clue by which to follow!"

All this while he was making his toilet. This done, he said, rather gaily—

"To-morrow! Well! 'The ides of March are come.' "

Was it a whisper of the demon in his ears, that concluded the quotation?

"Ay! but they are not yet over!"

He started and looked about him, as if he had really heard the words.

"Breakfast, sir!" said one servant; and, immediately after, as he sat down to breakfast, another came in, who said—

"A strange man, sir, in the yard, wants to see you."

"A white man?"

"Yes, sir."

"Well, sir, did you ask him in?"

"I did, sir, but he won't come in, and asks to see you outside."

"Is he a gentleman?"

"I don't think, sir! He's dressed up smart, but he don't stand easy in his clothes."

"Very well! Tell him I'll be out in a moment! Who the devil can he be?"

With some misgivings—some presentiment of evil, he went forth to encounter—Richard Gorham in the court!

He did not recoil—did not shrink; but there was a recoil of soul, as he fixed his eye upon the ruffian, and met his somewhat impudent stare.

Gorham had nerved himself to the encounter with his former master. Armed, as he conceived himself to be, with the power to crush, he had armed himself with the audacity to defy him!

Voltmeier did not yet conceive the full extent of Gorham's discoveries. He was yet to learn that his visit to the library and chamber had resulted in much more than the robbery of the good notes, and the adroit substitution of the bad. He calmed himself accordingly, and with that indomitable strength of will which constituted one of the chief secrets of his manhood, he took the initiative, and before Gorham could speak, he said, with admirable coolness, and seeming indifference:

"Ah! Mr. Martin, I think; come to see about cattle, eh?"

It will be remembered, that, on a former meeting of the two,

Gorham gave his name as "Samuel Martin," while Voltmeier called himself "George Clinton," and there was some talk of a cattle trade between them.

Gorham replied, with an impudent grin—

"No more Samuel Martin, than you are George Clinton."

With a growing consciousness, from this answer, that Gorham had something in reserve, Voltmeier yet replied coolly and evasively—

"Ah! well, sir, we both adopt wayfaring names when we are upon the highway. I am, as I suppose you know, Col. Voltmeier. Pray oblige me with your true name."

"I rather think you know that already. But as to *your* true name, I don't think you've got that, yit. It's very certain that you went by another for a long time. I know, when I first know'd you, you was a leetle older in looks than you air now, and they called your name 'Bierstadt!'—and some of your friends did go so far as to call you by sich pet names as 'Old Grizzly,' 'Old Graybeard,' and 'Old Satan,' himself."

There was a momentary struggle in the breast of Voltmeier, a rising in his throat, a deep crimson, blended with a turbid yellow, overspread his cheeks, and his eye looked forth upon the ruffian with that intense tiger-like stare which was apt to mark it whenever the passions of the man were greatly roused; and he spasmodically thrust his hand into his bosom as if searching for a weapon.

The action was so significant that Gorham receded a pace, and laid his hand upon the butt of a pistol which was now seen to protrude from beneath his skirt.

"Better not try it, Mr. Bierstadt! I know'd the danger of coming here, and I brought my barkers with me; and, as ef them wasn't quite enough, I brought a couple of my good friends along with me to see fair play. Ef, now, you'll jest look up to the side of yonder hill, you'll see a couple of hats, with two men onder them; both with their eyes drawing a fine bead along as pretty a pair of rifles as was ever made in North Carolina. I know'd *you*, you see; I know'd you was mighty quick on the trigger, and I guessed you mightn't altogether like what I had to say."

Voltmeier was weaponless. He did not look to see whether other parties were watching them or not, but took for granted that the ruffian had taken his precautions fully. He became more circumspect accordingly—more guarded in manner and action, and dismissing the frown from his brows, in an instant he substituted for it a look of surprise, as he said:

"Is the man mad? Pray, my good fellow, what are you talking about?"

"That cock won't fight any longer, Mr. Bierstadt. The old game's up, and you needn't try it on *me*. You play'd it beautiful, I allow; and 'twas the most beautifullest game, I guess, that ever was play'd; the kairds most beautifully stocked, and all the trumps ready to the hand. But I've looked into your hand, and found out the whole secret. So, you needn't try to put it on me as you does on the rest of the people; and it's for you to say if I shall shut down on the secret or shut down on you! That's the question, Mr. Bierstadt?"

Knowing Voltmeier as we do, we can more easily comprehend his emotions than describe them. How many times had he thought to himself, during this impudent speech:

"Why did I not slay this fellow long ago? Why did I not obey my first impulse to do so, when I met him at the cavern?"

But not a word of this did he say aloud. On the contrary, he continued in the *role* which he had adopted.

"Really, my poor fellow, you must be fresh out of Bedlam. I do not understand a word that you say."

"Well, I've come here, Mr. Bierstadt, to make you understand."

"Sehr schön! So soll ich denn diesen Elenden zu meinen eigenen Verderben verschont graben!"

This was said aloud, in German. It seemed as if Voltmeier required some vent for his passions, and found it impossible to keep from uttering somewhat, in some way, the feeling which most possessed him; and he lamented aloud, though in a foreign tongue, that he should have spared the ruffian to his own defeat and ruin.

"Now," said Gorham, "you are speaking what *I* kain't understand."

"Go on!" responded Voltmeier—"Go on; out with what you've got to say! We shall possibly understand each other after a while. Go on!"

"I guess we will! You see, Mr. Bierstadt, or Col. Voltmeier, or whatever you please to call yourself, I know'd, for a'most two years, an old gentleman named Bierstadt; and I sarved under him in doing a mighty smart chance of business. I was cute enough, and know'd a thing or two, but he know'd a mighty deal more, and he taught me more. Well, when I first know'd him, and for a'most two years after as I told you, he was quite old, and walked old with a great stoop in the back, and his head was bald a'most all over the top, only on the sides he had a little shock of white hairs. And I do believe he hadn't a tooth in his head; for when he talked, and he didn't say much, his lips used to sink into his mouth; and we called him 'old Grizzly,' and if twan't for his great strength—and we seen some smart shows of it more than onst—we'd ha' said he was as old a'most as that old fellow they talks of in scripter that lived a'most a thousand years! Well, one day, or rather one night, I happened to slip into a grand gentleman's grand bedroom, having a leetle money operation to carry on—and there I found the grand gentleman fast asleep. Now he was quite a grand gentleman that sate on a horse like a general, and rode beautiful, and wore fine clothes and was a rich man with a great name in the country; and to see him ride, or see him walk, and hear him talk, you'd ha' said that he wan't more than forty-five years, all told; and a mighty young and healthy looking man at that. Now, what do you think? I seen this fine gentleman in the buzzom of his family, so young, so fine looking, so tall and straight, and haird him talk and haird him sing; talk out of books, and talk like a book himself; and sing beautiful like a moosicianer; and I watched him tell he went to bed; and it was a long watch I had of it, before he went. But he went and I haird him sleep at last; he had a great snore of his own that told me; and so I slipt into his chamber and looked about me, and Lord love you, what do you think I found on the table, by the glass— the prettiest set of teeth you ever did see, as much like them you carries in your mouth, now, as one eye is like another; and then, there was the finest head of hair, as much like that you're a-wearing now, as if 'twas the brother twin to it; and there was bottles of dye stuff that could brown a man's face and beard beautiful; and there was a heap of sech things; jest ready to the hand, to convart an old gentleman into a young one; and then I turned to where the fine young gentleman was a sleeping, and I let my 'shady-glim' shine for a minute over his face, and what do you think! Why, there was the grand young gentleman, changed all at ons't into the old one; the youngish Col. Voltmeier was the identical 'Old Grizzly,' as we called him, that I used to know as Mr. Bierstadt! Then I onderstood the whole trick of it! It was the beautifullest game, I do think, that ever was played! I hopes you understands me now!"

"I' faith, a very curious and amusing history! and you really believe all this?"

Gorham stared with no little surprise, as he heard the question.

"Believe it! Of course I does; I'll take my naternal oath upon it, in any court in the whole country."

"Perhaps you have made oath upon it already?"

"No! no! Catch me at thet! whether I makes oath or not, you see, will depend upon what *you* says to me!"

"What should I say to you! I have nothing to say to you!"

"The devil you hain't! What! after all I've been telling you? Don't you see that I've found you out; that I knows you now to be Bierstadt, and not Voltmeier."

"That would be a grand discovery indeed! and you can't conceive, my good fellow, that you have mistaken my identity for that of another man; that there may be a score of old men, who, like myself, may wish to pass for young ones. You will hardly find any one to believe your story; and when you tell it, you will be required to answer for stealing into my chamber and robbing my house at midnight—a crime which goes under the name of burglary, and is punishable with the gallows!"

"No, no! Mr. Bierstadt, that cock won't fight. I've studied the case. I've seen your kairds. I knows my man, and kin swear to him, and clinch my affidavy with old Mother Moggs and Ephraim; and if you hadn't blowed up Brown Peters and Swipes!—ha! that was a nice transaction—a beautiful part of the game, I must say; well, I could ha' had *them* to jine in with my affidavy. They'd be quick to jine me, for they had a mortal curiosity to find you out, but didn't well know how to set about it. I was a leetle too cute to be blow'd up with 'em; but it was the prettiest contrivance! Now, you see, I could swear to a dozen beautiful contrivances, besides—"

"You talk wildly, my good fellow, about your Swipes's, and your Moggs's, and your Peters's! I do not see how their affairs concern me; and if, as I gather from what you say, you have been one of a gang of robbers, why, you are making your own confession all the while. You seem to be in as fair a way to the halter as anybody else."

The coolness of Voltmeier surprised the ruffian, but he felt himself too fully assured of his facts to be staggered in his purpose.

"Why, yes, you see I knows that; but then I knows what Lawyer Brownlow tells me, that there's sich a thing as being State's evidence, you see, if I makes confession; and then there's what he calls a 'non pros' for me that'll git me clear, and wipe out the whole score agin me."

"So you have consulted a lawyer in this matter?"

"Yes; jist on the hairbreadth of a line, letting him onderstand a case, you see, but telling no names."

"Yet, you have fellows, you say, watching now, on my grounds, and witnessing what takes place between us?"

"They only comes for my protection. You see, I knows you of old, Mr. Bierstadt, and—"

"Well, supposing that I should be willing to consider your case myself, *as* if it did concern myself—"

"Jest so! That's what I expects. That's your way to consider it, if you're a sensible wise man!"

"Well, I'm tired of standing out here. Come with me into my library."

"Thank you, sir; but you'll excuse! That's jest the sort of civil invitation that Jack Spider said to Jenny Fly! I'm sorry you're tired, Mr. Bierstadt, but all the business between us must be done out hyar, in the open air, and in the sight of my two friends you see watching their rifle beads over that hill. Hyar! I say, hyar! and nowhere else!"

"Well, sir, you have told your story, and you fancy you have made some wonderful discovery in which I am interested."

"I guess you air!"

"Now, will you please to say in what you expect this discovery to profit yourself? I take for granted that you have some notion that something is to be gained, and given, for the secret which you suppose yourself to possess."

"It ain't any suppose, Mr. Bierstadt; but jest the naked, and most solemn—consekential truth."

"Be it so! Go on!"

"Well, you see—"

"Stop! You have employed Mr. Brownlow to attend to this business? Don't you think you had better let him carry it on?"

"No, thank you. Lawyer Brownlow don't git the bird out of *my* cage, unless I finds that I can get nothing by keeping it. You understands?"

"I think so. Well?"

"Now, you see, Mr. Bierstadt, or Col. Voltmeier, it's my notion that, if I speaks what I knows, your utter ruination comes from it."

"Well! well! well!"

"You're a mighty rich man, with a great charakter, and a mighty fine riputation."

"Oh! d—n your preliminaries! I don't want to hear that stuff! Jump to your worst conclusion, man, and have done with your long faces and long preambles!"

Voltmeier was getting very impatient. He had been on the verge of madness for an hour.

"Don't be in a hurry, Captain! all in good time!"

"Now, would it not be the shorter process to blow this fellow's brains out at once?—no matter what the consequences!"

This was spoken aloud, but in German; but the look of the tiger, and the impatient action of the speaker, spoke audibly to the sense of Gorham, and he receded from before his victim and again grasped the butt of his pistol, and put himself in readiness for the attack.

"Oh! don't fear!" said Voltmeier, scornfully. "Were it my cue to put you to death, fellow, I could do so before your eye could wink twice! Only, go on, and speak to the point! Your price, scoundrel, your price!"

The passions which had been boiling in the soul and brain of Voltmeier were now over-boiling. Yet these words were spoken with stern, slow, measured accents, hardly above his breath; tone and manner all inconsistent with the tenor of what he spoke.

Gorham was not disposed to drive the tiger to extremity. He saw that the barb was in his side, and that there was a desperate purpose engendering in his brain that might defy all his surgery. His policy was to gain his object, not destroy his golden goose. Voltmeier conceived this to be money, merely; but when the ruffian said:—

"I am mightily pleased with that daughter of yourn! I must have her for my wife, and thirty thousand dollars to boot, that I may keep her up as a lady, as she is—"

The strong man, writhing with the passions which he was yet striving to control, with every muscle corded, with teeth set, and clinched together; with every vein in his forehead distended to bursting, shook like one in a violent ague fit. One moment he glared upon his enemy, as if about to make a tiger spring; then he turned aside, walked a few paces away, turned again, and, in hoarse, choking accents, he replied:

"Go hence, now. I can bear no more, now! Come to me again at this hour to-morrow! Away! Begone!"

He could hardly articulate these words, and having spoken them, he whirled about, and disappeared within the house.

Chapter LXIV

THE FATE IN THE MIRROR

Voltmeier stood alone in his library; stood in the center of the noble chamber, surrounded by his books—a large collection—and by furniture which illustrated the equal wealth and tastes of the owner.

But he saw none of these. His eye opened upon vacancy; and, though he stood erect, there were moments when a shivering fit passed through his frame, making the tall, strong man tremble like some giant pine under the angry pressure of the north-west wind.

So, for several minutes did he stand; so, at moments, did he writhe and shiver, never once speaking; and, with that look of vacancy, in which the eye, still dilating, is yet denied every faculty of vision, and sees nought but the vague creations in the mind.

All at once he strode towards one of the grand oval mirrors, two of which occupied spaces against the walls in the breaks between the windows. Before this mirror did he stand and gaze—still in silence—until, at length, the consciousness began slowly to grow within his eyes, and gradually to depict to his vision his features, in the glass.

Then he murmured, in low, but deep tones, as if spoken in the gorge of his throat, and between the closed teeth:

"Do I indeed see myself? Am I Leonard Voltmeier? Do I live, breathe, feel? Is it really a living consciousness that I have endured all this? Has my soul so shrunken of its old proportions, into pigmy size and weakness, that I have suffered this miserable villain to assail my ears with his damnable insolence and impudent propositions?

"Great God, these are thy Fates! To what have they brought me! Who would have dreamed that this would be the process through which to compel my repentance and lead to my atonement!

"And must the atonement be thus made to Fate, in shame and bitterness and disgrace? Am I then, after all the struggle, to succumb

353

at last? And shall this miserable reptile—this tool of my own crime, become the instrument of vengeance and my punishment? Great God! that he, the meanest, the vilest, the basest, the foulest wretch of all, should be the commissioned agent of Thy providence, to confound his master; to mock to scorn while he stings; to possess himself, by the veriest accident of chance, of a power to conquer, to crush, or, not crushing, to degrade!

"And have I lived to know all this—to look on this face, these features, with revolting sense, and feel that all their former manhood is shamed forever!

"How did I endure it all! Where was the WILL that once would have stricken dead the wretch, on the first breathings of his polluting demand!

"Ha! Ha! Ha! Ha!"

It was not laughter! The short, exclamatory syllables were separated by a gap in speaking; were so many spasmodic jerks of sound, breaking through the still closely-knitted teeth; and at each utterance the hands were clenched, as with fingers of steel; the shoulders were raised, the head buried between them, and there was a crouching of the whole figure, as if preparing for some tiger-like and ferocious spring upon a victim.

"My Mignon! my pure, my precious, my beautiful! that such a monster should even name thee to thy father's ears! Surely, I heard him not! I have dreamed all this! I look at myself, and still I am Voltmeier. Is the brain grown weak for thought; the will for purpose; the blood for action? Have I not the same sinews, muscles, limbs, and strength; and am I indeed shorn of will and courage?

"Try thyself, Voltmeier! Lo! the demon strikes at thy bosom— the accursed Fate! Defend thyself, if thou be'est indeed a man! He strikes at thee from the glass!"

And, with these words, driving, with gigantic force, both fists at his own image in the mirror; he dashed the glass into a thousand pieces!

With a scornful smile he looked at the fragments on the floor; at the jagged points and ends of glass still remaining in the massive and richly gilded frame; then, turning away, with arms folded, he strode to and fro, soliloquizing by fits and starts.

"And Fate is but an image in the glass! The WILL of a true man is capable of striking it down, if he will but brave it! I have weakly suffered this hound to track my footsteps! I have slept among my securities! My will has slept, and with it my courage! While I slept, the hounds of Fate kept wakeful!

"*I will sleep no more! I will* DO! I will MAKE the fate for this household, if I am no longer permitted to make my own! Yes, my children, ye shall be secure! And I say to ye, accursed Fate, I, too, will name a day! I challenge ye, this hour, to a trial of strength to-morrow! Ay, to-morrow! It shall be another sort of to-morrow from this; and ye shall see that Voltmeier is your master still!"

His hands were stretched out and clenched, as if in defiance of the invisible agencies which he summoned to that meeting of the morrow. His form was uplifted proudly. The eye shot forth a lurid fire; and, as one preparing himself for deadly battle, or for solemn sacrifice, in the eye of thousands, he stood up erect, the perfect embodiment of a brave soul and a perfect manhood, with every virtue of will, and thought, and purpose, stiffened and strengthened for a mortal conflict!

"BUT I MUST MAKE TO-NIGHT A PROPER PRELUDE FOR THE MORROW! I have it all! I grasp it in thought, and will fashion it with will! I must work a while! To see *what needs be done;* to *feel* the courage and resolve, and to be conscious of the *power* to *do;* and all the Fates that hound upon our heels are baffled and beaten down forever!

"This venomous cur will find his cunning all in vain! Nay, more —I feel, I see, I know, that he, too, hath HIS fate to encounter, and he will find himself no match for that wrestle.

"Fool! he rushes upon the spear, and will transfix himself! I see not how this will be; but that it will be, I know! My vision grows momently more clear for discovery. In baffling *my* Fate, I will turn its hounds upon the hunter!

"I must work now!"

He took one of his opium pellets from the box, swallowed it, walked the floor a while, in silence, then seated himself at the desk, writing with nerves as steady as if his soul had never been racked by any agonizing emotion.

Chapter LXV

INTO THE NIGHT

Voltmeier wrote for a goodly hour or more, the fingers coursing over the white sheets, and covering them with a lightning-like velocity. There were letters and notes for various parties—one to Col. Graham, which he sealed at once and made ready for transmission. The others were laid aside, in reserve, as fast as written. We note that Fergus Wallace, Mignon, Miss Gertrude, and Major Henry were all severally addressed, and these, with the one exception to Graham, were finally wrapped in one packet and thrust into one of the pigeon-holes of his escritoire.

From this he next drew forth a large packet which was already sealed, but unaddressed. He addressed it now to Major Henry. Other packets were drawn forth, apparently title-deeds. These were directed mostly to Fergus Wallace. These papers disposed of, he rang the bell, and when the servant appeared, he asked,

"Has Ben Harness got back from the village?"

"Jist this moment come, sir."

"Ask him to be so good as to come to me at once."

When Harness appeared, Voltmeier said:

"Ben, there are several matters upon which I wish to employ you, as the only one whom I can rely upon to serve me faithfully in affairs of some difficulty."

"To be sure, sir."

"Have you seen Fergus Wallace?"

"Seen nobody else, sir. It was that that carried me to the village; and I want to ask you, sir, is this thing going to trouble him, and why don't he speak out and say from what persons he got the money?"

"It is a point of honor with him, Ben, that he should *not* speak out, and a point of feeling, too. But I shall speak out for him, Ben, and I think it likely he will be discharged to-morrow. He got all that money from *me*."

356

"But, how did *you* get it, Colonel? all the cattle *I* sold for you was paid for in good money. They couldn't cheat me!"

"So I believe, Ben. But, you know, I had a dozen different graziers, and there were few of them like Ben Harness."

"Thank you, sir. And thank my mother, too; for if ever woman made a man honest, then my mother made us Harness boys honest, and I think sensible, too."

"I believe it, Ben. You are both! How is the old lady? God bless her."

"Smart, sir, and active. She's made a power of pickles and catchups and sweetmeats this year, and she says them spectacles you gave her have made her a young woman."

"I'm glad to hear it, Ben. And now, Ben, I wish you to attend to some business for me, to ask me no questions about the reason for anything, and to keep a shut mouth upon everything you do for me. You will know the reason for all in good time."

"Jist try me, Colonel."

"You've been tried already, Ben, and not found wanting. I can't tell you everything, or much of anything, my good fellow, for my affairs are something complicated."

Complicated was a word of difficult comprehension to Ben Harness. Voltmeier did not explain, though he saw the bewilderment of the other.

"It is probable, Ben, that my affairs will call me suddenly to Europe. I wish you to take charge of all the flocks and herds I have on these mountains. You will take charge of them in the name of Fergus Wallace, as his property. He is to marry my daughter Mignon."

"I'm glad of it, Colonel," was the hearty response of the mountaineer. Voltmeier proceeded:

"The titles are all properly prepared, and he will be the sole proprietor. He and his wife will probably follow me to Europe, and you will be the sole manager here at Keovala for a while. Col. Graham will give you instructions in everything except your own business. You know all about our grazing business, our cattle, and our mountains, a thousand times better than Graham."

"I reckon I does, Colonel," with a good-natured chuckle of self-complacency.

"But in all law business, Ben, Graham is your counselor."

"And a good one, too. But, Colonel, you talks as if you were making your will."

"When a man encounters the sea, Ben, he knows not what he encounters, and the great sea spreads before me. But, of all these matters, Fergus and Graham will consult with you, and you will look to them. Here, Ben, are five hundred dollars. I owe you something. I don't know what—"

"Not a third of this, Colonel."

"Take it, nevertheless, on account, and credit Fergus. Let us dismiss this more distant matter, and see to things more present. Ben, do you remember 'The Shades of Death,' through which I took you a year ago?"

"Like a book, Colonel, and a devilish dark, dreary tract it is, well desarving the name."

"You can find it in the dark?"

"Never lost the track I once seen. Can take it at midnight."

"Very good! Now then, I have a hard day's work before you. Take my white horse and ride slowly down to the village, and give this letter to Colonel Graham, and return. Is that clear to you?"

"As the noonday sun."

"Very good! Then be here before dark! There is no moon tonight. Saddle for me the bay mare, and have her ready at the entrance of the 'Shades' an hour after dark. You will come back here; and when I am gone four hours, take the stallion, Diomed, down to the 'Shades of Death,' and keep him there till I call for him. Meanwhile, in all your riding, ride my *white* horse. Now, to-day, as you ride him to the village, I wish you to note who meets you on the road; who sees you; whom you see; who stops you; who asks you any questions, and remember the questions; and report everything to me when we meet. You will lock up everything securely here when you return from the village; take possession of all the keys, and leave Clytus to occupy the basement. Having made everything secure, take the stallion by midnight to the east entrance of 'The Shades of Death.' Have some fodder along with you, and a feed of corn, and see that the beast is well saddled, and bitted with a strong curb."

"Why, you don't mean to ride him, Colonel. He'll fling you, sure as a gun. He's got all sorts of devil in his brain and belly."

"I will take the devil out of him. He will not fling me, and I mean to ride him. You will wait for me in the 'Shades of Death,' though I do not get back before daylight. You are to ride the white, yourself, you remember; you will have the bay filly ready for me, after dark, and the stallion you will have at midnight, in the 'Shades of Death.' Is it all clear to you?"

"Every bit of it!"

"Now, I wish you to remember, also, to note who sees or watches you along the road, who stops you, has anything to say to you, and what he says. You will find me here at dark, and for an hour after."

The motive for all these movements and precautions was all a mystery to Ben Harness, but, he was wont to heed all the directions of Voltmeier, without any questioning of their policy and wisdom; and he was willing, cheerfully and simply to obey. He was promptly in the saddle, mounted on the famous white steed of Voltmeier, and fulfilled his mission at the village, returning in due season to Keovala. Of his details along the route, we shall probably know all hereafter.

Meanwhile, and during his absence, Voltmeier was busied, without cessation, all the day, arranging papers, destroying papers, and never once leaving the dwelling. He was engaged in the solemn work of "putting his house in order," in anticipation of the probable encounter on the morrow, with his Fate!

What he conceived of plan, what he meditated of purpose, was closely locked up in his own bosom. He pursued his occupations without word, murmur, or soliloquy; but we do not fail to observe that he swallowed a frequent pill of opium, and that he put his pistols in perfect order for use.

The will of the strong man, resolute in his purpose, was evident in the dogged silence which he observed, in the promptness with which he turned to, the steadiness with which he pursued every object, and the stern calm and method with which he arranged his household.

There was a casket of jewels, which contained, among other things, the miniature of a beautiful young woman, on ivory, and set in a rich oval of variegated gold, illuminated with a circlet of small diamonds. This he pored over with saddest looks of longing, and finally enclosed in a paper and addressed to Fergus Wallace. On it he wrote the one name—"Catharine,"—and signed with his initials. The casket of jewels was sealed and addressed to "Mignon Wallace."

His work was ended only with the day; but not before Harness had returned.

When night had fairly closed in, the latter had conveyed the bay mare from the stables, to the particular spot which Voltmeier had assigned for it. There, Harness awaited him, and, in the deep darkness of night, and amid the silent, solitary, and well-shrouded hills, Voltmeier rode away in the direction of the county town.

But he did not take the ordinary road, almost the only one known to, or in use among the mountaineers. He passed from the hill-top into a great gorge, forming one of the entrances into the "Shades of Death." This gloomy avenue wound about the rear of the lands of Voltmeier, emerging into the main road at both extremities, some four miles on each hand from Keovala, by obscure mouths, imperceptible to those who were unfamiliar with the route. The obscurity of the pathway, the darkness of the night, were no obstacles to the practiced rider and the fearless man, and, riding as recklessly as if over a macadamized highway, he had reached the county town in less than two hours, lighted by one single star that still struggled among the clouds in the northern heavens!

Chapter LXVI

HAND IN HAND

It is just possible that we may find some clue to the meaning of those processes and precautions taken by Voltmeier, by looking into those which were adopted by Gorham, when he left the presence of the former. He retired in equal awe and dudgeon—the old feeling of fear operating to make him depart promptly, having so roused Voltmeier's passions as to make him apprehensive that, driven to desperation by his further provocations, he would proceed to violence; which Gorham not only feared instinctively, but which he felt would be well calculated to baffle his policy of gain. Still his self-esteem was vexed by the stern language of Voltmeier.

"I must begone, eh? 'Begone!' he said—he fairly roar'd it out, jist as if I was nothing better than a dog. But every dog, they say, has his day, and he shall pay for it all yet! 'To-morrow' is mighty sure and mighty soon to come! He kain't git away from me, as I will fix it."

So, muttering to himself, he rejoined the two detectives who had been watching from the hillside; and, as they rode away together, he gave them his instructions for the future.

"Now," said he, "men; I'm going to set you upon the watch for this Colonel Voltmeier, as they call him here. I've got a monstrous big claim of money against him, and there's no chaince of his dodging *me*, unless you let him dodge *you*. You've got to watch the two ends of the road closer than Mississippi Parson ever tried to do! Now, there's a fellow named Jacob Swales, that lives on the last hill, before you get to the river. It's about four miles from hyar. One of you can stop with Swales, and it's not possible for any man to pass you on the road, going towards the river, unless you sleep on your post. The other of you will go down with me to the house of Tom Watson, who's a grazier for this Voltmeier. Now, from Watson's, you can see any person that takes the track

361

going to the court house; and if this Voltmeier goes for the village, you've jist to watch him and let him pass. But, if you sees him pushing for t'other end of the road, then you're to stop him in the name of the law! You've got the warrant for it, you know, from Lawyer Brownlow; for you see the lawyer made it a bail-writ, to stop him from running out of the country. He's a sharp lawyer, that Brownlow!"

"That he is," said one of the detectives; "but suppose Col. Voltmeier won't stop? He's a very devil to ride, I know!"

"Well, you've got your rifles!"

"What! shoot him? I don't edzactly know that I'd have a right to shoot him in sarving bail process."

"Oh! don't you? Well, shoot his horse! It'll be a great pity, to be sure, for the horse is a most beautiful creatter, and I'd like to have him myself as part of my pay; but better kill the horse than lose the man! I'll see you safe!"

The two detectives here consulted together, and examined the writ; for such it was; the lawyer having intentionally filled all the blanks without calling upon clerk of court or sheriff. It was rather the loose practice of the profession in some of the county courts, to have on hand the signatures of these worthy officers, with the view to meet just such a case as the present. It appeared that the detectives were quite satisfied.

"All right?" asked Gorham.

Detectives and constables, familiar with the tricks of rogues of all classes, are apt to be unscrupulous in the manner of foiling them. They declared themselves ready.

"Well," said Gorham, "you can pay a trifle to Swales and Watson for their accommodations, and you know how to pump the truth out of a full mouth and a quick tongue. Do your best with eyes and ears, and let me know quick whatever happens. Hyar's twenty-five dollars apiece more. You've had twenty-five a'ready; and you shall have another fifty if the thing works right, and you put your spoke in this Voltmeier's wheel. I don't stint money, fellows, when business has got to be done. Business, you see, is so much virtue, and virtue deserves to be paid for. And you shall be paid well, if I get *my* pay. Hyar now, all along this road; you've got the watch, and must keep it day and night. Hyar's the road to the village, and hyar's the road to the river. He kain't pass you any way, by day or by night, if you'll keep eyes bright. You'll know him, certain sure, by that famous white horse. Do you see it clear?"

Well, both detectives thought they saw clearly what they had to do; but neither they nor Gorham knew of the passage of the "Shades of Death."

"You know where to find me at all hours. I'll be with you, bright and early, in the morning; for you see I'll want you again to-morrow, to go with me to the house, and keep good rifle-watch while this Voltmeier and me come to a right understanding of our business. You, now, Smith, remember you're to watch at Swales', the other end of the road, for that's the one that lets you over the river and into the 'gap.' Swales lives, as I tell you, on the height, the last rise of the road before you gits to the river. Be sharp on the look-out. If he passes you, and you can't bring his horse down with a bullet, one of you follow, fast as you can, jist to see the road he takes, and t'other one come back to me, and make report. I'll jine you pretty soon in the morning."

And so the parties separated, Gorham taking his way back to his lodgings in the village, after an ineffectual effort to find Brownlow, who had gone out to his farm for the day. The "Jack Leg" enjoyed the luxury of a country seat.

And thus we find these two men, Voltmeier and Gorham, each at his own game, arranging his forces; each making his calculations rather upon the play of his opponent than his own. Gorham was shrewd, and well knew the superior resources of his former master. Though taking his precautions as well as he could against the possible flight of Voltmeier, yet he was not willing to persuade himself that the latter meant to fly. It seemed to him much more natural to suppose that he would prefer any sacrifice short of his whole substance, if permitted to enjoy the rest. And Gorham was disposed to be magnanimous. He soliloquized thus, upon this weakness of his bosom:

"I don't mean to clean him out altogether. I kin make out with his daughter and thirty thousand dollars; and that'll leave him his fine place and a plenty besides to keep him up. I won't be hard upon him!"

And it was not strange that he should regard the scorn and anger, and the lofty tones, in which Voltmeier finally spoke to him, as not at all unfavorable to his demand. He could comprehend that these were the natural ebullitions of the proud man, bursting into passion at finding himself cornered and brought to bay! He persuaded himself that a night of reflection would teach Voltmeier the policy of submitting to his exactions, to escape a degrading exposure, public infamy, and the possible loss of life! How should he prefer to retain fortune at the peril of incurring all these probable dangers?

Did Voltmeier design flight?

The question, which, for some time, exercised the thoughts of Gorham, must occur to us also. Certainly, this was the obvious course, if he could effect it, to escape a danger which seemed possible, if not probable. He has given us no clues to his purpose; but it is certain that he wore not the aspect and manner of one who was prepared to become a fugitive and outlaw. He seemed to have sublimed himself, rather for a conflict, *à l'outrance*, with a thousand enemies, than yield one jot of dignity or position. His aspect and language were, perhaps, never more lofty, more marked by the assertion of a determined will, or less calculated to conciliate. He seemed rather resolved to conquer. He had looked the Fates fully in the face; and his mood was rather that of the man sworn to sacrifice in conflict with the worst, than one making a cowardly concession to escape any ultimate issue. But we need waste no further time in speculation when the issue is so near at hand.

It is with no misgivings of soul, no ducking of his head to fortune, that he gallops that night to the door of his friend, Graham, and enters the parlor, where he finds the Colonel, Mr. Graham, and Major Henry. They have another guest in the Rev. Dr. N. Shelton, rector of one of the Episcopal churches.

Mignon and her aunt are even now on a visit to Fergus at the jail. Here, the jailer, under the friendly auspices of the sheriff, accords to these visitors all the privileges which can be yielded to the prisoner.

"You have surprised us, Voltmeier," said Graham, after the usual courtesies had taken place. "This is a sudden, if not a strange determination!"

"It has been well considered, Graham. It is now proper. The relations of my daughter and Mr. Wallace are such, and have been such since she has visited him in prison, that I deem it only proper that they should receive the most solemn sanctions! Our friend, Graham, has apprised you, Doctor, of my wishes?"

"He has," replied the divine, "and I shall only be too happy to render my services, irrespective of place and time."

"Be it so! Let us proceed, my friends. Mrs. Graham has apprised Miss Leyfenholdt?"

"Yes, indeed, Colonel," answered Mrs. Graham; "but I am not prepared to say that the proceeding, under the circumstances, is at all grateful to that lady."

"I suppose not! You ladies find it difficult to pass behind or over the barriers of convention, at any time, especially on formal occasions like the present. May I beg you, Mrs. Graham, to be present, though the auspices may seem to you so unprecedented?"

"Oh! surely, Colonel, I should not have needed your invitation. We ladies, as you phrase it, rarely suffer such an occasion to escape us, when the opportunity is given us."

"Thanks! and, now, Mrs. Graham, with your permission, I will take a seat with you and the Doctor in the carriage. Graham, will you, or Major Henry, use my horse?"

"No! we will walk!"

"Then have the beast put up for the present, if you please."

And while the carriage was preparing, Graham and Henry departed on foot. As they went, Henry said:

"This is a very remarkable man, Graham."

"One of the most remarkably endowed men I ever knew."

"He is eccentric," said Henry.

"Somewhat, perhaps; but this seeming may arise from the very versatility of his talents."

"He is, I think, a diseased man," responded Henry. "He has undergone a wonderful change of aspect, even since I came up. Did you remark the wonderful, the almost unnatural brightness of his eyes? They seem literally to shoot forth fire."

"I noticed it, especially to-night."

"It is just the light and expression which I have noticed in the eyes of the insane, when under the influence of that suppressed excitement which usually precedes a paroxysm."

"No danger of such a thing in *his* case. He is the coolest, calmest, most methodical person I ever met, and with rarest powers of logic! With what grace and dignity did he move to-night in the parlor; with such perfect ease and readiness, and with such lofty and commanding carriage. He is a man to command."

"Yes! But—"

"But what?"

"There is, I think, a secret infirmity about him—a keen sense of suffering, which preys upon him in spite of the strong will and pride which keep it from expression. That man will probably die in a lunatic asylum, if, indeed, he does not commit suicide."

"Good God, Major, you confound me! But, here we are. We will speak further of this to-morrow."

"That gloomy house of morals called a jail," opened its massive doors to receive them; and the carriage, with the rest of the party, arrived almost at the same moment. In another, Voltmeier was clasped by Mignon, her arms twining tenderly about his neck, while she kissed him repeatedly, exclaiming at moments:

"Oh! papa! what does it mean?"

"That papa will make you happy, Mignon, if he can!"

"But, Leonard, this is all so sudden, so unusual; so out of the course of things; in such a place, too! and we have made no preparations. Mignon has hardly a change of clothes, and none made up for the occasion, and really—"

So Aunt Gertrude Leyfenholdt, with the natural prudishness of an old maid, fettered by the training of forty years.

Voltmeier silenced her in brief accents, cutting short her expostulations.

"Sudden, no doubt, Gertrude; but such is my determination;— unusual, no doubt, but such is what I deem the necessity of the case! The place, too, is not a palace or a church; but these walls, and these iron bolts and bars, confer upon it sufficient solemnity, if not sacredness! As for supper, and feasting, and fine clothes, and costly preparations, I have survived all these things, considered as essential to human happiness! And—" here he whispered in her ears: "when these people know that I have deliberately given to Fergus Wallace, my only and well-beloved daughter, with all her fortune; and under these circumstances, and in the walls of this prison, they will acquit him, in their opinions, of all suspicions of guilt. They will *know* that *I* should not do this, but for my own conviction of his perfect innocence. Remember, my dear sister, that the effort to obtain his release will be renewed to-morrow. The effects of his marriage to my daughter, this night, and here, will be conclusive to every mind!"

Was this a reason really entertained by Voltmeier? It does not matter. It was sufficient for Miss Gertrude.

Without any adventitious aids of dress, or pomp, or circumstance, of any sort, the marriage ceremonies were solemnized, and with sufficient solemnity. The dimly-lighted cell; the small company; the sheriff—who was a gentleman—being one of the group; huge gratings of iron across the narrow windows, had their effect. The scene was very impressive, and the clergyman no less so. And when the tall, stately form of Voltmeier, standing erect, placed the hand of his daughter in that of Fergus, saying, in slow but sonorous accents:

"Bear witness, my friends, that I give this, my only daughter, to be the wife of her cousin, Fergus Wallace, whom I hold to be one of the truest, best and noblest young men of the country; happy that I can bestow upon him such a gift, and happier still that I can give her so honorable a protector!"

The deep silence which prevailed was a sufficient proof of the natural pathos of the scene. The tears of Mignon flowed freely; the eyes of Fergus were suffused; Miss Gertrude sobbed audibly, and all hearts were touched and softened. There were few eyes looking on which did not glisten. The gentlemen came forward, and grasped the hands of the new-married couple, and Major Henry, the early patron of the young man, embraced him, almost sobbing, himself, as he exclaimed:—

"God bless you, Fergus! I am now as happy as if you were my own son!"

Thrice, thrice and again, did Voltmeier take Mignon in his arms and strain her to his bosom! Thrice and again he kissed her; kissed tenderly Aunt Gertrude, then hurriedly but graciously waving his hand to the company, he suddenly left the dungeon. Mignon darted after him, towards the passage, crying—

"Don't leave us yet, papa!"

But he was gone! He waited for no carriage, but proceeding to the stables of Graham, was soon mounted upon his bay, and pursuing the way he had come, to and through the *"Shades of Death."*

But once did he speak after he had mounted, and but one sentence did he utter aloud, as he waved his hands upward to the dark, mysterious, and starless sky—

"Now come, ye Fates! when ye will! I defy ye! I am still your master!"

Chapter LXVII

CLIENT AND COUNSEL

The sun was fairly risen, the next morning, when, without any formal preliminaries, Lawyer Brownlow burst into the chamber of Richard Gorham, where he lay, still asleep, in spite of his promise to himself and the detectives, to be with them "bright and early" in the morning. He certainly had determined, with himself, to do so, having so much at stake.

But, the truth is, Gorham had recently fallen into bad habits. When we knew him first, he was habitually temperate, and never would drink with the two vulgar associates, Swipes and Peters, both of whom he despised equally for their brutality and inferior intellect.

But a change had come over him with a change of fortune; and, with the accumulation of means and money, he seemed to think that he had a right to some of the enjoyments of this life.

It is one of the tests which the base nature never can endure long, that which brings it sudden prosperity; and, with a considerable sum of money, the accumulations of his outlaw life, with the discovery of Voltmeier's secret, and with the belief that he now possessed that "open sesame" which would unlock the swollen coffers of his late master, he became seized with a "sudden glory" which somewhat turned his head.

From the setting in of evening until his sleeping hours, his draughts were full and frequent, and he rarely found his slumbers satisfactory, unless the wand of Morpheus was duly succored by the *pipe* of Bacchus.

When Lawyer Brownlow burst so rudely into his chamber, the emptied bottle stood beside his bed, and tumbler and table gave equal proofs of the unsteady hand with which the last beaker had been poured out and swallowed ere he slept. His bloated features, as he awakened, his watery eyes, with their wan and wandering expression, were additional proofs to the lawyer, if any were necessary, that his client was hardly fit for the proposed duties of the day.

"Is it daylight yet, Squire?" was the question of Gorham, rubbing his eyes and yawning drowsily.

"Daylight, indeed! The sun's an hour high."

"The devil it is! I've overslept myself. I ought to have been on the road by the peep of day. So I promised them fellows. But, I reckon nothing's happened, or one of them would ha' been hyar to let me know."

"Well, what did you do yesterday?"

"I reckon I put a spoke in the right wheel, Lawyer."

"What did you do?"

"That's telling."

"Bah on your secrets. Do you think I care to know? But have you made any headway?"

"A good deal; but you see, Lawyer, that's atween him and me only."

"Pshaw!" was the reply. "Haven't I told you that I don't care to know your secrets, so long as you choose to keep 'em. The only question is, did you broach the business to him?"

"I reckon I did."

"And made your demands according to the terms you told me?"

"That's what I did."

"And he didn't throw you out of the window?"

"Didn't trust him there! Didn't trust myself to go into the house."

"And he showed no violence?"

"Axed me quite civil into the house."

"Wonderful! I can scarce believe it. You asked him for thirty thousand dollars, did you?"

"That was the exact amount."

"And—about his daughter? You said nothing about *her?*"

"*Didn't* I then! I axed for her the very first."

"Well?"

"Well—the truth is, Lawyer, it all put him in a roaring passion, and one time I thought he'd 'a' pitched into me; but I backed a little and let him see the butt ends of my pistols, and I p'inted to where your two fellows was a-watching us from the hill; and so he sobered down, and cooled off a little, and heard me quite patient all through, doing a little roaring to ease his feelings!"

"Well, but the end—the conclusion? What came of it all, and how did he satisfy you?"

"He ain't satisfied me yit! He's to do that to-day. I'm to meet him thar to-day, at the same hour, and he's to face the trouble, or I'm to know the reason why! I guess I've got him dead certain this time."

"You think so, do you?"

"Ay, that I do! I reckon you'll have a good job drawing up the law papers. You'll have the job, in course, Squire."

"And you really believe that you'll get that thirty thousand dollars?"

"Jist as sure as ef the gould was in my pocket."

"A very pleasant idea!—and how about the daughter? You're jist as sure about her, I suppose. She's to be your wife, is she?"

"Look you, Lawyer; the man kain't help himself! I've got him sure and fast, dead certain! He may squirm, and, indeed, he did squirm a good deal yisterday, and roar, too; and ef he could ha' got at me by himself, with no pistols in my belt, and no two officers looking on, and drawing a fine bead along their rifles, I guess he'd ha' tried to stop my tongue, by passing a sharp knife over my gullet. But he seed that wouldn't do now; so he got sensible, and we're to have the bargain struck to-day!"

"So! so! and you're sure, are you? Thirty thousand dollars!"

"That was it! I fixed that sum, and I stuck to it."

"And the daughter thrown in?"

"Exactly; though, I tell you, Lawyer, in confidence, I'll settle the half of that money 'pon her and the children!"

"That's magnanimous! It's a very pleasant reflection. In one day, to get a beautiful wife and thirty thousand dollars, simply by giving your father-in-law a very bad scare!"

"That's it! I guess 'twill do, and jist as I wishes it. That's my calculation. I was always cute, Lawyer. Fayther did say I should be a lawyer. He said I was a lawyer by natur. He was sharp him-

self, and he taught us boys the lesson every day. He had a sort of
song, that said—

> 'Jist git what you kin and keep what you git,
> And Dicky you'll be a rich man yit.'

"And one day—I was only fifteen then—I traded off his own nag,
blind of one eye, and mighty weak in t'other, for a pony, and
twelve dollars to boot, and borrowed the money from him with my
own consent only. Then he said to me:

"'You must go, Dicky, go down to New York. Two sharps
kain't live well together! Go down among the flats, and carry
on business for yourself.' So I went, but I had a key of my own for
the stable-door, and when the old man got up in the morning, he
found I was gone, and the pony too! He wrote me two years after,
when he haird whar I was, telling me all about it. But, he wan't
much vexed, or he'd got over the worst and the first of it; for he
said, at the eending of his letter—'Go on, Dicky; I see you'll do!'—
and hevn't I done? and I ain't done yit! I'm cute enough, Lawyer,
you see, to do without a lawyer, 'cept for drawing up them papers.
You'll get a good handful for that job."

"I hope for it," quoth the lawyer, somewhat dryly, "and I trust
the job will be soon in our hands; but—"

The dialogue thus far had taken place while Gorham was making
his toilet. This done, he drew from his trunk a quart bottle of his
favorite beverage, placed a tumbler before the lawyer, and proceeded, with a cup of honey, to make his morning dram.

"Shill I make one for you, Squire?"

"No! thank you. I always mix peach and honey for myself
to my own liking."

"That's the way! Here's to you."

"Your health, Mr. Gorham!"

"Whar waur you last night, Squire?"

"At my farm, five miles off."

"Didn't git in till late? I went to your house to see you."

"Pity we missed each other, Mr. Gorham. We may both miss
something by it."

"I don't see. How?"

"Well, that's for you to consider. You are cute, I'm willing to admit, Mr. Gorham, and it's just possible that you *may* make sure of your thirty thousand dollars. I hope so; and I don't like to make a friend uncomfortable, when he has such hopes, by having any doubts myself; but I confess, from something that happened last night, that you'll find Voltmeier a little more cute than yourself."

"What happened last night?"

"What satisfies me that even if you get the money you'll have to give up all hope of the daughter."

"One's as sure as the other, Lawyer."

"I'm sorry to hear you say so, Mr. Gorham, for, if so, you stand a pretty fair chance of losing both. Miss Voltmeier was married last night, by Parson Shelton, to Mr. Fergus Wallace!"

"Ha—ha! That's only your joke, Squire."

"It's a joke that'll hardly make you laugh. You'll find it more true than funny."

"Don't believe it! It's nonsense! The thing's impossible! The man's in jail."

"True; and the marriage took place in jail. Colonel Graham present, Major Henry, also, the great lawyer from South Carolina, the High Sheriff, Mrs. Graham, and several other ladies. The thing's all over town, and I hurried hither to see you about it."

The uplifted noggin dropped from the hands of the ruffian, and, for a moment, he stared upon his companion in speechless astonishment; then angrily he addressed the lawyer, with—

"And why didn't you tell me all this before, instead of keeping me hyar talking, and making a bloody and most ridickilous fool of myself? Didn't you see, don't you see, that Voltmeier means to slope? He'll be off for Europe, Jarmany, and other parts of the world."

"I think it likely, unless you have taken proper precautions."

"And didn't I take them? And didn't you git me the officers yourself?"

"I got you the officers, but you didn't employ me to take the precautions. You wouldn't trust me, being so good a lawyer yourself —born to be a lawyer, as your father said—and, as you say yourself, so very cute!"

"I'm a dern'd fool, I know."

"A good lawyer, nevertheless. I know many fools who think themselves good lawyers! I counseled you to employ counsel."

"Well, I got you!"

"Mr. Richard Gorham, there is but one way to employ good counsel, and that is by giving good fees. You have occupied a great deal of my time, and got my advice, so far as you wanted it, yet I have not seen the color of your money yet. You have beguiled me with promises based upon your expectancies of a rich wife and thirty thousand dollars. You have lost the former; and, by your own wits, being remarkably cute, and a born lawyer, I think you quite likely to come off *minus* in respect to the latter. Now, sir, one farther matter. This very day, Mr. Fergus Wallace will be brought before the court for bail in his case, and it will be granted him, let me tell you, unless you do get a lawyer, even if he be not quite so cute as yourself. I had good information last night, from a source that I can not question, that Colonel Voltmeier has furnished Colonel Graham with an affidavit, regularly sworn, that he alone is responsible for those counterfeit bills; that he put that very money into the hands of Fergus Wallace. And, on the strength of that affidavit, Mr. Wallace will be released—unless, indeed, some cute lawyer, like yourself, shall be employed to resist the application."

"If Voltmeier has sworn to that," said Gorham, hoarsely, "he has sworn to a most bloody and infectious lie! He knows tain't the same money, and I knows it, too; for didn't I"—

Here he stopped short.

"Ha! ah!—I see!" replied the lawyer. "You know, do you? And *how* do you know, Mr. Gorham?"

"Oh! none of your business, for that matter. It's money you want? I ought to ha' knowed that before! There! There's a good hundred dollars; take it and fight ag'in that fellow Wallace, curse him; ef I kain't git the woman myself, I'll keep him from her. No more words. He musn't get off; and Voltmeier musn't slope! I must be off. He'll be away for Jarmany and all Europe ef I'm not quick on trigger. Do your best, Lawyer. Send two more constables after me. I must be off at once. I kin stop him yit! I knows all his tracks now, and kin find him, wherever he runs, though it be into a rat-hole. I know *his* rat-hole, I guess. But he kain't well escape them fellows I set along the track."

"You'll get your breakfast before you go?"

"Breakfast? I kain't eat now. Ef I'm to breakfast or dine to-day, it must be on Voltmeier's liver!"

Brownlow chuckled and Gorham drank. He renewed his potations just as often as Voltmeier renewed his pills. But, under his present excitement, liquor did not seem to tell on him or enfeeble his energies; his mental excitement was now too great. He was quickly mounted, and his horse a fast one; and, though late, he was soon moving towards Keovala, at a speed which promised considerable recovery of lost time; cursing his Fortunes as he rode, but never once troubling himself about the Fates!

We must now follow the footsteps of Voltmeier.

Chapter LXVIII

THE VISION
OF THE HORSEMAN

Voltmeier found young Harness punctually at his post, deeply shrouded within the "Shades of Death," and ready to receive him. He lay upon a rock beneath the gloomy shadow of the "Devil's Pulpit," the rough, jagged ledges of this singular formation stretching over him, and the recess only dimly lighted by a lantern which he had brought with him, and which he had placed upon a smooth projection of the wall, forming a natural shelving for the interior, upon which a good housewife might have found room for all her crockery.

In the farther end of this gloomy recess stood the large black stallion of Voltmeier, which Harness, himself riding the white, had led, properly saddled and bridled, and ready for use.

Near him stood the white, both haltered to saplings growing out of crevices in the rocks. To the companionship of these was now added the bay filly which Voltmeier had ridden—a fine animal, but one which had been pretty well knocked up by the protracted labors of the night. Voltmeier usually rode fast, and the darkness of the night had not lessened his usual habit of speed. He was late—later by an hour or two than he expected or designed to be. He himself seemed jaded and wearied, as he threw himself down on the great flat boulder which had formed the temporary couch of Harness.

"Anything stirring, Ben, since you came?"

"Not even a wood-rat, Colonel."

"You have heard nothing?"

"Nothing, I think."

"How long have you been here?"

"Some three hours, I reckon."

"Have you slept?"

376

"Well, sir, I 'spose I have; but I can hardly tell. I had a good sound nap for two hours before I left Keovala, and was quite sound when old Jupe woke me. Then I started off, and think I must have done some sleeping here, for the red star has gone round a pretty long sweep since I first seed it over yon hill."

"Yes, you must have slept, or you would have heard. I think, Benjie, that I have been pursued somehow."

"Pursued, sir?"

"Yes; I heard the heavy sound of horses' feet behind me, from the moment I entered the shades and all along the park; and every now and then I heard the hounds giving tongue. Hark! Don't you hear them now?"

"No, sir! I hear nothing."

"Indeed! Yet your hearing is good. Clap your ears to the ground and listen."

Harness did so, and after a few moments rose and said:

"I don't hear anything, Colonel, and yet my ears are as keen after a hound gives tongue, as if they wanted to jine in the chase themselves."

"It is very strange! I certainly hear three dogs; a long, slow bay, a sharp, quick one, and a cry as of a lazy or lame hound, howling and hobbling in the rear."

"It is curious, if you thinks you hear, Colonel. It's something wrong about your head, I reckon, for I can hear nothing!"

"It matters not, but I do hear it."

"If you hear it, sir, then some hounds have got into the park, and are a-chasing the deer on their own account."

"No! no! Harness, if you hear nothing, then the dogs that I hear now are hounding after far other animals than deer! Let them hound it as they may! What need we care now?"

Much of this had no meaning for Harness.

"I'll see after them to-morrow, Colonel. I'll ride through the park—"

"Let them be for the present. You will have other riding to do! But did you meet with no one on your ride to the court-house to-day? You were not stopped or questioned?"

"I don't know who was to stop me, having any right to do so. I did meet with one stranger, who was stopping at Watson's, who looked curious at the horse, and asked who he belonged to, and wanted a trade with me."

"Did he ask after me?"

"No! He did ask who that beautiful place belonged to, p'inting towards 'Keovala.'"

"Ha!—well?"

"Well, there was nothing more said, and I went on."

"Did you find the packet of papers in the escritoire?"

"Yes, sir, and brought it with me, and the key, too."

"Well, you must take the packet to the court-house; start from here by daylight; and when you reach the court-house, open the packet, and you will find all the papers within it properly addressed. Lose no time in delivering them all to the several parties whose names are written on them; but the first person you are to seek will be Major Henry. You will find him at Colonel Graham's. Give the key of the escritoire to Mr. Wallace, and you will find letters for him, for Miss Gertrude, and Miss Mignon. By the way, Benjie, *she* was married this night to Mr. Wallace."

"What! is he out, sir?"

"No! they were married in the jail."

"Rather an ugly place, Colonel, for sich a happy transaction."

"Yes! perhaps! Those hounds—don't you hear them *now?*—first, a slow, deep bay; then a sharp, short, quick bark, and then a long howl."

"I don't hear a thing. My hearing must have something the matter with it!"

"No! perhaps not! Never mind it. Well, deliver those papers by nine o'clock if you can. You will ride the bay filly. She will be quite rested by daylight, and you must start by that hour. If you find that the lawyers get Fergus out of jail, as they hope to do by ten or eleven, then you must bring me word."

"To 'Keovala'?"

"No! You know the way to the 'great Whirlpool,' on the river!— the 'Devil's Cauldron'?"

"You showed it to me once, you remember, about two years ago, when we drove up the Paterson herds."

"Yes, then;—and the 'Jaws of Hell,' too?"

"The cavern—oh, yes!"

"And you can find the route to these places?"

"I'm like a horse, sir—never fail to find a way that I've ever traveled once."

"Seek me there, then, and bring me the news from the courthouse. If Fergus is released, as I am very sure he must be, the whole family, with Major Henry, will probably come immediately back to 'Keovala;' but you need not wait on their movements. Come to me quickly with all the speed you can. But, remember to ride the bay filly, and not the white. Leave the white here with me. It is just possible that I may need him."

"And the stallion too?"

"Both."

"You'd better not trust that stallion, sir. He's not been crossed by any of the people, since he broke Jack Barnes's arm; and he always had a spice of the devil in him!"

Voltmeier muttered, *sotto voce:*

"A very proper steed for one who is hounded by the devil!"

"What do you say, Colonel?"

"Those hounds again!"

"It's wonderful; and yet *I* can hear nothing."

Voltmeier swallowed one of his pellets of opium; then said:

"Can you watch for an hour, Benjie? I must try to sleep."

"I'm bright, sir, after my two sleeps, for the next twenty-four hours."

Then Voltmeier disposed himself at length on the flat boulder, and, covering his eyes with his arm, he subsided to silence, and after a little while, seemed to sleep. Harness walked for a time, to and fro, along the gloomy pathway; looked at the horses; strutted back to the sleeping man, and mused as he went, sometimes soliloquizing to himself upon events for which he himself was quite unable to account. His philosophy was wholly upon the surface, and did not often attempt to penetrate into the mysteries of human character, especially where the subject was one of such complications as Voltmeier.

"Something," quoth he to himself, as he strode up the gloomy avenue of the "shades," "something strange is gwine to happen! I never seed the Colonel so before. He's mightily changed in the last fortnight, and seems to forget himself at times. He knows it too! for what's he making all these preparations, jest as ef he was about to die? I reckon he's got a will made among these papers. And what's he got to be afeared of? He's afeared of something, that's certain; and yet, he was jest about the last man in the world I ever expected to see afeared of anything. It's something wrong with his head. How should he hear the tongues of dogs, and I, with all my listening, and good ears too, can't hear nothing? And then, who ever seed him weary before? Why, he was always a riding, a going, and a doing, as ef he was made out of cast-iron, and steel, and whalebone; and never did feel the weather, or the stretch of his sinews! I'm jubous something's going to happen, and he sees it too! I wonder—but twon't do to ax him any questions. Anyhow, it's none of my business, though he's been sich a good friend of mine that I can't help feeling jubous and oncomfortable, thinking something's wrong with him in his head."

In the midst of these musings, he was suddenly startled by a quick, sharp cry from Voltmeier, followed by a pistol shot.

He immediately drew his own pistol, and hurried to the spot.

He found Voltmeier standing up; erect, in gladiatorial attitude, his eyes staring wild, with a strange ferocity of expression, and his pistol still pointed as when he had fired. With his left hand he was even then engaged in drawing his second pistol from his belt.

"What was it, Colonel?"

"Did you not see him?"

"See who?"

"The man on horseback!"

"Man on horseback!"

"Great God! Benjie—he swept beside me like a tornado! Did you not hear the rush—wild as the winds coursing down our mountain gorges? He almost swept over me! He was on a black horse, as black as the stallion, and the rider was all in black; and when I challenged him, he laughed and pointed ahead, as if to say, 'Follow!' Then I shot! Is it possible you heard nothing—saw nothing! Why, where were you?"

"Not twenty paces off; just beyond the horses. There was no rush—no wind, that I heard! You see, sir, everything's quite calm now, and hardly a breath stirring."

"He went by like a whirlwind! Strange! that you did not hear him. Were you asleep, Benjie?"

"On my legs, sir, wide awake as a panther, and just as much on the watch! But you had been asleep, Colonel. I reckon 'twas only a dream?"

"A dream! Perhaps! Life itself is but a dream, Benjie; and half of its certainties are only dreams! One hardly knows that he lives, when living—still less does he know of earth's inhabitants; they fill all space! They can occupy all senses, in turn, and after what manner they please; and it is as *you* will, and as *they* will, that you can arrive at any consciousness of what they are and when they come! We *know* only as we *grow!* Better not *grow*, Benjie, if you would not know too much! I am weary, very weary of this strife to know! Is not that the dawn?"

"Where sir?" and Voltmeier pointed to the opening between two massive rocks.

"You're just directly opposite the east, Colonel. We must look for daylight on t'other side."

"True! true! Ah! there goes Lucifer, with his golden torch— that son of the morning, forerunner of the dawn! Bright one, I welcome thee! Yet, I fear I have followed too fondly on thy track! Lead on, thou Beautiful Bearer of the Torch! and usher in thy successor and thy foe, in whose grander rays thine are destined to be swallowed up! I will follow thee still, even though to be extinguished like thyself! Shall I know thy reawaking? Shall I, too, light my torch, as thou dost thine, by the never-failing fire of eternity?"

Voltmeier soliloquized, without, seemingly, a consciousness of the presence of Harness, on whose senses all his metaphysics must have fallen in vain. Suddenly he seemed to feel that he was nigh, and turning upon him quickly, he said:

"Bring hither your lantern."

When the lantern was brought, he reloaded the emptied pistol, as coolly and as deliberately as if he had undergone no excitement, and with a grim smile he said to Harness:

"It is just as well to be prepared, Benjie, whether we fight with a Hound of Hell, or only a sneaking panther!"

Thus speaking, he resumed his sleeping position, on the boulder, saying:

"Watch by me, Benjie, till daybreak! Then wake me, should I sleep! You must then be off, and so must I!"

Chapter LXIX

THE DEMON IN THE STEED

With daybreak both parties prepared to ride. When Harness was already mounted, Voltmeier stood beside him, with one hand affectionately resting on the thigh of the youth, while the other grasped his hand nervously. His eyes were fastened upon the features of the young man with a searching and tender interest; but he said nothing; and, after a warm pressure of the hand, he released it, and turned away abruptly.

Long after this silent parting did Ben Harness remember that earnest pressure of Voltmeier's fingers upon his own, and that long, earnest perusal of his face. He then knew that it was designed as his farewell.

He was out of sight in another moment, and Voltmeier stood alone, sole tenant of the "Valley and Shadow," so called, "of Death!"

He seated himself upon the stone where he had slept or tried to sleep; and delivered himself up to those successive thoughts, feelings and fancies, which absorbed equally his mind and his affections, and seemed, like so many billows of the sea, to roll in upon him, under the influence of capricious winds.

"Yet might I fly, and they might follow. We might all be secure in that other world beyond the sea, where I dwelt so long, and where I nursed the most innocent affections of my heart. Yes, they could follow. I have told them that! And the wealth which I have made securely theirs, might also follow, and all be conveyed beyond the deep, and away from these dangers.

"I have thought of all these things, all seems feasible—nay, the proper course of wisdom! But, we are not always free to accept the conditions, or secure the alternatives, which are laid open by our thoughts to our actions. Free agency, indeed! We are still fettered by circumstance, and the agency of others, in whose hands rest those leashes which keep in the Hounds of Fate till the moment when they are set free to dart direct upon the throat of the prostrate victim!

382

"Tell me not of will and aim and strength. I have had all these; but I have them no longer. By what impulse am I brought hither to these ominous shades? What is it that impels me to that gloomy cavern where every memory reminds me of my labors of guilt, which, for so long a season, were labors of love? Why linger here, or travel there, when the broad road for flight is open to me, and I have but to mount my courser and be gone; gone to safety, and, possibly, years of future happiness? Why am I disarmed of the will to do this, and instead of this, forced to succumb to that impulse which leads me as it wills, in despite of any will of mine?

"Here is the problem.

" 'Do this!' cries one voice.

" 'Forbear!' says another.

"We resolve *for* neither, perhaps—or resolve *with* either, and so mount the steed.

"But the Fate is not to be baffled. The reins are slacked within the grasp, and the steed goes forward, driven by our own spur, but under the guidance of a will more powerful than our own!

"Be it so! I will mount the steed, and it shall be at *his* will that I will ride. He shall have the free rein, though it is my spur that shall redden his flanks with blood!"

So saying, he went towards the cavity in which the two steeds had been fastened.

Why had Voltmeier retained both steeds? This was the unuttered question of Ben Harness, and he answered it after his own fashion.

"Who can tell what the Colonel's driving at? He's always too deep for me; but I reckon he'll try the stallion, and, if he finds he can't manage him, why he'll turn him loose and take the other. The stallion's sure to find the way back to his own stall by himself, and at a devil's gallop, too!"

Voltmeier first released from the halter his favorite white, and the beast, gentle as a dog, proceeded quietly to crop the dwarfish grasses that grew up through the stony beds of the valley. He next proceeded to transfer the saddle from the one horse to the other.

The stallion seemed quiet enough during this operation; but Voltmeier, a first-rate horseman, and well acquainted with the animal, did not fail to note the rapid movements of his ears, and the dogged, but fiery expression of his eyes.

He was a noble creature, sixteen hands high, beautifully chested, broad, full and swelling, the quarters admirably rounded, clean fetlocks, and all the limbs symmetrically perfect. He was of the best Arabian, through English stocks.

Already bridled and strongly bitted, the saddle on, and well girted, Voltmeier released him from the cover of the rocks, and led him forth into the open area between them.

Here he prepared to mount, and, while doing so, he whistled the white to follow.

But, scarcely had he put foot into the stirrup, and ere he could mount, the demon of the beast began to betray his temper and his qualities. He wheeled suddenly about, and strove to break away from the grasp which Voltmeier had upon the bridle.

A second effort to mount was equally unsuccessful. The beast seemed quietly to await the attempt, but, as it was made, he suddenly whirled about, and tried to break away as before.

But, Voltmeier was not the man to be baffled of any object which lay fairly within his strength, his experience, or his art. It was now a conflict between man and brute, and, just in degree with the opposition which he met from the animal, was the rider provoked to the trial of strength between them, which the stallion seemed to challenge.

The encounter warmed him to a forgetfulness of his philosophy. It seemed to him as if the Fates, in whose existence he believed as religiously, no doubt, as any ancient Greek, had already begun that ordeal through which, as he anticipated, he was now required to pass, and his soul rose to meet the exigencies of the encounter.

"It is very well!" he said, as he backed the beast against the rock, and looked steadily into his eyes. There was no quailing in the glance of either; and the stallion gave him look for look, nor did the eye close or shrink, when he suddenly waved his hand across it. The movement was answered by a snort of defiance.

"Now!" said he "could I believe in the Jewish doctrine of *"posses-sion,"* I should say that this beast was possessed by as malignant a demon as ever came hot from hell! and if the demoniacs could inhabit the swine; nay, if they could penetrate the brains and bodies of men as well, why not this beast?

"We must try our strength, Ashtoreth, or whoever you may be; I see you, too, are in the league against me. Let me see, if, in descending to the beast, you have not lost some of your demonic power. If I am to wrestle with angel or demon, I must put forth all my strength; and this, too, is a requisition of the Fates. Even in death we are to struggle against him!"

Thus saying, he swallowed a pill from his opium box, and proceeded to make new efforts. The stallion seemed to understand him. He stood *posed,* as it were for the painter, in a magnificent attitude of grace and power; his neck loftily arched, as if about to be clothed in thunder; his head elevated and thrown back; his form poised upon its center, with the legs slightly drawn toward each other, as if preparing for the spring; and from his nostril came an occasional deep snort, as if renewing defiance, from the very bottom of his lungs, and even from his eyes there shot forth a flash that seemed meant to express equal anger and contempt.

The bit was Mexican—the reins strong; the saddle was somewhat Mexican also, with high peak, but rather more near our McClellan model than the strict Mexican saddle. Voltmeier's heels were habitually barbed with great rowels.

He led the animal a few paces, so as to make him quite clear of the projecting rocks. He spoke to him in low tones, soft and low, but in words of irony, precisely as if he were speaking to an enemy by whom his language was understood.

"And now, Ashtoreth, my beauty, the question between us is reduced to one only. It is your neck or mine! I accept your challenge. You, too, are among my Fates, or I am yours! Now, do your best— for by the God that made me, I tame you as a beast this day, conquer you as a demon, or break your neck, or mine, or both! If you can break mine, well and good. It shall be fair play between us, according to our respective powers, and the game will then be at an end! 'So be it!' "

The *will* of Voltmeier had grown strong as of old, in the brief wrestle which he had already had. He was now himself once more— the mocking demon, Mephistopheles, to whom at certain moments, and in certain moods, he was apt to be likened, by his daughter, Mignon.

He led the barb out, walked him round a circle, in spite of several vicious efforts of the beast to break away from his grasp.

Meanwhile, the white steed, even as he had been bidden, followed every movement of the stallion, and when Voltmeier curbed in the latter, arresting the circling movement, the former ranged himself alongside of him, as an old cavalry horse takes his known station in the ranks.

But, the stallion was ignorant of the *esprit de corps;* and as soon as the white drew up beside him, he whirled his head about with demonic spite, and bit him severely in the neck. Upon which, in momentary anger, Voltmeier smote him savagely in the mouth with his fist, and the fierce beast turned upon him in the same instant, and bit him also, inflicting a slight flesh wound upon the arm.

Then it was that the passions of Voltmeier were fairly aroused, and setting his own teeth firmly, he seized the opportunity when the stallion had fairly turned a second time upon the white, to leap into the saddle, without any premonition, and making no use of the stirrup. He vaulted to his seat as lightly as if the weight of sixty years were not upon his shoulders, a very feathered Mercury, the practiced Hero of the Hippodrome.

The moment he had gained his seat, he struck the heavy rowels into the flanks of the beast. Then came the tug of war between the two, and verily, it did seem as if the demon had possession of both.

With a mixed snort and roar, the ordinary whinny of the horse,— raging desperate,—now almost seemed the utterance of a far more furious beast. The animal cowered first, and, for a moment, nearly to the ground; then bolted far and away, and, at a single bound, was rushing out of the track of the valley, and, darting up the slopes of one of the hills, seemingly bent upon reaching the summits of the great rocks that towered above them.

"Up, then, Hound of Hell!" cried Voltmeier, "as far and fast as you please."

But, as the ascent grew steep, the stallion changed his tactics, and stopping short, with head down, threw up his heels in the face of the white horse who had followed him as devoutly as if he had been his file-leader.

But for Voltmeier's experience in horses, and wonderful skill and dexterity as a horseman, he would have been cast out of the saddle like a stone, and over the head of the beast.

The snort of the stallion became an absolute bellow, as his rider drove the rowels relentlessly into his sides.

He now proceeded to vault and rear, so balancing upon his hind legs, finally, as to stand almost perpendicularly in air. But Voltmeier clung to him with the tenacity of death, driving the spurs into him without ceasing, and answering his sharp snorting cry with a few words of mockery, through his clenched teeth, the sneer being addressed rather to the foul fiend whom he assumed to be in possession, than the animal which he bestrode.

"Dog of a devil!" quoth he, "you must bring with you better arts of your own! Those of the beast will not serve you. Were I sure that my rowels were now ripping in your sides, I should be better satisfied. Do your best. You are matched. I am Mephistopheles enough for you!"

A series of rapid gyrations followed, the stallion spinning round as upon a pivot, with an occasional bound forward, or leap in air, or a sudden contraction of all his limbs and muscles, and sometimes, so sinking suddenly as to bring his belly almost into contact with the earth.

Meanwhile, the white steed kept pace with the black and his rider, quietly moving about him, prudently keeping clear equally of the heels and jaws of the former, but following his footsteps even as he had been bidden by his master.

Voltmeier, meanwhile, seemed to grow into, and become a part of the fierce beast which he bestrode. He realized to the eye the ideal of the Centaur. He laughed like a demon at the demonic efforts which the animal made to throw him; answered every snort and roar, and every new evolution, by the infliction of the terrible spurs, until the red blood coursed down clottily over the sable flanks of the charger, and dropped, at moments, in big gouts upon the ground!

Panting, flecked with mixed foam and bloody sweat, now leaping, now throwing out his heels, now vaulting so as to grow into the perpendicular, and to maintain this difficult position for a space of time inconceivably long even to the experience of Voltmeier—taxing all his strength and skill to keep himself in the saddle, the stubborn beast could maintain the contest after this fashion no longer, and he now proceeded to test his speed and strength, rather than his agility and dexterity.

On a sudden he darted away, like an arrow from the bow, and with head turned upwards, seemed once more to aim at the highest elevation upon the rocks.

Horse and rider, in all their several and various trials of strength, occupied an elevated table along the lower steppes of the rocks, with the sun streaming down upon them, making pictures of such intense action and fierce vitality, as would have yielded scores of wonderful studies for the tragic painter. The dramatic element infused with graphic vivacity every change of scene in this novel drama, in which the human actor so readily persuaded himself that he had found a demon in his beast antagonist!

"Up then, devil! up! up! and away! I have you now under me, and you shall feel me still."

And the rowel, at every word, ripped the sore sides of the flying steed; extorted every now and then his snort and cry of pain, but giving new impetus to his forward motion.

The blood was streaming from his sides, and blood and water issued together from his eyes. The balls of vision were protruding almost to bursting, yet he could no longer see! He knew not where he sped, but madly sped away, obedient to the spur, if not to the curb, and covering with wonderful lopes, rock and fissure, boulder and stump, while Voltmeier shouted, as in fiendish glee, as over a victory won, and still drove the beast forward, with a maddening spirit like his own. And he thought as he rode, of Bürger's ride of the demon with his bride.

"Now," said he, as he found the stallion staggering in his tracks, as if dizzied, though still bounding headlong forward; "now, would it be only well—a fit finish to this fight, if, literally, I should drive my demon to the wall! He seems bent on it himself. By all the Fates, he shall have it! It shall be so!"

He rose from his stirrups as he spoke, threw them from his feet, grasped the bridle which he had hitherto left loosely flowing, and for the first time giving the direction to the beast, shouted wildly as he drove the rowels—burying them fully in the flanks of the animal—then tore them out, and, at the same moment, with a dextrous bound threw himself out of the saddle to the earth.

He fell, slightly stunned only by the concussion, having chosen for the purpose a grassy spot which lay at the base of a mighty mass of rock. This mass stood up like a Cyclopean wall directly in the pathway of the steed.

The shout, with the keen pain of the rowel, had their effect. The momentum of the beast could not be arrested! He drove headlong against the wall of granite!

There was a crash!—a cry!—and a heavy fall upon the earth!

When the half-stunned Voltmeier opened his eyes, and could take in the objects about him, the stallion lay dead within twenty paces, his skull crushed to pieces; while the white horse was walking quietly around, curiously circling now about the dead beast, and now the living man,—with a nose of inquiry addressed to each in turn.

It required some half hour before Voltmeier even endeavored to regain his feet. His muscles had been so corded under the struggle through which he had passed, that time was needed for their relaxation. When he did rise, he walked to the dead beast, where he lay, and looking at him for a few moments, scowling in savage silence, he addressed him thus:

"And now, fiend of Fate, in what shape next shall I have to do battle with thee? I see that one foe must follow the other, till the end be reached! I am ready for any Fate, take whatever shape it please!"

He swallowed one of his pellets of opium, transferred the saddle from the dead to the living horse, and in another hour was upon his route, once more through the "Shades of Death," and riding in the direction of the cavern with the ominous name, which we have visited before.

Chapter LXX

WHAT DID IT MEAN?

When Benjie Harness made his appearance at the office of Colonel Graham, he found that gentleman, with Major Henry, in close consultation, preparing the argument in the case of Fergus Wallace. They were both at ease on the subject, satisfied that the affidavit of Voltmeier was quite sufficient for the acquittal and discharge of the prisoner from custody, and without the necessity of bail. To this moment neither party had any suspicions of the integrity of Voltmeier.

But they both were surprised by the tenor of the letters that were brought by Harness. As they severally read them, they handed the sheets to one another.

"There is something very strange in all this, Henry," said Graham, "and it seems to confirm the suspicions which you expressed to me yesterday, touching the mental condition of our friend. Why should he leave the country? He surely stands in no danger."

"His phrase is equivocal," was the reply of Henry. "He does not say that he is about to leave the country. He says that, in all probability, when we shall read this, he will be beyond the reach of all mortal hostility. This, to my mind, argues something more than flight. It may be exile, it is true, but the language is strong and significant, though equivocal. Where is the bearer of these letters?"

"In the hall."

"Call him in. He may tell us something."

Harness was called in, and Henry asked him the question—

"Where was Colonel Voltmeier when he gave you these letters?"

"In the 'Shades of Death,' sir."

"What!"

"That's the name of a valley," said Graham, smiling, "which runs directly in the rear of the park at Keovala. It is a dark and gloomy pass between the rocks which lie between Keovala and the river. I

390

have traversed this pass in company with Voltmeier, and it certainly deserves the name."

"When did you leave him?"

"At daybreak this morning."

"Did you leave him in that pass?"

"Yes, sir."

"And made he any appointment with you to meet him again, and bring our answers?"

"Yes, sir. He told me to come and tell him if Mr. Wallace was let out of prison."

"Ah! and where were you to meet him?"

"Well, now, sir, I don't know as how I ought to tell you. The Colonel was sort of confidential in the business."

"But we are his lawyers, you know—his personal friends; and you will be quite safe in telling us anything which may be of interest for him."

"I don't know, sir, but I'd rather not, as he didn't authorize me to say anything much."

"Well, perhaps you are right, Mr. Harness; but some questions you may answer, without violating any confidence. If he did not tell you to answer, he did not, if I understand you rightly, tell you *not* to answer. Now, as his friends, we tell you that it is important *to him* that you should answer a few questions, which I will ask you. You can decline answering them if you will; but when you hear them, I think it will be very clear to you that the questions are innocent. Now, was Col. Voltmeier sick, in any way, when you last saw him? was there anything strange about him?"

"Well, sir, I must say, I think there was. He talked, sometimes, in a way that I couldn't understand, and I did think, sir, that there was something wrong about his head."

"Ah!" said Henry, looking to Graham.

The examination was continued. It was not difficult, in the case of two such eminent experts in jury practice as Graham and Henry, dealing with one so ingenuous as young Harness, to extract from him, little by little, a very fair account of the events of the night, during that portion of it which found Voltmeier and Harness together; and their gravity increased, as they hearkened to his revelations. The details were quite sufficient to increase the apprehensions of

Henry, and awaken those of Graham. Yet Harness knew nothing of the subsequent mad scene with the stallion and its tragic finish.

When they had gathered from Harness all that he was able or prepared to deliver, Graham said:

"Well, Mr. Harness, you will remain here, until the case of Mr. Wallace shall be decided, when I will give you a note to Col. Voltmeier, and you can also make your own report. We are about to proceed to the Court House, and shall be there shortly. You can be present, also, if you think proper."

"Thank you, sir; I will be there, for I have letters also for Mr. Fergus, Miss Mignon, and Miss Gertrude."

"Ah!" said Henry; "then let me beg you, my good fellow, not to deliver one of those letters until Mr. Wallace is discharged. Nay, I *charge* it upon you that you do not deliver them till then."

"But, sir—"

"Did he tell you, sir, that you were to deliver them this minute or that; this hour or the next?"

"Well, no, sir; and, indeed, he told me particklar, that I was to deliver your letter *first*."

"Precisely," said Henry, "in order that I should counsel you about the rest."

This seemed conclusive to Harness, and he acquiesced in the requisition.

"See us," said Graham, "just as soon as the case is over."

The young man was dismissed.

"Graham," said Henry, suddenly, "I really feel as if I should set off this instant for Keovala, and see this man."

"Impossible, *now!*—the case—"

"Can just as well be argued by you as by me. Nay, there will hardly be any need of argument, armed, as we are, with Voltmeier's affidavit. That will be conclusive, and we claim the discharge, without bail, and as matter of right."

"True; but I am not sure that you will be doing right, in withholding your services and presence, especially employed, as you are, by Voltmeier. I am afraid that your absence at the trial will convey the impression that you are yourself doubtful, and abandon your client, because of this doubt. There may be some suspicions of complicity between the two; and, again, we are not to know but that an attempt will be made to obtain an order of Court for the arrest of

Voltmeier. Besides, where could you find *him*, now, unless under the guidance of this young fellow, Harness? It is clear enough, from what he says, that he will not be found at Keovala."

Henry submitted to the reasons of Graham, though still reluctantly.

"I am inclined to think," said Graham, "that he is at some point, on his route, for departure from the country; that this point is only made known to Harness; and that Voltmeier's final determination, whether to stay or go, will depend on our report, or that of Harness."

"If we could only know the contents of those letters to Fergus, and the ladies! Why should he write to *them*, at this juncture, if he did not meditate some act of extreme character—departure or death? The more I read this letter, the more pregnant it seems to be with the most mysterious meaning. Hear this passage." And he read as follows:

"Should my affidavit fail in procuring the discharge of Fergus, then, my dear Major Henry, you will open the larger packet, to your address, and make use of its contents before the Court. That, too, is sworn to before a magistrate, and, while its revelations may be most humiliating to myself, nay, even perilous, it will yet prove conclusive in behalf of Fergus Wallace. I shall not fear its consequences *to myself, as, when the revelation is made, I shall be far beyond the reach of mortal inquiry or injury; of human justice or human reproach!* If not needed for the extrication of my daughter's husband, I confide it to your good faith to destroy the whole document unread. It contains a painful history of a guilty and most unhappy life, for which it is now quite too late to atone."

"Well," said Graham, "the subject is one for after-thought. The clock is upon the stroke of ten. It is time to go; we will take this document with us, though I do not see that there will be any necessity for its use."

"Will you have a horse saddled and in readiness for me, just so soon as the case is over? I will set out with Harness, and seek Voltmeier myself. I have a notion that I understand the man, and can better deal with him than most persons."

"It shall be done; and I will follow you. It is quite probable that, in the event of Wallace's discharge, the family will desire to return home at once, and Mrs. Graham will put her carriage at their disposal."

Chapter LXXI

THE AFFIDAVITS

At the Court Hall they found seats already taken by Mrs. Graham, and other ladies of that class of people whom Brownlow was wont to sneer at as the Big Fish, the High Fliers, and nabobs of the country—the favorite *ad captandum vulgus* of the demagogue.

But, however jealous the lower order may be of the upper classes, they are yet pleased to see them at all popular assemblies, and they exercise a tacit influence over such people.

The array was quite imposing, made by the ladies; and when Fergus Wallace was brought into court, his young wife hanging on his arm, with all the fond solicitude of a truthful, loving, and anxious heart—when they saw that slight and fairy-like figure seated beside him, clasping one of his hands in hers, with her head nestling against his shoulder—beheld that beautiful angelic face, so fond and innocent; so girlish of form, yet so womanly in all expression and movement, there was a decided impression, indicated by a general murmur of sympathy, among the audience. The artist alone knows the effects of light and shadow. Graham whispered to Henry:

"We have Judge A—— this morning, instead of that miserable H——! A—— is a gentleman, as well as a good lawyer. We shall have no difficulty."

Nor had they. The affidavit of Voltmeier was submitted by Henry, who said he would not take up the time of the court by any attempt at argument upon a subject which the court would readily perceive required none, and he submitted the naked evidence.

Brownlow opposed the motion for a discharge of the prisoner.

"On what ground, Mr. Brownlow?"

"I have reason, may it please your honor, to believe that there is complicity between these parties."

"Are your reasons grounded in any knowledge of *your own*, as to the facts? If so, submit your affidavit."

394

"My reasons are based, your honor, upon the evidence of another party."

"Is he in court, or have you his affidavit?"

"I have not, your honor; but, if the court will postpone the consideration of the case for a single day, I hope to have my witness present."

"I do not see how the court can do this, unless you can assure me that your testimony goes to the conviction of the present petitioner before the court. If I understand you, the testimony of your witness bears wholly upon Col. Voltmeier; and here is Voltmeier's own affidavit, assuming the whole responsibility of the act charged; distinctly avowing that he, himself, gave the counterfeit money to Mr. Wallace, for a specified object on his behalf, which he, Wallace, fulfilled as an unconscious agent."

"But the presumptions, your honor—"

"What presumptions, sir?"

"Mr. Wallace is the son-in-law, your honor, of Col. Voltmeier!"

"Well! I see not the significance of this fact, unless it be good doctrine that, if there be one black sheep in a family, we must make it the ground for hanging the whole flock. It will be a sorry condition for society, and humanity, if, because a father proves a villain, we are to suspect all his children; or, *vice versa*, if the son turns out a rogue, we necessarily refer his offenses to his father."

"Sir, your honor, we could, perhaps, establish all this to-morrow; —a brief delay, sir,—only a day—"

"A day and night in jail, on a mere conjecture, is, to an honorable gentleman, no small evil, and indeed, a great indignity. To you, who are free from this 'durance vile,' it may be nothing. But, in this case, much evil has been done already. The prisoner has already been held in custody, in the common jail of the county, for a long time; a time sufficiently long to have enabled you to have subpœnaed all the witnesses in the county. It does not appear that you have made any efforts to this end. Nay, you have no affidavit to offer to show that you have a witness at all. Meanwhile, it appears, from evidence now before me, that criminal appeals have been made to popular violence, in this very case, by which a shocking riot has taken place in the county, in which many persons have been hurt, their lives endangered, and the high sheriff of the county himself has nearly fallen a victim to this violence! Were there before me now, any proper affidavits, it would give me the greatest satisfaction to commit all persons who participated in this riotous affair. According to the popular rumors which have reached my ears, there were persons notoriously engaged in stimulating the popular passions to violence, which, for the honor and credit of the profession itself, I should be glad to punish! I should like to show to the people, as to the professions, that no social or professional position shall be allowed to shelter such offenders, or give tacit sanction to such offenses. It appears to me, from all that I can learn, that this young man has been cruelly dealt with. Here are affidavits from several of the first men in our sister State, who bear the warmest and highest testimony equally to his attainments and moral character. Scarcely does he enter our State, but he nearly falls a victim to the murderous aim of a highway robber. Recovered from this injury, he identifies himself with the brethren at our Bar, and at once establishes a high claim, by his talents and his conduct, to our esteem and admiration. The court, itself, perfectly remembers his most creditable examination before us, when asking admission to the practice; nor is the court ignorant of the very able legal arguments which he has since made within these very walls, to justify the anticipatory judgments of the court. I should be sorry to think that the hostility which seems resolute to pursue him so vindictively, should have its origin in any miserable feeling of envy, on the part of any member of the North Carolina Bar. I have possessed myself, Mr. Brownlow, of much testimony in regard to this young man, and here, in the person of one of the most eminent of the lawyers of our sister State, is a living witness to his uniform integrity, great moral worth, and mental ability. But, apart from all this testimony, and were there nothing before us, speaking to his personal character, the affidavit of Col. Voltmeier, taking upon himself, without reservation, the whole responsibility of this counterfeit money, is conclusive, and compels our discharge of the prisoner, without bail, in the absence of any well-founded and attested allegations against him. Neither your conjectures, Mr. Brownlow, nor mine, can possibly justify his further detention; and I herewith make the order for his immediate discharge from custody."

There was a prompt and loud murmur of applause from the assembly, and from mouths which, but a short time before, were most clamorous for hanging and lynching the same person. Such is the consistency of popular impulse!

Mignon sobbed on her husband's shoulder. The sheriff ordered silence in court, and the judge proceeded.

"The sheriff will at once release Fergus Wallace from all constraint."

"And is Col. Voltmeier to escape, your honor?" said Brownlow. "Upon his own affidavit, it seems to me that the court may well issue an immediate order for his arrest, and before he flies the country, which I have reason to believe he meditates. Nay, he is supposed to be even now on the road. He is certainly missing from his usual haunts."

"He was in town for two hours, at least, only last night," said Graham, dryly, "in a large circle, in the jail itself, to witness his daughter's marriage, in the presence of numerous witnesses, the high sheriff himself being one."

"Yes," was the quick reply of Brownlow; "but the honorable gentleman does not tell you that it was a sort of fashionable surprise party—Col. Voltmeier coming under cover of the night, without beat of drum, and departing as silently, suddenly and secretly as he came."

"There was no surprise about it, your honor. We were all properly apprised of his proposed visit, and its objects. The Rev. Dr. Shelton was spoken to, during the day; so was the high sheriff, Major Henry, myself, and other parties, all of whom were duly written to or spoken with on the subject."

"And the secrets confided only to these parties?" said Brownlow.

"I know not, may it please your honor," answered Graham, with look and language of equal scorn, "that we have yet reached that degraded social stage when it is requisite that the populace, generally the rag-tag and bobtail of a country village, must be advised and consulted with, when we give away a daughter in marriage, or entertain our guests at a domestic festival. One would suppose that this affair was sufficiently notorious, with a large circle of ladies and gentlemen present, and the high sheriff himself among them."

"I renew my suggestion, may it please your honor, that an order from the court issue to instruct the sheriff promptly to arrest the person of Col. Leonard Voltmeier, on his own confession, as a criminal, as having passed this counterfeit money, knowing it to be such."

"This affidavit contains no such confession," said the judge.

"It admits the emission of the counterfeits, and the presumption of guilt follows."

"Not where the same affidavit disclaims the knowledge. We have to take all the parts of the affidavit together, as a whole; and, unless met by positive testimony of other parties, showing the knowledge and intention, the affidavit becomes our best evidence, especially in the case of a person occupying the social position of Col. Voltmeier, and seemingly totally without any motive for such a crime."

"Your honor has, but a little while since, said that no social or professional position can be allowed to serve as a shelter or excuse for offender or offense. Were it an ordinary man, *without* social position, I take it that there would be no hesitation on the part of the court, in issuing the order for arrest. Now, sir, I am prepared to offer my own affidavit, which I think will suffice to justify the court, even against its own scruples, in issuing this order. I have the best of reasons for believing that Col. Voltmeier was not only the circulator, but the fabricator of this counterfeit money; and, with proper time allowed me, I think I can bring proof of it from the mouth of one of his own associates."

"Make your affidavit, Mr. Brownlow. It is at your own peril."

"Be it so, sir."

The affidavit was submitted. The lawyer, desperately struggling to the last, and driven to extremity, transcended the intimations and even the confidence of Gorham. He was apprehensive that the flight of Voltmeier would lose him all those fine fees and pickings which the cunning of Gorham had held out as lures to his cupidity.

The order for the arrest of Voltmeier was accordingly issued, and placed at once in the hands of the sheriff, and the court adjourned.

It was with great difficulty that the indignation of Mignon could be kept from ebullition by Fergus, while Brownlow was speaking of her father—things and suggestions so atrocious in her thought, as to sound as little less than blasphemy.

It was now that Benjie Harness darted forward and grasped the hand of Fergus, with his congratulations. He then delivered his letters to the members of the family severally. They were all tender and affectionate—passionately so, indeed, but of a startling nature to each. To Fergus, the pregnant portions were these:

"You will follow me at once to Germany. Miss Leyfenholdt will know where to find me. We shall meet there, God willing! Col. Graham has charge of your affairs and mine. Ben Harness will take care of 'Keovala.' All is assured to you and Mignon. Be of good cheer, and God's blessing upon you till we meet!"

To Miss Gertrude, after certain preliminaries, he said:

"You have long been anxious to see Germany once more. You will now have the opportunity. Some very pressing and present exigencies call me thither. You will show the young people the way, and will know how to find me. You need not write, but follow promptly. If safe, *across the great deeps that now spread before me*, we shall meet again. You will seek me at the old quarters, with Bertha, Walter, and all the rest," &c.

To Mignon, after some pathetic and fond expressions, he said:

"Follow me fast, beloved! Follow me soon! There is no need for delay. You shall see Germany once more; and my Mignon shall guide her Fergus over the well known 'pillared halls' of her Italian associations. Yes, you can guide him where the 'Dragon still rears her brood,' where the 'crags are still riven by the flood,' and the patient mule still strives upward through the fog! Oh, my child, my best beloved Mignon, pray that we may pass safely these black waters, and meet, for perfect happiness, in happy lands, at last! *adiós! adiós!*"

THE HOUNDS IN FULL CRY

What happy hearts were in that little group until they had received and read the letters of Voltmeier! That they should miss him, after the release of Fergus—that they should fail to meet and receive his congratulations and embraces, after that term of doubt and trial—that months would probably pass away before they should join him in Europe; all these vexatious thoughts passed through the breast of Mignon; but neither she nor Aunt Gertrude suffered from the apprehensions which troubled Major Henry—which, by the way, he did not express to them—nor did they know the anxieties which Fergus felt at the mystifications of Voltmeier's proceedings.

But when it was known to them that Ben Harness was to meet with him that very day, in order to carry him the tidings of the discharge of Fergus, they were reassured. They felt that they would certainly be in time to prevent his departure; and Fergus, with the family, set off in the carriage of Mrs. Graham for Keovala, as soon as the horses could be put to the vehicle.

The ladies, at least, had no reason to doubt that Voltmeier would be found at home, Harness having taken care, under Major Henry's instructions, to say nothing to them on that subject. Henry himself, by the way, was already on horseback, prepared to accompany Harness as soon as the proceedings of the court were over.

Thus we find nearly all our *dramatis personæ* on the road that day, and pursuing a like direction.

We have seen Richard Gorham, aroused to intense eagerness for the pursuit of Voltmeier, some few hours before.

We have seen Voltmeier himself vainly battling with his demonic stallion, in the endeavor to goad him forward, under a *will* that seemed without any aim or purpose.

We see the family following, in part, their footsteps, and bound for Keovala, while Major Henry and Harness ride before.

And, following fast on the track of these, is the Deputy Sheriff, bearing the order of the Court for the arrest of the supposed fugitive.

And he—Voltmeier?

We left him threading the gloomy avenues of the "Shades of Death," and shaping his course in the direction of the river, by an obscure road, which, at a certain point, will conduct him into the main trace, or common highway of the country.

And here, at a short distance in the rear of this point of the junction, is stationed, on the watch, the constable or detective, in the employ of Gorham, whom we have heard called by the unfamiliar name of Smith.

Smith has in him enough of the pride of the detective, irrespective of the profits of his business, to do his watching narrowly, even though his wits failed him in his watch. We will suppose the other detective, employed in watching the route leading from Keovala to the Court House, to have done his duty also. But he has been baffled by the maneuvers of Voltmeier, who, from sheer habit, will play the politician in all his operations, and for the very pleasure derivable from his art, will prefer the circuitous to the direct. He loved mystery as, in itself, a most fascinating agency for thought. He had sent another on his famous white horse, by the ordinary route of the country. He had traveled himself by a road but little known beyond his own family, and rarely traveled by any but himself. But we have noted these things in detail already. Enough that, when Gorham reached the place of watch of that detective who had been stationed at Watson's, he gained no information upon which he could base a single conjecture.

Had Voltmeier left Keovala? Was he still there? To ascertain this point was Gorham's first necessity.

Leaving strict injunctions with the detective, privately, to be on the alert, and to ride to and fro between his own and the station of Smith at Swales', Gorham disappeared among the hills, seeking those recesses by which he had hitherto wormed his way into the precincts of Keovala.

Once hidden from sight in these obscure recesses, he dismounted and secured his horse, as of old, among the great boulders and deep thickets, which were not likely to be sought, save by the mountain hunter in pursuit of game.

"And now for the stables," said he to himself. "If the horses are gone, he's gone! On that famous white, he'd distance any nine horses in ten of all this country."

Working his way about the precincts with all the dexterity and caution of an Indian scout, he succeeded in making his way to the stables unseen. Into these he found no difficulty to look. He found some colts and work-horses, *but no white!* The stallion was gone; the bay filly; in brief, the stables were stript of all save the well-known pair of carriage horses, which, after conveying the ladies to Col. Graham's, were brought back with the carriage.

"He's made a clean sweep! He's off somewhere. But where? If he hain't passed the officers, then how did he git off? That's the question."

It now dawned upon him, for the first time, that there might be another and a secret road. Such a man as Voltmeier, pursuing such a life, would, no doubt, provide himself with some such mode of escape.

"What a fool I was, not to think of that! But, to cross the river, he *must* git into the main trace somewhere by Swales'. There's a nigger now; I'd like to ask him; but 'twon't do to risk it."

Retreating as he came, he returned to his own horse, remounted, and soon rejoined the detective.

"Now," said he to the latter, "git up and push on with me. Is your nag a fast one?"

"Pretty good trotter."

"Can he *run?*"

"Tolerable."

"Well, we'll try him with a trot, to begin. We mustn't push our beasts at first. We may have a starn chase, as the sailors say, and that's always a long chase."

So they rode, Gorham taking the lead, and sullenly brooding as he went, over his own mistakes, and cursing his own eyes and head for his *"oversteeping"* himself in whisky the previous night, and oversleeping himself that morning.

"Now," said he to himself; "now, I could ha' had the whole thing fixed beautiful, and made certain, if I could have trusted that catamaran, Mother Moggs, and that poor devil, her son! I could ha' blocked up the 'gap,' and caught him in a perfect trap. But he's not the man to run and leave all that property behind! No, no! He'll try to dodge about, and lie low, till he thinks the thing's blown over, or I'm blown up! at least, we'll have a look for you, 'Old Grizzly,' in your beautiful cavern and about. It's the way with the old fox, to double about till he gets tired, and then make for his hole. It'll do no harm to feel for him there, though I guess he's got a dozen other holes for hiding. To be sure he has! And yet a something seems to tell me that I'll catch him *there;* though he'll be a great fool to go to a place which he now knows I knows all about!"

Gorham had his monitor also.

He and his companion rode at a trot till they came to Swales'. The detective, Smith, had taken post about half a mile beyond Swales' cabin, which occupied a little hollow of the hills a few hundred yards from the road, and quite out of sight from it.

Smith was on the watch, apparently, as vigilantly as any employer could discern; but it was with disgust, wonder, and anger that Gorham heard him reply to his question—

"Yes, there was a man on a white horse, that I seed, just for a minute, on the top of yonder hill you sees to the left. In a minute he was out of sight and gone. I reckoned he was some person living on a farm thereabouts, for you see 'twan't on the road at all, but jist out thar among the hills, a'most a mile off."

"And you didn't put out after him? Hell and brimstone, man, what are you good for? Where's your sense? Why, that was he, for all the world! Among the hills—yes; to be sure, among the hills! Ef a man's got to go over a hill, why, he'll cross it and a dozen hills to the back and sides of it! Now push for that hill; take the lead, and a thousand to one you'll find a track there, and one that'll lead us into the main trace for the river. Drive ahead, and lose no more time. How long ago was it that you seed him?"

"I reckon about an hour."

"How did he ride when you saw him?"

"Why, I told you on a white horse."

"I mean at what *gait* did he go."

"I seed no gate—'twas on the naked hill, I tell you."

"Curse you, man, can't you understand? was the horse going fast or slow—in trot, or canter?"

"Oh, that's it! Why, he was going in a long lope; and I reckon it tuk him only three lopes to git out of my seeing."

Gorham looked as if he could have brained the simple constable where he stood. He grasped his rifle with the gripe and action of one who was prepared to deal a mortal blow, exclaiming, "You most eternal bloody ass!"

"Don't strike him, Mr. Gorham," said the other detective.

"Strike me!" cried Smith, lifting his own weapon defiantly; "let him only try it if he durst! What's he making a fuss about? I watched the road he put me to watch. He didn't expect me to be watching every hill, and shooting every farmer that happened to be on a white horse? Besides, neither his rifle nor mine, I reckon, is the we'pon to reach a person half a mile away."

"Oh," said Gorham, with a more refined irony than could have been expected of him, "your name is Smith, and I guess you'll never be the better for it. But push on, Smith; I'm not going to strike you."

"I reckon not; you're sensible, Mr. Gorham, for it takes two on us to play at that rifle game; and if my name is Smith—and I don't know what you've got to say agin that name—I can show you as big a bunch of the whipcord in this arm hyar as ever handled a sassy fellow when he had more tongue than teeth."

"Oh, don't be angry, Smith, but push ahead!"

Smith sullenly led the way. The hill was reached. The tracks of the horse were fresh over what was a blind path.

Like a hound, Gorham, having dismounted, coursed about, and soon found the obscure passage, leading through circuitous boulders and thick clumps of laurel, down into a hollow, where the obscure avenue opened at once to the hilltop on one hand, and the "Shades of Death" on the other. Following the tracks of the white horse, he found, half a mile beyond, where the rider had emerged—rounding other great boulders which obscured the route—into the great traveled road from the river to the court house in one direction, and to the "Mills' Gap" in the other. All was clear, and Gorham now chuckled.

"We'll earth him now!—I guess I know where to find the fox. I see the end of his tail! let's go ahead. Keep close to me, men, and be ready with your rifles the moment you hear me call!"

There was an exulting demon now speaking through all the tones of his voice, and giving a fearful impulse to his blood, which he imparted through his spurs to his steed. Gorham rode a fine, high-mettled and fast horse, very far superior to the steeds of his followers. His steed was not equal to the white of Voltmeier, but it soon went ahead of his companions. Possessed by his demon of greed, Gorham gave little heed to the detectives; and, like other fox-hunters, dashed ahead, never stopping to ask what saddles were emptied in his rear.

It does not much matter what passion it is that impels, whether avarice, or lust, or hate, and the thirst for revenge; but when it gets the bit fairly between its teeth, it is very apt to ride to the devil. If Voltmeier had a demon riding with him on his saddle-bow, and whispering him as he goes, Gorham was not less well provided with his evil spirit; and while the one brooded gloomily over the prospect of meeting and wrestling with his Fate, the other was hardly less insane with his dream of grappling with his Fortune. Both were fast riders, but Voltmeier was in the lead. Knowing this, Gorham used his rowels freely, calling ever and anon to his followers, "Come on, men, come on!"

And miles behind him came other riders, who cried to each other at each turn of the road, "Come on! come on!"

So Major Henry led Harness at a pace even faster than that honest yeoman thought necessary. So the deputy sheriff rode a few miles further in the rear, and he called to the constable, who followed on a lean jade, "Come on, Bullwinkle!"

And the impatient spirit of Fergus Wallace murmured, even as he rode, to itself, "How slow are these horses of Graham!"

And Mignon ever and anon would clap her little hands and cry, "Oh, how happy it will make papa! He is not gone yet! Harness says so; how happy he will be!"

And when Major Henry and Harness had reached the hill at Swales', there might be seen three horsemen, at equal distances, crossing a mountain spur a mile or two ahead, one after the other rising to the top of the height, and passing out of sight till all had gone down into the valley, to ascend still other heights beyond.

These were dimly descried by Harness, and the sight troubled him, as he saw the direction they were taking; but he said nothing of his fears to Major Henry, but put a new spur into the flanks of his horse, and cried out, "Come on, Major! a leetle faster, if you please!"

There was a vague apprehension rising in the bosom of Harness, that his friend and patron was in danger from these three men; and he had heard of the order for Voltmeier's arrest.

Chapter LXXIII

ABOVE THE GULF

With the headlong haste of hate and cupidity, Richard Gorham pursued the chase with an eagerness which became more and more reckless at every forward bound of his horse. He already had distanced the detectives, who only occasionally caught glimpses of his outline, as he ascended the successive eminences before them, which happened to be naked of woods. Once, twice, and even thrice, at the beginning of this wild scour, had he reined in his steed and held up for a while, till they approached within speaking distance; then, shouting to them to "Come on!" he resumed his race, his thoughts too much possessed with the idea of having earthed his fox, and of dragging him from his hole, to allow him time for any prudent considerations.

Meanwhile, Major Henry and Ben Harness overhauled the detectives, and finally passed them. From these they learned who was the pursuing horseman ahead, and what was his and their mission. It somewhat surprised Henry that the order of court for the arrest of Voltmeier had *preceded* them in the hands of the Sheriff's officer, and he expressed his surprise to Harness. The latter found it a subject of surprise also.

"I don't see," said he, "how this fellow, Richard Gorham, should be made a Sheriff's officer. He had a very bad character in the country, long ago, and was suspected of being one of a gang of robbers all along the forks of the river. Some of our people had a thought of lynching him."

"Set a thief to catch a thief," said Henry. "The Sheriff, no doubt, found out his virtues, as a thief, and employed him as a thief-taker; but how he should start ahead of us to-day, I don't understand! Let us push on and see!"

And so they sped; the detectives following more slowly in the rear.

407

Gorham, meanwhile, was wholly out of sight of both parties, and was probably quite a mile or more ahead.

And what of him whose tracks were thus followed with such tenacious purpose—Voltmeier?

He has long since gained the rocky pass leading to the cavern. He has paused before the grim entrance and dismounted, leaving the famous white steed without, standing quiet, bridled and saddled as he came; with no halter—the trained veteran, who could be relied upon to maintain his post.

Voltmeier strode into the thick darkness of the cavern, dark and gloomy of soul as its own shadows; folded his arms over his breast, and stood erect and silent in the center of the dismal chamber, in which nothing could be seen.

Yet Voltmeier gazed steadily into the obscure vacancy around him, and, after a brief pause, spoke aloud, as if to one standing before him.

"Why have you brought me hither? For what purpose—what final consummation—what sublime sacrifice? I have fought against this coming, with all the will of my soul—with all the reasoning of my brain! Yet you have withstood me! And you have prevailed! I am here! What would you have of me now? I see not!"

He was answered by a low, rumbling sound, which issued from the dark recess of the cavern, where the artist, Gellert, had found his couching-place for so long a season.

Looking in this direction, Voltmeier beheld two small red, sharp eyes, twinkle and flash in the extremity of the cave—then, as he advanced fearlessly towards them, there was a rustling noise, and he was conscious of the vague outline of some beast rushing close beside him; rushing past him with the fleetness of wings, and making for the mouth of the cavern.

He struck at it as it passed, but without effect. It might have been fox, or wolf, or wild cat—he cared not which; but, in his imagination it was his embodied Fate.

"It takes what shape it will!" he muttered, as it went, and as he followed to the entrance of the cave. There, it was no longer to be seen; but the white horse stood, with his ears erect; and, with a great snort greeted the reappearance of his master.

In this incident, as in almost every other, now, Voltmeier's imagination beheld an omen; all things, sights and sounds, seemed to sublime his fancies, and inform his brain with a fearful signification.

"That beast," he said, looking to the still trembling steed—"is not one to be terrified by any outlaw—whether fox or wolf—of the forest!"

He took a pellet of opium from his box. He had taken more than one that morning, already; and since the fearful conflict with the stallion. He recalled the events of that conflict.

"Why should that brute have so madly struggled to resist me— fighting against this progress—unless he had some consciousness— some blind terror, informing him of unknown and incomprehensible dangers? Why so resolute to rush even among the pathless boulders, and up the difficult heights, unless to avoid the *one* route to which I turned his head? And whence that midnight rush of the strange horseman, that swept by me like a hurricane; whom Harness could neither see nor hear? And why the goading impulse, which I, too, have fought against in vain, which has brought me hither, now? And why should I linger here, now? Fergus Wallace must be released by this time. Why should I wait the intelligence by Harness? Why not pursue my way, as my reason prompts and counsels, and hie to the seaboard and across the seas? What prevents? I can hear as well in Germany as here. We can meet there. We can once more reunite; I shall live to behold and to bless these dear children, and, under a more gracious destiny, perchance, behold *their* children rising beneath my eyes, each bearing those features of Catharine, my beloved, which gleam on my sight in nightly vision. Surely, this is the right reasoning, the wise counsel; it is the conviction of my mind. Why then delay? I have but to *will* it, and my good horse awaits my will! I will go. I will not be resisted now! Seek not to keep me back, ye Fates! I am still your master!"

And so saying, he took but one step forward, in the direction of his horse when he sank down, as with a sudden weakness, on the spot where he stood at the moment of speech—upon the great boulder, on the edge of the river, which overhung the precipice and gulf.

We have seen him with Gellert, bestriding that very rock, and hurling down into the boiling waters which raged in the abyss below, all the mysterious implements and materials of their secret workings within the cavern.

The gulf had swallowed them from sight, and still its jaws were open wide, as if ready for other treasures. Still roared the cataract above, with its eternal rush of waters, which, churned into perpetual foam among the rocks, kept up a continuous chant of fates and destinies.

Voltmeier stretched himself out feebly upon the huge boulder, which, presenting an inclined plane to the shore, rose gradually above the rapids, and terminated in a great cliff, projecting over the abyss.

Here he lay, sensible, and much wondering over the sudden weakness which seemed to paralyze all his limbs. He resorted again to his opium box, and murmured again his old philosophy.

"It is the Fate! The Destiny! As my *will* conquers, my sinews shrink. As my resolve strengthens, my muscle fails! Who shall tell me of this *free will* of manhood, when a power which he can not resist thus interposes at a moment, paralyzing the physical when it fails to combat the intellectual man! For a time my intellect failed me! I obeyed an impulse! I am here; dragged, driven here by that impulse! And now, here, when my will reasserts my manhood, lo! my limbs fail me! I can neither fight nor fly. What shall come of this?"

At that moment the white steed whinnied cheerfully.

"The brave beast! He summons me! I will obey *this* impulse! I can surely ride! We will go! I will not succumb! I will be strong. Hence, potent enslaver, I will succumb to you no more!"

With these words, he threw his opium box into the gulf, and, with desperate effort, rose to his feet; rose to his horse and mounted, though feebly. Then, looking wan and wild, he twitched the bridle nervously, and the beast and rider moved slowly away from the mouth of the cavern,—taking that backward path which we have seen them travel of yore, when, changing his black steed for the white, Voltmeier took the easier route from the cavern to the farmstead of the Harness family.

Scarcely had he started on this route, when he arrested the motion of his steed, and eagerly bent forward, shading his eyes, and gazing afar off, up the plane of a small mountain, which closed the valley where he then stood.

There came a horseman, riding fast along the mountain. His course was for the valley, and he was then, when discovered, about to cross the last ridge, which led to the descent. Voltmeier exclaimed:

"Can it be? Gods, Fates and Devils,—I understand you now! Ha! ha! ha! These are your mysterious ways! Thus ye bring about your processes for atonement; for revenge! Thus hound on your victims, one to the other, neither knowing what rein it is that guides, what spur it is that goads! and all the while, ye look down from your eminences, laugh at the blind fools as they hurry headlong—they too, perhaps, laughing all the while—to the precipice, and the eternal doom! It is well! and ye are welcome! Now shall I drink hot blood! Now do I comprehend ye all! I see my way! I know the task which is assigned me! I am again strong! The Fates second my will! I am again their master!"

The horseman speeding down the mountain was Richard Gorham! He was alone, far in advance of all who followed him; and, reckless as before, he plunged forward, obedient to *his* Fates!

Chapter LXXIV

THE CROUCHING TIGER

Voltmeier was once more strong as a lion. His courage came back to him. His muscles were newly corded for strife. His nerves no longer failed. In a moment he seemed to recover the best energies of his nature. In a moment, all doubt and despondency, all fluctuation of purpose, was at an end, and his whole soul was concentrated upon a single thought. The pangs, goadings and vexations, the torture of pride, and the mortifications which he had suffered, because of the hounding hate and mercenary passions of this invader of his happy home, were all to be avenged, and the tiger appetite absorbed all of the moral and mental nature of the diseased, but powerful man. He was the embodiment now of an insane appetite, which had been growing within his bosom for a long season, and which now resolved every purpose of his life into one, and that one sublimed by a demonic intensity.

With his keen falcon eyes he had discovered the horse of Gorham. He knew the beast well. It was one of his gifts to discern at a glance the peculiar physical characteristics of beast and man, and once seen, neither was ever forgotten. He possessed a wondrous power of vision. He was sure of the steed of Gorham at the first glance; and a few moments more enabled him, with like certainty, to recognize and be sure of the person of the rider.

It was with a hoarse chuckle that he ejaculated:

"Ha!—I have it! Ho!—about, good steed! about! One task more, and you shall have rest! About! about!"

He wheeled the animal out of sight, passing around a group of rocks which effectually concealed him from the approaching horseman. He could circle this group of rocks, and find his outlet into a narrow gorge, among isolated spurs of the group, which opened upon the valley through which Gorham was forced to pass.

Here, completely hidden from all eyes, in a region which he well knew, he felt himself fully the master of the situation; and, though raging inly with a tiger passion, he was able, in that moment, to recall all the cool, deliberate aim and resolution which enabled him to keep himself and steed grimly erect, with stonelike stillness, waiting the moment when he should spring upon his prey.

Behind those rocks, standing thus,—boiling with passion as we know—his self-constraint was wonderful. As they stood, horse and man, immovable as if wrought of the massy granite grouped frowningly above them, they made a study for the sculptor.

While the *features* of Voltmeier exhibited an almost demonic agony of impatience, every muscle was made rigid under his will, as if horse and man had suddenly become petrified, the very moment when every vein and artery was glowing with the most fiery sense of life!

Verily, they made a monumental group in repose, as perfect as the sculptures of the churchyard; but the repose was that of the tiger, crouching, with all his muscles gathered up, prepared and ready for the spring upon his prey; and the moral of the study brought with it the grandest images of Death.

Chapter LXXV

THE SHOCK OF STEEDS

Richard Gorham had his insanity also!

We doubt if any passion, wrought to intensity, is without its insane element. The mind ceases to govern; the thought becomes sluggish; there is a feverish irregularity of the blood, and the whole temper of the man is wrought up to a general recklessness, which leaves no moment for the reflective mood, or for that calm of mind which is capable of self-restraint.

So the fool exults in his cups; so the fox-hunter goes rushing through the thick forests, witless, in the absence of thought, whether his brains are dashed out or not, against the impending branches of the tree. So men provoke what they call Fate—in other words, make their own destinies, and charge their several insanities upon the gods!

The sources of insanity in the case of these two men were very unlike; the one elevated by education, by fine tastes, the love of art, a naturally brave and beautiful intellect; yet morally and mentally corrupt, having certain morbid characteristics, which were heightened by peculiar studies, and, perhaps, by the very sensibilities which belonged to his endowments.

The other was endowed with the fox brain. He had cunning in high degree; the devil's wisdom; and that which, as it is the one most apt to bring with it worldly prosperity, is most preferred and honored among the great portion of mankind.

Cunning is the quality with which Mammon endows his worshipers. Wisdom is the gift of the great God only.

Gorham's cunning kept him superior to the subordinates of his outlaw associations; superior to their gross appetites and lower impulses. But he, too, had his lusts and passions, which he indulged only when these were not in conflict with his policy of cunning.

This property and policy of cunning prompted his curiosity, in the discovery of Voltmeier's secret. When found, the same cunning suggested the profits to be derived from the fears which he naturally supposed Voltmeier would entertain, at the betrayal of that secret. Voltmeier's treasures were to be drawn upon *ad libitum,* according to his desires.

His lusts were awakened into unwonted activity by the beauties of Voltmeier's daughter.

He was not the person to rise to any adequate conception of the character of Voltmeier. He did not know or conjecture that the sense of annoyance, pursuit or persecution, was to him a keener pain and a greater terror than any he could ever entertain of human law or social opinion. Goaded on these points, he would rather brave the worst issues and perils of life than linger under the annoyance of a single fear.

With prosperity, the head of Cunning is apt to turn as quickly as that of any other fool! Cautious and circumspect, till he had realized money in abundance, and had become the possessor of Voltmeier's secret, Gorham then grew profligate and vain; and, as we have seen, soon passed into those brutal excesses which fully developed the purely animal in his nature. In his present chase of his victim he had given free vent to his indulgence, by which his brain was blunted to all sense of danger, and only accessible to the one leading idea, of securing the fugitive whose escape from the country was the loss of his treasury.

He drew repeatedly, as he rode, upon his flask of mountain whisky, and as he cantered up the last ridge, looking down upon the valley, in whose bosom, unsuspected, lay the great cavern of Tselecè, he drew the flask from his pouch, took a deep swallow of the naked and fiery draught, and, waving his hands backward, he shouted—

"Come on!" as if his detectives were close at his heels; then plunged rapidly down the slope of the hill, while the valley opened silently and innocently before him.

But for the intensity of his passion, the liquor he had swallowed would have laid him prostrate and senseless along the rocks. But there is a degree, beyond which, while passion is triumphantly employing human energies, when alcohol seems to lose its effect, or asserts it only in the last moment, when, the conflict over, the whole system collapses, from the very exhaustion of nature.

"Come on, fellows!" murmured, rather than cried aloud, the

frenzy-goaded inebriate, as he plunged over the hillside. "Come on, brisk, fellows, and be ready! we'll smoke the old fox out of his hole. You'll git your pay, fellows—good pay—all in good money; no '*nums*' (shams); no '*queer*' or '*kone*' (counterfeit bills); good '*flimsies*' (bank notes) or the genuine yellow gould! Every man that does his work shall have his share. Once I git hold of the old fox, he shall bleed; and, jist as he bleeds, you shall all drink. Come on! we'll have him soon!"

Did you ever see an urchin, feeling for a rabbit in a hollow tree, take hold of the tail of a snake? Did you ever witness the countenance of an old hunter who enters the cave of a bear, hoping to kill her cubs, and finds himself in the embrace of the she bear? or did you ever, pursuing the antelope, find yourself suddenly confronted by a panther? Imagine your own sensations, at such experiences, then try to divine those of the hitherto exultant Richard Gorham, when, chuckling with glorious anticipations, he descended the heights, down into the gorge which opened upon the valley leading to the river, he heard a wild yell, accompanied by the rush of what he thought a mountain torrent, when he saw, but for an instant, a great white shape, too rapidly rushing on for his senses to define, and felt, an instant after, such a concussion as lifted him, for the moment, high in air, then hurled him headlong, in the next moment, stunningly to the earth.

Such was the sudden, unexpected, wild surprise of Gorham, in the very midst of his most grateful reveries.

Grim as death, gloomy as the grave, remorseless as hell, Voltmeier waited for the moment for his victim to descend the hill and penetrate the gorge leading to the valley. He knew every foot of the ground, and, whether he could watch and did see the several successive movements of Gorham, or could so distinguish them by the ear, he so timed his own movements as to put the rowel to his steed at the critical moment. He was an old soldier, and, by the way, would have been famous at a charge.

Suddenly, the grouped statues of man and horse became animated with life. The steed sprang forward with a bound, which increased in length with every touch of the rowels; and by the time he had rounded the piled rocks which had concealed him, and came within leaping distance of the gorge, Gorham was emerging from it into the valley.

It was then that the shout of Voltmeier—rather the howl of a wolf or tiger than the cry of a man—burst upon the senses of Gorham. Then it was that, driving the goad still deeper into the flanks of his steed than ever, Voltmeier drove him forward with an impulse which nothing could resist—drove him forward headlong, full against the breast of Gorham's horse, as he had, that morning, impelled the stallion against the rocks.

The momentum given to Gorham's horse, coming down the mountain slope, was such as to prevent him profiting by that howl of warning. Instinctively, he strove to swerve aside from the vague, undefined bulk and force which he felt were coming upon him with the rush of the whirlwind. In an instant the two steeds thundered against each other, and both went down in the terrible concussion.

Gorham's horse lay insensible. That of Voltmeier was soon again upon his legs, but looked astare as if staggered by fright, stunned, and only half conscious. Both men, however, were quickly upon their feet. Both were good horsemen, and at the moment of collision, Voltmeier, cool as reckless, had extricated his feet from the stirrups, and thrown himself to the earth in safety.

Gorham was almost as quick of movement, and it so happened they had thrown themselves off on different sides, and the horse of Gorham, apparently insensible, lay between them, while Voltmeier's was struggling up from the ground.

In that moment, Gorham recognized his ancient master, and the old instincts of fear and deference prevailed. A single glance of the eye showed him the demonic fires in that of Voltmeier; and in the next moment, the lithe and athletic form of the latter had leaped across the body of the fallen steed, while he shouted terribly:

"Now, hound of hell, we will settle this long account between us!"

Gorham did not wait for the assault. That eye—that voice—that action—infused him with a sudden and inexpressible horror. Though armed with pistols, he did not think to use them, but darting onwards in the direction of the heights along the river, he fled in silence, terror lending wings to feet which were still those of youth, and always possessed of strength and fleetness, which did not desert them now. And, strange to say, this strength and fleetness under the impulse of his surprise and terror, seemed in no degree to suffer from the potent draughts, which, while on horseback, had goaded him to recklessness. He fled like a deer, bounding first along the valley, then taking the direction for the rocks along the river.

In taking this direction alone, did he show the absence of that cool sense and resolute possession which might have saved him. The rocks which bounded the river constituted a terminus which forbade escape. He could not leap the gulf nor climb the cataract; and, unless able and prepared to stand at bay, there was no hope for him.

Voltmeier was already at his heels. Though twice his age, this lithe and powerful man, under the impulse of such a mood as then fired him, was, perhaps, quite as fleet as the fugitive. But terror has a wondrous power of wings, and at no period in his life had Richard Gorham ever shown himself more sensible to fright, or more agility in flight. Never looking behind him, or, if thinking to do so, that occasional howl in his ears—"Hound of hell, I have thee!"—drove him again forward, till, half breathless, when they had sped nearly the whole length of the valley, were parallel with the cavern, and the great boulder ledges along the river rose conspicuous before them, did he pause and confront his pursuer, this time with pistol cocked and ready in his hand.

Voltmeier saw no pistol, and heeded no weapon. He saw only a victim of the Fates. With the pause of Gorham, and upon his turning, the pursuer bounded forward.

The pistol was fired.

Did the shot tell?

There was no recoil in the pursuer. On he came; and yet the calm looker-on might have seen, what Gorham did not—that his breast was covered with blood in an instant.

The fugitive resumed his flight—turned again at the foot of that great broad boulder, plain of surface, which, rising from the rocks, stretched up and peered over the abyss of waters—turned, and again fired.

The shot was answered with a shout of scorn and rage, as Gorham, throwing away his empty weapons, darted up the slope of the rock, hardly knowing whither he went, and now doubly given to despair, as he seemed to have made no impression upon his foe. Did he indeed bear a charmed life?

Voltmeier, in another moment, bounded up the rock after him, howling again and again, as he came on, the one terrible cry, "Now, hound of hell, I have thee!"

Richard Gorham could no longer escape or evade the mortal conflict. The cataract was plunging down before him, a mighty waterspout; the abyss was boiling and raging like a cauldron, covered with foam, all around and beneath him. He stood on the very brink of the precipice, and his mortal foe confronted him, barring the only passage to the shore. He now saw that Voltmeier was covered with blood, and he leaped towards him to anticipate the leap of the latter, and baffle its momentum. Another moment found them grappling together in deadly embrace.

Chapter LXXVI

THE LEAP OF THE CATARACT
AND PASSAGE OF THE GULF

It was at the very moment when the apparent climax had been reached, that Major Henry and Ben Harness had attained the summit of that last mountain spur, which looked down over the gorge and into the valley leading to the cavern and the rock.

All the scene lay open before them, and, as they paused for a moment, to trace out the pathway for easy descent, an excited exclamation from Harness drew Henry's attention, while his finger pointed to the still prostrate situation of Gorham's horse. That of Voltmeier, meanwhile, was seen slowly marching on in the direction which his master had taken. At length, the eye of Harness ranging to the rocky terminus of the valley, he cried out:

"Good God, Major Henry, they are fighting!"

"Who are fighting—where?"

"See, there! Look over the valley to where the great boulder glistens under the spray from the cataract. Two men are fighting. It must be the Colonel and that scoundrel, Gorham."

"I see—I see! They grapple!"

"And it is a death-grapple, you may be sure, for one or both! That fellow, Gorham, has the bone and muscle; but the Colonel has the heart! Ha! see! They are down together, one atop of the other."

"Which is uppermost?"

"I can't tell yet! They twist about like snakes! Now, I see! The Colonel has him down. No! He is uppermost—the wretch—Gorham —he is uppermost now!"

"Look again, Harness—my eyes are too old to distinguish."

"There's no telling which is which—now one appears atop, and now the other! I know it by the Colonel's hunting shirt. God! they must be on the very edge of the rock, and over the gulf! The

420

smoky spray from the cataract seems to cover them. How they twist, as if they knowed the danger!"

"Let us hurry forward, Harness; we may be in time!"

"Not possible, Major! It'll be all over before we can git through the gorge. It's too close a hug, there, of them two men, in that place, to hope to reach 'em now to do anything. It's death for one or both on 'em, or I never see'd men in a desperate fight afore! Ha! the Colonel's up—they're both up, and on their legs, and apart; but the Colonel gives a spring, and now they clinch again! Lord God! Major, could we ha' got here an hour sooner!"

"Let us hurry down now, Harness! I can't stand it any longer here. I am in agony! Hurry down—hurry down! It is possible we may be in time to prevent mischief."

"As you say, sir; but there's no time left for them two men! They're both of 'em on the leaping-off p'int—on the very varge of eternity!"

"Do you see them now, Harness?"

"I see nothing, Major! My eyes are all blinded with water. As you say, let us hurry down; although we'll be too late, I reckon."

Putting spurs to their horses, they made their way down the hill and into the gorge, whence, until they should enter the valley, nothing more of the combatants could be seen. Let us return to them, and anticipate the arrival of Henry and Harness.

The momentum obtained by Gorham, in his forward leap, to encounter the panther-like bound which Voltmeier had made towards him, on first ascending the rock, had not saved him! The fierce impulse of Voltmeier had borne him down, and he himself had gone down with him in the gripe of Gorham; but Voltmeier remained uppermost.

Gorham had fallen heavily; but his senses had come back to him; his mind, spite of drink, was fully in hand of his will. He felt the desperate situation in which he stood; he fully comprehended the deadly nature of the conflict, and nerved himself to the uttermost.

Voltmeier, pressing down upon him, breast to breast, now seized him by the throat, and with his face thrust into Gorham's—his eyes glaring close, with fiery glance, directly into his, he gnashed the words through his teeth—into the very ears of the other:

"Hound of hell, thou shalt have thy reward! Thou hast hunted after it long enough! Oh, wretch, brute, dog of hell, thou'st dared to speak to me of *my* daughter! Ha, ha, ha! That insolence dooms thee! Thou shalt wallow in all the sulphurous fires of hell, ere an hour shall pass over thee! Ha! dost thou feel me now, villain? I am on thee! I am thy Fate, dog of damnation, and thus—thus—"

His speech was arrested. Gorham had drawn his knife, and answered the imprecations of his enemy with a stab in the side! It would seem that Voltmeier had no weapons. He had used none. As he felt the wound, which momentarily checked his speech, he cried:

"Ha, ah! villain! but it will not save thee! Thou shalt die!"

And, regardless of another and another stab, he continued the effort to strangle the other by throttling. He had nearly succeeded, when Gorham, by a desperate effort, and the concentration of all his strength, shook him off; and both staggered to their feet, apart; but only to reunite, in another moment, in the same deadly embrace.

Voltmeier was now covered with blood. The stabs, delivered awkwardly, and with an arm half paralyzed by the incumbent body of Voltmeier, were hardly well directed, and did not, perhaps, penetrate very deeply; and though drawing blood freely, were little more than flesh wounds. The pistol shots had one or both told upon him, but to what degree, and how far fatal, may not be said.

But pistol shot and dagger stroke seemed equally ineffectual to lessen the demonic strength or subdue the demonic will of Voltmeier. Not a moment of respite did he yield his victim.

Gorham presented the naked knife to his breast as he came on; but he either seemed not to see or to regard it; rushing upon his enemy with that desperation — that utter recklessness of life, which, of all other aspects, is most apt to make an enemy quail, if not despair.

Gorham, with pistols empty, and reduced to defend himself with the knife only, against one who seemed to bear a charmed life, might well be supposed to feel like Macbeth, when made to "despair *his* charm;" finding the prophetic speeches of the witches to be mere fictions, keeping "the word of promise to the ear," but "breaking it to the hope." But he nerved himself, as well as he might, like Macbeth, for the final issue.

At the next bound of Voltmeier, Gorham's knife entered his arm. Was his own palsied, that he had failed to reach the heart? But the action of Voltmeier was that of a maniac, and every look and shrieking cry which he gave forth, as he made his bound, was that of a maniac!

No knife, no sinewy effort, could prevent that deadly grapple which followed, and which bore Gorham to the very edge of the gulf, while the blinding spray of the cataract was showered freely over both.

They writhed together in the new struggle, as Harness had described, like snakes enveloped in each other's folds! Even as the king, or thunder snake, drops from the tree upon the war rattle, and ties him up in his muscular embrace, so grasped Voltmeier in his sinewy arms, the venomous — but, in that embrace, the almost powerless victim! Desperate, indeed, were Gorham's last struggles to avoid the precipice to which he was rapidly being borne. Again and again he stabbed, but with no result promising safety. Then Voltmeier, possibly finding his own strength failing, grasped Gorham in his arms about the waist, and, with Herculean effort, lifted him up— away from all support—and suspended him for a moment over the gulf in air.

It was then Gorham's turn to cling to the neck of his enemy; to cling and cry aloud for mercy.

Voltmeier laughed bitterly, as he cried:

"Hold fast, dog of hell! Hold fast; and we make the acquaintance of the Fates together!"

With these words he plunged forward, into the shower of the cataract; into the boiling bosom of the gulf; while his howl of exultation silenced the roar of the falling waters.

Terribly piercing was the one shriek of Gorham, as, still clinging wildly to his enemy's neck, he was borne by his embrace into the deep waters.

The cataract caught them beneath its ever-tumbling torrents. The gulf received them in its ever-boiling cauldron of white foam and mysterious depths. They were whirled about helplessly in its circling eddies; in the resistless whirlpool, helpless as starlings with shut pinions and borne before the storm.

Gorham tried to extricate himself, but Voltmeier kept him down! Once he rolled uppermost, but could not shake himself free of that constrictor fold, which, in his death-spasms, the latter had taken upon him!

And then Voltmeier rose again above him; rode above him; rolled over him, with shout and shriek, and with ever-tightening folds, with his chin buried in the beard of the victim—and his eyes glaring hate into those which looked up only with terror—he pressed him down, down, down, into the gulf, which swallowed them both from sight.

Two arms for a moment appeared above the waters, one hand still grasping a knife, and striking wildly; the other thrown up in air, and grasping vaguely, as if seeking for some support, and then all disappeared.

The cauldron boiled on as before, without impediment! The torrent of the cataract poured over them; and when Major Henry and Harness reached the spot, there was no sign of human life on rock or water!

There was blood, however, a perfect stream of it, from the base of the boulder to its upper ledge, where the spray of the cataract was vainly striving to wash it out. A slouched hat lay upon the stone, which was supposed to be Gorham's. But, with all its voices, the ever-rolling torrents bounding from above, and the ever-chafing waters boiling in the gulf below, neither made report. The tragedy had no chorus.

But Henry and Harness had seen enough to conceive fully the catastrophe of the fearful drama. The Furies had done the work appointed of the Fates.

Chapter LXXVII

COLOPHON

While Henry and Harness were still examining the scene of this fearful drama, the detectives, now overtaken and joined by the Sheriff's deputy, made their appearance on that neighboring hilltop which had been the Mount of Vision for the former.

"Say as little as possible to these men," said Henry to Harness. "I will communicate with the Sheriff hereafter. We have no need to waste words on these subordinates. Let them find out what they can for themselves. We need not impart our conjectures to everybody. Let them do their own guessing."

"What does it all mean, Major Henry?" asked the Sheriff's officer.

"You see for yourself, sir, and may form your own notions. Here, you see, are blood stains enough to show that a fight has taken place between certain parties unknown; that some one, or both of these persons have been slain; that, if one survives, seeing us, he has fled! This horse, with his jaw broken, is a well-known horse of Col. Voltmeier. The horse which lies yonder, seemingly dead, with his neck broken, I suspect, must have had an owner. Whether that owner be living or dead, we can not say; but it may be well for you to explore all this neighborhood, and report to the Sheriff."

The detectives now explained that the dead horse was Gorham's, and further reported the objects of their mission; gave, in brief, all those particulars with which we are already familiar.

Henry and Harness left the Deputy Sheriff and detectives in unprofitable search after the supposed fugitive, whether Voltmeier or Gorham, whom they supposed to have sought shelter and a hiding-place, on foot, seeing the approach of other parties.

We may say in this place, that the search was pressed for several days without avail, Henry and Harness suppressing, for the sake of the family of Voltmeier, the details of the struggle they had witnessed, and their conviction as to the manner in which it ended.

Henry and Harness proceeded to "Keovala."

It was easy to impress the family with the belief that Voltmeier, as his letters had said, was on his way to Germany. Under some strange freak, or infatuation, he had fled the country, at the very moment when his interest in it had grown stronger than ever.

Mignon, and even Aunt Gertrude, were noways surprised at any of Voltmeier's caprices. He had trained them to perpetual surprises, and, though greatly regretting the freak which had kept them from a common progress together, in that tour of travel to which they all looked forward with enthusiastic desires, they were yet perfectly prepared to believe that Voltmeier would present himself as soon as they should reach the continent of Europe.

Fergus was not so easily satisfied, but he was somewhat bewildered. He could see that there was a mystery, and believed that Graham, or Henry, or both, possessed the clues to it; but his good sense taught him the propriety of waiting for a while on them, assured that they had good reasons for present silence, and that, in good time, all would be made known.

This policy was made the more apparent to him by the urgency of Henry and Graham, in pressing the immediate departure of the family for Germany. And this urgency was enforced to Wallace by that equally of Mignon and Aunt Gertrude.

A few days found them prepared, and setting forth; the business of the estate, and the charge of "Keovala," being confided to Harness, under dispositions previously made by Voltmeier, himself.

It was found that the whole property was secured, jointly, to Mignon and her husband; with the single exception of certain possessions conveyed to Gertrude Leyfenholdt.

Graham and Henry were both apprised by letter, of their safe arrival in London; their transition to Paris, and thence to Germany.

But, no Voltmeier!

Mignon mourned and wondered, and Miss Gertrude, familiar with all his ancient haunts, and searching all of them, could find no traces of him. She, too, wondered. Old friends and associates, to whom he would surely resort, had heard nothing of him; and, with daily search, and daily question, and constant anxiety, months passed; then a year; and it was only after Mignon had become the mother of a beautiful girl, that Fergus Wallace was apprised by Henry, of her father's fate. It was only then that Mignon could endure to hear of it—then, when another being of love had found a central place within her affections.

She moaned and wept, for a while; would frequently moan and weep, and refuse to be comforted, until they put the baby in her arms! They gave to the child the name of Gertrude Voltmeier; and the weight of the name had no evil influence in retarding her growth!

After near three years of absence in Europe, chiefly in Germany and Italy, the family returned home, the young couple bringing with them two beautiful pledges of their fond and pure affections, a girl and a boy.

But, when they came to "Keovala," then the grief of Mignon burst forth afresh, as she thought of her father, and she buried her face in her husband's bosom, exclaiming:

"Alas, Fergus! that he can not behold and bless these beautiful and dear ones! How happy would it have made him!—and this boy, how he would have hugged him in his arms, and dandled him on his knee, and—and—oh! Fergus, the boy does so look like both of you!"

"He *does* see them, my Mignon, and bless them too, if our spiritual belief be worth a straw!"

"It must be so, Fergus!"

And the two hung over the little pallet where the babes were sleeping so sweetly, then sunk upon their knees in prayer.

It was their happy fortune that neither of them had sufficient self-esteem to possess a Fate! No Furies followed *their* footsteps, and their children, numerous and noble, grew, in turn, also to become fathers and mothers in the land!

Part II

EXPLANATORY NOTES

TEXTUAL APPARATUS

EXPLANATORY NOTES

1.1–5   The references to the "present population" of Spartanburg and to "the period of our narrative, some forty years ago" may cause confusion as to the intended time of the setting. By the "present population" of Spartanburg village, Simms presumably refers to the actual date of the writing of *Voltmeier*, 1868, although J. B. O. Landrum in his *History of Spartanburg County* (Atlanta, 1900), p. 37, gives the figure in 1870 as only 1,050, about one-fourth of Simms's estimate. Possibly Simms meant "the period of our narrative, some forty years ago" to refer to the period forty years prior to 1847 (the year when he first made the notes or initial sketch from which the novel derives), since the actual case in the United States Courts upon which the counterfeiting story is based was tried between the years 1805 and 1815. (See Introduction, pp. xix-xx.) However, Major Henry, who figures in the novel, and who was actually born in 1796 (see note for 3.15), is said to be "apparently of thirty years of age" (3.15-16), which might be an indication that Simms was thinking of a date some forty years before the publication of *Voltmeier*.

3.15   Major James Edward Henry (1796-1850), of Spartanburg, was a lawyer, and a member of the South Carolina House of Representatives from Spartanburg (1832–34 and 1840–50). Simms and Henry had served together as delegates in the Union Convention in Columbia in 1832. In 1844 both were members of the South Carolina House of Representatives Committee on Federal Relations. Henry had been Simms's companion on his 1847 expedition into the North Carolina mountains.

13.2–3   Fergus is mistaken; the quotation comes not from Shakespeare, but from Dryden's *All for Love*, I, 1.

15.27   The Bobos were a prominent Spartanburg family. Simpson Bobo (1804-1885), a leader of the Spartanburg Bar, was president of the Board of Trustees of Spartanburg Female College when Simms made the inaugural address at this institution on August 22, 1855. See S. Bobo, Esq., *Inauguration of the Spartanburg Female College* . . . (Spartanburg, S.C., 1855).

26.33 Jacob Dechard (variously spelled, e.g., "Deckard") of Lancaster, Pennsylvania, came from a noted German family of gunmakers. The familiar "Kentucky rifle" was well-known as a Deckard product. See A. Merwyn Carey, *American Firearms Makers* (New York, 1953).

28.23 Cherokee money: In a series of treaties between 1791 and 1805 the United States Government agreed to pay the Cherokees for cessions of land. (Charles C. Royce, *The Cherokee Nation of Indians*, U.S. Bureau of Ethnology, 5th Annual Report, 1883–1884, Washington, pp. 159, 169, 171, 175, 184, 189.)

53.1 Mills Gap: When Simms made his 1847 journey into the Blue Ridge, he visited at the home of Dr. Columbus Mills near the town of Columbus, N.C., the county seat of Polk County. Simms always spoke of Mills as "my kinsman," but actually Dr. Mills's mother, Sarah Robison Mills, was a sister of Simms's wife's grandmother. Columbus Mills was the grandson of Major William Mills, who after the Revolution moved from Rutherford County, N.C., across the Blue Ridge and settled on Clear Creek. "He cut the wagon-road across the mountain at this point, and hence it was always called, and is to this day, Mills Gap. He was the pioneer of that country and gave names to the mountain streams and places of that section. The most beautiful river in Western North Carolina, Mills' River, was named for him. He named the stream on which he lived Clear Creek and named the following mountains: Bear Waller, Sugar Loaf, Look Out, Bald Top, Pilot Point and Black Mountain. . . ." (Isabel C. Patterson, *Builders of Freedom and their Descendants*, Augusta, Ga., 1953, p. 164.)

69.35–70.12 The meter and stanza-form of these moralistic verses utilize a rhythmical pattern common to Goethe, Schiller, and other German poets of the period, but the poem is not characteristically Goethean.

88.27 Baldface whiskey is fresh from the still, without any aging.

Simms's sketch of "Part of the Range of Mt. Tryon, N.C." (See p. 433.)

Simms's sketch of the "Highest Peak of Mt. Tryon."

94.14 Old Tryon: See illustrations facing this page and p. 432 for the two sketches of Mt. Tryon which Simms drew in his 1847 notebook. The first he labeled "Part of the Range of Mt. Tryon, N.C." Below it he wrote "From the West porch of Dr. Mills's House." The second he labeled "Highest Peak of Mt. Tryon." Below it he wrote "Sunday Mg. 26 Sep. 1847. Went to Tryon Mountain — Tryon Mount. 3700 feet above the level of the surrounding country. The South view spread before us is South Carolina — 5 miles across the line."

103.12 grand cavern: A few lines in the 1847 notebook indicate the source upon which Simms was drawing when he made counterfeiting an important part of the plot of *Voltmeier*. "Friday mg. Off for Hickory Nut Gap—pass Green River and Broad river — residence of Allen Twitty, the famous counterfieter — his farm — his cave—& anecdotes of his career — his character—his *virtues*".

The Twitty family was prominent and highly respected in this region, and several of its members were known for their services to the country in the Revolution. Allen Twitty's marriage bond, dated February 27, 1787, is recorded in the Rutherford County Courthouse, as are deeds to large tracts of land on the Green River. A tract bought in 1801 (Deed Book 15-17, p. 255) and another bought in 1803 (Deed Book 20-21, p. 85) were acquired from General James Miller, possibly a relative of Twitty's wife, as the marriage bond gives her name as Martha Miller. In a deposition made on May 12, 1812, during Allen Twitty's trial on charges of counterfeiting, General Miller stated that he had known Twitty for forty years, "or from his infancy" (United States District Court, Raleigh, N.C. FRC # 83387, General Service Administration, East Point, Georgia). The records in Rutherford County also disclose that the first tract of land which Allen Twitty acquired on Green River was bought in 1795 from William Twitty and is described in the deed as being a part of the estate of Ambrose Mills, inherited by William Mills, the grandfather of Dr. Columbus Mills, Simms's host during the 1847 trip. It is interesting to note that on his 1842 trip to this region Simms had visited an inn at Rutherfordton where his host was one William Twitty.

103.31 It is possible that a German by the name of Christopher Bechtler living within about three miles of the town of Rutherfordton, N.C., may have served as the prototype for Simms's Gellert. A marker at this point states that Bechtler's Mint was established there in 1831, minting over $2,250,000 in gold before it closed about 1849. Bechtler and son and nephew were skilled German metallurgists, natives of the Grand Duchy of Baden. The elder Bechtler is described as being "rather mystical and imaginative, most Germans are, and superstitious to a marked degree." His will, written in German, was probated in 1844. At the time of Simms's 1847 trip to this region the business was being operated by the nephew as minter, gunsmith, miner, and jeweler. (Charles W. Griffin, *Western North Carolina Sketches*, Forest City, N.C., 1941, pp. 52-53.)

138   MICHEN-MALICO: The chapter title is from *Hamlet*, III, 2: "Marry, this is miching mallecho; it means mischief."

148.8   well known choral chant: From the Song of the Spirits in *Faust*, Part I, Scene 4. The translation at 148.10-36 and 265.12-13, 265.17-20 is probably Simms's own.

178.11   five beautiful cascades: Probably the five cascades of Pool Creek, above Lake Lure, a few miles from Chimney Rock, N.C.

190.7   circular mound: Such a mound, supposedly Indian in origin, still exists at the spot which Simms in 1847 located as the estate of the counterfeiter Allen Twitty. (See note for 103.12.) For Voltmeier's ascription of the building of these mounds to another race than the Indian, see Simms's comment in *Views and Reviews in American Literature, History and Fiction*, Second Series (New York, 1845), p. 80: "The vast mounds [of the southeast] . . . indicate a dense and stationary population—a people in possession of a considerable degree of science . . . . These works . . . were not works in the use of the red man . . . and must have belonged to a race having . . . far greater endowments and far greater necessities—by whom he was preceded, and whom he, in all probability, not only overthrew, but massacred. . . ."

216.12   Johann Kaspar Lavater (1741–1801), Swiss theologian and author, was father of what was called in Simms's time the science of characterology.

232.12 In 1742 Colonel William Graham settled in that portion of North Carolina which became Rutherford County. (Griffin, *History of Old Tryon and Rutherford Counties,* Asheville, N.C., 1937, pp. 46-48.) Simms may have used him as a prototype for the Colonel Graham of his story. The records of the county courthouse at Rutherfordton show a marriage bond of William Graham and Susanna Twitty dated December 29, 1806, just at the period when Allen Twitty was first indicted for counterfeiting.

240.2 the great gorge of the Tselica: Sims took "Tselica" to be the Indian name for the French Broad River. See the introductory note to his poem "The Syren of the Tselica," *Simms's Poetical Works,* I (New York, 1853), pp. 324-327.

246 The following synopsis of the preceding installments was supplied at the beginning of Chapter XLV in the *Illuminated Western World.* (See p. 444 for two emendations made in its text.)

> To those who have not had the pleasure of perusing this truly admirable work of the celebrated author, we will give the following synopsis, that the succeeding chapters may be read and enjoyed:

The "hero" of the romance is young Fergus Wallace, whose mother, dying, sent him up into the mountains of North Carolina, to seek out his Uncle Voltmeier. In following out this dying wish, the young man goes up into the wild and magnificent "up country," amid whose fastnesses, at the date of the story, dwelt a set of desperadoes, who, by horse-stealing, pillage, highway robbery, and the circulation of counterfeit money, became the terror of the whole region. Into the hands of these Mountain Men the youth falls, wounded almost unto death, and he is robbed and left for dead. Voltmeier, his uncle, under an impenetrable disguise, is, in reality, chief director of this gang of villains. He ascertains, by the property and papers found on the young man's person, who he is, and at once becomes his most tender nurse, under whose skill and the unremitting kindness of the Harness family, Fergus recovers. Voltmeier, in his true character, has a splendid estate further down the mountain range, in South Carolina, called Keovala, where he lives the princely gentleman planter. His family consists of himself, his beautiful daughter, Mignon, and his sister, Gertrude. Into this home Fergus is introduced. All are unconscious of Voltmeier's relations to the Mountain Men. Fergus becomes beloved by every member of the household, and in turn becomes so deeply attached to Mignon as to finally ask her hand in marriage. This greatly pleases her father, whose love for Fergus' mother had been very deep and strong.

Voltmeier having resolved to break up and scatter the villains comprising his band, had, by various arts, done so, but was followed by one of them like a fate—a scoundrel named Gorham, who, by accident, makes his way to the vicinity of Keovala, but is wholly unconscious that Voltmeier and his "old man" leader are one and the same person—so clever had been the leader's disguise and so subtle his movements.

At the point of the story where we now introduce the reader, Fergus, plighted to Mignon, has made a promising debut as a lawyer, in the neighboring county town, and is enjoying the smiles of all the Keovala household. Mignon—a maiden of exquisite mold in mind and body, gives him of the richness of her love, and all promises well. Voltmeier—a man of truly royal intellect, a scholar, and an accomplished gentleman—is outwardly calm, but inwardly is haunted by the shadow of his evil life. Gorham is on his trail; the very forest paths seem to lead him into the toils of his destiny. What that destiny is—what the fortunes of the lovers— what the career of Gorham, and of one of Voltmeier's old comrades and confidants, named Gellert, who fled to Germany when the mountain band broke up—it remains for the succeeding chapters to tell.

258.5   Furze must be one of the *seven. I only knowed four!:* The four are Bierstadt, Moggs, Brown Peters, and Swipes. Gorham, speculating upon the meaning of the figure 7 on the amulet, has in mind Bierstadt and his employees rather than Voltmeier's aliases.

265.12-13, 265.17-20   See note for 148.8.

347.24–25   The German may be translated as follows: "How nice! Then I shall bury these miseries in my own exempted ruin!"

388.21   Bürger's ride: The ballad "Lenore," by Gottfried August Bürger (1747–1794), was widely known during the "Gothic" phase of the Romantic movement.

399.21-22   The quotations are from the lyric at the beginning of Book III of Goethe's *Wilhelm Meister,* "Kennst du das Land."

D.D.
M.C.S.O.

TEXTUAL APPARATUS

INTRODUCTION

The textual history of *Voltmeier* is simple. No manuscript is known to have survived, and before the publication of the Centennial edition in this volume, the only printed form of the novel was that in the *Illuminated Western World*, which appeared in twenty-six weekly installments, beginning March 6, 1869.

The original serial form, which thus becomes copy-text for any subsequent edition, undoubtedly differed from Simms's manuscript in a great many details. Perhaps all of the differences were minor, the result of inevitable house-styling and emendation, conscious or unconscious, by the printers, and of the further changes that always occur if proofs are corrected without being read against copy. But possibly there were more significant changes, editorial in origin; Simms feared that cuts might be made in the text in order to make it fit serial format (see Introduction, p. xxv), and there is no evidence, and little likelihood, that the author saw proofs and thus could have corrected major editorial or compositorial blunders. The many obvious minor printer's errors in the text prove that no great pains were taken with its accuracy, and probably indicate that no greater pains were taken to follow copy faithfully.

A good many corrections and emendations, therefore, have been necessary in the Centennial edition of *Voltmeier*, and a good many further emendations were considered. But as a rule, changes were kept to a minimum, in order to avoid the danger of carrying the text a step further from the lost manuscript in a misguided attempt to bring it closer. When justification could be found for retaining the original form of the text, either in its accidentals or its substantives, no change was made. If in retaining a doubtful reading from the *Illuminated Western World* text the Centennial edition has occasionally preserved a compositorial error or editorial idiosyncrasy, rather than some actual feature of Simms's prose, the odds are that a more liberal policy of emendation would have lost a greater number of authorial readings than it recovered.

The same principle has been followed in avoiding, whenever practicable, regularization of the many inconsistencies within the text. A good many aspects of punctuation have been left irregular; for example, the placing of colons both before and after quotation marks. Both forms have historical justification. If the texture of Simms's prose was inconsistent in some respects in the *Illuminated Western World* edition of *Voltmeier*, it remains inconsistent in the Centennial edition. To bring his accidentals into greater conformity could conceivably affect the meaning of Simms's text, losing the flavor of some archaic or obsolescent form, altering the tone or rhythm of his prose. Spelling too has been allowed to remain inconsistent. In dialect the reasons for retaining irregularities are obvious; for example, there would be little justification in making consistent the spelling of *clark* and *clerk*, even though both appear in the speech of the same character (33.2, 33.8). It is possible that Simms spelled both the same way in his manuscript and a printer mistook an *a* for an *e*, or vice versa, but it is also possible that Simms was recording a variant pronunciation. Nor is there real justification for regularizing *leatle* and *leetle* (e.g., 54.28, 87.21). Although it is unlikely that Simms, if indeed he spelled the word differently in these two places in his manuscript, intended to indicate a difference in pronunciation, to regularize dialect, even when it is eye-dialect, is hardly more defensible than to correct it.

It might be argued that inconsistencies in form, spelling, and usage in Simms's own language, the descriptive portion of the narrative, should be considered in a different category from his dialogue. And it could be further argued that since the original serial publication of *Voltmeier* doubtless permitted a greater number of inconsistencies than would have occurred if the manuscript had instead been first published as a book, it is an editorial obligation, in now bringing the novel out in book form, to impose a greater degree of uniformity upon the text. Nevertheless, lacking manuscript authority, regularization runs the risk of losing manuscript readings.

In a few details—the spelling of proper names is an example—
inconsistencies have been removed. But to have eliminated the inconsistency between *Fates* and *fates* would have been to alter emphasis;
to have restored the accent to *role* or omitted it from *rôle* would
have been to lose some sense of a language undergoing change, of
a foreign word still in process of adoption into Simms's English.
With one exception, the rule followed in editing the Centennial
text of *Voltmeier* has been to preserve, despite inconsistency, any
feature of the original text for which there is demonstrable precedent
or justification in the published form of fiction in Simms's time, and
to preserve obsolescent and archaic spellings throughout. In order
to establish precedents in leaving doubtful readings unemended, the
standard historical dictionaries have been consulted. Simms's dictionary is not known, but several editions of Webster's and Todd's
Johnson-Walker dictionaries published during his lifetime have been
consulted for spelling and word-division.

The one exception to the principle of adhering to the form of the
copy-text, whenever possible, despite inconsistency, is in the italicization of punctuation before and after italic words. In the font used
by the *Illuminated Western World*, there is apparently no distinction
made between roman and italic commas, apostrophes, and quotation
marks. However, as is usual at this period, a clear distinction exists
between roman and italic colons, semicolons, question marks, and
exclamation points. Following italic words, these four marks of
punctuation, as a rule, are italicized in the original text. The Centennial text of *Voltmeier* follows this rule; and in addition italicizes
commas, apostrophes, and quotation marks both before and after
italic words. Not to do so would, in effect, imply an emphasis not
present in the original, where these punctuation marks are either
italic or roman according to their context. In the font used by the
Centennial edition, the existence of both the italic and the roman
forms of all punctuation marks except the period means that one
form or the other must be chosen; neither can do service for both
without calling undue attention to itself. In the one case (120.24)
where, in the original text, an exception is made to the rule of
following an italic word with an italic tall punctuation mark, it has
been emended to follow the general practice of the original. There
would appear to be little chance that such an inconsistency in the

original printed text was due to an attempt to follow faithfully the vagaries of an inconsistent manuscript. Simms's own practice, discernible in other manuscripts dating from this period of his life, was to indicate italics by drawing a short line under the middle of the word or phrase involved. Obviously he intended the whole word or phrase to be italicized, not just the letters immediately above his line, and there is no reason to suppose that the underlining was not also intended to apply to punctuation immediately following the italicized words. Finally, the Centennial edition italicizes parentheses around italic words. Although in the original text such parentheses are invariably roman, the font used by the *Illuminated Western World* did have italic parentheses, and they appear elsewhere in issues containing installments of *Voltmeier*. But the failure to use them in the original text of *Voltmeier* is an irregularity not likely to reflect an irregularity of Simms's manuscript.

The apparatus provided below for the Centennial text of *Voltmeier* has been kept as simple as possible. All textual notes, including those explaining refusals to emend, are included with the list of emendations in Table I. The three parts of Table II deal with compounds divided at the ends of lines in the original or in the present text. In Table III are listed the dates of the original serial installments.

Printer's copy for the Centennial edition of *Voltmeier* was a typescript prepared from a negative photostat of the file of the *Illuminated Western World* at the New York Public Library. Proofs were read four times against this photostat and once against a negative microfilm of the New-York Historical Society file. No textual differences between these two copies were revealed in the proof-reading process; nor were differences found when a number of passages were checked against the negative microfilm of a partial file of the *Illuminated Western World* at the Lilly Library. Galley proofs were read by five teams, page proofs by three. Proof was read by all members of the Editorial Board; and by Dr. William S. Kable and Dr. Gordon Lindstrand, and the following graduate student research assistants, of the University of South Carolina English Department: Mr. A. K. Butterworth, Mrs. Mary Meats, Mr. Stephen Meats, Mr. Noel Polk, Mrs. Miriam J. Shillingsburg, and Mr. Peter Shillingsburg. Special acknowledgment is due Mrs. Shillingsburg for her work upon the text and the notes.

J.B.M.

TABLE I: EMENDATIONS AND TEXTUAL NOTES

Listed here are all changes made in the copy-text, with the exception of the italicization of punctuation marks (see textual introduction pp. 439-40). The original reading appears to the left of the bracket, the emended Centennial edition reading to the right. Where no bracket appears the reading is the same in both texts and the refusal to emend is explained in parentheses.

Where an explanation of the change is necessary it follows in parentheses.

Heading: Foragers] Forayers (This error in the title of a Simms novel was left uncorrected in the heading of all twenty-six installments of *Voltmeier,* a probable indication that Simms did not see proof.)

3.3 day?"] day?
3.22 Bingham] Brigham
3.32 late?"] late?
4.2 pretext (Possibly Simms wrote "pretense" here, for "Pretense" at 4.5 sounds echoic; but the two words would not be easy to confuse in Simms's hand.)
6.22 had.] had."
7.29 Watty] Wattie (Cf. 15.33 and 336.15.)
17.17 docter] doctor
22.10 either.'] either.' "
22.15 Customers.] customers,
23.1 This] "This
24.13 flute.] flute."
27.6 Mogg's] Moggs'
27.10 *Mogg's*] *Moggs'*
28.2 want's] wants
28.17 togither.] togither."
28.24 Government.] Government."
29.22 Mogg's] Moggs'
34.5 "stand."] 'stand.' "

35.32 drink."] drink.
39.27 speak off] speak of (The possibility that Simms intended "off" to represent a mispronunciation seems slight, even though this is dialect; it does not occur elsewhere in the book.)
45.37 Methusaleh] Methuselah (cf. 81.4 Methuselah.)
46.23 horses] horses'
48.36 "monkey rock."] 'monkey rock.'
49.22 "The] The
53.1 Gap"] Gap'
53.10 Harness'.] Harness'."
56.6 Walter] Wallace
59.25 Harness'.] Harness'."
61.30 bnsied] busied (Turned "u".)
65.36 Hou] How
67.9 yeoman] yeomen
69.29 country.] country."
71.27 indeed!] indeed!"
73.20 kein] kin
73.24 kein] kin
74.10 any.'"] any."
77.22 "den"] 'den'
77.23 "den"] 'den'
78.17 git's] gits
79.38 "den"] 'den'
80.11 be] he

85.4   boiling] broiling (Cf. 87.9, "brile".)
86.4   its] it's
93.2   "good night,"] 'good night,'
93.24   witch!] witch!"
95.8-9   "Tumbling Terrapin"] 'Tumbling Terrapin'
96.30   Peter's] Peters'
97.10   now!] now!"
97.39   Moggs,] Moggs,"
98.12   Swipes] Swipes'
99.23   as goes] as it goes
103.21   advanced] advanced.
103.32   You.] You,
104.21   boson] bosom
105.3   intervals. Sometimes] intervals, sometimes
107.16   life.' "] life.'
110.16   electrial] electrical
110.34   me.] me."
116.23   see-] see, (The hyphen occurs at the end of a line in the original text; cf. the emendation at 116.24, where the comma, also occurring at the end of a line in the *Illuminated Western World*, obviously should be a hyphen. It appears very likely that in making a correction a workman confused the two lines and the comma and hyphen were exchanged.)
116.24   some, thing] something (See above.)
116.26   "It] It
120.12   fool's] fools
120.24   *them;*] *them;*
120.28   panther.)] panther.)"
121.2   *"jest a leetle"*] *'jest a leetle'*
129.31   night-fall.] night-fall."

130.4   "Here] Here
130.8   journew (Though it is quite possible that the "w" is simply a printer's error, perhaps Simms was attempting to render dialect pronunciation, or even a deliberately exaggerated mispronunciation.)
131.4   *blink—*] *blink—*"
132.20   tegether] together
134.20   you've] you're
139.4   satisfied.] satisfied."
143.32   wan't] want
144.24   its] it's
152.18   "den,"] 'den,'
153.2   mill-to-morrow] mill to-morrow (Another possible emendation here would be to replace the first hyphen with a dash instead of omitting it.)
155.24   *cachés*] *caches*
157.4   "Old Grizzly"] 'Old Grizzly'
157.13   "Old Grizzly's"] 'Old Grizzly's'
157.28   "Old Grizzly"] 'Old Grizzly'
158.6   let's] lets
158.30   swipes] Swipes
160.9   drink—] drink—"
160.26   to night] to-night
161.26   Augusta.] Augusta."
161.33   "den"] 'den'
171.1   I'll] "I'll
181.10   Swananoo] Swananoa
181.12   Henderson (Although the shortened form may have been intended, surely the town referred to here is Hendersonville, in Henderson County, rather than Henderson, which is in Granville County, an-

other part of the state entirely.)
185.15   twired] twirled
201.35   longer.] longer."
215.17   'Well] "Well
219.13   morning.] morning."
221.5   Tyron] Tryon
221.30   And] "And
223.8   allaboy'?] allaboy'?"
224.5   goood] good
229.10   Mill's] Mills'
230.34   Harnesss] Harness
233.12   sprinkt] sprinkled
234.16   deceived.] deceived."
236.5   sooth] soothe (This occurs at the end of a line in the original text, and the final "e" may have
been crowded out.)
238.36   him] him.
244.19   rifle] rifle.
251.11   Goneial] Goneril
254.22   comfortable.] comfortable."
262.32   his] her (The dog has
been identified as a "slut", 262.28
—i.e., a bitch.)
274.4   "Voltmeier] Voltmeier
275.29   him | self] himself (Hy-
phen missing at the end of a line in
the original text.)
288.6   "go,"] 'go,'
288.6   "go,"] 'go,'
302.8   sueing] suing
303.7   oi] hoi
308.18   an (Perhaps dialect; perhaps a "d" was dropped, as the
word occurs at the end of a line.)
312.7   hot.] hot."
312.26   "lynch him,"] 'lynch
him,'

312.28   "pose . . . us,"] 'pose . . .
us,'
321.26   "big fish"] 'big fish'
321.26   "nabobs"] 'nabobs'
321.37   awyer] lawyer (Letter
missing at the beginning of line in
the original text.)
322.37   want.] want."
323.29   "knock] 'knock
323.30   out!"] out!' "
328.24   Mignon] "Mignon
344.6   There] "There
344.7   to-day] 'to-day
344.23   moment s] moment's
347.9   stocked (Simms may have
written "stacked", but "stocked"
was not an unusual nineteenth-century spelling of the word for a fraud-
ulently arranged deck of cards.)
347.24   schon] schön (Here
and below at 347.25, the context
makes clear what German word is
required.)
347.25   braben] graben (See
above.)
347.35   guss] guess
348.38   "Old Grizzly,"] 'Old
Grizzly,'
355.25   This] "This
355.28   Fool] "Fool
356.7   Wallace] Henry
363.11   Swales] Swales'
363.13   "gap."] 'gap.'
372.4   yit,] yit.
374.6   power] former (The
passage calls for emendation; the
parallel construction of "former
. . . latter" fits, and "power" for
"former" is an entirely possible mis-
reading of Simms's hand.)

384.37   Ashtorath] Ashtoreth
385.23   Ashtorath] Ashtoreth
386.5   *esprit du*] *esprit de*
386.12   siezed] seized (A frequent misspelling of Simms's.)
387.16   sinkingly] sinking
388.21   Burger's] Bürger's
393.3   Keovala.] Keovala."
399.26   *àdios*] *adiós*
399.26   *àdios*] *adiós*
402.21   What] "What
403.37   him?'] him?"

404.4   'Curse] "Curse
416.4   *"nums"*] *'nums'*
416.4   *"queer"*] *'queer'*
416.4   *"kone"*] *'kone'*
416.5   *"flimsies"*] *'flimsies'*
421.3   Let] "Let
423.8   others] other's
427.25-26   had . . . No (This line
was repeated in the original text.)
435.32   Calolina] Carolina
435.37   houshold] household

TABLE II: WORD DIVISION

1

The following possible compounds, hyphenated at the end of a line in the Centennial edition of *Voltmeier,* appear as one word in the 1869 *Illuminated Western World* text. All other compounds that are hyphenated at the end of a line in the Centennial edition (except those listed on p. 446) are hyphenated within the line in the 1869 text and are omitted from this table.

29.33-4   land-|lord
35.24-5   land-|lord
36.21-2   land-|lord
40.3-4   hill-|side
91.4-5   South-|west
114.14-5   night-|fall
129.30-1   church-|yard

154.2-3   hill-|side
178.13-4   sun-|beam
220.4-5   horse-|back
262.16-7   store-|house
267.37-8   house-|keepers
324.18-9   head-|long

2

Listed here are the compound words that were hyphenated at the end of a line in the *Illuminated Western World* text of *Voltmeier* but fell within the line in the Centennial edition. Where other examples of the same compound appeared consistently in the same form, either as one word or hyphenated, within the line in the *Illuminated Western World,* that form was adopted in the Centennial text. Where there was inconsistency in the form of a compound in the *Illuminated Western World* text, a simple majority rule was followed in establishing the form for the Centennial edition. In the few cases where there was no clear majority for either possible form, the Centennial edition follows the form of the nearest example of the same compound occurring within the line in the *Illuminated Western World* text. In such cases, and in all others where cross-reference to other examples of the same (or related) compounds seemed useful, page and line references are supplied in parentheses.

2.9 shopkeeper (33.8)
9.1 sweetmeat (357.11)
11.37 wrongdoing
15.37 death-bed (11.34)
27.24 haystack
33.19 breadstuffs
34.23 look-out (97.30)
34.33 to-morrow (34.15)
39.19 to-day
40.28 death-like
51.11 blanket-cloak
52.32 buffalo-sling (59.14)
54.29 over-drinking
63.33 half-blind
64.36 empty-handed
66.14 countersigns
68.7 overall
73.12 to-night
73.21 to-night
77.21 sundown
77.22 to-night
79.12 ill-drawn
90.27 gray-beard
99.11 overhanging (100.6 and 100.18)
109.9 mountain-tops (41.28)
109.21 undergone
115.7 reappeared
119.11 hiding-places
126.14 to-night
137.23 To-morrow
138.17 overpassed
143.7 *michen-malico* (cf. chapter title)
152.19 to-morrow
155.27 hiding-places

156.17 well-known
162.36 starlight (183.26)
177.7 alongside
220.27 humdrum
226.19 look-out (97.30)
236.16 bridal-bed
267.25 farmstead
267.36 pick-locks
268.3 hunting-shirt
271.23 hiding-place
275.5 horseback
277.4 horseback
278.26 opium-box (cf. 385.5 and 410.14, opium box)
280.7 opium-box (cf. 385.5 and 410.14, opium box)
280.17 midnight
280.31 bedclothes
285.2 dyestuffs (cf. 110.13; but see also 348.31, dye stuff)
292.6 to-morrow
303.30 court-house
304.14 cold-blooded
305.21 court-house
322.30 To-morrow
343.29 To-morrow
361.17 hillside
366.2 to-night
366.12 to-morrow
371.26 to-day
380.9 whalebone
413.15 churchyard
414.8 fox-hunter
419.8 waterspout
425.4 hilltop

3

Listed here are compounds, or possible compounds, which are hyphenated at the end of a line in both the original and the Centennial edition.

78.24-5   gray-|beard (i.e.,   164.14-5   how-|come (i.e.,
gray-beard)   how-come)
91.24-5   to-|night (i.e., to-night) 297.32-3   stock-|sale (i.e.,
101.38-9   over-|hanging (i.e.,   stock-sale)
overhanging)

TABLE III: DATES OF ORIGINAL SERIAL INSTALLMENTS

Listed here are the dates and page numbers in the 1869 *Illuminated Western World* of the twenty-six installments into which *Voltmeier* was divided.

chap.	date	pp.	chap.	date	pp.
1-3	March 6	1,2	41-44	June 5	6,7
4-6	March 13	1,2	45-47	June 12	7
7-8	March 20	1,2	48-49	June 19	6
9-11	March 27	5,6	50-52	June 26	6,7
12-13	April 3	5	53-55	July 3	6,7
14-16	April 10	5,6	56-58	July 10	6,7
17-20	April 17	5,6	59-61	July 17	2,3
21-23	April 24	5,6	62-63	July 24	6
24-26	May 1	5,6	64-66	July 31	6,7
27-29	May 8	5,6	67-68	August 7	6,7
30-33	May 15	5,6	69-70	August 14	6,7
34-37	May 22	3	71-72	August 21	6,7
38-40	May 29	5,6	73-77	August 28	6,7